**"We're barely back on our feet. The last
thing Indrana needs is a war between two alien
races throwing everything into chaos."**

"Just when we thought things were going to get quiet around here,"
Caspel replied with a grin.

"True enough." I got to my feet and the pair followed. "Keep
an eye on it. I'll send a message to the Farian ambassador. I don't
mind saying to you that I don't like this feeling in my gut, but in
the meantime I should go get ready to make this hard-won peace a
reality."

Praise for K. B. Wagers

BEHIND THE THRONE

"This debut ranks among the best political SF novels in years, largely because of the indomitable, prickly Hail...[a] fast-paced, twisty space opera." —*Library Journal* (starred review)

"Taut suspense, strong characterization, and dark, rapid-fire humor are the highlights of this excellent SF adventure debut." —*Publishers Weekly* (starred review)

"Full of fast-paced action and brutal palace intrigue, starring the fiercest princess this side of Westeros." —*B&N Sci-Fi & Fantasy Blog*

AFTER THE CROWN

"*Crown* is fast paced, and its focus on a female action heroine defined by her decisions rather than romance is refreshing and fun." —*Washington Post*

"Craving a galactic adventure? K.B. Wagers's second Indranan War novel is just the ticket." —*Bookish*

"Two books in, this series has exemplified political plotting as compelling as the badass heroine at its center." —*B&N Sci-Fi & Fantasy Blog*

BEYOND THE EMPIRE

By K. B. Wagers

THE INDRANAN WAR

Behind the Throne

After the Crown

Beyond the Empire

THE FARIAN WAR

There Before the Chaos

THERE BEFORE THE CHAOS

THE FARIAN WAR: BOOK 1

K. B. WAGERS

www.orbitbooks.net

Copyright © 2018 by Katy B. Wagers
Excerpt from *Down Among the Dead* copyright © 2018 by Katy B. Wagers

Author photograph by Donald Branum
Cover design by Lauren Panepinto
Cover art by Stephan Martiniere
Cover copyright © 2018 by Hachette Book Group, Inc.

Orbit
Hachette Book Group
1290 Avenue of the Americas
New York, NY 10104
orbitbooks.net

First Edition: October 2018

Orbit is an imprint of Hachette Book Group.
The Orbit name and logo are trademarks of Little, Brown Book Group Limited.
The publisher is not responsible for websites (or their content)
that are not owned by the publisher.

The Hachette Speakers Bureau provides a wide range of authors for speaking events. To find out more, go to www.hachettespeakersbureau.com or call (866) 376-6591.

Library of Congress Cataloging-in-Publication Data

Names: Wagers, K. B., author.
Title: There before the chaos / K. B. Wagers.
Description: First edition. | New York : Orbit, 2018. | Series: The Farian war ; 1
Identifiers: LCCN 2018026314| ISBN 9780316411219 (trade pbk.) |
ISBN 9780316411202 (ebook)
Subjects: | GSAFD: Space operas | Science fiction.
Classification: LCC PS3623.A35245 T48 2018 | DDC 813/.6—dc23
LC record available at https://lccn.loc.gov/2018026314

ISBNs: 978-0-316-41121-9 (paperback), 978-0-316-41120-2 (ebook)

Printed in the United States of America

LSC-C

10 9 8 7 6 5 4 3 2 1

This one is for the librarians.

We are haunted by ghosts. The shadows of the choices we don't make can hover in our vision for a lifetime. Or they can dissipate like smoke in a sharp wind. Those choices that were negligent and easy to forget without much—if any—regret.

Sometimes they follow us, stalking our steps like a hungry wolf. Every snarl and snap a reminder of our failure, a caution to stay vigilant.

I live with my ghosts. They are an endless reminder. A tally of those I have loved and failed to save. A thousand lives of unanswered potential and discarded dreams. They whisper counsel, condemnation, and occasionally love into my ear. With every choice I make, their ranks grow.

Despite my failures, this army of the dead follows me, loyal for eternity; striding without question into the chaos before us.

1

"Are you sure I can't shoot him?" Crown Princess Alice Gohil, heir to the throne of Indrana, sighed with such exasperation that it took me a full minute before my surprised laughter echoed through the room.

"Alice!"

I was the one with the royal blood, the second daughter of Mercedes Aadita Constance Bristol, and yet my time in the black as a gunrunner—first for one of the most dangerous gangs out there and then as the captain of my own crew—had made me something of an anomaly among the noble families of Indrana.

Alice, by contrast, had been born and bred to take over the leadership of her family from the moment she'd taken her first breath. It had been one of my many reasons for choosing her as my heir.

Six months of daily interaction with me was starting to show on Alice, as evidenced by her entirely improper suggestion. I figured Indrana deserved it for dragging me back to the home I'd run from all those years ago. The Hail they got back wasn't a princess, she was a hard-drinking, foul-mouthed gunrunner with all sorts of crimes under her belt.

"I'm just asking." Alice's grin was wicked.

I shook my head with a smile and held my hands up. "I am not taking the blame from Nila if you do that, I want that on the record now."

"Who are you and what have you done with my empress?" Alice laughed at my look and held her hands up, pressing them together and shaking them in my direction. "Okay, I surrender. I promise I'll behave at the dinner. I wish we didn't need this deal to go through. He's so oily."

"I don't disagree with you. Mr. Hanson is, ugh." I shuddered. "Emmory doesn't like him either." Ignoring my half-finished breakfast in favor of my blue chai, I mulled over the truth of Alice's words. However, I also knew that my personal dislike of one Mr. Peter Hanson—and honestly it was just a combination of his face and my gut instinct—wasn't enough to throw away this impending deal with one of the largest businesses from the Solarian Conglomerate.

A deal we needed to get Indrana out of this financial hole the last few years had put us in. My return home hadn't been a triumphant one, but rather a wild mess of murder, attempted assassination, partially successful coups, and having to fight tooth and nail to recover the throne of Indrana from the hands of a man who'd been determined to see my whole family and the empire itself burned to ashes.

The Indranan Stock Exchange was already responding favorably to the news of the deal and yesterday had posted its highest closing level since before the end of the Saxon war. The steady improvements had started almost immediately after my victory over the attempted coup and the traitors who'd taken my throne.

"However, Penib Industries is a highly respected corporation, and allowing them to build several thousand factories across the empire plus the mining rights they're willing to pay us for is a huge win. We need this, you know we do."

"It never fails to amaze me how you just settled into this, Hail," Alice continued with a smile of her own, and set her cup down by her plate with a sigh. "You really need to stop discussing politics with your *Ekam*, though." The rebuke carried little heat, and I ignored it the same way I had for the last six months.

I was settling into the role fate had assigned me, and while I was privately surprised at how well the last six months had gone, a tiny part of me was still convinced everything was going to go to shit in the blink of an eye. I was the only choice to save Indrana from the fires of war and the desperate destruction of men who'd wanted to overthrow the matriarchy, simply because I was the only member of my family still alive.

I'd named Alice my heir in an act of desperation that had provided temporary relief about the question of succession and then married her off to my childhood friend Tazerion before the dust had settled from the devastating coup that had nearly brought Indrana to her knees.

There'd been less fallout from that than I'd expected, given Taz's status as the head of the *Upjas*—a sect of rebels who'd fought my mother's government almost her entire reign. Their calls for gender and class equality were still raising eyebrows, but I'd granted amnesty to Taz and as many of the *Upjas* as I could in exchange for their assistance during the war and their help in rebuilding Indrana after.

I was empress, and would remain so until I felt their daughter could take the throne. Alice and Taz were popular with the people but she wasn't from my family, and he was a rebel. With peace a reality just over the horizon, they were little more than the parents of the future empress. Unless, Shiva forbid, something happened to me in the next several decades.

Thankfully my chosen heir was a consummate politician and had understood her role even better than I in the beginning.

Her temper was also better, or it used to be. I was fairly sure she was only joking about shooting the head of Penib Industries.

Despite Alice's initial protests over the dubious honor I'd bestowed upon her, she'd been invaluable at juggling an endless list of acts and deals and appointments as we cleaned out the government of anyone who'd been associated with the former prime minister Eha Phanin.

Phanin was dead. Wilson, the man ultimately responsible for the coup and for the deaths of too many Indranans—including my entire family—was dead. My hand tightened of its own accord around my mug, and I had to force myself to release it even though crushing the sturdy ceramic cup would have been an impressive feat.

I was still alive and that was supposed to be victory enough.

"Hail?" Alice asked, her voice laced with concern.

"I'm fine." I forced a smile. "Just remembering. So, the dinner with Penib is in a few days, but it's all under control?"

"Yes. I know you have a lot to deal with because of the Saxons arriving for the treaty signing, but I appreciate you spearheading this also." Alice pushed to her feet, hissing a little at the effort, and my heir rubbed at her swollen belly. "Three more months."

"You know I would have backed you if you'd wanted to go the tube route," I said.

"You know they're sticklers for that sort of thing." Alice shook her head. "There's enough fuss still bubbling about you naming me heir to begin with. Believe it or not, it's easier to do it this way in the long run." She smiled softly, her hand lingering on the place where her unborn daughter was growing. "Besides, I never thought I'd have the chance."

Tubed-babies were common around the galaxy, but here on Indrana it would have been a step too far for the future empress to have been anything but a natural birth.

"It agrees with you," I said, surprised by the softness of my voice. A well-placed gunshot on Candless, a dusty world on the edge of nowhere, had nearly killed me and killed any chances of me having children.

"Oh, shit, Hail, I'm—" She looked up, horror on her face, but I got to my own feet before she could apologize and wrapped her in a hug.

"I made peace with what happened to me a long time ago. Don't apologize for your joy."

At the time I'd just been glad to be alive, and the thought of children, let alone empires, hadn't been on my scans at all. I'd been Cressen Stone, feared gunrunner, not Hailimi Bristol—second daughter of the empress of Indrana.

Now I was neither.

Now I was Hailimi Mercedes Jaya Bristol, Empress of Indrana, long may she reign. I snorted in amusement. Some days it was still hard to believe I wasn't caught in an endless dream.

"Hail—" Alice hesitated at my look and whatever she'd been about to say went unspoken. Instead she smiled. "I should get going. I have a meeting across town before my doctor's appointment and I don't want to cut into your run time."

"I appreciate it," I said with a smile of my own. "Have a good day, I'll talk to you later."

I watched her leave, stopping to exchange a few words with my *Dve*, Gita Desai, at the door. The second-in-command of my Body-Guards was a lovely, statuesque woman with black curls a shade or two darker than her skin.

Gita had been one of my new BodyGuards when we'd traveled to Red Cliff for the first attempt at peace with the Saxon Kingdom. An attempt that had fallen well short when Wilson convinced a drug-addled King Trace to try to bring a building down on my head. Emmory had appointed her *Dve* after Cas's death, a move that showed he was not only focused on my protection but politically savvy enough to appoint a woman as his second-in-command. Which was a large part of why I ignored anyone's complaints about me discussing imperial business with my *Ekam*.

Gita was also the second daughter of the late Matriarch Clara Desai, a woman I'd deeply respected who'd backed me from the moment I'd been dragged back home. Matriarch Desai, like so many others, had been murdered by Wilson. It was a calculated move on his part designed to hurt me as much as possible and force me to come back to Pashati.

It was his own fault Wilson hadn't counted on the rage I'd brought with me when I returned.

I could still remember the look in her eyes. Clara had been right in front of me on the com screen, but with light-years between us there'd been nothing for me to do except stand there while he killed her.

I had a sudden, desperate desire to resurrect Wilson from the dead so I could cut his throat with a wineglass again. If I messed with my schedule I'd have to cancel my run, and right now the movement was the only thing keeping me sane.

The wind gusted in off the Lakshitani Sea, battering at us with the sharp scent of salt and the spray of the waves. Golden streaks of sunlight cut through the city, lighting up the new skeleton of my palace. The sound of the crews already hard at work raising it from the ashes of Wilson's explosion echoed through the early dawn air.

I dug deeper against the resistance of the sand under my bare feet, my stride matching Gita's and Johar's.

Johar had joined up with us when our flight from Wilson's forces landed us at the pirate stronghold of Santa Pirata and she, along with Bakara Rai himself, had helped us take back Darshan Station in the Canafey system.

Intrigued by the idea of an empire run by women, Johar ended up coming back to Pashati rather than heading home with Rai after the battle for Canafey. For the moment the tall, pale woman with black hair and icy-blue eyes had made herself at home in my empire and I certainly enjoyed her company.

At the very least she kept the nobility of Indrana on their toes even more than I did.

I loved running the beach, and now that the wind coming off the water was no longer frigid, and the daylight ran longer, it was even more pleasant. It was also an excellent place to talk about things I didn't want people overhearing.

Plus the steady breaths and the sound of the waves were a balm for my nerves.

The opposite was likely true for my primary BodyGuard and the rest of his people, but my *Ekam* indulged me in this habit because he knew keeping me cooped up in the hotel led to a restlessness that ended poorly. It spoke to Emmory's trust, not only of me but of the other BodyGuards, that he let me outside at all.

Six months had passed since the end of a long and bloody coup that had taken the lives of my sisters and my mother. Almost a year since my Trackers had dragged me back to Indrana to take a throne I'd never had any interest in sitting on but had somehow managed to not only retain but turn into something of a success given Indrana's precarious position in galactic politics.

I didn't have a reason for my overtaxed nerves, not really. It had also been six months since anyone had tried to kill me, which was a blessing, I supposed. And though habit prevented me from truly letting my guard down, anyone involved with the coup was either locked up, dead, or long gone out of my empire.

I glanced at Johar. "What's the news?"

Jo scratched at the black swath of a tattoo curling along her upper arm without breaking stride and squinted out at the water. "Things are weird. There's a lot of talk about a big payday, but no one will fess up and tell me what it is. Invitation only, from what I've been told, and if you don't have an invite you're in the dark."

"What's Rai say about it?"

"Nothing." She shook her head at my eyebrow. "He's in the dark, or he's lying to me."

"He'd lie to his own mother if he thought he could get away with it," I said.

"True." Johar chuckled. "But last time he lied to me I cut off a toe and promised to go further up if he did it again."

Gita choked on a laugh and I grinned. "Fair enough. I don't like weird, Jo. It makes me nervous."

"The fact that the Farians and Shen are tangling again makes me nervous," she replied. "It's been years since things frayed to the point of actual conflict. You know I was on Colony 17 when everything went to shit?"

"I did not know that." I heard Gita whistle next to me. It didn't surprise me that Johar had survived the notorious attack. She had made a name for herself for her uncanny ability not only to sense when things were about to go sideways but to somehow survive the shitstorm that usually followed as well.

"I was there to deliver a shipment, ended up cramming five families into my ship and running like hell." Johar looked out over the ocean again, a faraway look in her blue eyes. "Word was the Shen were chasing someone—a Farian, I guess? I never heard anything more than that. They didn't care in the slightest that there were a bunch of humans in the way. I don't want to see what happens if they decide to really hammer at each other in our space."

A chill worked up my spine despite the sunshine, and I suddenly felt the need to run. "Race?" I asked, and lengthened my stride, pulling away from Gita. Sensing rather than hearing her surprise, I knew the moment she adjusted her speed to keep up with me. It wasn't that difficult; my *Dve* was as long-limbed as I was, nearly matching me in height, and she'd put on several kilos of muscle in the last six months.

Johar chuckled and passed us both, her long, loping strides powered by genetic and technological augmentations. I dug into my last reserve of strength in an effort to catch up, but Johar was the fastest of our trio.

We sprinted. The sound of the rising tide and our breaths mixed with the singing of the dolphins in Balhim Bay. Indranan dolphins were cousins to the ones back on Earth, their hides a darker gunmetal gray with unique white markings. They were also smarter than their Earth kin and sang sweet songs like a chorus of angels.

I slowed to a walk when we reached the jagged rocks and walked to the water's edge to watch the dolphins leap and play in the rising sun. The trio of BodyGuards waiting for us approached, their conversation carried away by the breeze.

"I swear I will beat you one of these days," Gita said, the breeze snatching her laughter away as she came to stand at my side. Her loose black curls danced in the breeze.

"Only when she stops cheating." Johar dodged my swing. Her laughter was deeper than Gita's, belly-deep and unapologetic.

"You won, how can you accuse me of cheating?"

Johar gave a shrug that said *just like that?* and grabbed for my arm on the next swing, but I dodged behind Gita, who held her hands up.

"Hiding behind your *Dve* is cheating," Johar declared. "Zin, she's cheating."

I turned as Zin, Indula, and Iza reached us. The BodyGuards of Team One were splayed out in standard formation; Zin faced me while the other two kept their eyes in the opposite direction. They were all dressed in matte-black uniforms and wore Hessian 45s on their hips.

"You get used to it," Starzin Hafin replied, a grin on his broad, handsome face.

Emmory's husband was an imposing figure. The former Tracker was shorter than me with wide shoulders and a jovial face. His smile could light up a room and ignited his gray-green eyes with a twinkling quality I'd only seen in the sands of Granzier. If you didn't know him well, you'd assume he was never serious, but I had seen his grim determination during our fight to regain my throne, and he was one among a handful of people I trusted without reservation.

"Cheating or not, I wasn't sure I could keep up with you at the end there," Gita said, her dark eyes sparkling with mirth as she took the towel Zin offered.

"It was a good sprint." I faked a smile in Zin's direction as he handed me a towel and scrubbed at my face. The fabric hid my worried frown as I replayed our conversation and my gut twisted at the thought of two powerful alien races going to war anywhere near humanity. The Shen and Farians could kill or heal with a touch. But the Farians were Indrana's allies and had been for centuries, which meant any escalation of their long-standing conflict with the mysterious Shen potentially involved my empire.

"You are improving," Johar said, knocking me out of my thoughts. "I don't remember you being quite that fast before."

"What are you talking about? I used to outrun you all the time."

"I have no memory of this." She sniffed, grinning when I punched her in the arm again.

"It occurs to me, Majesty," Zin said. "If you'd wanted to get away from us you could have outrun Emmory and me. I can run well enough, but not that fast with this." He gestured at his left leg, the prosthetic from the knee down hidden by his uniform pants. "And Emmory is fast, but you're faster. Though if you tell him I said so I'll deny it."

Laughing for real this time, I threw the towel back at him and shrugged into the blue jacket Gita passed along as I pushed thoughts of the Farians and Shen to the back of my mind. "You know Emmory would have just shot me in the back, but I'll remember it for my escape plan."

"*Uie Maa*, you're not leaving us now and we all know it," Zin teased. He put a hand on my back as we headed for the aircar.

"You could definitely outrun Indula," Iza said, her grin flashing white against her dark skin. "I'm not sure I could catch you in a short sprint, but my endurance is decent."

"Hush, shorty," Indula replied. He threw me a wink, long lashes falling over his pale blue eyes as he struggled to keep his smile from spreading over his pretty face.

This pair of Guards had come to us late, during the chaos of my return home and fight for my throne against my cousin. Iza had been a policewoman in the capitol, and Indula had been one of my mother's BodyGuards. Initially they'd been on Team Two, but over the last six months Emmory had been shifting teams around as he solidified my BodyGuard teams with new recruits.

The three BodyGuards at the vehicle were all new. Muna Vandi was yet another volunteer from one of the noble families of Indrana, while Riddhi and Sahil Gupta came from more humble origins.

I knew their names now and even extra details not found in the BodyGuard files stored in my *smati*. The collection of computer chips embedded in my brain provided me with the information from the files Emmory had given me one night after a timely piece of advice Cas had managed to issue from beyond the grave.

It meant getting attached, and I wasn't sure I could do that, but my former *Dve* insisted: *I also know you'll have distanced yourself from your new BodyGuards to try to avoid the pain of losing them. Don't. Make yourself vulnerable. Treat them the way you treated me, and Jet, and Will. It's why we loved you, it's why we didn't hesitate when the moment came.*

He'd been right and I'd been wrong and though it was hard, over the last six months I'd opened myself up to the women and men responsible for my safety even though it meant carrying around more pain in my heart when one of them died.

And they would, they always did. Just like Cas. Just like Portis.

I'd thought the man who'd rescued me from a gang of street punks on New Delhi was a rogue, a former member of the Imperial Tactical Squad, an arm of the Indranan military, who'd been dishonorably discharged for theft and smuggling. As it turned out, Portis Tresk had been sent by my childhood BodyGuards to keep me safe out in the black. His crimes were fake. His whole life given in the service of Indrana to keep a wayward princess safe. For twenty years he held to that charge. In the end it had cost him his life.

Zin closed a hand around my upper arm, squeezing gently and then letting me go. My *Ekam* and his husband had the benefit of their Tracker talents and a generous file on my gunrunning exploits provided for them when they'd hunted me down to explain their uncanny knowledge of my moods. However, they'd also proved to be quick studies of my body language, and it took more effort than it was worth for me to hide how I was feeling now.

I smiled and nodded to the two young women and lone young man standing by the car. "Good morning."

"Good morning, Majesty," they echoed.

"Riddhi, how's your father doing?"

Riddhi replied before her brother did, a smile hovering on the edges of her full mouth. "He's excellent, Majesty, thank you. He said the customers are coming more steadily."

"Is he going to send more of that pandolce?" I didn't even try to keep the little thread of hope out of my voice, and my BodyGuards laughed.

"I will mention to him you enjoyed it, Majesty."

"You do that." I winked at her. "Muna, how's your mother?" Muna's mother was the daughter of Mila Vandi, the general in charge of the Imperial Tactical Squad, and she'd been injured during the fighting in the capital chasing down Wilson's forces in the final engagement.

"She's recovering. The doctors say she will be out of the hospital by next week."

"I'm glad to hear it." I patted her on the shoulder as I got into the aircar. "Tell her I'll be by to visit soon."

"I will, ma'am." She closed the door with a smile.

I leaned my head back and spotted Johar grinning at me. "What?"

"Nothing," she said, shaking her head. "You're good at being an empress."

"Shut up."

2

Good morning, Majesty. Johar." Alba Tenaka greeted me with a smile when I slid from the aircar. My chamberlain was a brilliant woman with straight black hair and dark eyes. She'd been a member of Clara Desai's household before I hired her and sometimes it felt as though we'd been together for years instead of only these past chaotic months.

If it weren't for her I'd have run away from this job the moment an opportunity presented itself and never looked back.

"How was your run?" she asked.

"The weather was lovely, and Johar kicked my ass on the final sprint," I replied with a grin. "What do we have on the schedule today?"

"You've got an hour and a half, and then the daily intelligence briefing. After that is a meeting with the Tarsi delegation to finalize the trade agreements," Alba said, falling into step with us, her heels clacking on the pavement as we headed up to the door of the hotel I called home while my palace was rebuilt.

We'd moved from the tiny hotel on the outskirts of Krishan—used during the fight to reclaim my throne—to something larger in the middle of the city that could handle the needs of my ever-expanding staff. The Indranan Star Hotel was better able to bear the burden of an entire floor shut down for the empress and her crew. The cluster of buildings in the middle of the capital were tall, fluted structures that billowed outward and then spiked toward the sky. We'd settled into the smallest of the three buildings as I tried my best to minimize the disruption of my presence.

I'd read the briefing she'd sent me last night about the Tarsi, but couldn't resist the tease. "Trade agreements? What trade agreements?"

"You were up late reading Admiral Hassan's reports again instead of mine, weren't you?" Alba sighed.

"I was, but I read yours first." I'd learned my lesson early on to pay attention to the things she did for me and to value her hard work by putting in my own time in response.

"Good morning, Majesty."

"Good morning," I replied, using the greeting from the hotel doorman and the BodyGuards just inside the doors to dodge Alba's reproving look and continued across the foyer to the lift.

The lift dinged and the doors opened. Alba and Zin stepped into the tiny space, Johar following. I closed my eyes for just a second, my humor vanishing when faced with the tiny metal box, and dragged in a breath before I followed them. Gita, Iza, and Indula joined us and I squeezed my eyes shut as my claustrophobia sank its dagger-sharp claws into my chest. "You could shoot me now, Zin. I wouldn't complain. Sorry, I'm in a strange mood this morning. Continue."

Alba cleared her throat. "After the Tarsi delegation, Caterina Saito has asked if you'll sit in on the Matriarch Council meeting. They're discussing the budget and the topic of integrating eldest sons into the Ancillary Council today. She thought your presence for such a historic occasion would be worthwhile."

"Not to mention quelling any potential ruckus," I muttered.

Alba nodded with a sigh. "Most likely, Majesty; you do tend to have a calming effect on objections."

"It's because everyone is still so Shiva-damned convinced I'm going to shoot them if they disagree." I shot her a sideways glance. "I should tell them to be more afraid of you."

"You tend to suggest shootings more than your mother did, Majesty," Alba replied, ignoring my accusation with a tiny smile.

"Mother seems more likely to have suggested they go do the deed themselves."

The elevator came to a stop, the doors sliding open with what seemed like excruciating slowness after the little ding of our arrival. My BodyGuards stepped out of my way with practiced ease, no one commenting on the fact that I went straight to the large window in the foyer and stared, unseeing, out over the capital until I could trust myself to speak without screaming.

I'd suffered from claustrophobia since my childhood and an unfortunate incident that had left me trapped in a tunnel under the old palace for several hours before my father had rescued me along with Mother's *Ekam*, Ven. Then Wilson, in his madness, had locked me in a metal coffin and drowned me. That I survived it was a testament to the gods' foolishness and my own stubbornness. However, the doctors told me that I'd have issues with enclosed spaces for the rest of my life, and the past six months had been a rather haphazard game of chance as we discovered my new limits.

A train zoomed by on the rail system that ran past the window, and fifteen stories below people moved along the street, going about their day. A sense of normalcy had returned to Krishan since Wilson's takeover and the battles that followed. Most days I was better than I'd ever been, but some days I swung wildly from one extreme to the other.

"I'm going to go get cleaned up," Johar said, slipping her hand around my upper arm and giving it a squeeze. "I'll see you later. Thanks again for the run."

"Thanks for joining us," I replied, and managed a smile now that my panic had dissipated. "Is Alice going to be there? She didn't mention it at breakfast." I turned from the window and headed toward my rooms.

"No, ma'am," Alba replied. "Your heir has a doctor's appointment and then she and Taz are presiding over a memorial dedication down at the docks this afternoon before they head for her estate."

Alice and her husband, Tazerion Shivan, trapped back here on Pashati during Wilson's attempted coup, had joined forces to fight the traitors. What had started as dislike between my new heir and the leader of the *Upjas* bloomed into love. I'd seen it clear enough, though even if the affection hadn't been there it was likely I'd have married them to each other anyway.

It turned out I was as ruthless an empress as my mother.

The marriage of the pair cemented the new direction for Indrana's future. One of equality and progress. One where sons and daughters were seen through the same lens. My heir and her husband would never rule Indrana—but their daughter would once I died. Until then I would be with her every step of the way, guiding Indrana into a brighter era, bullying when necessary.

The reactions to the wedding had been mixed. Though the predictable outrage to putting a former rebel leader like Taz that close to the throne had been less than the reaction to the return of the former gunrunner who currently occupied it. Eventually the news reports had settled back into something resembling pre-coup Indrana, and these days all they talked about was the impending signing of the peace treaty with the Saxon Kingdom.

Which was why Alice and Taz were headed for the safety of her family home in the country. Promise of peace aside, that ever-wary part of me didn't trust the Saxons not to try something, and I was going to make sure my heir and her child were as far away from danger as I could put them.

Our enmity with the only other government in this arm of the galaxy was a long and sordid tale. One that had come about in part because of Wilson's machinations, but also due to Saxony's habit of expanding into territories that didn't belong to them.

My threat to take the Indranan Navy and wipe them off the fabric of the universe even though I'd just been knocked off my throne had been taken seriously by Jaden Toropov. This afternoon I would welcome their delegation, complete with the new Saxon king, to Pashati to sign a treaty heavily weighted in favor of my empire.

It was the peace and stability Indrana so desperately needed. A return of our lost planets and with them lost industries that would bring a much-needed boost to our economy. And once Saxony was back on their feet we would also see some sizable cash reparations.

The newslines were lauding me as a peacemaker, but the truth was I was as desperate for peace as the Saxons. Indrana's people deserved a future freed from war.

If I was going to be honest—I deserved it as well.

"Have the reservations at Shivan's been taken care of for the dinner with Mr. Hanson?"

"Yes, ma'am." Alba's steps didn't falter as she checked the information into her *smati*. "Your lunch is free today and the afternoon has been set aside for the Saxon delegation's arrival." We stopped at the door to my rooms, and I greeted the two Guards on the door as they came to attention with a jumbled chorus of "Your Majesty" and "*Dve* Desai."

My maid was also waiting, and Stasia smiled up at me. "I spoke with Fasé this morning, Majesty," she said by way of a greeting. "She said to tell you to pay attention to the little things and she will see you soon."

I raised an eyebrow. "Really?"

Stasia smiled, pushing a golden curl away from her face. "I know you are still angry with her—you have every right to be. But listen to her, please?"

I couldn't ignore the sting of pain. Fasé Terass—a valued member of my circle since the beginning—had been released from her service in the Indranan military and sent home to atone for breaking the faith.

Farians could heal humans. They could also kill us and bring us back to life, though both those things were forbidden by their

17

religion. Fasé had saved the lives of so many of my people with her ability to heal and had violated her people's most sacred laws for us not once, but twice.

She'd also killed, though not directly with a hand to my former *Dve*'s skin, but by telling him of a future where Indrana burned unless he sacrificed himself.

My anger at what Fasé had done was fading, replaced with a sadness I couldn't find words for and tangled in forgiveness I couldn't grant. She'd sent Cas to his death, claiming it was the only way to save us all. She'd sacrificed him without thought or care. I still couldn't forgive her for the loss of my previous *Dve*.

The grief over Cas was still so painfully fresh, and I pushed it aside with difficulty as I headed into my room on the all clear from Gita without a response for Stasia. There was a flutter in my gut at her words, the instinctive knowledge that Fasé's reappearance would herald some form of trouble. When coupled with the news about the increasing fights between the Farians and the Shen, even the more logical part of me could see the danger crawling over the event horizon.

I feared that this hard-won peace wasn't going to last for long, and I hoped we were ready for whatever storm was coming.

"Gita, I'm taking my bios off-line," I said.

"Yes, ma'am. We'll be back in an hour." The quiet sounds of Alba and Gita ushering everyone else from my suite followed until I closed the door of the bathroom, cutting it off.

I turned off my *smati*'s bio-link with my BodyGuards; normally this would set off a loud series of alarms for all my Guards, but Gita had already issued the warning.

About a week after Wilson's death, I'd discovered a rather nasty side effect of his little box stunt. My claustrophobia notwithstanding, being drowned in a metal box in front of the entire galaxy had led to an extreme difficulty with most enclosed spaces. Adding water only made things worse.

Which meant showering was . . . difficult.

The first time I'd tried it had been in the hospital, and my break-down had resulted in a truly epic scene I only knew about because Emmory had relented and allowed me to watch his digital record-ing of the event.

I'd started shutting off my bio-link the next day. Gita had pro-tested. Emmory had only nodded and offered me the compromise of an hour of time, or more if I needed it as long as I checked in both before and after I went off-line.

For four months afterward I'd bathed out of the sink.

The hotel shower was even worse. A box—with clear glass sides—but still a box, and the sound of running water had left me breathless and sweating and curled into a corner of the bathroom every time I'd tried to use it.

Two months ago I tried to turn the water on again. The sound of it falling on the tile reduced me to a shaking mess and I'd thrown up twice before I could get back up to turn it off.

I reached into the shower and tapped the water on, jerking my hand out before it could get wet.

Breathe in, breathe out. Portis's voice was calm in my head. My former lover and Emmory's younger brother had accompanied me out into the black and died there—trying to protect me from Wil-son's vendetta. I could still hear him, or at least liked to pretend I could, and took what comfort I could in his fading memory.

My fingers shook as I tied my hair back, and the air was thick in my lungs. "I can't." The words tumbled out even as my hands oper-ated of their own free will and stripped my clothes off with ruthless efficiency.

It's just a shower, baby. You can leave the door open.

It wasn't just the door. It was the water on my skin. The feel of it brought everything back—from the cold damp air of that box to the rushing sound of water in my ears and finally the feeling of water sliding into my lungs.

Muttering a curse, I gritted my teeth and grabbed for the washcloth, wetting it and swiping it across the soap as I stepped halfway into the shower and washed as fast as I humanly could.

I rinsed off and turned off the water, the silence broken by the sound of my heart thumping in my ears and my sobs slicing through the air.

The tile was cool on my cheek where I'd sunk to the floor, a towel wrapped around me and prayer on my lips. "...never did I do fire sacrifice. Chanting millions of mantras." The words tumbled unbidden out of my throat, jagged-edged and painful. I'd never been much of a faithful devotee, but when Wilson locked me in the box the only thing besides Portis that had kept me from screaming was reciting the Aparadha Stotram. "O Lord Shiva who is all compassionate, please forgive me. You are the Lord of all deities and one whose nature is to bless all."

Praying brought me so little comfort it was useless, but for some stupid reason I did it anyway.

"We appreciate all that Your Majesty's people have done over the past few months." The head of the Tarsi delegation, a stately older woman wrapped in a rust-colored chador, sat with a poise that reminded me of my mother. "We realize how difficult things have been, and there would have been no complaint had you asked us to return at a better time. Even though the fighting on the horizon is worrisome for us all."

I folded my hands and shook them lightly in her direction. It would seem I wasn't the only one concerned about the newest reports of fighting between the Farians and the Shen. "We are grateful for your compassion, *Essa* Donya, and your patience with us. This agreement was important to my mother, and it's a worthy way to honor her memory."

Donya returned the gesture, and the young woman and man flanking her echoed it. "*Bark Allah laha*, Your Majesty." Her clear amber eyes were on mine.

May God bless her.

I swallowed back the lump in my throat. My mother could have used those blessings years ago, not only for the troublesome second daughter she'd had to wrangle after my father's death but for the monsters that crawled into our home and stole everything from her.

"Thank you." Pressing my hand to the data pad in front of me with a smile, I shook away the sadness and then passed it across the table to Donya. "I am most pleased to announce the beginning of our partnership. May it be the first days of a long and beneficial friendship between Indrana and Tarsis."

"As Allah wills it." Donya pressed her hand to the pad, and then, like the consummate politician she was, stood. "We know you are extremely busy, Majesty. If there are other things you need to attend to, do not feel as though you are rude to do so."

I stood with a grateful smile as they left. The numbers flashing in the corner of my eye told me I was going to be late for the Matriarch Council meeting. We'd spent longer in casual conversation than I'd expected. I'd enjoyed it, though; *Essa* Donya's presence had been a soothing blanket on the raging fire still burning across my raw nerves.

The Tarsi were a small contingent within the wider Sulimain Alliance and generally didn't do business with anyone outside the alliance. However, something about Mother and Indrana had piqued their interest, and the Tarsi had approached with an offer of some very interesting farming technology and a desperately needed influx of cash in exchange for Indrana lobbying the Farians on behalf of the alliance for a treaty and allowing Tarsi students to come to our universities for study.

It was a win-win and the bulk of the work had been done before I'd even arrived home, so there had been no reason to reject the Tarsi's offer. No one seemed quite willing to breathe that idea out loud for fear of cursing the opportunity; however, I suspected it was the first step to an alliance with all the Sulimain worlds, and that was something I was very interested in. Especially if the Farians approved the pending treaty. So I followed their lead and kept my mouth shut.

For six months I'd been finding my feet as empress, searching for a way to balance the gunrunner I had been with who I was now. It was surprising to everyone, I think, but especially to me just how well I was adapting. There was no time for wistful reflection or moping about the loss of my freedom. It was not at all how I'd thought my life would turn out twenty years ago.

My flight from home had started off as a mission to find my father's killer. When my search dead-ended, I decided to stay away and build a life for myself: first, as one of Cheng Hao's crew, then as the captain of my own ship.

The empire didn't need me. It was safely in Mother's capable hands and set to be passed along to my older sister, Cire. I was free out in the black, not Hailimi—second daughter, princess by accident of birth—but Cressen Stone, a person of my own making, a woman answerable to herself and the laws she'd chosen instead of the ones imposed on her.

Until Wilson, the very man responsible for my father's death, directed his fury at the rest of my family. With my younger sister Pace dead and my mother unstable, the Trackers Emmory and Zin were tasked by Cire to bring me home.

I hadn't wanted to go, but I was all that was left to save the empire.

Now I was here, days away from peace with the Saxons, something my mother had never been able to accomplish. I was proud of myself for juggling busier days than we'd ever seen out in the black—even if there were a lot fewer people shooting at me. And even if I occasionally missed the freedom I'd had out in the black, I was happy right where I was.

Fasé's message cast a shadow over all that. If she was coming back to Pashati, my gut whispered, it meant trouble was following in her wake.

3

M ajesty?" Gita touched my arm. "Are you all right?"

I realized I was alone in the room and the numbers flashing in the corner of my vision were pronouncing me even more late for my next meeting.

"I'm fine," I said with a smile. "Just musing on the unexpected turns a life can take. Let's move."

"You're not wrong, Majesty," my *Dve* said with an answering smile. "I'm reasonably sure none of us ever expected we'd be where we are now."

The shouting reverberated down the hallway as Gita and I approached a repurposed suite down the hall where the council meeting was taking place. My *Dve* stepped in front of me, her hand going to the Hessian 45 on her hip.

"I doubt we need backup, Gita," I said, knowing she would ignore me.

Moments later Riddhi and Sahil Gupta, twin BodyGuards, arrived sporting a pair of identical concerned frowns. The twins were in their midtwenties. Their dark hair, eyes, and skin made them look like shadows against the white hallway wall.

The shouting had only grown in volume while we waited, and I arched an eyebrow at the words that spilled into the hallway through the doorway.

"Clinging to our antiquated way of life is what got us into this mess in the first place, Heela!" Caterina Saito's voice rang with frustration and anger.

"Antiquated? You want to talk about ancient history? We could stumble back to the old days of Earth if you'd like. When we were nothing but property? We don't treat men anywhere near as badly as they have treated us."

"Do you want to go in, Majesty?"

"No, let's hang out here for a moment, Gita," I murmured the order as a third voice cut into Caterina's reply. My *smati* identified the voice as Gita's older sister, Adi Desai.

"There are males in positions of power all over the empire: governors, in the military, here in the government. Even half the empress's BodyGuards identify as male. I don't see what the fuss is about equality. They've already got it. Forcing even more diversity on us before we are ready is a recipe for disaster."

Sahil's indrawn breath was sharp, and I was unable to stop myself from sliding a look in his direction.

"Thoughts on that reasoning, Sahil?" The question slipped out before I could stop myself. I wasn't supposed to be asking my Body-Guards for political advice, a request from a number of people that I frequently ignored.

Plus, Portis whispered in my head, *Fasé told you to pay attention.*

Sahil swallowed, his dark eyes wide and conflicted while I waited patiently.

"A scattering of important positions isn't the same thing as equality, Majesty. It doesn't change the system that's already in place."

"Correct." I grabbed him by the back of the head and pressed my forehead to his. My older BodyGuards were used to me treating them more like crew on equal footing than empress and Guard, but Sahil jerked a little in surprise before he grinned at me.

I released him and slipped into the room, Gita's hissing displeasure following on my heels.

Heela Maxwell had her back to the door, so she didn't see me as she continued her tirade. Several other matriarchs did, but I held up my hand and shook my head.

"Whatever the empress has planned with her *Upjas* friends, it's our duty to preserve the empire. The empire, Caterina, as it has stood for thousands of years. Not some half-baked notion of equality based on her gunrunning exploits and the *Upjas*'s ridiculous demands."

"Really, Heela, if we were doing this based on my gunrunning exploits I'd just kill everyone and start over," I said, grinning as I shook my head.

You'd have thought I'd set off a silencer nuke. Heela's strangled gasp dropped with her to the floor as she went to her knees. I moved into the room, my BodyGuards behind me, and all the other women within the room dipped into curtsies.

"I am disappointed in you, Adi," I said to Matriarch Desai as I passed her. I hadn't thought Gita's older sister was against the reforms.

"And you, Heela," I said over our *smati* link so no one else could hear. "Your mother *would be disappointed in you.*"

Heela jerked as though I'd kicked her.

"I was kidding about the killing," I said aloud. "I think you'd all agree we've had plenty of that already. I apologize for my tardiness, ladies; it took longer with the Tarsi than expected. What have I missed?"

"We seem to have reached an impasse concerning elder sons on the Ancillary Council, Majesty." Caterina's face was neutral in its expression, but I could see the amusement lurking in her eyes. "The council is split."

"Everyone have a seat. Heela, get up off the floor and put your ass in a chair," I said, stepping around her and taking my seat at the head of the long table.

The lump in my throat made its appearance as the women settled into their seats, seven on each side of the table, and I blinked to clear away the faces that should have been there: Clara Desai, Loka Naidu, Irit Waybly, Madhashri Acharya, Tare Zellin, Ola Surakesh, and Ipsita Maxwell. They were all gone, now nothing but memories to be carried by those of us unlucky enough to still be alive.

Wilson had executed the matriarchs of half of Indrana's noble families—more than half if you counted my mother and sisters among the dead. He'd stolen away decades of experience and leadership in the span of a few heartbeats. Even six months out, we were still fumbling with the loss, the council trying to find its feet in the ever-shifting landscape while Indrana staggered out of the traditions and customs that bound us toward something better.

Now there were eldest daughters, or in the case of Lani Gohil, second daughters. Lani had taken Alice's spot on the Matriarch Council upon her sister's elevation to Crown Princess.

"The issue under discussion, Majesty, is the proposal to allow elder sons onto the Ancillary Council," Caterina said once everyone was seated. "I and six others feel that this is a good step toward the reforms proposed by the *Upjas* without causing further disruption to the government. The others argue that because we are still recovering from the war and Indrana is on unstable footing, it's best to wait to enact any sort of changes until things are settled."

"Majesty, we merely think it's best to move slowly." Adi spoke up, gesturing at the matriarchs on her side of the table. "Everything is in flux; the people are uneasy about the reforms. They should be focused on the recovery and reconstruction from the war. Now is not the time to make changes that will only increase the instability of the empire."

"So they should just be patient?" I rested my elbows on the table and steepled my hands in front of my mouth. "Wait their turn?"

"Our issue isn't with the changes themselves so much as the timing," Adi replied, shifting in her seat at my slow smile. I hadn't been quiet about my support of the reforms, and she had to know she was treading on dangerous ground.

"How long?"

"Majesty?"

"How long should they wait?" I waved a hand in the air. "Six more months? A year? Five? Fifty?" I slapped the same hand down on the tabletop and nearly everyone jumped. "I'm sure you think your argument so very logical and sensible, but the reality is there will always be another catastrophe, another time when things are unsettled, and the people are uneasy. Would we be where we are today if my ancestor-grandmother had waited for things to settle down before she took power?"

"Majesty, that's not the same—"

"It's exactly the same," Zaran Khatri cut Adi off; the young, blond matriarch had her hands folded on the table in front of her. "If we wait, if we ask them to wait, it will never happen. There will always be some reason to put it off. We acknowledge that things are unstable right now, but that makes it easier, not harder, to do more than pay lip service to equality. You were in support of this when we met with the leaders of the *Upjas*, Adi. Don't back away from it now just because you're scared."

"How dare you," Heela snapped, dark curls bouncing with her fury. "This isn't about being scared, Zaran, though we have every right to be. We watched our mothers die at the hands of a madman who wanted to turn this empire upside down. And if no one else will say it, I will—my issues are with the changes. It was men who got us into this horror. Wilson, Phanin, your nephew, Your Majesty. If anything proves that men are untrustworthy, it is these new faces around the table."

"How dare I? How dare *you*, Heela." Zaran slammed a fist into the tabletop. "Your mother went to her death in support of this empire's future and the equality we seek! Now you'll stain her memory with your cowardice."

The room devolved into chaos. I kept my face carefully blank at Zaran's harsh words when what I really wanted to do was stare at her in shock. Matriarch Khatri had been a shy youngster when I'd first met her, her timid support of the *Upjas* a result of falling in love with one of the members. It appeared that the last few months had put some steel into her spine, and I felt a little sparkle of pride in my chest at how well she'd taken the older matriarch to task.

"Well, that went downhill quickly. I thought you were supposed to be here to keep this from happening," Caterina murmured under her breath, and I snorted.

Caterina Saito had also changed. The stately matriarch was fourteen years my senior but had done better than I'd expected from a noble when the negotiations with the Saxons exploded and we'd fled from Red Cliff. Her time away from home opened her eyes to a galaxy outside Indrana.

Which wasn't to say that she hadn't been outspoken and determined when we'd gone to Red Cliff to negotiate with the Saxons. It was one of the reasons I'd chosen her for that trip.

However, she had been a matriarch, born and bred in the very system we were now trying to tear apart. Our flight from the unexpected attack and our time on the run had hardened her into a woman a bit more like me and slightly less like a noblewoman of Indrana.

Heela slammed a fist into the tabletop. "Your arrogance is astounding!"

"I'm being arrogant?" Saba Hassan snorted. "All we're asking is for fair treatment for our brothers, Heela. How is that arrogant?"

"The empire teeters on the brink of disaster and you—"

"Enough!" My voice echoed through the room, cutting off the arguments and shocking everyone into silence with the force. "That is quite enough. Reconstruction from the war damage is almost complete—with the exception of the palace—so now is the time for us to focus on the future.

"Since the council is deadlocked, I will put in my vote. Integrate the Ancillary Council, ladies. That's an order from your empress."

A large part of my decision to stay was the knowledge that I was the only one who could move Indrana in the direction she needed to go. I had the spine to weather the storm against the nobles' protests on equality and the social capital as the "gunrunner empress" to push through enough legislation at the lower levels for a solid foundation.

"The people will not approve of this."

"Seventy-nine percent of them already do," I replied, raising an eyebrow at Heela's response. "Or do you think this gunrunner hasn't read the reports?"

She swallowed. "Your Majesty—"

"You are behaving like spoiled children who are mad that others among you were also given toys. Learn to share"—my patience gone, I snarled the order over the top of Heela's protest—"or I will turn you over my knee and spank you until you do. You are the leaders of your people. Behave like it."

There was a moment of awkward silence as I settled back in my chair and tapped a finger on the table. "Caterina, move on to the next item on the list."

"Yes, ma'am." She cleared her throat.

The remainder of the meeting was more subdued and wrapped up without further argument. The women filed out with murmured good-byes until only Caterina and Adi remained.

"They mean no disrespect in their opposition, Majesty," Adi said, her eyes pointed at the floor.

I lifted a hand before Caterina could say anything. "Adi, look at me. Heela was being deliberately disrespectful, and while I am getting gods-damned tired of it, that's a matter between me and her. Do you really think this is about me feeling disrespected?" I asked. "Is there anything about me that suggests my feelings are easily hurt?"

Her dark eyes flicked to her sister standing silently behind my chair and then back at me. Adi shook her head. "No, Majesty. I just don't want you to think we are being disloyal—to you or to the empire."

"I'm not worried about enemies lurking under my bed, Adi." I tried and failed to keep the amusement out of my voice. "Nor am I so arrogant as to think we've caught everyone who was involved in Wilson's scheme. Someone always escapes, slips through the cracks. If they have any sense they have run far from here like Elsa Khatri.

"That said, the matriarchs have my trust, even when I don't agree with them." I held out a hand to her, pleased when she took it. "I understand very well your concerns about integrating the council. However, I don't share them and I'm going to overrule them. Everyone is invested in this, from my BodyGuards to the people on the street. You will have to learn to be uncomfortable for the good of Indrana."

"Yes, ma'am."

I snorted and squeezed her fingers. "You say that like I just ordered you to eat peas. Talk to Caterina. Talk to your sister, Adi. Fires of Naraka, talk with your brothers. You have one who will be on the Ancillary Council if my memory is right. Find a way to see past your discomfort and work for a solution instead of just pushing it away. If you love Indrana, Adi, love her people, too. All of them."

Adi blinked at me as if she were seeing me for the first time. I released her and she curtsied again. "Yes, ma'am. I will."

Caterina watched her go. "You're going to bully them all until they agree with you, Majesty."

"I'll do no such thing." I shot her a smile. "Though what good is a reputation if you can't cash in on it from time to time?"

She laughed, shaking her head as I got to my feet. "Thank you, Your Majesty, for your support today. All joking aside, I think it did make a difference."

"You have it whenever you need it." I patted her shoulder. "Would you like to join me for lunch? Or do you have plans?"

"I'd love to." She gestured at the door and we headed back down the hallway toward my rooms.

"Stasia, we've got a visitor for lunch," I said over my *smati.*

"Yes, ma'am. No trouble."

Stasia was setting out another place at the table when we returned to my rooms. My head maid had been with us since I'd set foot back in the palace. The quiet young woman was now made of steel, forged in the same crucible we'd all endured over the last year. She was still quiet, but she ran my staff with a firm hand. Even Alba didn't dare to challenge Stasia when she put her foot down.

I squeezed her arm on my way to the screen on the far wall. Caterina stopped to exchange greetings with my maid, and I heard the door open and close again as my BodyGuards went through their shift change. A few taps of my fingers and the news came on, adding to the noise in the room.

"The attack was carried out by the new leaders of the Shen, and though no one was killed, it appears the rebels took possession of several ships." Serita Gupta, lead anchor for Indranan National News, faced the camera with the calm composure she'd carried through the coup. Her steadfast commitment to the truth even in the midst of Phanin's takeover was being hailed as the best reporting in decades.

Several images flashed on the screen, stock footage and stills of the pair of siblings now in charge of the Shen—Mia and Aiz Cevalla—and I hummed thoughtfully as the camera returned to Serita.

"The Farians are being understandably tight-lipped about the security breach, but we will have more as the story develops. Indrana is bound up in a collective defense treaty with Faria, and there is concern we will be required to join the fight against the Shen. However, there's been no word from either government as to the state of that treaty and whether the Farians will request Indranan help in the matter."

"Majesty." The bass tone of my *Ekam* dragged me away from the news report. Emmory Tresk had a few centimeters on me and at least a dozen kilos. My primary BodyGuard was an imposing figure, made all the more impressive by the matte-black uniform and the silver star tattooed onto his left cheek.

"That's the sixth attack in three months," I replied, pointing a finger at the screen as I turned on him with a half smile.

"Seventh, actually, though the skirmish three weeks ago didn't do any damage, so I think most people are discounting it."

My smile vanished as Fasé's warning resurfaced and I wondered again just what she'd meant. The Farians wouldn't have sent a message through Fasé. They would have sent it through the ambassador here on Pashati. "There hasn't been a sound from the Farians about needing our help."

"You could send Fasé a com and ask," Emmory said.

"I could." I sighed. But we both knew I wouldn't. My issues with Fasé aside, as the empress of Indrana if I wanted answers I'd cause far less of an uproar by messaging the Farian ambassador instead of a former Imperial Tactical Squad medic.

The Shen and the Farians had been at war for longer than the existence of human civilization; the few encounters in human space had all happened after the great exodus into the black. For the most part they kept their fight contained to the interior arm where the Farian homeworld was rumored to be. I doubted they needed our help; despite this long-running war with the Shen, the Farians never gave the appearance they needed or wanted outside assistance.

"Should we be worried?" I asked, still frowning at the screen, which had moved on to a news story about the upcoming marriage of one of Krishan's sports heroes and her movie star girlfriend.

"At the moment I don't have it on my list, and I don't think it will pose a problem during the tour," Emmory replied, glancing away from me to the screen.

I was slated to leave on a welcome tour of the empire shortly after the treaty signing. An eighteen-month ordeal that would send me in a big loop around our arm of the galaxy. There were plenty of stops at friendly planets, but just as many that had sided with Wilson during the coup. PR was careful to edge around that point, but I knew enough about shows of force to know what the real purpose of the tour was.

The fighting between the Farian and Shen had never come this far, though, and I thought back to Johar's comment on the beach. A worried Johar made me nervous for no reason I could articulate to my *Ekam*, so I pushed it aside and went for the easy response.

"Your list?"

"Of things to worry about, Majesty."

I laughed. "Oh, I'd love to get a peek at that list," I teased.

My *Ekam*'s smile had been a rare thing in the early days, but now it appeared more frequently. It creased the tattoo on his left cheek, the Imperial Star, our empire's highest award. Given for those who walked the road to temple in service of the empire, it was almost always awarded posthumously.

I'd have given him another if he'd allowed it, but despite my outranking him, my *Ekam* refused to admit that dying while trying to keep me safe was anything more than part of his job.

I'd hated the silent, barely civil man who'd dragged me home to become empress, at least at first. Then I'd realized he had more honor than the entire Indranan court and was my best hope of staying alive.

I hadn't been wrong. Without Emmory it's likely I would have died long before my showdown with Wilson, but try as I might he refused to let me repay him. I still didn't know what I'd done to engender such loyalty from these men and women who were my BodyGuards, but I was endlessly grateful for it.

"Matriarch Saito." Emmory nodded to Caterina.

"*Ekam*, how are you?"

"Thankful for peace, ma'am."

"Aren't we all?" Caterina smiled.

"Lunch is ready, Majesty," Stasia announced.

I took a seat at the table where I could keep one eye on the news and one on the door because old habits die hard and even surrounded by peace and protection I was forever going to keep my back to the wall.

4

Majesty, are we friends?"

I raised an eyebrow at Caterina's curiously worded question. We were alone in my room; Emmory and the others had departed as soon as the food was served. The conversation during lunch had revolved around the gender reforms and some of the easier laws we'd been able to enact without a lot of pushback from either the Matriarch or the Ancillary Council.

Now, judging by the tone of her voice, something was bothering Caterina, and I settled back in my chair. "I assumed so. What is it?"

Caterina swallowed, obviously thinking the words over in her head before she allowed her mouth the right to speak them. I didn't push, content to let her wrestle with whatever it was that bothered her enough to preface the question with a reassurance of our friendship.

"There is some concern, Majesty, and I've been asked to speak with you on the subject. However, I'd like you to understand that I do so as a friend, not as a matriarch, and that I also share these concerns." She stopped and inhaled, then met my eyes. "There is some concern, Majesty, as to the company you have chosen to surround yourself with."

"I see. You could just say you're worried about Hao and Johar."

Caterina winced at my tone but continued. "I understand they are your friends and Indrana owes them a debt of gratitude for the fact that they fought by your side during the coup. There is no doubt that they helped us win; however—" She looked down at her hands and tried to collect her thoughts. "You continue to ask them for advice on policies that will have no impact on their lives. You share information with them that could be used against Indrana."

"I know better than to throw classified information around, Caterina." I kept my eyes on her as I picked up my chai and took a sip.

"I know, Majesty." She held her hands up. "I'm not accusing you of that; no one is accusing you of that. Sometimes there is information that, while not classified, could not be easily obtained."

"You're asking me to believe that Hao would do something to put me in danger, Caterina. If I believed that, he'd have been gone a long time before I ever set foot back here."

She shook her head. "I'm not suggesting he would, Majesty. The man clearly adores you, and he's loyal to you or I would eat my sari. But to him, you are not Indrana, not in the same way you are to those of us who have lived here all our lives and given ourselves to this empire. I know you trust him, but this is not a gunrunning operation. It is an empire. Can I ask you to consider trusting those of us who have experience running the empire over those you call friends?"

I stared unblinking at the screen on the wall without really registering the newscaster's report about Chennai Pharmaceuticals' new expansion plans. Alice's gentle rebuke this morning floated up out of my memory and I sighed, uncrossing my arms to rub a hand over my face. There wasn't anything to be done about it beyond me taking the advice for what it was—in the best interests of Indrana—and moving on.

"Majesty, I'm sorry. I—"

"Don't." I held my hand up. "You're not wrong, Caterina, and if anyone should apologize it's obviously me. I'm sorry I put you in this position. I won't apologize for trusting the people I trust, but I realize how it looks and I promise I will do better at least to keep things to a minimum and out of the public eye." I smiled. "I do realize this isn't a gunrunning operation. For one thing it's far more disorganized."

Caterina sighed, but smiled. "Majesty, I—"

"Alice said something similar this morning," I said, cutting her off again. "She was right to bring it up and so were you." I got to my feet and she followed me up. "I know when I'm out of my depth, Caterina. My business is fighting and war, not peace and politics. I'm learning the latter things. All I can ask is that you continue to support me as we try to do what's best for Indrana."

Caterina smiled. "You will always have my support, Majesty, though I think you're wrong. I think you are more than capable of peace and politics, as you call them. I would never have supported you in the beginning if I believed otherwise."

I sat alone in my room after lunch, cursing over the budget figures, when Hao and Dailun made an appearance.

My gunrunner mentor and his younger cousin were matched in height and build, but the slight family resemblance in their faces was drowned out by Dailun's Svatir heritage. The pretty, pink-haired pilot wouldn't ever achieve Hao's more rugged look thanks to his Svatir mother's genes.

The Svatir were a withdrawn alien race whose homeworld was somewhere on the very edge of the Perseus arm of the Milky Way. Their contact with humans was mostly facilitated by those who came our way while Traveling—a rite of passage for young Svatir. It was a chance for them to see the universe, to add to the collection of knowledge they already carried for their entire race.

"Hail," Hao said after the door had closed behind him. He'd accepted my title more easily than even I had, but he still defaulted to my name in private.

I didn't mind it. Truth was I missed the days of companions on mostly equal footing with one another. Even though over the last few months I'd gotten the majority of the nobles and others in my vicinity to stop bowing and scraping, no one was going to forget I was the empress. Hao gave me some of that quiet companionship, and it was an invaluable gift.

Dailun's hero worship of me was something else entirely, and I still hadn't been able to pry a good reason for it out of him. I'd accidentally stolen Hao's cousin shortly after we met. He'd piloted Hao's ship and asked to Travel with me while we fled from the Saxons. My agreement meant he would follow me for as long as his Traveling lasted, and he was loyal to me for the duration of his journey. In turn I was responsible for his welfare and making sure he had as many experiences as he wanted. Since I was stuck on Pashati, he tended to go off with Hao a great deal, but he never seemed to complain about the arrangement.

"When did you get back?" I turned my cheek upward as Dailun leaned in to kiss it and reached a hand out to squeeze his forearm.

"*Jiejie.*" Dailun's dark eyes were like stars, the silver running through them a result of his Traveling.

"Little over an hour ago." Hao stretched his lithe arms above his head. His tattoos ran the length of both limbs, a calling card of his life as a member of the Cheng gang and his status as a member of Po-Sin's family.

"Thanks for the use of the ship. Fair warning, though, you may have to pry it out of Dailun's hands when you want it back." He leaned his hip on my desk and scratched at his metallic-streaked hair, the strands now a deep bronze among his natural black.

"It is an excellent ship," Dailun said.

"You're welcome to it," I replied. "How's Henna?"

Dr. Henna Brek had saved my life several times when I was on Hao's crew and when I'd been injured on Candless.

"Settled in with her mother." Hao narrowed his golden eyes at me. "I can pay her stipend."

"I owe you anyway, it all comes out in the wash."

"The empire of Indrana is paying for my doctor's retirement?" Hao asked.

Dailun chuckled and wandered over to the window.

"It's coming out of Cressen's accounts, not that it's any of your business," I said.

"You kept your accounts?"

"Mind your own business." Desperate to avoid the curious look he was giving me, I fixed my eyes back on the tablet. Much like sleeping with a gun under my pillow and sitting with my back to the door, I couldn't find the strength to move all the money from my gunrunning days to Pashati. I might have to run—someday— and it was better if I wasn't caught off guard when it happened.

I'd tried during those first few months at home to settle in and forget the instinctive need to be prepared for any eventuality, telling myself that I was home and that nothing could possibly happen that would require a safety net like that. Of course, I couldn't undo twenty years of habit and gut instinct through sheer willpower and worked myself into far too many sleepless nights.

It had been Zin who'd finally sat me down—with his customary practicality—and told me to leave the accounts where they were if it helped me sleep better at night.

"Because we all sleep better when you do," he'd said.

I still couldn't figure out how he'd even known the accounts existed, let alone how that was what had been bothering me, but he was a former Tracker and they lived and breathed instinct. Regardless, the permission worked, and I stopped worrying about it and started sleeping at night.

Hao smirked. "Do your BodyGuards know you still have an exit plan?"

"They do, thank you very much."

The talk with Caterina was loud in my head and I smacked Hao's hand away when he reached for the tablet on the desk in front of me.

Hao shrugged, studying me curiously over my rebuke. "Indrana is hard up for cash, that's not exactly a secret, little sister."

"True, but you're not a member of my government so you don't get to look at our financial records."

"Ouch." He pressed a hand to his heart in mock hurt but raised it in surrender when I glared. "All right, all right. Have it your way. I can't do much about Indrana's money problems, but I could pay for that new palace of yours, if you'd let me."

I couldn't do much more than blink at him. This wasn't a frivolous offer, but Hao's fortune was nothing to sneeze at. The reconstruction budget for the palace was giving me a massive headache. I'd put it off for as long as I could, forcing them to rebuild and repair everything else in the capital before we tackled the palace. I would have skipped the structure entirely, but everyone else insisted it had to be done.

Here was a way to get rid of this particular headache. My former mentor's wealth rivaled that of what the agreement with the Tarsi had just brought into the empire—if you mixed his legitimate businesses in with everything else. It wasn't anything compared to the treasury of Indrana, even on a bad day, but it was still impressive.

It wouldn't fix anything, not in the long run, but for a moment I was so very tempted to take the breathing room he offered and at least get this headache over with. Except Hao was, for all intents and purposes, still attached to his uncle, still a gunrunner.

"I can't." I looked toward the window and watched the clouds float by, little tufts of cotton in the blue sky, before I met Hao's raised eyebrow with a soft smile. "Thank you, for the offer, Cheng Hao. It is more appreciated than you know. However, I am no longer a gunrunner."

"You are the empress of Indrana," he said without a hint of a smile and the tiniest of nods. "However, you are also my little sister. Nothing will change that. The offer will remain should you decide otherwise."

Nodding, I swallowed down the lump in my throat.

My relationship with Hao had always been a strange, undefinable thing. Something caught between love and respect with only one awkward moment of attraction that unnerved both of us so badly we vowed never to open that door again. I loved him like a brother; there wasn't a need for any more of an explanation than that.

Hao had always been fond of me, a fact that worried Portis from the outset and seemed to amuse everyone else we encountered over the years.

After my—albeit brief—death at Wilson's hands, Hao had decided to stay in Indrana. He hadn't said anything about his plans, so I had no idea how long he was going to stay. But for the moment, at least, I got to enjoy his company. Him doing strange things like offering to bankroll the construction of my palace and my occasional ass chewing from the matriarchs about letting him into my inner circle seemed to be the price I had to pay for his presence.

"Anyway, I hear you are busy being an empress for the next few days, and I have some other things to look into." Hao smiled and executed a bow as Emmory came into the room with Stasia behind him. I got to my feet.

"The Saxons are inbound, Majesty. They should land in about an hour."

"Thank you, Emmory."

"I'll go get your things ready, Majesty," Stasia said, and I nodded to my maid.

Offering up a smile to Dailun as I walked them to the door, I squeezed his hand. "Henna is really all right? You know how Hao is."

"She is fine. It is a lovely place for her to settle. Her mother lives out on the edge of a small settlement on Thory V."

"Good. If anyone deserves the peace and quiet, it's her."

"She said to tell you she'll miss you and to come visit sometime."

"I'd like that," I replied. "I'll talk with you later."

Dailun smiled and dipped his pink head, then followed Hao down the hallway. I rubbed a hand over my inexplicably misty eyes and headed for my bedroom to change.

5

The beads of my heavy cream-and-gold sari danced in the breeze. I stood on the edge of the landing pad, watching as two smaller, but far more powerful, Jal fighters escorted the unarmed courier ship carrying the new king of Saxony and his retinue to the ground. The fighter craft were under orders to fire upon them should they deviate even a meter from their assigned path, and I imagined the pilot was sweating buckets.

The good part of surviving the attack on Red Cliff and winning the war against the Saxons was that it had enabled me to set the rules for not only this meeting but all the terms of the final peace treaty.

In all but the most official and technical terms, the Saxon Kingdom was surrendering to Indrana. I had agreed not to wipe the Saxon Navy off the galactic map and allowed Ambassador Toropov's people the space to run a bloodless coup against King Trace, putting his younger brother Samuel on the throne. In exchange, they were about to sign a document that returned all the planets the Saxons had taken from Indrana in the War of '84, in addition to the ones that Indrana had relinquished in the peace treaty we'd signed in 3001.

There would be reparations, though Saxony was nearly as broke as Indrana. The money would come, but it was a long way off, and the more cynical part of me didn't hold a lot of hope we'd ever see a single credit. But maybe Alice's children would.

Even more importantly, King Samuel would admit, in front of the entire galaxy, that Saxony was responsible for starting the War of '84 and for my attempted assassination. He was also going to offer a full apology.

That was almost worth more than any concessions we were about to receive. No longer would history claim that Indrana had started the war that brought both powers to their knees, killed millions, and required the might of the Solarian Conglomerate to bring it to a halt. My planets were returned to the empire, their resources and people back where they belonged after more than twenty years under the control of a foreign power.

Indrana was whole again and I would use that to our advantage. Brokering deals with powerful Solarian businessmen was just the start to bring credits and jobs into our economy. I would build my empire back up and make it even better than before the war started. Once we were on solid footing again, we could focus on the second phase of the reformations and by the time Alice's daughter took over, Shiva willing, the citizens of Indrana would know equality and peace and prosperity.

Not bad for a former gunrunner.

Caterina shifted at my side. The two of us, along with my Body-Guards and a full platoon of Marines, were the only ones here to greet the king. Alice would stay well away from the signing, safe at my country house at the base of Mount Rishabha, her absence a pointed reminder of how little I trusted the Saxons to keep their word.

My other conditions were also in place to put the Saxons in the most disadvantageous position possible. It was petty of me, maybe, but I wanted everyone to remember what had happened on Red Cliff, and the best way to do that seemed to be my continued insistence that the Saxon party come to Pashati, that they fly in on a courier ship, and that they remain unarmed at all times.

It was the sort of thing that gave a bodyguard heartburn, and even Emmory winced in sympathy when I had laid my terms out to Toropov.

Jaden Toropov, former ambassador to Indrana, had known better than to argue with me, and he bore the demands with a resigned sigh and a promise to do his best. As we watched the courier ship drift downward and come to rest on the landing pad fifty meters away, I smiled. His best, as it turned out, had been enough.

"I'm not going to lie," Caterina murmured. "It is a relief that we won't have to keep an eye on the Saxons if things start to get worse with the Farians and the Shen."

"You're still thinking about that news story from lunch?" I murmured back.

"That and the recent messages from a number of our freighter captains expressing concern about an uptick in mercenary presence around the shipping lanes."

"I read those." I only just managed to keep from frowning as the ramp for the courier ship came down and the four Saxons descended to the tarmac. My Guards and Marines all came to attention. "You think there's a connection?"

"You know as well as I do that the criminal syndicates will take advantage of the Solarians' distraction."

"Fair point."

"They brought a woman," Caterina said, changing the subject. "Interesting."

Saxony wasn't as oppressively patriarchal as the Ganymede Oligarchy, but it was more so than the Solarians, and certainly I couldn't remember ever having seen more than a handful of women in a position of power in their government.

"Very," I replied. The young woman walking by King Samuel's side was nearly as tall as the king, though both were shorter than Jaden Toropov walking on the left and the strange man on their right.

"Bodyguard on the right, Majesty," Emmory murmured. "Jakob

Utkin, former Saxon Shock Troop of thirty-three years. Honorably discharged just a few months ago to take over as King Samuel's guard."

"We expected as much; is he armed?"

"Not that I can tell. Zin is doing a more thorough sweep."

I nodded, keeping my eyes on the approaching group. They stopped in concert a meter away.

"Your Imperial Majesty." Jaden Toropov folded his lanky frame into an elegant bow. "Thank you for your gracious hospitality. May I present to you King Samuel Gerison and his bride-to-be, the Crown Princess Thora Bogdan."

Turning my gaze from Toropov to the young couple, I was pleased they both stood their ground, as obviously nervous as they were.

Samuel Gerison shared his brother Trace's features, but they still bore the innocence of a sheltered royal sibling who'd never expected to take the throne. I could sympathize, though my innocence had burned away a long time ago in the black.

His navy-blue eyes were filled with a wary respect as they met mine. "Your Imperial Majesty, thank you for having us." Those same blue eyes flicked to Emmory and then he extended a hand, taking a step forward to close the gulf between us. "I hope this is the beginning of an era of peace between our nations—and possibly in the future something more like friendship."

I took his hand and shook it firmly. "Peace is in all our best interests, King Samuel. Indrana also hopes for a day when our people can step away from the pain of the past and look on Saxony with friendship. Congratulations on your upcoming wedding."

"Thank you." Samuel smiled, the expression brief before he resumed his neutral look. "Thora is one of my most valued advisors."

"Your Majesty." Thora's smile was more genuine, and she held her palm up in an Indranan greeting instead of extending her hand.

Her braided, white-blond hair hung over one shoulder to her waist, while her eyes, a lighter blue than Samuel's, were filled with genuine warmth.

"Your Highness." I pressed my palm to hers. "Welcome to Indrana."

"I have been looking forward to it," she said. "I hope to learn more about your empire and perhaps even encourage some changes at home based on your example."

Toropov unsuccessfully swallowed a chuckle, while Samuel sighed, suggesting that this was not a new discussion between the three of them—and that some of those changes were going to give these men heartburn.

I grinned.

"Let me introduce Matriarch Caterina Saito, head of the Matriarch Council."

As the royal couple moved on to greet Caterina, I turned my attention to Jaden. "You have moved up in the world, Prime Minister Toropov."

His own grin was as unrepentant as mine had been. "It is a pleasure to see you in your element, Your Majesty."

"That's a kind lie. How is Trace?"

"Stable." The smile faded and Toropov shook his head. "Most days he is himself, and better than half of those he is his old self, which is a greater blessing from God than we could have hoped. The rest of the time he is lost either in his own world or in one that is rather nightmarish, I'm afraid."

"I'm sorry to hear it." I truly was. My fond memories of Trace from my childhood before the war between us tore things apart had pushed me to accept his offer of talks on Red Cliff once I'd returned home and taken the throne. What we hadn't known at the time was that Wilson had his claws in the Saxon king in the form of an extremely addictive and deadly drug known as Pirate Rock. It had made him unstable and Wilson's willing pawn in the scheme to destroy my empire.

I looped my arm through Toropov's and followed behind Caterina and the others. "Will you give him my wishes for more good days than bad back home with you?"

"Of course, Your Majesty."

"How are things at home going?"

Toropov's smile was slow, the older man studying me for a long moment before he answered. "Settled, if tentatively. We are watching the news about the Farians and the Shen with some concern. You?"

"Same," I replied with a smile of my own. "The quiet is nice, isn't it?"

"Very much so, Majesty. Very much so. I hope it continues."

"Good morning, Your Majesty." Admiral Inana Hassan gave me a short bow and then stepped into the room, making way for the shorter man behind her.

Caspel Ganej, director of Galactic Imperial Security, was a hawk-faced man with gray hair and a deceptively easy smile I'd learned early on hid an extremely devious mind. "Empress." His bow was equally brief and I hid my smile. Everyone was catching on to my dislike of pomp, and functional while still technically proper greetings were becoming the norm. "We're early, if you'd like to finish your breakfast?" Caspel asked.

"I'm done with it," I replied, waving a hand at the nearly empty plate on the nearby table and then nodding at my maid standing in the doorway. "Thank you, Stasia; tell Yun Li it was lovely."

"I will, ma'am." My maid nodded her blond head with a smile and started clearing the plates. "Did you want the rest of your chai? Or can I bring you a fresh one?"

"This is fine, thank you." I snagged the cup and followed Admiral Hassan over to the seats near the fireplace. The elegant commander of Home Fleet and victor of the battle of Pashati folded herself down onto the blue-gray couch and adjusted her uniform.

Caspel sat next to her, looking like a Great Banded Eagle from Pholsus IV with his lean face and hooked nose. He was probably as dangerous as one of the carnivorous beasts, which could take off with a young child in their talons if given half a chance.

I smoothed down my own top after I sat, the cut similar to Hassan's but minus the military accoutrements and in a matte black the same as my BodyGuards.

"What have we got?" I asked, cradling my mug in both hands.

"Things are quiet, Majesty," Caspel replied. "Though I think in part because everyone is holding their breaths until the treaty signing is completed." A smile appeared briefly on his lean face, and I could see the slight difference in his prosthetic left eye from his real one as the silver shone through the brown. He'd lost the eye during Wilson's coup, though the intelligence operative had mounted a successful defense of Krishan as I fought my way back home. "It is not just the Saxons and the Indranans who would like to see peace happen."

"None of the rest of them have borne the brunt of all these years of war," I replied, rolling my eyes.

"True enough. It will open up a number of doors to us, and likely the Saxons. I'm seeing suggestions that the XiXu will approach us about trade possibilities." He raised an eyebrow. "It was their fuel tech in the *Likho*."

I whistled. The *Likho* had been a monster Saxon ship that King Trace had chased me down in as we'd made our way from the Canafey system back home to the Ashvin system. The behemoth of a vessel could do a thousand warp floats without stopping to refuel, and even though I knew part of that was due to her size, it was also the tech from the XiXu that had allowed for that kind of range.

"Can you imagine what we could do if we could get that to work with the *Vajrayanas*?" Inana asked with a grin.

"Will they be willing to offer up military tech, though? Surely something in their alliance with the Saxons prevents it."

"Maybe." Caspel's shrug was terrifyingly nonchalant. "But opening up trade means more people in and out of their territory, which means more chances for information to come out. And for the right price one can find out anything."

"I am going to pretend I didn't hear that." Inana looked at the ceiling with a sigh, and I chuckled.

"There's been some unrest along the border between Hyperion and Ganymede," Caspel continued, his real eye unfocusing only slightly as he consulted his *smati*. "Honestly, I don't think it will come to anything. You know how the Hyperions like to poke at their neighbor, but it would be suicide for the current leaders of the oligarchy to attempt anything. They've only just solidified their own power base."

"Not to mention the Hyperion Royal Marines would wipe the fucking floor with whatever ragged group they've got for a military right now." I snorted into my chai.

Ganymede was an oppressive nation in a constant state of revolt. No sooner did one group take power before the infighting started and then the revolution happened all over again. There were times when I wished the more powerful, not to mention more egalitarian, nation of Hyperion would just step on their rambunctious neighbors.

To this date no ruler of Ganymede had been dumb enough to take on one of the Milky Way's most powerful fighting forces.

"Sign me up to front-row seats for that shit-show," Inana said with a laugh that I echoed.

"It would be one for the ages. Okay, business as usual for that sector. If the Solarians aren't too fussed about it, I'm not worried. They're closer to the action than we are anyway."

There was a wealth of space—mostly starless, planetless space—between Indrana and the Solarian Conglomerate. Indrana was located in the Perseus arm of the Milky Way near the Orion-Cygnus arm that was home to the Sol system and the vast number of systems and planets making up the SC.

"They're not," Caspel replied. "Though it could be because they've got more pressing things to worry about. All of these recent engagements between the Farians and the Shen have happened either in or near their territory."

"Why aren't they pressuring the Farians about it?"

"I think they have been, Majesty, but you know their influence has never been as strong with the Farians as ours has. Without any success. I've sent some feelers of my own out and haven't gotten any response." He shook his head. "The lack of response from the Shen doesn't surprise me; we've been Faria's ally for a very long time. However, I'm not hearing a thing from the Farians, either, and frankly that worries me a little."

I finished off my chai and set the mug on the side table, then crossed my arms over my chest. "You think they might be losing the fight?"

"I don't know, Majesty. We know next to nothing about this conflict except that it's been ongoing somewhere in the Scutum-Centaurus arm of the galaxy for a very long time. And believe me, I have tried to find out more."

"I could ask the Farians directly if you think it'll help," I said. "It's a big galaxy, but if things get bad in the Solarian sector it will impact us even if the fighting doesn't spill our way."

"I think it would, Majesty," Caspel said after a moment's thought. "The Solarians haven't asked us to intervene yet, but as I said, we have more pull. Maybe the Farians will listen to you."

"I agree," Inana said. "Let's take the offensive diplomatically on this and see if we can't have an impact. We're barely back on our feet. The last thing Indrana needs is a war between two alien races throwing everything into chaos."

"Just when we thought things were going to get quiet around here," Caspel replied with a grin.

"True enough." I got to my feet and the pair followed. "Keep an eye on it. I'll send a message to the Farian ambassador. I don't mind saying to you that I don't like this feeling in my gut, but in the meantime I should go get ready to make this hard-won peace a reality."

6

There was no fanfare, no big gathering later that morning; just me and Caterina in the downstairs conference room sitting across the table from the three Saxons.

Lunch was planned for after. I hoped it would be less somber than this situation and that we truly could start to build that friendship Samuel and Thora both seemed interested in.

Samuel cleared his throat, straightened his spine, and met the news cameras with a look that reminded me of his older brother. "Ladies and gentlemen. Citizens of Indrana and of Saxony. People of the Milky Way. I am King Samuel Gerison, duly confirmed and sworn leader of the Saxon Kingdom. Hear my words.

"In the Indranan year 2984, my father, going against the words of his advisors, and despite the best efforts of Empress Mercedes Bristol, threw away hundreds of years of friendship in favor of war. My own brother, drowning in his addiction and his grief over the death of our father, furthered that war in 3001 after a peace treaty was duly negotiated and followed by the Indranan Empire."

I kept the smile on my face and my hands folded at my waist as Samuel cleared his throat again and continued.

"The Saxon Kingdom accepts and admits our fault in starting this war. We are at fault for the deaths of millions. We are at fault for breaking a friendship through greed and blindness. The first step to forgiveness is admitting this, and I pray that Her Majesty and the people of Indrana will find it in their hearts to accept our apology and allow us to work to make things right between us."

"The Empire of Indrana gladly accepts your apology, Your Majesty," I replied. "We look forward to a new friendship, one that will be stronger with the lessons learned from our past conflict and one that will endure throughout the years."

The signing itself was formulaic. All the details had been hashed out in advance, and both Samuel and I had read through the treaty a dozen times at least.

I pressed my hand to the screen and passed the tablet to Samuel with a smile. He did the same, with a firm nod in my direction.

I extended my hand, and Samuel took it, his grip cool in mine. "Thank you for this, Samuel. Thank you for saving lives."

"To peace," he said. "And a new day."

I turned to Toropov and took the hand he offered as Samuel turned to Caterina.

"Peace benefits us all, Your Majesty," Toropov said with a smile. "Thank you for being wise enough to realize it."

"We dishonor the dead if we don't seek peace at every opportunity. There's lunch in the room next door, if you'd like to follow me?"

"Now that business is attended to," Toropov said as we passed through the doorway into the neighboring room. "I feel it's a good idea to inform you that the Farians approached us about an alliance."

"Did they now?" The Farians were notoriously selective about their alliances with humans, and I had often wondered why they'd never approached the Saxons—though Trace's unpredictability and the constant war with Indrana was probably a huge obstacle to securing any kind of relationship.

But now they were reaching out to the Saxons when Caspel couldn't get anyone to tell him what was going on with the Shen. My gut rolled. I faked an easy smile.

"Why do I feel like you give Director Ganej sleepless nights, Jaden?"

The other man's smile made him look fifteen years younger, and he patted my arm with a scarred hand. "He knows he does the same to me. Though we had a most enjoyable time, given the circumstances, while I was here during the coup."

"What are you going to tell the Farians?"

Toropov considered me for a long moment and then pulled out my chair for me. "We are still considering the offer, Your Majesty. I won't lie, it is beneficial for Saxony. The money alone would prevent us from a complete financial collapse. I don't need to mention that the Saxon kingdom staying financially solvent is also to Indrana's benefit."

"I feel like there's a *but* hanging around that needs to be said." I sat down and waited for Toropov to take his own seat before he answered me.

"We are not in a position to go to war again—not for ourselves, and certainly not for the benefit of another. This increase in the conflict with the Shen is extremely worrisome." He frowned and lowered his voice, though Samuel and Thora were deep in discussion with Caterina and the news cameras had been blocked at the door. "I don't understand what it is about the Shen that scares the Farians so, and that, quite frankly, concerns me."

"You're not alone on that front," I murmured. "You have to do what's best for Saxony, Jaden."

"I know. I will." He paused, collected his thoughts, and then continued. "It will not impact our relationship with Indrana if we say yes?"

"I cannot see how it would," I replied with a smile. "We are allies with the Farians and will continue to be so even if we can't assist them in this war with the Shen. It is Indrana's official position that the fight between the Farians and the Shen is their affair alone. We have no desire to involve ourselves in a war that does not concern us and will only do so if the conditions of our treaty with Faria are met—namely if the situation escalates beyond what has been these consistent conflicts involving both the Farians and the Shen, or if this conflict directly impacts Indrana."

Jaden relaxed and returned my smile. "That is good to hear, Majesty. Now, before I ruin lunch completely with this talk, let's find a better topic. I hear you recently cashed in on some good odds concerning how long you'd be staying with the empire."

My laughter bounced up to the ceiling. "You are an awful man, Jaden Toropov; I knew there was a reason I liked you."

Lifting a slender shoulder, he smiled at the server as they laid a plate in front of him. "I made a decent amount myself, I confess, and put most of it down for this time next year."

"I'm not going to tell you if I'm staying that long or not," I said with another laugh. "You'll get us in trouble with the gambling commission."

"You and I both know you're in this for the long-term." He winked at me. "However, don't get so settled, Your Majesty, that you forget how much fun trouble can be." Toropov lifted his wineglass. "Ladies and gentlemen, a toast, to a new era of peace and prosperity for both our peoples."

I lifted my own glass, a smile on my lips. "To peace and prosperity."

I said our good-byes to the Saxons late the next morning at the Saxon embassy before Emmory and Caspel escorted them back to the landing pad and their ship. I headed out for a visit with the soldiers being treated at the Alix Kavi Hospital with Zin and Gita. They'd renamed the Royal Indranan Hospital after my father's assassination. His death had been the opening shot of Wilson's private war against my family and the Empire of Indrana, though at the time no one had realized just how twisted the conspiracy was.

On the way back to the hotel I'd sent the message to the Farian ambassador requesting that she make an appointment with Alba to see me. If things were escalating with the Shen, I wanted to be prepared for whatever the Farians might request. They had to know we weren't in any position to run headlong into another fight, but I was certain Indrana could offer some kind of assistance to one of our oldest allies. Even if it was simply on the diplomatic front, as Inana had suggested.

"I was promised lunch now that you are done being empress," Hao said with a smile when we met him and Dailun in the lobby of the hotel.

"I am never done being empress," I replied with a laugh. Slipping my arm through his, I leaned against him, his solid presence chasing back the panic of being in the lift and the sadness that always clung to me after my visits to the hospital. "Do you remember when we crashed that highbrow party on New France?"

Hao chuckled and Dailun raised a curious eyebrow.

"I danced with a bona fide prince," I said with an exaggerated wink, and Zin burst into laughter along with Dailun. "He was also a thief and a liar and we stole several million credits from him shortly after."

The lift doors opened and Hao started forward without urging, smiling at me when I released my grip on his arm. But I noticed the way his eyes strayed to my *Dve* and the way Gita had somehow managed to end up on the opposite side of the lift from Hao and swallowed a sigh. My *Dve* had been briefly involved with Hao during our time out in the black, but the return to somewhat normal life had driven a wedge between them not long after. I'd asked Hao once and he'd snarled at me to mind my own business. I could have ordered Gita to tell me, but that seemed an awful abuse of power. So I let them sulk and awkwardly avoid each other in public and pretended I didn't see the wounded glances when the other had their back turned.

If Portis were still alive he'd have wondered at my self-control. "Majesty." Alba dipped her head in greeting and fell into step with us down the hallway. "Stasia has lunch waiting for you, and Caspel will come over after seeing the Saxons off for the daily briefing."

"Good." I headed into my rooms after the sweep, exchanging greetings with Stasia and the other servers still fussing over the table.

"After lunch your schedule is empty except for the visit to the palace construction site."

I swallowed down the lump in my throat. I wasn't looking forward to going to the palace. The place where Wilson had executed the matriarchs, where Cas had sacrificed himself. "What about the evening?" I asked, shaking away the ghosts clamoring for attention in my head.

"*Ekam* Tresk asked me to keep your evening cleared, ma'am."

"Did he now?" I glanced in Zin's direction.

He shook his head and lifted his hands. His grin, however, belied his ignorance, as did the fact that I knew Emmory wouldn't have planned anything without his husband's input.

Or his second-in-command's. "Gita, what's this about?"

"I couldn't say, Majesty."

"*Uff,* is there a point to being empress if you're all going to lie to me? If I'd wanted that I could have stayed out in the black."

Chuckles met my protest and I grinned as I dropped into my seat.

Dailun laid a hand on my shoulder on his way by. I reached up, my fingers on his for a moment before he moved on to his seat. "The islands were very beautiful, *jiejie,*" he said. "I have not seen water that clear for a long time."

"Johar seemed very enamored of the area," Hao added, taking a seat. "We looked at several properties down by the beach."

I laughed. "I can't believe she's actually thinking of buying property here."

"Santa Pirata isn't exactly a resort planet." Hao smiled up at the server who put his plate in front of him, and the young man blushed.

"True. Thank you, Zin."

"Of course, Majesty." He winked at me. "Emmory said to let you know the Saxons are off-planet and headed home. He'll be back here in twenty minutes."

I inhaled and then exhaled, feeling some of the tension leaving me. "That's one thing accomplished."

That pessimistic voice in the back of my brain whispered that there wasn't any guarantee that peace would hold for the day, let alone for years. I shook it off as best as I could. It was done for now and my people were safe.

"To the Indranan Empire," Hao said, raising his cup. "And Her Majesty, Empress Hailimi Bristol."

Clearing my throat of the unexpected tears clogging it, I raised my own cup. "To the Indranan Empire and an age of peace. Not too bad for a former gunrunner, eh?"

Hao winked at me and we settled into friendly chatter as Dailun pushed for more details of the Paris heist, which I gladly provided while Hao interjected his own version of events along the way.

We were just wrapping up when Emmory and Caspel arrived.

"There you are. I thought for sure you were going to hide from me all day."

"I had some things to take care of." Emmory waved a gloved hand, his dark eyes scanning the windows behind me out of habit.

"Yes, your mysterious surprise for this evening." Waving my own hands in the air, I got up from the table. "Have I mentioned I don't like surprises?"

"I promise no one will be shooting at you, Majesty."

Hao chuckled as he got to his feet.

"*Jiejie*, do you mind if I wait around and join you this afternoon?" Dailun asked.

"Not at all," I replied, and hugged him. "I'd love your company. Hao, you want to join us?"

"Thank you," he said with a shake of his head. "I have some business to deal with. I'll see you this evening."

"He has plans." I waved a hand in my *Ekam*'s direction.

"Yes, I know," Hao said, his laughter following him as he sauntered out of the room with Dailun on his heels.

"He knows?" I shot Emmory my best betrayed look, and Caspel laughed.

Emmory shrugged. "It's Hao. Keeping a secret from him is challenging."

"Tell me about it," I muttered, but then I grinned. "I managed it for twenty years, though."

My *Ekam* shook his head with a sigh.

"Majesty? I just received a message from Ambassador Ussin." Alba frowning was never a good sign, and my amusement slid away as quickly as Emmory's did. "She regrets that things are so hectic at the moment she won't be able to come see you any time soon."

I blinked once in shock. "That's cowshit."

"She's not a citizen, Majesty," Emmory said. "She doesn't have to come when you order her to."

"I didn't order," I replied. "And the cowshit is less about her being extremely unprofessional by refusing. It's about claiming she's too busy to see me. She's blowing me off just like Caspel's contacts blew him off." I muttered a second curse, this one in Cheng, and Emmory raised an eyebrow at me. "He's been trying to get information from sources familiar with the Farians about what exactly is going down with the Shen, but so far it's just been silence in response."

"Silence may mean they just don't have an answer for you, Majesty."

"You know as well as I do, Emmory, that's not how this works. Silence means they're scrambling for answers, or planning something they don't want to share with us. Silence means whatever is going on is nothing good."

My *Ekam*'s grim look told me all I needed to know.

7

My BodyGuards headed next door for shift change, and I followed them, the twins staying out in the hallway as Stasia finished clearing the room. My maid handed me a fresh cup of chai and a smile, pausing on her way out to exchange quiet words with Dailun. Judging from the quick shake of his head, she was checking to see if he needed anything.

What had become my rooms in the new hotel occupied the entire fifteenth floor. My suite was in the back corner, close to an exit with empty rooms on the opposite side and a block of rooms Emmory had converted into BodyGuard barracks in the last six months between me and the elevator and stairs.

I hadn't been in those rooms for the first month, unlike my brief time in the palace when I'd spent as many hours in the Body-Guard barracks as my own space; where I'd laughed and joked with Willimet and Jet and the others; where I'd had countless meals and cups of chai, sat through briefings, and debated the art of bluffing at Antilan poker.

Now it was almost, if not quite, what we'd had. Zin smiled at me, his gray-green eyes sparkling with delight, and went back to the report he was typing.

"Majesty." Indula had his back to the others, and he winked at me. "Did you get to see the end of the baller game last night?"

"I did, and it didn't seem like the Queens were going to pull off that win."

Indranan rugby, more commonly called baller, was an odd mishmash of Old Earth rugby and cricket—thankfully without the bats the latter sport employed back in the SC.

"Iza bet on the Water Bugs." He nudged Iza as he passed, and she kicked him in the back of the knee in response.

Johar didn't look up from her cards as I passed, simply holding out a fist to me that I tapped on my way by. The smuggler had made herself at home with my BodyGuards, and Emmory seemed content to let her stay. Dailun pulled up a chair on her left, peeking at her cards. She hissed and smacked him away.

"Majesty." Zin finished his typing as I sat in the chair on the other side of the desk. "Have a good lunch?"

"It was lovely. Did you get something to eat?"

He grinned and winked. "Emmory does feed us."

"Shift change, people. Let's get this moving," Emmory said, rapping his knuckles on the desk. My *Ekam* gave the tiniest smile as the Guards came to attention. "At ease, everyone."

Johar had also gotten to her feet, but not braced to attention with the rest of them. Instead she crossed to me and rested a hand on my shoulder. "We need to have dinner soon."

"Yes." I peeked at my schedule on my *smati*. "What about next week?"

"Good. I will confirm with Alba." She nodded and turned toward the door, Dailun on her heels.

"You're not staying?"

"Security protocol," she said with a shrug and an easy grin. "I am technically still a gunrunner. This one is whatever he is, mostly a pain in the ass."

Dailun rolled his eyes at the ceiling.

Johar winked at me. "Your *Ekam* would be foolish to let us sit in on security briefings, and he is certainly not foolish." She tapped Emmory on the arm on her way out the door.

"Huh."

"What is it?" Zin asked.

"Nothing." I shook my head. "I guess I just wasn't expecting her to be so . . . okay with it?"

"That's been the routine for the last six months," Zin said. "She was fine with it from the very first shift change. I guess she thinks it's a small price to pay to get to spend time with you."

What really surprised me, but what I wouldn't voice out loud, was that Johar seemed much more at ease with being the outsider than Hao did. My brother hadn't settled into life on Pashati like Jo had and was off-planet as much as on these days.

"I never pegged Johar for being sentimental," I said, because Zin seemed to be waiting for a reply. "It's an interesting look on her."

"All right, people, listen up." Emmory tapped a fist on the desk again and moved to the front of the room.

It hadn't been all that long since the fateful Pratimas day when I'd leaned against the wall with Zin listening to Emmory run a security briefing for my BodyGuards, but so many faces were missing now. So many faces were new and nervous.

"How many teams are we taking with us on the tour?" I whispered as Emmory ran through the shift briefing.

Zin glanced away from Emmory. "Three on the ship with us and four more scattered throughout the fleet."

I raised a curious eyebrow, and he flashed me a grin, answering before I could ask the question. "That's in addition to the battalion of Royal Marines and three additional *Vajrayana* ships."

"Such fuss. Wouldn't it be better if I stayed home? It'd certainly be cheaper," I muttered, crossing my arms and settling back in my chair. I knew better than to disagree with Emmory's security plans for the trip, though, especially since we were going to several planets that had been less than enthusiastic about staying in the empire. And even more so now with the additional risk of the fight between the Farians and Shen spilling out of their playground.

After the briefing, I rejoined Dailun in my rooms. A light schedule only meant I didn't have to be anywhere, and I settled into the chair at my desk in the corner of the room to dive into the endless stack of files in my inbox.

So much of it just required my approval, or for me to suggest the best person to handle whatever the issue was. However, it was a relief to discover that I wasn't responsible for the daily workings of the Indranan government even if I did have a tremendous amount of power. I was constantly on the lookout for ways to further reduce our dependence on the throne as the final stop for decisions in the empire. If Wilson's coup had taught me anything, it was that Indrana was entirely too vulnerable with things as they were. My sister's death and mother's poisoning had created enough chaos to allow Phanin to gain more control than the prime minister should have had, and the councils had been so stuck in their ways that they hadn't realized what was happening until it was too late. There needed to be more balance, more offset in who was making decisions.

I hadn't breathed a word of it yet. I didn't know anything about ruling an empire, but I knew you didn't tell a crew you were changing things up while you were still out in the middle of the black. You told them once you were safely in port and they were well paid and preferably drunk off their asses.

With all the turmoil swirling over Taz and the *Upjas* reformations, I knew better than to throw this pot of oil onto the flames. We'd deal with it later.

I signed off on three requests for funding from the General Assembly and glanced Dailun's way. "You doing okay? I'm sorry there's a lot of work to do even during my supposed downtime."

"I'm fine, *jiejie*." He smiled. "I am writing my family."

Stretching, I got to my feet and wandered out onto the balcony. Closing my eyes against the warm sunshine and letting the sounds and smells of Krishan surround me. The scent of the sea lingered on the breeze coming in from Balhim Bay, tangled with something sweet—jalebi, maybe, from a street vendor—and the heavy spice of the noodle shop just around the corner from the hotel.

I exhaled with a sigh as Dailun joined me on the balcony. "You are happy here, sister." It was a statement, not a question, and I turned my face to the sun again.

"I am. I didn't think I would be. Thought I'd chafe at the restrictions. Naraka, I did chafe in the beginning. But this?" I opened my eyes and gestured at the city around us. "This is actually interesting, not stifling."

Dailun smiled and leaned his forearms on the railing; the breeze ruffled his pink hair as he squinted up at the suns. "I suspected you would be better at this than you thought."

Bumping his shoulder with mine, I snorted on a laugh. "Know it all, do you?"

He raised an eyebrow and chuckled. "I am Svatir, sister, that's a given."

"I think what surprises me most is I enjoy this. There was something to be said for not having every second of my day plotted and planned." I heaved a sigh. "But I don't have someone trying to kill me at every port and I sleep in a Shiva-damned bed every night."

"The hospital trip was hard on you." A second statement. Dailun was good at those. So sure for one so young.

"I am responsible for them," I replied.

"You mean you're responsible for their injuries." Dailun made a shushing sound as he reached for my hand. "Do you mean as a gunrunner or as their empress?"

"Both. I guess? This fight was justified; those warriors carry their scars proudly." I looked at the buildings across from my balcony. The sunlight reflected off the petal-shaped arches. "But I have lied to myself about the jobs I chose while out in the black, trying to reframe them as the best choice I could make under the circumstances. Trying to tell myself that the path I started down was about my father's killer even though I continued it long after I'd given up finding Wilson.

"The truth? I was a gunrunner. We ran other cargo, but I sold weapons. Weapons that dealt death and destruction. That caused injuries like those soldiers had. The same soldiers who sat there and stared at me with expressions too much like worship on their faces."

"Are you looking for forgiveness, *jiejie*?"

"I don't know." I truly didn't. Polite society dictated that I should feel guilty and ashamed for the choices I'd made. Some days I did. But those choices had led me here. Without them there would be no Emmory or Zin, no Gita or Jo, no Hao or Dailun. Everything about my life would be different. How could I forsake all that?

"There will be more war." The third statement was a knife between my ribs, cold and painful, and I closed my eyes to the tears that threatened. "Are you ready for it?"

"Are we ever?" I rubbed both hands over my face before I dropped them and looked at Dailun. "Do you know something I don't?"

"No," Dailun said, settling against the railing with a shake of his head. "The Farians and Shen have been at war for a very long time; these escalations are familiar. The Svatir have stayed out of it because we are pacifists. It is a natural by-product, I think, of carrying the memories of all those who come before you. The Farians and Shen could stand to do that a little more."

"I don't want to go to war again."

Dailun smiled at my quiet confession. "I know you don't, sister. I am not Fasé and I cannot see the future, but I see things clearly enough to know we are headed back into the very place you don't wish to go." He wrapped a hand around mine. "I asked my mother once why she'd fallen in love with someone like my father. I didn't understand it. She said sometimes we make a bad choice, but we play it through to the end because there are things bigger than ourselves at stake."

"Your mother sounds like a wise woman."

Dailun smiled. "She would have liked you."

"Even though I was a gunrunner?"

"Possibly because of it." He laughed softly. "She fell in love with my father, after all. I miss her, even though her voice and her memories are in my head. Her dreaming came too early. I should have had more years with her."

I wrapped an arm around his shoulders and leaned against him. "I know how much that hurts."

"Majesty?" Emmory's voice floated through the open door. "Matriarch Khatri is here with a representative from the General Assembly; do you have a moment?"

I checked my *smati*; we still had an hour before the palace tour, so I pushed away from the railing with a sigh. "Duty calls."

"You can close the door," Dailun said. "I think I will sit out here a while and be with my mother's memories."

Nodding, I slipped through the doorway and tapped the panel to close the sliding door to the balcony, tapping it again to darken the glass and give both Dailun and myself a little privacy.

"Let them in, Emmy."

He nodded and as Zaran and a shorter young woman came through the door I was hit with a memory. My heir and Zaran, their roles reversed as Alice led a nervous newly placed Matriarch Khatri into an audience with the empress.

Now, just like the meeting days earlier, Zaran was calm and composed. Her companion slightly less so, the darker-skinned representative twisting her fingers nervously in the edge of her patterned teal sari.

"Your Majesty." The pair dropped into curtsies.

"Good afternoon." I crossed the room. "Up, both of you."

I took Zaran by the shoulders and pressed my cheek to hers. "How are you?"

"Very good, Your Majesty. May I present Representative Priti Qureshi."

"Your Majesty," Priti said from the floor.

I raised an eyebrow. Zaran gave me a suffering smile and then nudged the young woman with her foot. "What did I say about groveling?" She hissed and I laughed.

"It's all right, Zaran. Priti, welcome." The young woman's shoulders were stiff under my hands and her cheek was cold with nerves. My *smati* gave me the necessary details as I ushered them to the couches. Priti was the youngest new representative, elected from Yamuna A. The planet was four systems away from Pashati, and its main city of Delhi was where I'd met Portis.

But Priti was from one of the outer districts, and judging from her wide dark eyes, Krishan was a whole other world to her.

"What can I do for you two?"

Zaran glanced at Priti, who was still staring at me slightly awestruck and chuckled. "I seem to recall being in her seat, Majesty, so I'll have some patience for her. Priti was elected from District 43 in the special elections. Given the somewhat chaotic nature of the government, the Matriarch and Ancillary Councils thought it best to assign mentors to the newcomers."

"I remember something about it coming across my desk." I nodded. The special elections held just a month after my defeat of Wilson had been necessary to fill empty seats caused by the war. I'd wanted to make sure that the government was up and running as soon after my victory as possible. Even the façade of stability was enough to settle things and make our transition even smoother than I'd hoped.

Zaran's lead-up was unnecessary, but I didn't prod for more information, content to sit back in my seat and wait for the matriarch to put a hand on Priti's knee and squeeze. "Tell the empress what you told me."

Priti swallowed, hesitated, and then her words came out in a rush. "Yesterday before session started I was coming into the building and happened to pass the prime minister in the hallway. She was talking with some other, older representatives and made an awful comment about the Prince Consort." She dropped her gaze back to her lap.

I waited a beat for Priti to elaborate on just what the comment was and when she didn't, I looked Zaran's way.

"She said it was a dangerous precedent to allow *Upjas* trash that close to the throne." Zaran's voice was flat.

"I see."

Priti's shoulders jerked at the fury sliding under the surface of my words, but then she looked up. "I thought it was going to be different here, Your Majesty. We'd heard such great things about how you were going to bring change to the empire. Yamuna A is committed to change; we've spearheaded several equality programs already. That's why I ran for this seat. I thought I could help, but—" Her face fell, and she shrugged a defeated shoulder. "If the prime minister holds such beliefs, what good can I do?"

"You can give me your recording of the incident," I said, holding a hand out. When Priti took it, I smiled, closing my fingers around hers. "You can go back to work with the knowledge that there are more of us who believe in equality, and we are not going to stop working for a better future for all Indranans. Don't quit when the task seems daunting, Priti. Work harder."

She smiled back. "Yes, ma'am. I will."

Letting her go, I got to my feet. "I'll handle the rest of this. Thank you for bringing it to my attention."

"Of course, Majesty." Zaran nodded as she and Priti both rose.

I followed them to the door and stopped Zaran before she could follow Priti out. "I want to know how widespread this is."

"Yes, ma'am. By tomorrow?"

"End of the week," I replied. "And, Zaran?"

"Ma'am?"

"Don't tell Alice about this. I'll handle it."

She nodded grimly, and I closed the door behind her, suppressing the urge to scream into the empty room. It had been the height of naïve arrogance for me to expect we'd make it through the reformations without significant obstacles, but the election of Prime Minister Shivali Tesla had been something none of us expected.

The representative from the third district on the northside of Krishan was a brilliant molecular biologist who'd won the PM slot by a narrow margin in the General Assembly after the special elections had been settled. At the time I hadn't been particularly opposed to her candidacy, even though I preferred Representative Oena Jani. The more genial and well-known candidate from Canafey Major's District 55 was openly in support of the reformations.

I'd mistakenly believed Shivali was also, just to a lesser degree, and it was only after her election that we'd realized just how much of a hard line she was going to take against not only the practical reforms but the very idea of equality for half the population of the empire.

Had I known, I would have had more quiet conversations with members of the General Assembly.

Once the urge to scream was gone, I turned my attention to the actual problem. As much as I wanted to com the PM right that moment and chew her to pieces, I knew I couldn't. There was a fine line to be walked between direct intervention by the empress and delegating the job to someone with just as much influence but slightly less visibility.

Alice would normally be the first person I spoke to about something like this, but I didn't want to upset her so I sent the file to Caterina with a note that said, *Call me.*

Five minutes later my *smati* pinged with the incoming message, and I answered the com as I headed for the bedroom.

"Where did you get that recording?"

"Zaran brought Representative Qureshi to see me."

Caterina sighed. "It figures it's from a junior representative. Someone with more experience would have gone straight to the press."

"Maybe," I replied with a shrug. "Priti's concerned with being stonewalled over the reforms. We know the prime minister has been dragging her feet over them and from the looks of it getting bolder about voicing her opinions in public. I'm not going to stand for it, Caterina."

"No, I'll handle it; you shouldn't be involved." Caterina thought for a moment and then smiled. "I know just the person to speak with our prime minister."

I nodded in reply. "Keep Priti's name out of it if you can. I don't want her career to suffer because she did the right thing."

"That was my plan, though I have a few favors I can call into the GA if necessary. Plus, if she's got Zaran on her side already, she'll be fine." Caterina chuckled at my snort of laughter. "I'll let you know how it goes."

"Do that." Time flashed in the corner of my vision. "I've got to go, Caterina; we're headed for the palace construction tour in a few minutes."

Caterina's hard look softened into sympathy. "Take care of yourself, Hail. I know this is hard on you."

I nodded sharply and disconnected the com.

8

The new skeleton of the palace crawled from the ground like a wrathful spirit, and it took every ounce of self-control I had to not turn and sprint away from it. I didn't want to go inside. The ground was littered with ghosts. They were going to wrap around my ankles and drag me under the second I set foot through the doors.

But there were news cameras and an architect with shining eyes, all of them watching me, so I pretended my pause was to adjust the gold-and-green sari wrapped around my waist, and my *Ekam* bent to assist me without a word while Dailun stood like a shield.

I gave him a little nod and straightened, forcing a smile for the cameras and following Emmory through what would one day be the front doors of my palace.

The workers had been cleared for the visit, and a platoon of Royal Marines patrolled the grounds, but only our group went inside and the voice of the architect echoed off the partially finished walls.

"We are, of course, replicating a lot of the original style, Your Majesty. Though, as you instructed, we've been strictly sourcing materials from the empire rather than looking to outside vendors."

I'd agreed to the palace reconstruction only after a great deal of pressure from both councils; however, during the fight and with Alice's help I'd secured the right to have the final say on all building materials and contractors for the job itself. That had allowed us to hire only local Indranan firms and source building materials from the empire rather than the Solarians. If I was going to have to spend money, I'd spend it at home and do everything I could to get our economy back on its feet.

"We salvaged a great deal of material from areas farthest away from the throne room." The architect smiled over her shoulder at me. "The door into the throne room was only partially damaged in the blast. We'll repair it and use it for the new throne room, which is just through here."

My gut clenched, an icy fist of pain and fear, as we crossed over the threshold. It wasn't the same room, I tried to tell myself, and yet all I could see was Cas's golden head bent before my throne as he sacrificed himself for me, for Indrana, in a way I could never repay.

All because Fasé had told him it was his life or Indrana in flames. I remembered how angry Hao had been over what she'd done. He'd nearly killed her. I'd been equally angry but so caught up in trying to get my throne back that there hadn't been time to really process just what she'd done.

I'd have to face her soon and make the choice to either forgive her or turn my back on her forever.

The architect chattered on, unaware of my sudden rapid breath and how I fumbled for Emmory's gloved hand.

"I can't, Emmy. I can't do this," I said over our *smati* link.

"It's all right, Hail, just breathe."

His fingers closed around mine, hidden from the news cameras by the other BodyGuards—Guards who, I realized, were all familiar faces: Kisah and Ikeki, both expected since the others had gone off duty, but also Zin, Gita, Indula, and Iza. There were none of my newer BodyGuards, only those who'd been with me through the fight, those who'd survived.

Those who understood.

None of them were looking at me, but it felt as though they were all in my head saying, *"We're here, Majesty. You're not alone."*

Alba had led the architect off to the other side of the room and was asking questions about the buttresses.

I blinked, scattering unshed tears and the vision of my previous *Dve* from my eyes.

"Anyone who thinks you don't carry the weight of your choices with a great deal of awareness, *jiejie*, is a fool," Dailun murmured from my other side.

Emmory squeezed my hand and then let me go when I exhaled.

"What are we doing tonight?" I asked once I could trust my voice not to waver. "Give me a distraction, Emmory, or I can't promise I won't run out of here screaming."

"My parents are in town, Majesty."

"Oh, that's lovely, why aren't you and Zin taking time off to—" The realization hit me before I finished the sentence. "Oh Shiva, no."

Only the presence of the news cameras kept me from staring at my *Ekam* in shock.

"It was your idea, Majesty."

"What?" Even as I shook my head, the memory of saying something about how long it had been since Emmory had been home filtered into my brain. "I said you should go see them, Emmy, not that you should bring them to see me."

My *Ekam*'s grin was startlingly unrepentant. "My mother wanted to come to the capital, Majesty. She said it's been too long since she's been here."

"I'm holding you personally responsible for my impending heart attack, *Ekam*."

"You wanted the distraction."

"*Dhatt.* I'm fairly sure that doesn't count as a proper distraction." I hissed at him and headed across the throne room to rejoin Alba and the architect.

*   *   *

Thanks to Emmory's news, I managed to find a balance between panic and grief that lasted me the remainder of the palace tour and through most of the remaining afternoon.

As the late summer sun began to set, I paced the confines of my room, waiting for Emmory and his parents to arrive.

I'd driven Stasia crazy, changing outfits twice—from my shimmering gray sari to my customary black uniform and back again—before she'd told me if I wanted to change a third time I'd have to do it myself and she wasn't fixing my hair again.

My green curls had grown out some from the impromptu haircut Emmory had given me when we'd been exposed to Mustard T-18 at the Naidu estate and were now brushing my shoulders again. Stasia had twisted them up around a simple silver circlet and I knew if I tried to mess with it the whole thing would end up a disaster.

"Hail, sit down," Hao ordered.

The snap of command, something he hadn't used on me in a very long time, did the trick. I dropped into a chair, my back ramrod-straight and my hands in my lap. I stared at the door, dreading the moment it would open but needing this to all be over.

"Relax your damn shoulders. You're taking the regal bit too far." Hao spotted the look on my face and stopped his teasing. "Hail, seriously, breathe before you pass out."

"She's going to hate me," I whispered.

"What?"

"I killed her son."

"Hail—"

"Portis would be alive if he hadn't gone with me."

"You have no guarantee of that." Hao dropped to a knee at my side and took my hands in his. "Yes, he's gone, but he could have just as easily died here. You were not responsible for the choices that he made, so stop trying to shoulder that burden. You and I both know Portis would be furious at you for it." The door opened and Hao rose to his feet. "And I suspect his family would feel the same."

I swallowed my nerves and pasted a smile onto my face, rising as Emmory and his parents entered the room followed by Zin.

"Your Imperial Majesty, if I may present Anah and Haris Tresk."

The pair in front of me bowed. What Emmory's mother lacked in height, she made up for in an elegance I could never hope to achieve. Anah's gold-tipped braids flashed in the light of the setting sun. Her husband's dark head was as bare as his son's.

"Please, get up. It's a great pleasure to meet you," I said as I crossed the room. They both rose, Haris towering over his wife and son, his eyes filled with a calm warmth that reminded me so much of Portis my heart stuttered in my chest.

"It is our pleasure, Your Majesty; thank you for having us," Anah said, her voice smoky and soft, carrying the weight of a trusted leader. I could hear echoes of it in my *Ekam*'s own voice.

"Anah, Haris." I took their hands and went down on a knee, ignoring the indrawn breaths and the way Anah tried to pull her hand from my grasp.

"Majesty, no, you shouldn't—"

"Thank you," I said, unable to keep the tears from my eyes or my voice. "Thank you for the gift of your sons. There is nothing I can give you in return that is equal in worth. All that I have and more is yours; you have only to ask."

"Majesty." Anah flexed her hand in mine, glancing at her husband, tears standing in her eyes.

The sad smile on his face echoed his wife's, and Haris Tresk pulled me to my feet with a gentle tug. I landed in his embrace, feeling Anah's arms tighten around my waist as I buried my face against his chest and wept.

I don't know how long we stood there as pieces of my wounded heart slowly fused back into place, only that when we separated and

I turned away to wipe the tears from my face I caught a glimpse of Hao smiling.

"Anah, Haris, if I could introduce Cheng Hao." I made the introductions as Emmory opened the door and a trio of servers entered behind Stasia. With the same efficiency of a general on a battlefield she had us settled and served by the time I'd finished the introductions.

Muffling a smile at the way my *Ekam* sat awkwardly in his chair, I raised my glass before anyone else had a chance to. "Ladies and gentlemen, to the empire."

"To the empire."

"And to Her Imperial Majesty, long may she reign." Anah beat her son to the toast, a mischievous sparkle in eyes that were so like Emmory's. The table echoed the words.

Dinner was pleasant. Anah kept the conversation rolling with practiced ease, and the topics were as light as the meal.

"You have turned over the running of your company to your manager?"

Anah nodded. "It's been almost five years. I am technically retired, but—"

"Mother decided to try her hand at growing spices in addition to selling them because she doesn't know how to relax," Emmory said with a grin.

"Sounds like someone else I know," I countered, unsuccessfully hiding my smile behind my glass when he gave me the Look.

"Whose fault is that, Your Majesty?"

The laughter that followed reminded me of my childhood and the family dinners before Mother became empress. The sadness that curled in my heart was a faint echo of what it had been. Warm memory was now tangled among the shards and I could listen to the stories of Emmory and Portis's childhood without pain.

After the meal, Anah joined me on the balcony, where the sounds of Hao telling some wild tale to Haris and the others wafted out into the night air.

"There is a storm coming," Anah said, leaning on the railing and rolling her wineglass between her palms. "You can smell the ozone ahead of it." She smiled. "And according to my manager it has already hit down in Assamin."

I knew she was talking purely about the weather, but something about it shook me to the core and I realized a large part of my unease during the day had been my gut trying to warn me—but of what I had no idea.

"You expanded your operations to include several farms in the region?"

"I have been experimenting with peppercorns." Her dark eyes lit up with delight. "Five years ago, I got my hands on some heirloom plants from Earth and crossbred them with our own Indranan peppercorn. The *piper indus* are, of course, plants descended from Earth's *piper nigrum*, but the soil here changed the taste and—" She broke off, shaking her head. "My apologies, Your Majesty, I am a bit obsessive about this. Emmory is right. I don't know how to relax."

"I'm not bored, if that's what you're thinking." Sipping at my drink, I leaned on the railing next to her. "What is it about our soil that changed the taste?"

"I don't quite know, Majesty." Anah smiled. "I am not a scientist, just a dabbler. Time, the composition of our soil, the radiation from our suns? From what I've read there are many factors at play. The end result is that our pepper has a more bitter aftertaste than Earth's. I was hoping the reintroduction would add some of the sweetness back in." Her smile grew. "It did. It has also increased the spiciness, possibly a hair too much. I'm not entirely sure how to fix it."

"It might be time to call in some of those scientists," I said. "I just signed a trade agreement with the Tarsi that would interest you. They have some very good agriculture specialists. I'll let you know when the documents are available."

"That would be lovely, Your Majesty. Thank you." Anah took a drink and stared out into the darkness. "I know my son is eavesdropping and might interrupt me, but I wanted to ask you: Was Portis happy?"

Most days it was too easy to pretend it had been less than a year since his death, but at Anah's question all those feelings came rushing back. I couldn't stop the gasp as a thousand images of Portis flashed through my head: the love in his eyes that would appear without warning over dinner or something equally mundane, the smile on his face as we'd stepped onto our new ship, even the frustrated glare he so often pointed in my direction when I put my life at risk.

"Mother." Emmory's protest was hushed and faded when I held up my hand.

"Before he died, he told me he wouldn't have traded a single day," I whispered. "I loved him." Tears tangled themselves into the words. "He loved me."

Anah's cheeks glistened in the moonlight. She reached up, touching her crossed middle and index finger to her lips and then to my heart. "Good. It does not ease the loss of his light, but I will rest better knowing he was where he wanted to be and that you were with him at the end. You are a good woman and an empress who will lead us into a bright future."

I returned the gesture, my own cheeks wet with tears, until Anah wrapped her arms around me and held me close. I wasn't going to get to spend the rest of my life with Portis like I'd wanted to, but I liked to think he was proud of me and the world I was trying to create.

9

Several days later I sat curled in a chair out on my balcony. The afternoon breeze cut through some of the humidity that still lingered from the series of storms that had swept in the night Emmory's parents visited and the background sound of traffic rushing through the air.

Taran chattered about his day via a com link routed through my *smati*. My former nephew's eyes shone with the thrill of discovery that not even the events of the past year could extinguish.

He was technically no longer my nephew, since the councils had insisted we remove my sister's son from the family tree to prevent any further attempts to seize the throne; but I felt responsible for him. When Father Westinkar, an old priest from my childhood, had offered to take Taran to Ashva, I'd agreed.

Taran would live in a Buddhist temple on the other habitable planet in our home system that was run by a friend of Father Westinkar's. Tefiz Ovasi and Fenna Britlen would keep an eye on the boy, and anyone stupid enough to come after him would have to face the pair of them. I trusted my childhood *Dve* and the former GIS director not only with my own life but with Taran's, and with their help he'd grow up to be a good man.

In the meantime, I stayed in touch to give Taran some measure of consistency in a life gone mad, and what started as awkward weekly *smati* calls had evolved into something I looked forward to a great deal.

"Put Father Westinkar on," I said with a smile once he'd wound down. "I'll talk to you next week."

"Bye, Aunt Hail." Taran waved, the picture fuzzed and Father Westinkar's kind face filled my vision.

"Your Majesty."

"How are you, Father?"

"I'm good, child, you?"

"It's been quiet," I replied, thinking of how I still hadn't resolved the incident with the prime minister and of the report I'd seen an hour ago about yet another skirmish between the Shen and the Farians near a Solarian port. No one had been injured in what amounted to a situation where the previously stolen Farian ships had warped in, fired on a group of Farian vessels, and then warped out again before anyone could return fire.

I couldn't tell the old priest any of that, even though Father Westinkar had secrets he would take to his grave. The ongoing issue with Prime Minister Tesla was still Caterina's problem, and Father Westinkar would be the first to tell me he didn't know anything about fighting a war so there was very little point in talking about my worries over the Farians.

Father Westinkar laughed, unaware of my wandering thoughts. "A blessing, then; Taran is doing well. His nightmares seem to have lessened and he has been quite open in therapy. He has a bright mind, Majesty. He will do great things for this empire."

"Cire would have been proud." Thinking about my sister didn't bring as much of a knife-sharp pain now that we were almost a year out from her death, but I touched my hand to my heart, lips, and forehead in remembrance, and Father Westinkar echoed the gesture. "Thank you, Father."

"It is always a pleasure to serve both you and Indrana." He

smiled. "Fenna asked if you would message her once you finished here."

"I can do that," I said after checking my schedule. I didn't have anything else to do until dinner with Alice and Taz.

"I'll speak to you next week before you leave." Father Westinkar waved good-bye and the image went dark.

I cued up Fenna's contact, at the last second deciding to run it through the higher-level encryption com link rather than my regular one. If the former director of Galactic Intelligence Security wanted to talk to me, I figured the odds were better than fifty-fifty it was about something important.

"Majesty." Fenna Britlen dipped her graying head briefly in my direction after she answered.

"Father Westinkar mentioned you'd like to speak with me. What's the matter?"

Fenna's blue eyes were sober, and she didn't even bother with a denial. "I overheard some Farians talking the other day, thought you should know what their conversation was about. The young men were being rather candid. I suppose they assumed none of the humans around them could really understand." A smile pulled at her narrow lips, the smile interrupted by a scar that cut through the corner of her mouth and ran down her jaw.

The Farians kept many secrets, including their language, which had been withheld from the databases for any translation software used by our *smatis*. Unfortunately for this pair, the former head of my spy network had more than a passing acquaintance with Farian.

On our side of things, Gita had been teaching me the language when we had time. Her natural command of languages and time spent as a guard for the Farian consulate had given her a working knowledge of the alien language. I wasn't sure why I was doing it, if I was going to be honest, but Fasé had said we needed to learn, and despite my tangled feelings for the Farian I'd once considered a friend, there were some things I still believed in.

One of them was that Fasé could see the future.

"I was out with Tefiz the other day for lunch," Fenna continued. "She's doing well, by the way, and sends you her love."

"Send her mine back," I replied with a smile. My childhood *Dve* had lost her wife in the early days of the attack on the throne—the same attack that killed a number of my mother's BodyGuards—but she'd survived and gone into hiding with Fenna's help. When I returned home the pair's assistance had been invaluable in the recovery of my throne.

"I will, Majesty. There were a pair of Farians at a nearby table." Fenna shook her head. "I wasn't even listening at first; it was just casual conversation. Then one of them dropped their volume, just enough to catch my attention."

I raised an eyebrow. "Go on."

"I've sent the recording to Caspel. It's not good, Majesty," Fenna said instead with a sigh. "The gist of it is that something is going on back on Faria. I can't get a good read on it, but there appears to be a new faction on the Farian homeworld that the Pedalion is very concerned about. From what I've found when I started looking into it, there appears to be a prophet—not all that unusual for the Farians—who's calling for an end to the war with the Shen and for Faria to open herself up to humanity. The message is very popular among the newer generation of Farians. These two young men were talking what I'm reasonably sure is heresy, but they're so unhappy with the way the Pedalion is handling relations with humanity that they're willing to consider open revolt." She frowned. "Part of me feels like we should pass it along to the Farians, but—"

"We'd have to tell them why you know Farian," I finished and dragged a hand through my hair with a sigh of my own. Our *smatis* translated every human language in the galaxy with the exception of a handful of obscure dialects, but even after all these years the Farians hadn't agreed to putting their language into the database. Their objection was religious in nature, leaving us with no choice but to attempt to learn it the old-fashioned way, and that was harder than it should have been with no Farian willing to teach it to us.

"Not to mention answering a few other questions I know we don't want to get into right now. All right, Fenna, thanks for this. I'll talk to Caspel about how best for us to proceed. Did you see the news about the hit on the Farian outpost?"

"I did. That's why I thought I should tell you about this as soon as I could, but I didn't want to call you directly. It seemed better to wait for your regular com with Taran. I apologize for using your nephew like that."

"It's all right, Fenna." I waved a hand in the air in dismissal. "Your instincts are on point. If anyone is watching, it's better for them to at least have to work to keep up with us."

Fenna grinned. "Keep making them work, Majesty."

"Tell Tefiz I love her. I'll talk to you both later."

"Yes, ma'am."

I disconnected the call and got to my feet with a heavy sigh. It seemed things were far more complex than just the war heating up between the Shen and the Farians. I hoped the two alien races kept their war as far away from Indrana as was possible, but if Faria was facing unrest at home, it could impact their ability to fight off the Shen.

The Farian homeworld was somewhere in the Scutum-Centaurus arm of the Milky Way, closer to the center of the galaxy. We didn't know exactly where it was because no human on record had ever been to their homeworld.

Neither did I know if the Shen lived anywhere close to the Farians, or even if they had planets of their own. I double-checked my *smati* for any information on the Shen and found it sadly lacking. According to the Farians, they were heretics, renegades who'd been at odds with the Farians for more than a thousand years before humanity had begun our evolution on Earth.

All we knew about the Shen had been funneled through the Farians, and it didn't take a genius to realize how biased the accounts were.

Leaning on the railing, I called up Caspel Ganej's direct line and watched a train car pass by outside the privacy screen as I waited for the current director of my intelligence agency to answer. The area we were in hadn't suffered damage during the battle for Krishan, and if I hadn't known any better it would look like just another late-summer day in the capital. Indranans went about their business on the street below me and in the fluted buildings arching toward the sky across from me.

"Good afternoon, Majesty, what can I do for you?" Caspel asked.

"Director. Fenna sent you a recording. I thought you should have time to look at it before tomorrow's briefing."

"It's encrypted. I'll need to decode it."

"Do that, we can talk about it more in-depth tomorrow." I gave him the quick rundown.

Caspel frowned. "If this is accurate, Majesty, it's the first I've heard of it. It could be an indicator that things are shifting against the Farians."

"Between that and the news about the latest attack, I'm starting to wonder why we haven't heard a thing from the Farians."

"I know, Majesty. We've sent out several feelers, both official and unofficial. There continues to be no response. There have been several visitors to the embassy lately, and a new arrival early this morning."

"I haven't heard from the ambassador since she very politely told me she was too busy to see me. We're used to these little flare-ups, but they almost always settle back down. What's changed now?" I asked, blowing out a breath as I paced the balcony.

"If you recall from a briefing back at the beginning of Kartik, the Shen's leader, Javez Cevalla, was assassinated several months ago," Caspel replied, and an image of a bearded older man with dark brown eyes filled my vision as Caspel's video feed moved to the bottom right-hand corner. "I'd put even money on that being the catalyst for this escalation."

"Did we ever get confirmation on who was responsible?" I raised an eyebrow.

"No, Majesty." Caspel shook his head.

"Any guesses?"

"It's hard to say, Majesty. No one has claimed responsibility for it. I mean, the Farians wouldn't admit to it even if they were capable of something like that. According to the Shen, he was murdered. All the reports I could get from my operatives say he died in his sleep, but that was all secondhand hearsay. I don't have people in with either the Farians or the Shen." He swiped a hand in front of him, removing the image and replacing it with two other pictures.

"You already know that his children, Aiz and Mia, took over the leadership of the Shen. Officially, they are in joint control of the Shen forces. What little I can find on them indicates that Aiz is about ten years older than his sister. I have full dossiers in process if you would like to see it when I am finished."

I leaned against the railing again, tapping my fingers on it. We'd covered this when news of Javez's death broke, and I remembered seeing both these photos on the news report the other day.

Aiz was bearded like his father had been, and the family resemblance was strong. His hair was longer, a rich brown that matched his eyes, and it brushed the edges of his sharp jaw.

Mia's hair was darker, her chin rounder, and her eyes a piercing gray. They were filled with a determined anger that was echoed in the set of her mouth. She was stunning, and I felt an odd little flutter of attraction in my stomach that hadn't made itself known for a long time.

"Quite the pair," I said, pursing my lips. "Yes, let me see it and keep it updated."

"Yes, ma'am," Caspel replied, swiping again to bring up several news articles. "In the three standard months since Javez died, the

Shen have hit five Farian colonies. Wiped them out, burned them to the ground. There was a minor skirmish at a research station with a mix of Farian and other nations on board, but no one was injured. Then a week ago they walked into a Farian outpost and stole more than a dozen ships."

"I saw the news report on that ship theft. It said no one was killed?"

"Correct." Caspel lifted a shoulder. "I don't know why they didn't kill everyone in the outpost. That would have fit their modus operandi more closely."

"Well, let's just be grateful they didn't and hope that pattern continues." I reached up and brought the photos of the Cevalla siblings back. "Is this going to be a problem for us, Caspel?"

"My professional opinion, Majesty?" At my nod, Caspel continued. "I don't have enough information to make a proper risk assessment. We all know it's imperative for Indrana to get her feet back under her, and obviously getting involved in another war is not going to accomplish that."

"Tell me about it," I muttered with a bitter laugh. "Caspel, Fasé told me to watch for the little things."

"Did she elaborate?"

I shook my head. "No, but coupled with all this it makes me uneasy. What does your gut tell you?"

Caspel swallowed. "My gut says there's a storm coming, Majesty, and like it or not we may be right in its path."

I blew out the breath I'd been holding. "I'm right there with you. The last time I felt like this and ignored it, Portis and I were ambushed on a shitty little outlier world and I almost died."

"Candless, Majesty?"

Nodding, I studied the photos for a moment longer before sharing a grim smile with Caspel. "Find out what you can, as fast as you can. I don't want Indrana to get caught up in any fight, but this one looks like it's going to be particularly nasty."

*   *   *

The sun was setting, streaking gold across the sky that evening when Emmory came through the door of my rooms as I finished dinner with Alice and Taz.

"Apologies, Majesty."

"What is it, Emmory?" My *Ekam* had that look on his face, the careful non-expression that meant he was trying very hard not to let anything show. Taz set his wineglass down, sharing a look with Alice.

"Majesty, Colonel Morri is here with another Farian. She apologizes for not contacting Alba about your schedule and wonders if you have a few moments to speak with them."

The reason Emmory was upset was suddenly clear: no Body-Guard wanted an unvetted Farian to show up unannounced, even one vouched for by a Royal Marine, who was herself a Farian. And even if said Royal Marine had acquitted herself with a great deal of honor during our push to retake my throne.

The fact that the heir, her unborn child, and her consort were also here just made things even worse.

"What did Nila have to say?" I asked.

"The Heir's *Ekam* is understandably concerned, as am I, about having all three of you in the room with an unexpected visitor."

"The room across from us is empty, isn't it?"

"Yes, ma'am."

"Have Nila put them in there with Team One and then bring her team over here. We'll go see what's so important that it's got Colonel Morri risking Alba's wrath—and mine—to show up like this."

"Well, now I'm curious," Alice protested as I got to my feet and smoothed both hands over my gray-and-black sari.

"You sit there with Taz and be curious; I'll show you the recording when I get back."

"The Farians are our allies, Hail; their fight is with the Shen, not with us."

"I realize that." I smiled, shaking my head. "But I didn't survive the last twenty years by assuming my friends were always going to be on my side. Don't argue, Alice. Stay here."

The hallway was filled with a silent pantheon of grim-faced Body-Guards, and I stepped hard on the sudden panicky racing of my heart.

"Go in, lock that door. You two on guard in front of it. Anyone besides me or the empress comes out of this room, you start shooting, understood?" Emmory said.

"Yes, sir."

I exchanged a nod with Emmory and he opened the door again. Lieutenant Colonel Dio Morri and an older woman in a pale green dress turned from the window facing the interior courtyard. Zin and Gita were on opposite sides of the room. I stopped close to the door, with Emmory slightly in front of me. Iza and Indula were on either side of the door, hands on their guns. All my BodyGuards were tense, and I couldn't blame them. An unvetted Farian was enough to make everyone nervous.

Even though the Farian scriptures specifically forbade killing with their powers, it wasn't something anyone wanted to test with me in the room.

The aliens could heal or wound with just a touch to bare skin. They could also kill and bring someone back to life, and though both those things were forbidden by their gods, all of the humans in the room had seen Fasé bring Emmory back to life on Hao's ship and then revive Admiral Hassan on Ashva after a sniper had blown a chunk out of her heart.

I stayed where I was, with my hands folded together at my waist. Even were it appropriate for me to offer the proper Indranan greeting of a palm out, there was no way my BodyGuards would let an unvetted Farian touch me.

"I am sorry for interrupting your evening, Majesty."

"This explains why the ambassador refused to come see me." I waved off the apology. "But we're here now. What do you need?"

"Your Majesty, may I present *Itegas* Adora Notaras. She just arrived from Faria and wanted a chance to speak with you."

"It's a great pleasure to meet you," I said.

"Your Majesty. It is an honor. I am Ambassador Notaras." The elderly woman bowed low, and I glanced past her to where Lieutenant Colonel Morri stood, tight-lipped, at her side.

"Welcome to Indrana, Ambassador. I didn't hear anything about your arrival from the embassy. If I'd known you were coming, we would have been better prepared to greet you."

"It is quite fine as it is. There is no need for elaborate ceremony. And time is of the essence." Adora rose, her platinum eyes serious. "Fasé sends her deepest regards."

"She's well?"

"As she can be. She's atoning for her sins."

Whatever my issues with Fasé were, the edge to Adora's words made me uneasy. When Fasé's father had taken her home, it sounded simply like she would spend some time alone contemplating the magnitude of what she'd done. She'd had plenty of access to Stasia since her departure; surely she'd have said something if things were that bad.

I wondered if I should pull a trick from Fenna's book and slip into a com link from Stasia to speak with Fasé directly. Adora's reply carried a heavy weight, reminding me how much I owed Fasé, how much Indrana owed her. Fasé had sacrificed everything for us by violating her people's most sacred beliefs when she'd brought Emmory back from the dead, and I'd repaid her with cold fury at the end of it.

Because Cas would be alive if it weren't for her. Or we'd all be dead.

"She's a criminal?"

"Oh no, Majesty." Adora waved a hand. "She is voluntarily undergoing penance for breaking faith."

The words went to war in my head, drowning out everything

else, because I knew Adora was talking about Fasé bringing Emmory back to life when she said that. I felt Emmory's fingers brush against my arm, returning my focus to the Farians in front of me. I forced a smile as I released the breath I was holding.

"What is it we can do for you, Ambassador?"

"I have come to extend an invitation to you, Your Majesty. Indrana and Faria have been allies for a very long time. The Pedalion would like to meet with you to discuss a stronger alliance between our people."

10

The shock that Dio failed to hide told me all I needed to know about this unprecedented offer, and I remembered Fasé's words about how the Pedalion had never met with a human in all the years they'd been in contact with us.

"I would be happy to talk with the Matriarch Council and put together a delegation. We would need to select an ambassador—"

"The Pedalion would like to meet with *you*, Majesty. No one else. I am here to bring you back to Faria with me."

"Me? Why?" Something about this whole situation made the hairs on the back of my neck stand up, and I couldn't stop myself from shaking my head. "No. Indrana values our relationship with Faria, Ambassador. However, this is an incredibly difficult time for us and I am needed here. I'm sure the Pedalion can respect that there is no way for me to leave my empire. We've just forged a fragile peace. I have things that I must handle here at home before I head out for a tour of my empire. I do not have time to be traveling all the way across the galaxy."

"The Pedalion requested you, Your Majesty. If they had been willing to meet with anyone else, they would have said so."

"I'm sure they will understand my position," I replied with a smile, and watched as her eyes narrowed a fraction. This was a woman not used to being refused.

Not an ambassador, then. Interesting.

I wondered if that was just an easy title for the Farians to convey their wishes or if there was some awkwardness in the translation from a Farian title to Indranan and Adora had chosen the easier, more understandable term.

Colonel Morri's behavior was the most curious. Her tense shoulders and the barely controlled muscle twitching at her jawline screamed her unease. She kept her eyes glued to the floor rather than looking my way.

"I will send a message home and let the Pedalion know of your concerns," Adora said finally.

"That sounds like an excellent idea. I'll let Alba know you'll be contacting her for any future meetings. Do you need accommodations?"

"No, Your Majesty. Colonel Morri has already taken care of that for me." Adora's smile was tight, the woman so clearly perturbed by my refusal that it was all I could do not to laugh out loud. "Thank you. Good night."

"Night." I turned and went through the door Indula opened, waiting for it to close behind me before I blew out a breath and looked at Emmory. "That sounded an awful lot like a summons," I said.

"It did, Majesty. And one they weren't expecting you to refuse."

The door to my rooms opened and the Guards stepped aside so Emmory and I could enter. Alice stopped her obvious pacing as we came into the room, and I grinned at her demand of "What happened?"

"You'd think they'd know me a little better than that," I said to Emmory instead.

"They've obviously not been paying attention over the last year."

I punched him in the arm with a laugh, but my amusement was fleeting and was soon replaced with a hissing curse. "Give us a minute, Emmory. I want to talk to Alice and Taz alone."

My *Ekam* nodded, ushering out Stasia and the maids who were cleaning away the remains of our dinner. He paused at the door. "Hao and Johar are here; do you want to see them, or should I tell them you're busy?"

My first thought was an immediate *Have them come up*. But the words didn't make it out of my mouth. "Tell them I'm busy," I said instead, and continued over to the bar.

"Hail, what is it?" Alice whispered.

"Come here." I held my hand out, passing over the clip of my conversation with Adora. "Let Taz see."

Ice clinked into my glass, competing with the quiet direction of my staff as they cleared the table and with Alice and Taz's reaction to the recording of Adora's demands.

Shocking didn't even begin to cover what had just happened. On any other day, under different circumstances this would have been exciting. I would have said yes to Adora's invitation and become the first human to set foot on Faria. Something was off about this whole thing, and as I sent a copy of the encounter to Caspel I realized what it was. Why hadn't the Farians just sent a message to Ambassador Ussin about the trip? Why send an entirely new ambassador who didn't behave like one? Who was Adora and what did she really want?

I poured whiskey onto the ice and stared down into the amber depths. *"Hai Ram."*

The Farians were at war. Indrana needed me here. And the invitation was a poorly concealed demand to fly far too many light-years away from my home for reasons unknown.

The audio on Fenna's recording of the two Farians talking was better than I expected, not that it did a whole lot to help me understand what was being said. Instead I followed along with the text translation Gita had provided.

Which was fine, but it meant I couldn't watch their faces as they spoke, and after several minutes I hissed in frustration and paused the playback.

"Gita, come in here."

The hallway door cracked open. "You're up early, Majesty."

"I've been up for an hour, as you well know." I stuck my tongue out at her when she grinned and pushed the door open further for Stasia to come through.

"Morning, Majesty," she said, putting the tray on the table in front of me and passing along the cup of blue chai before I could answer.

"Morning, Stasia. Thank you."

"Let me know when you're ready for breakfast."

I murmured a reply, inhaling the steam from my chai before I opened my eyes again and looked up at my *Dve*. "Sit," I said. "Do you want some?"

Gita's lips twitched. "With respect, ma'am, it tastes like the bowls of smelly flowers my mother's staff would leave around the house."

"Potpourri?" I snorted, nearly inhaling my chai when I laughed.

"Sure," she replied, lifting a shoulder.

"You are too like Hao at times." The smile fled Gita's face and I cleared my throat at the sudden uncomfortable silence. "Gita, you need to talk to him."

"Majesty, please don't."

I stared at her. I knew Hao was hurt by the sudden distance, and even though Gita was nearly as good as I was about hiding her emotions, I suspected my *Dve* was suffering equally. However, the pleading in her voice was enough to push my advice back down my throat and I sighed heavily. "Fine. Read Fenna's translation of this conversation for me." I tapped at the tablet with the text portion. "I can't read it and watch at the same time. I want to see their faces."

"Yes, ma'am. May I?"

I handed the tablet over, reset the image on the screen on the wall, and started it again.

Miles and Lucca were both students at the Ashva branch of Indranan Royal University and had been on Ashva for three years.

They hadn't known each other before coming to my empire but had become fast friends shortly after their first meeting, according to the files Fenna had composed on each of them.

Miles was slightly taller than his companion, his red hair straight and clipped short. Lucca had wild red curls and both of them had the same golden eyes as Fasé.

"All I'm saying is that it's worth listening to. Call it a thought experiment if it makes you feel better," Miles said, via Gita's murmured translation. The Farian gave off a good show of being relaxed for his friend, but I spotted the ticking muscle in his jaw and the way he fisted one hand under the tabletop.

"It's less about feeling better and more about what my father would do to me if he found out I was involved in heresy." Lucca leaned forward over the remains of his meal. He wasn't even pretending to be anything other than tense, every muscle taut like a prey animal waiting for the decision to flee to finally connect from its brain.

"He's been living a lie, Lucca. Are you going to keep doing the same thing just because you're scared of your father?" It was a carefully designed jab and I watched it hit its mark.

"I'm not scared of my father. I'm scared of the idea of spending twenty years atoning for my crimes instead of getting to be here. Look, I agree with you about the Pedalion, they're overstepping. Things are changing, but they refuse to see it. We should get more involved with the humans. We should consider putting this ridiculous feud with the Shen to rest. But—"

"The Pedalion and their enforcers are going to be so busy with the Shen they're not going to have time to round people up, especially all the way out here. Relax some. I'm just saying we should meet with the local group and listen to what they're saying. This prophet knows things, Lucca. She's special. We're not alone, and there is a much wider universe we should be a part of. The Pedalion doesn't understand, or worse, they don't care."

"Fine. When's the meeting?" Lucca slumped back in his chair, the battle of wills with his obviously stronger friend lost.

"Tomorrow night. Finish your drink. Class starts in an hour, and I wanted to swing by the shop on the corner."

"You just want to flirt with that Indranan girl behind the counter."

"Meeting new people is a large part of the reason I left home, Lucca."

I leaned back against the couch, cradling my chai in both hands as the recording ended and Gita fell silent.

"Didn't Ambassador Notaras say Fasé was 'atoning for her sins'?"

"She did, Majesty."

"Bugger me. That conversation sounds more ominous than I first thought, Gita." It also highlighted how little we knew about our Farian allies, and I felt more than a little concerned that lack of knowledge was about to turn around and bite us in the ass.

Before I could say anything else, Alba stuck her head in through the open doorway, knocking on the frame. "Good morning, Majesty. Hao would like to see you, if it's convenient?"

"Morning, Alba, that's fine, we're just finishing up. Make sure Emmory sees this," I said to Gita, who nodded and stood.

"He's watched it once, Majesty, but I'll fill him in on our conversation."

"Good, tell him I'll want to speak with him about it when he has time."

"Yes, ma'am."

I watched as Hao came into the room, and my *Dve*'s posture shifted almost imperceptibly. She changed direction, avoiding him, and took up a spot on the other side of the room.

Hao didn't change his expression, and no one else noticed the moment, so I forced my attention and my concern away from the pair.

"Morning."

"Lot of activity around here," Hao said, settling onto the couch. "And a bit more security."

"We had some excitement last night."

"That you're not going to tell me about." His grin faded when I didn't smile back, and he stared at me for a moment. "You're really not going tell me?"

"I'll let you know when I can. Are you going to tell me what you were talking to Po-Sin about yesterday?"

He blew out a breath and muttered under his breath. "Family business," he said.

"Ah. Did you need something?"

"I thought we'd have breakfast."

"I already ate. I'll talk to you later, though," I said to Hao, who raised an eyebrow at me.

"A dismissal, how imperial."

"Would you let me do my job?"

"Don't let me get in the way." He got to his feet and headed for the door Gita had opened, pausing as if he wanted to say something to her, but she refused to meet his gaze and he left the room with a muttered curse.

"What have you got for me this morning, Alba?" I pulled up my schedule for the day as she took the seat Hao had just vacated, refusing to feel the guilt clamoring for my attention.

"I received a request from Ambassador Notaras first thing this morning, Majesty." Alba cleared her throat, a smile curving her lips. "She is most insistent that I allow her to speak with you."

"I'm sure she is; however, today is pretty packed." I scrolled through my schedule. "Tell her today won't work, but that I'll see her tomorrow afternoon."

"I can do that."

"Majesty, Director Ganej is here for your daily briefing," Gita said from the doorway.

"Let him in."

"Morning, Majesty. My apologies for the delay."

I waved him off. "We were just discussing Ambassador Notaras's request to meet with me. Have a seat."

"I brought you some reading material." Caspel sat down next to Alba and handed over a book.

"*A History of Indranan/Farian Relations*? Interesting."

"It seemed like it might be a good place to start." He cleared his throat. "Also you need to see this, Majesty." He held his hand out and I raised a curious eyebrow at the chip in his hand. If the director of my intelligence service was reluctant to pass something over the network, it had to be important.

I slipped the chip into the slot at the base of my skull and cued up the playback.

11

The slender Farian on the screen had the golden eyes and distinctive red curls of so many of her kind, but her heart-shaped face and smile were painfully familiar to me. My breath hitched, and I tightened my hand around my mug.

"Your Majesty." Fasé Terass dipped her head in greeting, the Farian's smile so soft it took some effort to remember she'd engineered the death of one of my BodyGuards with ruthless efficiency. "I suspect you have already met with the Farians who came to see you. I thought it best you have an unbiased opinion of them to start with. It is vital that I speak with you; if you will meet me at your country estate this afternoon at eighteen hundred hours, I will explain everything then."

Caspel lifted his hands slightly in a helpless gesture when the message ended.

"I have reports of a Farian ship docking on Ashva at a warehouse supply depot," he said. "The timing matches. If she boarded a freighter headed for Pashati, she'll land here a few hours before the meeting."

My hands were cold and I rubbed them together. I wasn't afraid of Fasé, quite the contrary; I still cared about her as much as any of my BodyGuards. And I knew I couldn't turn my back on her. Adora had spoken of her as though she were still back on Faria, but that obviously wasn't the case, and the fact that she'd gone to such lengths to conceal her return meant something important was on the line.

When a Farian who could see the future wanted to meet with you, you couldn't say no.

"Alba, figure out a way to get us to the country estate by eighteen hundred hours without raising a lot of eyebrows."

"Today?"

"Yes." I waved a hand at the door before tapping my fingers and thumb against my lips. Alba read my mood easily and left with a smile and a good-bye to Caspel. I waited until Gita closed the door behind her before I started speaking again. "The Shen have been a thorn in the Farians' side for longer than any of us have been alive, but it's always been something the Farians could handle on their own. Now we've got rumors of a schism within Faria, Fasé is here, and I have a feeling she's tangled up in all this."

"You need to tread very carefully, Majesty," Caspel replied. "I don't know what the Farian rules are in regard to Fasé. It hasn't had the feel of someone who's a prisoner, but Adora's reaction when you asked about Fasé made me feel like we're missing something. Adora's mention of Fasé was pure political propaganda with an edge that I disliked."

"You and me both." I got to my feet, waving Caspel back down before he could rise. "Damn it, Caspel. It's obvious something has rattled the Farians enough to make them approach me about a visit to their homeworld. The question is why? Why now?" I exhaled. "And why Indrana when there are half a dozen other governments the Farians have alliances with?"

"Two reasons, I think: Whatever is going on back on Faria has them rattled enough to ask us for help. And two, the other governments don't have Hail Bristol in charge, Majesty."

I snorted at Caspel. "Outside of the empress of Indrana, I'm nothing."

"You are far from nothing, Majesty." It was Caspel's turn for a look. "You are the woman who survived an attack on the royal family. You are the woman who rode a fleet into the Ashvin system to liberate Indrana from Wilson's grip. You are the empress who just negotiated and signed a historic peace treaty with the Saxons. And you were Cressen Stone, one of the most dangerous gunrunners out in the black. The only reason you weren't on Fenna's radar was that she knew who you were. And that was information she didn't share with me, so I was keeping an eye on you even though you seemed to have an aversion for Indranan space. I was waiting for the day you changed your mind and made my life miserable."

I couldn't stop the grin that spread across my face. "Bet that was a surprise, huh?"

"One of the few in my life." Caspel's amusement faded. "Indrana is hurting, Your Majesty. We've gone to great lengths to keep just how badly a secret, but we couldn't afford to get involved in another extended war. Maybe something quick, but—"

"There's no such thing as a quick war."

"True." He nodded. "The Shen have always been a relatively small faction of—according to the Farians—heretics. I've pressed for more information recently, but again it's been nothing but silence from my sources familiar with the Farians. What I have been able to figure out on my own is that the Shen often recruit directly from Farians. We've seen Farians among them in some of the more recent footage and some who look—odd."

"Define odd," I said.

"The Farians are distinct, Majesty. They're all pale-skinned, small, the pointed ears and eyes the color of gold or silver. It's easy to spot them in a crowd. The Shen look like humans." He lifted his hands. "Which makes them harder to spot, and that makes me nervous. But I've caught glimpses in the footage of Shen forces that I would swear were Farians with coloring much more in line with the Shen physiology."

"You think they've been having children?"

"I would," Caspel replied. "The Shen have always seemed to be at a disadvantage on the population end of things. But there's obviously more of them now, and I think that's a big reason for the escalating violence. Before this they were not willing to confront the Farian navy directly. They'd do a lot of hit-and-runs and then disappear. The only time they've ever attacked anyone other than the Farians was the attack on Solarian Colony 17 sixty-three years ago. Since then they've both gone to great lengths to keep the fight in their own backyard, so to speak."

"Bugger me." I muttered the curse as I rubbed a hand over my face.

"In the last six months they've enlisted the aid of mercenaries. It's added considerable bulk to the Shen forces, and their tactics appear to have completely thrown the Farians for a loop."

"Why? They've been fighting a running battle with the Shen all this time, haven't they?"

"Yes," Caspel said. "However, I think the Farians are so used to fighting the Shen, they don't know how to react to human fighting tactics—especially mercenary ones."

"Majesty?"

"Yes, Gita?" I watched Caspel closely to see how he reacted to my *Dve* speaking up. I wasn't above admitting when I was wrong about treating the people around me more like members of my crew, but Gita had experience with the Farians and I wasn't about to let that go unused.

Caspel only turned to my BodyGuard with a surprisingly deferential nod, and she continued.

"Not only do the Farians not know how to respond, they can't respond. Their moral code prevents them from associating with criminals, so they can't hire mercenaries of their own to help them fight or understand the tactics."

I laughed. "How on Pashati are they even allowed to talk to me, then?"

"You are a complicated case, Majesty." The fact that Caspel could say that without even a hint of a smile only made me laugh harder. "You are the Empress of Indrana. You were born royal, and you are officially recognized as the empress. It may be that they choose to overlook your past in favor of that." He glanced over his shoulder at Gita, who nodded in agreement.

"That would be my guess: official approval from the Pedalion to ignore the fact that you were a gunrunner for twenty years."

Rolling my eyes, I snorted before I picked up my chai again. "Religions seem to love nothing so much as a good excuse to break their own rules when it suits them. What do we do, Caspel? The ambassador has been politely harassing Alba about meeting with me, but we both know that meeting with Fasé is likely to throw any plans we make into the bin."

Caspel's brown eyes unfocused as he considered the options. Then he looked at me. "I would suggest you go talk to Fasé first, try to get a handle on what's happening. Did you set a time to meet with Ambassador Notaras?"

"Yes, tomorrow afternoon."

He nodded. "That will work. See if you can get them to tell you what's really going on. I trust your gut on this one, Majesty. They're not being entirely honest, and we need the truth before Indrana can even consider getting involved in another conflict. Though if you're wanting my opinion, I think we should do all we can to avoid committing to anything until we're on stable footing."

"Agreed. All right." I finished off my drink and set the mug on the edge of my desk as Caspel got to his feet. "I'll message you as soon as we're done. Hopefully we'll have some answers."

"Yes, ma'am."

I turned away to the window as Gita led Caspel to the door, their voices lost to my heartbeat humming in my ears. As I stared out at the gleaming city in front of me, it was all too easy to envision it in flaming ruins. I'd spent most of my life neck-deep in violence, and it seemed like no matter what I did, no matter how hard I worked, I couldn't get clear of it.

"Majesty?"

"This is bad, Gita," I said without turning to look at her. "I don't know how I know, I just do."

"You don't have to explain it, ma'am. We all trust your gut and we'll follow wherever you lead."

I hadn't been back to my family's country estate at the base of Mount Rishabha since my showdown with Wilson six months prior. Part of me, the more sane and sensible part, knew that the box he'd drowned me in was gone, as was the pool of blood he'd left behind when I'd cut his throat with a wine stem. Staff had come in and cleaned it up, and no doubt Alba had supervised to make sure it was done right.

However, that wasn't the part that was in charge as I stepped from the aircar, Emmory and Zin at my sides like a pair of imposing bookends. The part in charge remembered that awful moment when I thought Hao's dead body lay in front of me and the rush of relief when I saw him take a breath. The part in charge remembered Wilson's maddened rush at me and the easy way skin and artery split under the razor-sharp edge of a broken wineglass.

"House is clear, Majesty. Two life signs, both Farian, in the library." Emmory scanned back and forth across the terrain, listening to the chatter from Gita and her team as they made their way in through the back. "Do you want me to have them meet you somewhere else?"

"No, if Fasé is there she has a reason for it. I'll be fine," I murmured, and climbed the stairs to the front door.

He gave me the Look, and the whispered "liar" was for my ears only. I smiled at him and reached for the door.

"Let me go first," Emmory said, and vanished into the house.

We waited what seemed like an eternity but wasn't more than a handful of minutes before Zin touched a hand to my back. "We can go in, Majesty," he said, and pulled open the door.

As we stepped into the foyer my panic faded somewhat. The sight of the double staircases arching up past cream-colored columns brought with it memories of running up and down those stairs until someone—usually Mother—yelled at us to stop. The yell had been laced with laughter and we never did stop because Father would distract her, and my sisters and I would be left to our own devices for hours.

The summer estate was a rare slice of happiness, and we stopped going after Father's death. I hadn't set foot in it until Wilson.

"Are you okay?" Zin's voice was low, his hand warm on my back through the black uniform shirt I'd changed into before we left the hotel.

I nodded wordlessly and continued down the hall, my heart pounding in my chest. The last time I'd seen Fasé, I'd been more than a little cold to her, but now I knew I was going to have to put my feelings aside and do what was right for the empire. Whatever was coming at us, I'd much rather Fasé be at my side than on the opposite side of whatever field I was going to end up fighting on.

Taking a deep breath did almost nothing for my nerves, but I ignored my shaking hands and nodded to Emmory when he pushed the door open.

The floor was spotless, but I knew exactly where Wilson had fallen, clutching at the wound on his neck and staring at me in disbelief. I knew where Hao had lain and where I had collapsed when Emmory and Zin rushed into the room.

Fasé stood by the wide window, the mountain bathed in the late-afternoon light behind her. Her hands were clasped at her lower back, and an unknown Farian stood beside her in an identical pose. She was dressed in a white top that hung to her knees with white leggings underneath. The sleeves stretched down past her knuckles, almost obscuring her hands, making the whole outfit look a bit like clothing she'd stolen from someone much larger than her. Given the circumstances, I wasn't entirely sure that assumption was wrong.

"Star of Indrana." Fasé turned and went down on a knee, her head bowed. The woman at her side followed her.

"Welcome back." It surprised me to realize I meant it. The universe felt like an engine with the last piece of a rebuild slipped into place. She was where she was supposed to be.

"It was time for me to come back. This is my jailer." Now Fasé lifted her head and an impish grin split her face. "Or rather, my former jailer."

"Get up." I held a hand out and helped her to her feet. Fasé's hand was cool in mine, and a faint humming worked its way up my arm when our skin made contact.

"This is Sybil. She's on our side but I've told her to keep her hands covered."

"Your Imperial Majesty, it is a great pleasure to meet you." The slender woman was a third of a meter taller than Fasé, with long red hair cascading over one shoulder and eyes such a pale silver they were almost clear. She had stayed where she was when Fasé moved forward, probably because Emmory still had a hand on his gun.

"Fasé said you are her jailer?"

"I was tasked with Fasé's reeducation and penance." A slight smile fluttered over Sybil's face. "The Pedalion has"—she searched for a word—"misjudged matters concerning the gods' will for Fasé. I suppose they will call me a heretic, or the first convert to the unexpected future-seer, depending on who wins."

"Wins?"

"The civil war, Your Majesty."

A cold weight settled into my stomach.

"We will speak on it more later." Fasé slipped her arm through mine. "If it is all right with you, I would have Sybil and the others wait outside. Emmory can stay." She smiled. "Because I know he will anyway. I have some things to tell you. They will not be easy to hear but they are necessary."

I shared a look with Emmory and found myself nodding.

"Sybil, go with Zin. Behave yourself. It will make everyone less anxious, and while I have complete faith in the empress's Body-Guards, I would hate to lose you now." Fasé smiled and I noticed how much she'd changed since I'd seen her last. There was something sure and solid about her presence.

"Yes, *Mardis*."

"So," I said. "*Itegas* Notaras—"

"*Itegas*, is it?" Fasé laughed, following me toward the fireplace. "Listen to you, sounding like a proper Farian, speaking about a member of the Pedalion with the right honorific and everything."

12

ugger me, what?" I jerked to a stop, and Fasé dodged to the side to avoid colliding with me. "Colonel Dio called her that. I just thought it was another Farian word for *ambassador*. She's a member of the Pedalion?"

"She's the one who came to see you?"

"She is still here." I stared at Fasé in shock. "She said she was an ambassador and that the Pedalion wanted to speak with me."

"Huh." Fasé pursed her lips. "That changes things somewhat. Your Majesty, I realize this may put you in a somewhat difficult position, but I would like to request political asylum for myself and Sybil."

"Fasé, you know I can't just grant that. I have to run it through the councils."

"That's perfectly fine. I just need the process started before Adora realizes I'm on Pashati."

"You're going to get me in trouble, aren't you?"

"Maybe." She smiled and lifted one shoulder. "But it's not any trouble that's not already on the way, and you know I'm an advantage you want in your corner."

She was right. My personal feelings for Fasé were a tangled mass of affection, guilt, and anger, but I knew without a doubt from a tactician's standpoint that she could mean the difference between winning a fight and going down hard.

"Zin, have Sybil fill out a request for political asylum for herself and Fasé, please." I issued the order over the com link.

"Yes, ma'am."

"And you," I said to Fasé, pointing at one of the chairs by the massive fireplace. "Sit and start talking."

Fasé settled into a chair, pulling her legs up underneath her and leaning on the arm. "The future-seers of the Council of Eyes do not share the things they see without good cause. They know that to even breathe of a possibility can have impact on the outcome. So they do so only when not speaking of it is worse than speaking of it."

"Like when they told the Pedalion not to wipe out humanity?"

Fasé smiled and looked down at her lap for a moment. "Yes, Majesty. Those futures are told to the Pedalion, but the Council of Eyes still makes an effort to not share the details, only the idea of it. From there the Pedalion takes over. Farians are told of these outcomes from birth, taught them in our schools. One of them deals with Indrana, and it is the reason your empire was sought out to be our ally long before any of the other human collectives were considered." She sighed and lifted a slender shoulder before dropping it back down. "This may end in fire no matter what we do, but I and others are committed to the preservation of a balance in the universe."

"And the Pedalion isn't?"

"The Pedalion wants what anyone with power wants, to hold on to that power. The Shen want that power, or they think they do." Fasé got that faraway look that I knew was her seeing a future none of the rest of us could grasp. "They won't like what happens if they get it, but that's a problem for another time."

"What do you want, Fasé?" I asked.

Fasé gold eyes went soft. "I want my people to be whole again instead of split over a faith that was never meant to divide us. I want an end to this endless war with the Shen. I mean to disband the Pedalion and give Farians the option of not living an endless life."

"You can't die?"

"We can't die, well—" She wiggled a hand. "We die, we come back. That's the way of it. The only way a Farian can truly die is by petitioning the Pedalion. It is almost unheard-of for them to grant such a thing and they should not have such power. The Pedalion was never meant to be more than a temporary fix to guide us through the loss of our gods. However, they consolidated their power during that tumultuous time and have become a group that is intent on holding us back rather than moving us forward."

"You're the fucking prophet," I blurted, then squeezed my eyes shut. "Sorry." When I opened them again, Fasé was smiling at me.

"Where did you hear of it?"

"A conversation overheard on Ashva between some Farians. Fasé, are you leading a revolution against the Pedalion?"

She pressed both hands to her mouth, tears in her eyes. "I didn't dare dream it would reach so far so fast, but Farians are waking up to the truth, and if my message has reached as far as Indrana there is hope for us all."

"The Farians want me to come visit the Pedalion," I said. "Is it because of you?"

"I doubt it," she replied. "It's probably because of the Shen, though the unrest I've caused is no doubt weakening the Pedalion's ability to manage the war. We've been at this for so long, Majesty, and my people are exhausted. We want peace." She looked down at her lap. "And I want your forgiveness, Majesty. I am so sorry for what I had to do."

I fisted my hands in my lap at the pain in her voice. I didn't doubt the strength of it, but my own grief protested her right to feel anything at all when she was the cause.

She wasn't, ma'am. Wilson set the bomb. I made the choice. Cas's ghost whispered in my ear words I desperately wanted to deny.

But I couldn't. They were the truth.

"Cas said I should forgive you," I whispered with a sad smile.

"He left another message for me with his grandmother. She gave it to me a while ago. I don't know if I can. But I am willing to try."

Fasé launched herself out of her chair and into my arms with a sob. A thousand tangled feelings went to war in my head, but love won out in the moment and I wrapped my arms around her, hugging her tight. I held her until her tears slowed and then let her go, wiping the tears from her face. "I've missed you," I said. "Let's start over."

"Thank you, Majesty," she said, returning to her chair.

"If all I have to do is stay out of this fight between the Shen and the Farians, Fasé, I'm all for it," I said, ignoring the lump in my chest and steering the conversation back on topic.

She shook her head. "I wish it were that easy, Majesty, but I doubt it will be. There are futures—" She dragged in a breath, the air shaking in her throat. "It is hard to see."

"You mean false futures?"

Fasé allowed for a small smile and shook her head again. "No. No future is false. No future is true. They're all just possibilities. The Pedalion's problem is they're too focused on the future when they should be looking at the choice. Same for the Shen, though they are less predictable."

"So they're both focused on the end result?"

"Yes." Fasé nodded her head and held up her hand, thumb and forefinger pressed together. "The moment is a thousand times more important than the outcome. It is the choice that defines the outcome. You chose to give your life for this empire, Majesty. Cas chose the same. Two identical choices. Two very different outcomes. See?"

"No, I don't see. Cas chose to die, Fasé, and maybe it was for me. Although that is hard to bear. I made no such choice."

"Didn't Cressen Stone die when you acknowledged who you were, Majesty?"

I jerked in shock and a smile spread across her face.

"You changed the path of this empire when you decided to stay."

"I didn't decide. I was dragged home." I flipped a hand at Emmory.

"You made a choice, Majesty. You may not realize it, but it was there. Would you like to see one of the other options?" She held her hand out, wiggling her fingers at me, and before I could stop myself I laid my palm on top of hers.

I backed straight into the sixth intruder before I had time to remind myself what I-F stood for.

He was hidden by the shadows I was trying to blend into, as still and silent as a ghost. He didn't make a sound when I spun and drove my right hand into his ribs. The blue shimmer of his personal shield flared and I swore under my breath. It would smother any strike I threw at him, making the damage laughable. But the kinetic technology didn't extend to his unprotected head, so I swung my left up toward his throat, blade first. He caught my wrist, twisting it back and away from his head.

I matched him in height, and judging by the surprised flaring of his dark eyes, we were nearly equal in strength. We stood locked for a stuttering heartbeat until he drove me back a step. Sophie's emergency lighting made the silver tattoo on his left cheekbone glow red.

My heart stopped. The Imperial Star—an award of great prestige— was an intricate diamond pattern, the four spikes turned slightly widdershins. But what had my heart starting again and speeding up in panic was the twisted black emblem on his collar. He was an Imperial Tracker.

"Bugger me."

The curse slipped out before I could stop it—slipped out in the Old Tongue as my shock got the better of me. There was only one reason for a Tracker team to be here. The reason I'd spent the best part of twenty years avoiding anything to do with the Indranan Empire.

Oh, bugger me.

Trackers always worked in pairs, but I couldn't break eye contact with this one to check for his partner. Instead I eased back a step, my mind racing for a way out of this horrible nightmare.

My captor smiled—a white flash of teeth against his dark skin, just enough to bring a dimple in his right cheek fluttering to life. The fingers around my wrist tightened, stopping my movement and adding a high note of pain to the symphony already in progress.

"Your Imperial Highness, I have no wish to hurt you. Please let go of the knife."

Oh, bugger me.

"I don't know what you're talking about," I lied easily. "I'm just a gunrunner."

He tapped a finger next to his eye, just missing the tattoo, and now I could see the silver shadow of augmentation in their dark depths. "I see who you really are. Don't try to fool me."

A stream of filth that rivaled any space pirate poured out of my mouth and blistered the air. The modifications I'd paid a fortune for after leaving home had stood up to every scanner in known space for the last twenty Indranan years, but of course they wouldn't stand up to this one.

Trackers were fully augmented. Their smatis were top of the line. The DNA scanner had probably activated the moment he grabbed my wrist, and that, coupled with the devices in his eyes, had sealed my fate.

Bluffing wasn't going to get me out of this. Which meant violence was my only option.

"Highness, please," he repeated, his voice a curl of smoke wafting through the air. "Your empress-mother requests your presence."

"Requests!" My voice cracked before I composed myself. "Are you kidding me? She fucking requests my presence?" I wrenched myself from his grasp and kicked him in the chest.

It was like kicking the dash when Sophie's engines wouldn't power up—painful and unproductive. Fucking shields. The Guard stepped back, his suit absorbing my blow with a faint blue shimmer as the field around him reacted to the impact.

Hard hands grabbed my upper arms.

There was the other Tracker.

I snapped my head back, hoping this one was as helmetless as his partner. The satisfying crunch of a broken nose mixed with startled cursing and told me I'd guessed correctly.

I spun and grabbed the man by the throat with one arm as I flipped the knife over in my hand and smiled a vicious smile at Tracker No. 1. "You come any closer and I'll cut his throat from ear to ear."

"Highness." The Tracker took a step forward, a hand up; but my hand was already moving and the coppery bite of fresh blood joined the stale charnel-house reek of the cargo bay.

"No!" I jerked my hand away, falling out of my chair, scrambling to get away from the horror I'd just been presented with. "Dark Mother, no."

"Majesty." Emmory caught me under the arms in my mad scramble away from the Farian and followed me to the floor, completely unaware that she'd just shown me cutting his husband's throat in our first meeting. "Fasé, what is it? What did you show her?"

"She'll be fine," Fasé replied. "I showed her another option, another choice she could have made but didn't during that first meeting on her ship. I'm afraid none of us survived it. Cressen Stone was badly wounded in the fight but managed to escape. You are truly a terror when your life is at stake, Your Majesty." She climbed out of her chair and knelt on the floor next to me. "I stopped watching after a while because it was a dark future. You died a drunk in some desolate space port while most of the rest of the galaxy was at war."

"I wouldn't have—I didn't—" I pressed a shaking hand to my mouth, unable to say the words, and Emmory's fingers tightened against my sides.

If I had killed Zin out there in the black, Emmory would have died. Trackers were bonded from young ages by a special talent; so partner became lover or siblings grew so close they could practically read each other's thoughts. The cost of it was that they couldn't survive without each other, and the death of one led to the death of the other. I'd almost lost Zin when Emmory had been shot on Red Cliff, and Fasé admitted it was his cry that pushed her to save my *Ekam* on the floor of Hao's ship.

"The you in that future made the choice to kill Zin in the cargo bay of your ship. She did so without hesitation or remorse and changed the history of the galaxy forever."

There was a quiet inhale from my *Ekam* as he finally pieced together what was happening.

"You chose not to kill Zin. Maybe it wasn't a conscious choice." Fasé continued, ignoring him and tapping a finger against my forehead for emphasis. "However, it doesn't change the fact that the choice was there. That's my point. You made the choice to come home, to give your life for Indrana; conscious or not, it was made."

She got to her feet and held her hand out. I hesitated before I took it. With her help I got back on my feet, Emmory's hands a comforting presence on my back.

"I'm still not sure I understand."

Fasé smile was slow and she folded her hands together, pressing them to her heart, lips, and forehead before bowing to me. "You can't change the future if you don't know what moment needs to change."

"What moment needs changing so desperately that you busted out of prison to come tell me about it?"

"You have to say no to the Farians. No matter what they offer, no matter what promises they make. Indrana cannot agree to join in this fight with the Shen. You cannot fight for either side, Majesty. You must remain neutral or the future that happens will make the one I saw a dream by comparison."

"What future?"

Fasé shook her head. "You know I won't tell you, Majesty. This is one of those moments. You'll have to make the choice—trust me or don't."

"With the fate of the galaxy apparently hanging in the balance? That's not much of a choice."

"Of course it is, we just both know what choice you're going to make." She held out her hand again and this time there was no hesitation in me when I took it.

"Ambassador Notaras." I inclined my head at the Farian as she came into my rooms the next day with Emmory at her side. Dio was conspicuously absent, but I contained my curiosity, gesturing for Adora to have a seat on the other side of my desk.

"Your Majesty." She bent her head briefly. The gesture was awkward, unfamiliar to her and more telling than anything so far that this woman was not who she pretended to be. "I appreciate you taking the time to see me."

Her unspoken *finally* hung heavy in the air, and I resisted the urge to suggest we talk about this tomorrow in front of the Matriarch Council.

We sat in silence. I was content to wait for Adora to start, especially since it was clear she expected me to ask what message the Pedalion had for me.

"Majesty, I have spoken with the Pedalion and they wish me to convey their respects. They understand your concerns and promise to take no more of your time than is necessary. That is the reason I was to bring you back on my ship; the flight would be considerably shorter. They don't wish to interfere with Indranan affairs; however, this issue doesn't only impact Faria. If it is not handled the repercussions could spread across the galaxy."

Arching an eyebrow in the air, I offered up a cool smile. "So you said earlier. Ambassador Notaras, I have several other meetings today. Could you get to the point?"

Her metallic eyes narrowed and the muscles in her jaw twitched.

"We have a problem, Your Majesty, that we are hoping you can help with."

"You realize Indrana is not able to help anyone? We just fought a civil war. My noble families are decimated. We are rebuilding, but it will be a long road back. I don't know what we could offer in assistance."

"The Pedalion wants *your* help, not your empire's, but we realize the two are rather tangled together. Even with her recent troubles, Indrana is a mighty force in the galaxy. Your own reputation is"—she paused, and a curious smile curved her lip—"impressive enough to give the Shen and their allies pause."

"You want *me*?" I glanced at Emmory.

"The situation has escalated with the Shen to the point where we want Indrana to honor our alliance, but we understand you cannot provide monetary aid and that your military—though recovered— is no match for the Shen forces. What we will require is that you provide your personal knowledge and experience. It is not acceptable to send an ambassador or proxy in your stead; we will need to speak with you directly. This is important, not only for the fate of Faria but for all of humanity. The new leadership of the Shen are employing mercenaries. It is creating some difficulty for us. We are not able to follow their tactics. We need someone who thinks like them and maybe even could speak with them directly. You know these mercenaries. They might listen to you. It would give you a chance to get out of this quiet existence you've ended up in."

I hid my shock. The Farians clearly thought I was still a gunrunner and that I desperately wanted out of this choice I'd made. How wrong they were.

It didn't escape my notice that Adora had messed up and said *we* when speaking of the Pedalion, proving Fasé's statement that she wasn't just an ambassador but a member of the Pedalion. I glanced quickly at Emmory before I replied. "I can't fight a war for you, Ambassador. I'm not sure how many different ways I can say that. I am the Empress of Indrana, not a gunrunner for hire. Furthermore, I am no longer a gunrunner; any connections I may have had out in the black—" I spread my hands wide. "They will not speak with me now."

Adora sighed, her face pinched as though the entire thing were distasteful to her. "Your Majesty, the Farians are prepared to compensate Indrana for their help."

The figure she named had me whistling, but I still shook my head. Fasé's warning was ringing in my ears. "I'll speak with the council. I can't promise you they'll agree to this. In fact, I can almost promise you they won't. I have an empire to think of and people to answer to."

Adora started to respond, thought better of it, and nodded at me. "I'll wait for your reply, then. Thank you, Majesty."

"You're most welcome, Ambassador. Please don't hesitate to let Alba know if you need anything."

Nodding again, Adora let my chamberlain lead her from the room.

"So Caspel was right," I said to Emmory as soon as the door closed behind them. "Not that I doubted him." Sighing, I rested my chin in a hand and stared at the spot Adora had occupied. Emmory was quiet, and I appreciated the space he seemed to know I needed.

The Farians wanted Indrana, or rather the Empress of Indrana, purely because they thought I could help them understand how mercenaries fought? Or was it because of Fasé's rebellion? I wondered if Adora knew Fasé had escaped and what the repercussions of that would be once the request for asylum went through. Fasé seemed convinced the councils would approve it despite the obvious difficulties it could cause for Indrana. It should be such a simple choice—the Farians were our allies and had never done anything but help Indrana. But the more I learned, the more I started to worry that what Faria wanted might not be in our best interests.

"What is it, Majesty?" Emmory asked after several minutes of silence.

"I'm staring down a charging Hagidon." The massive beasts of Nugwa XIII were reminiscent of the mastodons of Earth's Pleistocene period, but with more teeth. Faced with an attack, you had two choices: Try to outrun it, or stand perfectly still and hope it got confused enough by your bravado that it wandered off in search of better sport. Both options had a fifty-fifty chance of death.

Movement seemed necessary and I shoved out of my chair to pace the room. "You'd think I would be concerned about refusing to help an ally and harboring fugitives. But I'm not." I turned to look at him, throwing my hands helplessly into the air. "And ironically that concerns me. This whole thing smells like a three-day-old corpse, Emmy.

"I don't care what anyone tries to claim—if *I* get involved in whatever cowshit is about to go down between the Farians and the Shen—my empire will be involved.

"Are the Shen moving now because of Fasé? Can we risk another massacre like the Solarians saw at Colony 17 if we don't act to put a stop to this?" Hissing air between my teeth, I shook my head as my thoughts collided. "That's a lot of money, Emmory. We could put it to good use."

"It's not worth it, Majesty. You heard what Fasé said."

"I know. Bugger me, I know. I won't lie and say it's not tempting. But my gut says I'd be better off taking the money Hao offered me before I take anything from the Farians."

"Hao offered you money?"

"Yes." I laughed. "*Hai Ram*, Emmory, don't look at me like that—it was just an offer to pay for the palace reconstruction. I turned him down. As much as I adore Hao, I'm not about to let it cloud my judgment and do something like take money from Po-Sin's second-in-command."

The look on Emmory's face was a mix of surprise and what I was reasonably sure was pride. It made me laugh again. "You'll notice I also didn't let him in on what has been going down with the Farians, even though I'm going to catch Naraka from him for it later. Look at me, growing up and being a dutiful empress." I punched him in the shoulder as I headed for the door; lifting my face to the ceiling, I sighed. "Mother would be proud."

"She was proud of you already, Majesty."

I pretended not to hear him. "Did you catch that insinuation from Adora that I'd be happier away from here? Everyone apparently thinks I'm still going to run away."

"Not everyone, Majesty."

Leaning into him for just a moment, I let his solid warmth ease some of the tension in my chest. "Thanks," I whispered, clearing the emotion stuck in my throat before I reached for the door.

The message from Caspel came in that afternoon while I was going over the tour details with Alba and Emmory, reading simply: *Message sent.*

After a great deal of deliberation with my intelligence director, I'd sent a message of my own to the Shen's new leaders offering my condolences on the loss of their father and requesting that they tell us what in the fires of Naraka was going on.

I'd phrased it better than that at Alba's insistence, but it was essentially the intent behind reaching out to the Shen directly. I was walking a fine line between empress duties and something that probably should have been discussed with the Matriarch Council; however, I was following my gut rather than wading through a debate about contacting the Shen.

We needed more information. With three sides to the fight but only two sides of the story, I felt like I was feeling my way around a pitch-black room. Fasé had been right; I didn't have a whole lot of choice but to trust her about the dire prediction of a deadly future, and I understood her refusal to tell me just what that involved.

It just wasn't going to stop me from getting all the information I could about this conflict—even if I had to do something as risky as contacting the Farians' enemies directly.

"Majesty, are you listening?"

"No, sorry," I admitted. "I got a message from Caspel."

"Sixteen planets in eighteen months," Alba replied. "You've got more than a few multiplanet systems where you'll be doing day trips to every planet. And then a few long-haul trips through warp."

"It's like you're all trying to get me to abdicate the throne. Do you have money on me bolting or something?" I didn't try to hide the grin that accompanied my dramatic flop onto the couch next to her, since the only other person in the room with me besides Alba was Emmory.

My *Ekam* raised an eyebrow at me from his position by the door and chuckled. "You'll do fine, Majesty."

"You've got an awful lot of faith in me, especially considering how much you know I don't like people."

"I'm sure there will be a few you could safely punch."

Alba choked on her tea. "*Ekam*, please don't encourage her."

Laughing, I patted her on the back. "I promise to behave myself as much as possible, Alba."

"It's the qualifier that concerns me, ma'am." Alba sighed and set her cup down on the table. "Anyway, yes, sixteen planets in eighteen months. Several of the planets are in the same systems, and we'll just be spending a day on each, but there are multiple-week or longer transit times. I promise you'll be able to recover between stops."

"I'm teasing, Alba—mostly." Looking at the schedule again, I rubbed a hand over the back of my neck. "I understand the need for this show of force. I just wish it weren't necessary."

In a month I was leaving for what was officially being called a tour of the empire but was in reality a reminder to those planets who'd picked the wrong side of the conflict that betting against the Empress of Indrana was a very bad idea.

Several planets where Phanin had laid the groundwork for revolt had taken advantage of the chaos of the coup and tried to break with the empire. While all of them had been brought to heel—either by the force of my military or by the local population—their disloyalty meant I got to spend the better part of a standard year away from Pashati.

The discussion over that three months ago had been ugly. It hadn't been a matter of my *Ekam* being wrong about how dangerous some of the stops were, but more that we really had no choice in the matter.

Alba and the others responsible for the list had at least taken pity on me and my *Ekam* by tossing in more than a few easy landings on the tour. I was looking forward to visiting Admiral Bolio and 8th Fleet at Draupadi Station, as well as my trip to Mathura, a planet orbiting an F-class yellow-white dwarf that served as a major trading hub for Indrana.

Overall it seemed like an awful waste of desperately needed resources and money, but I was doing my best not to question everything those with far more experience in government had planned.

"I wish it weren't necessary either, ma'am. That's life, I guess." Alba offered up a small smile as she got to her feet. "Do you need anything else from me this evening?"

"No, I'm fine. I'll look over the schedule and do my homework on our itinerary so I don't embarrass you out in the black."

My chamberlain seemed to think a nonverbal murmur of assent was her best option as she gathered up her things and headed for the door. I watched her go, my fond smile slipping some as I looked at Emmory.

"Between you and me, I'm tempted to cancel this tour," I said. "I know you won't argue with me."

"Everyone else will." Emmory's smile was surprisingly apologetic.

"Caspel sent my message to the Shen." Making a face, I got up from the couch and rubbed my hands over my arms. "I want them to reply, but I'm afraid of what they'll say."

"Why?"

"I don't know." I threw my hands in the air in frustration. "And that's the worst part of it. How am I supposed to keep my people safe if I don't know what's coming?"

"No one expects you to be able to see into the future, Hail." Emmory's quiet use of my name was a rare enough event that it shook me out of my growing panic. "We'll handle it as we always do—when it's there in front of us."

I smiled. "So that's where Portis got that saying from."

"You can blame our mother for it," he replied, and held a hand out to me.

I took his hand and gave it a squeeze. "She gave me both of you; I'd never blame her for anything."

13

"You know I love you, right, Cress?"

I slanted him a sideways look. "What are you on about? How much of that have you had?" Snatching the bottle out of Portis's reach, I laughed when he grabbed me and pressed his lips to my throat. "Cheater."

"I haven't had anything to drink," he said, skimming his lips up to my ear. "I love you."

"Is this about that pretty little Solie who owned the casino on Windenheim? She was too damn adorable and a whole lot of fun, but you know I'm not leaving you to settle down on a planet."

He laughed and kissed me again. "I'm too damn adorable *for you to leave, we both know it."*

I melted into the kiss, and after a long moment surfaced for air. "I know you love me. I love you, too."

The dream I woke from slipped away; only the lingering feel of Portis's breath on my throat and murmured words in my ear remained, and the sweeter side of grief wrapped itself around me in a comforting embrace. He'd been in my head a lot more lately, but without the sharp pain of loss, and I smiled up at the ceiling for a moment as I remembered that drunken night right before my past had kicked its way back into my life and changed everything.

I slid out of bed and shrugged into the robe lying over the back of a nearby chair. The main room was quiet, the lights dim as I padded across the floor to the balcony window. Gita looked up from the tablet in her lap when I put a hand on her shoulder.

"Morning, Majesty. Sleep well?"

"Well enough, I'm getting some air."

She nodded and went back to her book. I pulled my robe closed and pressed my hand to the panel, slipping through the open door and out onto the balcony into the cool morning air. The city was awake, even at this hour, and the sounds of aircars and ground transport filled my ears in an easy hum.

The sunrise coated the buildings in a wash of purple and blue that faded the farther east it went until it disappeared entirely into the golden light.

As I pulled up the files Caspel had sent me overnight, the background of Krishan's buildings faded to almost nothing at all with a few blinks.

Mia Cevalla
Daughter of Javez Cevalla and unknown human woman.
Approximate age: early thirties.
Height: 180 cm
Weight: estimated 85 kg
Brown hair. Gray eyes.

I studied the photos as I cued up Caspel's audio notes. "Based on our limited interaction with the Shen, building profiles on the new leaders has been somewhat difficult, and nothing in these files should be taken as absolute unless specifically stated. According to my resources, Mia oversees the military side of things. Recent encounters between the Shen and the Farians leads me to believe she's relatively inexperienced and somewhat reckless, though it's hard to say for sure if that's due to the influence of the mercenary forces or just in her nature. At the present her strategy seems to be to harass and confuse the Farians as much as possible. Running battles and quick strikes are going to be preferable for their out-numbered forces."

There were three photos of Mia: the one Caspel had shown me earlier, and two others that were long-distance shots. That pair was of poor quality, grainy and out of focus, but I could see Aiz standing next to his sister in one of them. Their fingers were brushing, a moment captured as Aiz smiled at his sister.

It made me ache for my sisters.

I blinked, partly to clear away my tears and partly to switch files.

Aiz Cevalla
Son of Javez and Estella Cevalla
Approximate age: early forties.
Height: 185 cm
Weight: estimated 91 kg
Brown hair. Brown eyes.

"Aiz appears to be the diplomat of the pair," Caspel said in my ear. "He's had more interactions with the Farians that we can track and more face time in the press, though even that is limited." My intelligence director's sigh was so heavy as to be audible on the recording. "I wish I had better profiles on both of them, Your Majesty, but I don't. I'll continue to see what information I can gather and update these as that becomes available. Until then—"

"Her Majesty is on the balcony." Gita's voice drifted out to me. "It's a little early, though. Let me see if she's—"

"I didn't come to talk to her." Hao's reply had me stopping Caspel's recording entirely, but I didn't turn toward the door.

"You should go," Gita said, her voice even more formal, though I wasn't sure how that was possible.

"You should tell me why you've been avoiding me since I got back, and don't lead with the Saxons because we both know it's not because of that." Hao's voice was clipped, a tone just this side of annoyed that I was extremely familiar with, having been on the receiving end plenty of times myself.

"I have been busy." Gita sighed and I could picture my mentor staring her down with that implacable golden gaze of his. "Look, Hao. What we had was fun."

"Fun?"

"Okay, maybe it was more than fun. But it was easy. The rules were different. We were outside." Gita paused and I imagined she was shoving a hand into her short hair the way she did when she was frustrated. "Now we are home, Hao, and you...whatever Her Majesty was, you're still a gunrunner."

Part of me wanted to cover my ears while I sang loudly. The other part stood frozen as my BodyGuard broke up with my brother.

"Are you saying I am not loyal to her?"

"Keep your voice down."

My eyes went wide at the snap of command in her voice, and I suspected Hao's face wore an identical look of surprise.

"I know you. Her Majesty knows you. Others? People talk, Hao, and the fact is you are still marked as Po-Sin's." I knew she was gesturing at his arms and the ink proclaiming his loyalty to his family. "It means you are not one of us. You never will be. You've made your choice same as all the rest of us have. I care for you, but I'm her *Dve*. I can't risk anyone suggesting my loyalty might be split from her by a gunrunner."

"Understood."

My heart broke. So much hurt in a single word.

"Hao—"

"No, it's fine, Gita. I understand. It explains the last few days." Hao would be smiling: that careful, formal smile reserved for deals with strangers. "Far be it from me to interfere in Her Majesty's protection or the running of her empire. Whatever you think of me, I care for her and I would sooner cut off my own hand than see her come to harm."

"Hao, don't do this—"

Unable to stand it any longer, I stretched my arms over my head and turned back to the balcony door with more noise than was necessary. "Morning!" The false cheer in my voice as I came through the door made me wince, and I rolled my eyes at the ceiling.

Hao was closer to me, standing at the window, his back to both of us. His shoulders straight as the lines of traffic under Solarian orbital control.

Gita was trying, with relative success, to hide the sorrow on her face. For just a moment I considered saying something, anything, to ease the hurt in the room, but the door opened and Stasia came in, bearing a tray and chatting with Zin. Others followed, and any hope I might have had of talking to the pair was lost to the morning bustle.

I didn't miss the look that passed between Gita and Zin, or the gentle hand he wrapped around her forearm for just a moment as he passed by her.

"Good morning, Majesty."

I took the cup of chai Stasia handed me with an answering nod and joined Hao at the window.

"If I were looking to hire mercenaries to go up against a foe that was superior in both technology and numbers, who would be worth the money?"

"Is this about the Farians wanting you to come fight for them?" He lifted his hands when I gave him a stern look. "People talk, little sister. I didn't even have to ask anyone important and I pieced most of it together myself. Hell, it'll probably be in the news tomorrow."

"That's not reassuring."

Hao frowned in consideration. "Since I assume we're taking about hiring someone to go up against the Farians, the Shen had better have something really worthwhile. You know as well as I do it would depend on the payout." He rubbed his thumb and forefinger together. "That said, the Barton boys would probably do it for kicks. Half a dozen other smaller outfits would consider it a good payday. Jamison could be persuaded with the right amount."

"Ugh." I made a face and sipped my chai. "I hate that guy." Jamison fancied himself something special, dressing the part of a gentleman and scholar even though he was neither.

"I hear the feeling is mutual. Word out there in the black is you cheated him."

Shooting Hao a sidelong glare, I set my mug down on the windowsill. "You know I would never. I stopped him from snaking a job out from under us. He didn't want to admit that he'd been bested, so he started spreading that stupid story around."

And now that I was the only one left of my crew, there was no one else to tell the truth of it.

"I didn't say I believed him, just that he was telling the story differently."

"He hates me." I rolled my eyes. "Always has."

"I'm pretty sure the three broken ribs you gave him that time he grabbed you has something to do with it, too." Hao grinned at me.

"Possible. Portis warned him not to touch me. Jamison just thought the punch was coming from him."

Instead it had come from me. I'd kicked his feet out from under him and put my boot into his side hard enough to snap three of his ribs before Portis pulled me off.

"I'd actually pay good money to have seen his reaction when the news about me hit," I said with a smirk.

"Majesty, breakfast is ready," Stasia said, and I waved a hand in acknowledgment.

"Has Po-Sin said anything about the Shen making him an offer?" There was no delicate way to ask that question, and only I could see the flinch that echoed in Hao's utter stillness.

"They have. He hasn't given them an answer." He shook his head. "Don't ask me anything else, little sister. You know I can't tell you specifics." A wry smile twisted his mouth. "And it occurs to me I owe you an apology, or at the very least an acknowledgment." He pressed a hand to his heart; despite his numerous tattoos, that spot had always been oddly blank. "You have an empire to run, one I am not part of, and just like there are things I cannot share with you, so it is the same with me."

"I appreciate your understanding." I leaned against him briefly, enjoying the warmth. "You know I have a place for you in this empire I'm rebuilding, if you wanted to join us."

Hao sighed, and I told myself I was imagining the longing held in his exhalation. "You know how Po-Sin would react. I think we have enough troubles at the moment, *sha zhu*."

"Do you think Rai would work for the Shen?" I asked, rubbing a hand over my heart as I changed the subject. His refusal stung for reasons I couldn't quite understand.

"If the money was good enough?" Hao wiggled a hand. "Rai will do anything if the numbers work out. Best to ask Johar about it, though. You're not actually thinking of getting involved in this, are you, Hail?"

"Even if I were, the Matriarch Council is going to say no. I'm not about to fight them on it. I know I'm needed here. We're headed out for this whole victory lap in just a few weeks. What?"

Chuckling, Hao shook his head. "Nothing, I just never expected—" He waved a hand in the air. "For you to want to stay."

"So everyone keeps telling me." I tapped a hand on the window-sill and made a decision I knew would raise more than a few eyebrows. "You want to join me at this meeting? We could use your knowledge about the various merc factions."

"Even though I'm not part of your empire?" Hao's tease had an edge of bitterness he couldn't quite hide, and I reached out, laying my hand on his forearm.

"You're important to me, *gege*, and I value your advice."

"You need your head checked." But my words had chased the rest of the sadness from Hao's eyes, and he nodded. "I don't have anything else to do today."

"Besides, it'll be fun."

He groaned. "The last time you said that to me I ended up getting shot by an Earth cop."

"That was in no way my fault." I punched him in the shoulder and headed for the table before Stasia dragged me to it.

"Admiral Hassan." I held a hand out to Inana, gripping her forearm and feeling the solid weight of her hand on mine in return. "Thank you for coming."

"Of course, Majesty. It was the right call to involve the Raksha in this. This is a matter that concerns all of Indrana."

Last night I'd sent a message to the Raksha with a brief overview of the situation for the five members of Indrana's military council and an invitation to join us at the meeting. Inana's words confirmed my intuition that no matter what the Farians were saying, involving me meant it would impact my empire in the end. I exchanged greetings with others as they filtered into the hotel conference room, watching how they interacted with each other.

When Heela came in with the prime minister trailing behind her, I hissed out a breath that had my *Ekam* tensing.

"Majesty?"

"It's nothing," I said, and caught Caterina's eye across the room, jerking my head toward the pair. She nodded once in acknowledgment and went back to her conversation with Alice and Taz.

"What's that about?" Inana asked.

"I'll tell you later. Caspel?"

"Yes, Majesty?" He bent in at my beckoning finger.

"I don't want to mention Fasé just yet. I think it's better for all of us if the Farians don't know she's here, and some of us in this room enjoy speaking with the press a bit too much."

He followed my gaze over to Shivali and nodded in understanding. "It's not written down on the agenda, Majesty. I won't say anything if you won't." He glanced at Inana, who shrugged.

"I don't know what you're talking about, Director."

I laughed softly and then murmured, "Would you look at that?"

Adi Desai came into the room with her younger brother Valmiki following her.

"Surprised, Majesty?" Inana asked.

"A bit," I admitted. "Though Adi's protests over integration were more moderate than the others. If anyone from their side was going to offer that kind of conciliatory gesture, she's the one I would have put money on."

"Majesty," Adi said, dropping into a little curtsy. "May I present my brother, Valmiki Hon Desai."

"Your Imperial Majesty." Valmiki Desai had close-cropped brown hair, and his bow was practiced perfect, if stiffly formal.

In the heartbeats of the exchange, I debated my response. Everyone in the room was watching—some of them more obviously than others—and my reaction to this would no doubt set the tone for the integration and our continued path to equality.

When Valmiki came up from his bow, I reached out and gripped his forearm the same way I had Inana's. I felt his jolt of shock, knew it was rippling through the rest of the crowd. "Valmiki, it's a pleasure to meet you. I hope you're ready to be Indrana's future."

"Yes, ma'am—uh, Majesty." He fumbled, squeezing my forearm back as he stammered, and I couldn't resist the wink.

"If everyone is here, take a seat and let's get started," I said as I released him and moved toward my chair at the front of the room. "Director Ganej, if you will proceed?"

Caspel cleared his throat and stood. "As stated in the briefing you should have all received yesterday, Her Majesty was approached by a Farian ambassador several days ago with a request from the Farian ruling body, the Pedalion."

We'd planned on also discussing Fasé and Sybil, who was still at my country estate with Indula and Iza to look after them. But the unexpected appearance of the prime minister was enough to make me change my mind. Shivali liked to run her mouth on nightly news programs, one of the many reasons I didn't make it a habit of inviting her to meetings like this one despite my desire to increase the General Assembly's participation in Indrana's governing. We couldn't run the risk of the Farians finding out about Fasé before the request for asylum was officially relayed and granted.

Capel cleared his throat. "The Pedalion requested that the empress travel to Faria to discuss strengthening Indranan's ties with Faria. Her Majesty refused, citing the impossibility of her leaving Pashati when there is still much work to do—"

"Never mind we're not in a position to help anyone at the moment," General Vandi, head of the Imperial Tactical Squad, muttered. Heads nodded in agreement around the table.

"Her Majesty also pointed that out," Caspel said with a smile. "What was not included in the briefing is that Ambassador Notaras spoke with the Pedalion and returned to the empress with a more honest reason for their request yesterday afternoon. They want to call on our alliance—and the assistance they are requiring to fulfill the terms of our alliance is for Her Majesty to provide her experience and knowledge to the Pedalion. They are willing to compensate Indrana for the empress's absence."

I rested my elbow on the table and my chin in my hand as Caspel continued, watching the reactions around the room. There was a little shock, a matching amount of amusement, and frowns of concern from all of the military members present.

"That is a lot of money," Caterina said finally, her dark eyes flicking in my direction, trying to gauge my reaction. "Can they afford it?"

Looks were exchanged around the table and it was Taz who leaned forward, his forearms resting on the edge. "There's no reason they couldn't. The Farians have their fingers in a lot of trading, not just here in our stock market but with the Solarians. They run one of the largest medical technology companies in the sector and we import about forty percent of our tech from them. Rumor has it that for some reason Indrana's prices are far lower than those of any of the other human governments."

"We were the first to sign a treaty with them," Alice said. "That's always been the reason I heard."

"Assuming they can pay us, that much money always has strings attached, even if it's promised as a fair exchange." Masami Tobin was the eldest member of the council, her life spared from Wilson's violent retribution on the matriarchs only because she'd gone to Red Cliff with me for negotiations with the Saxons.

"I'd say. The Farians would own us," General Aganey Triskan said, shaking his head.

"We have been the Farians' allies for centuries longer than any other humans; even the Solarians can't claim that kind of longevity. We are technically in a position where we could honor the treaty with the terms they set forth. Princess Alice has been prepped to take over while the empress is on tour, and we all know it's a tour that could be put aside for something more important like this." This protest was from Inana, but it was halfhearted, and the frown on her face matched that of her comrade in charge of the army.

"It feels like they just want you, Your Majesty, but you are Indrana. This makes me uneasy. They want to take you tens of thousands of light-years away from us on what? Just the promise they will bring you home? The fact that they weren't up front about it in the first place gives me a bad feeling about the whole situation. Why the subterfuge?" Matriarch Vandi asked the question from the far side of the table.

Sabeen Vandi had been the youngest member of the Matriarch Council before the tragedy, and she'd also been spared thanks to her presence with me for the negotiations with the Saxons. Her time out in the black had wiped some of the naïveté from her personality, and I kept my face carefully neutral when I wanted to grin at the matter-of-fact way she now spoke to me.

"They think they know you because of the story the newslines all over the galaxy have been playing." Few people in the room could have gotten away with saying what my heir just announced. Alice's dark eyes sparkled with amusement as she waved her hands in the air. " 'Intrepid princess becomes famous gunrunner who is dragged home to take the throne' gives people all sorts of misconceptions about who you really are. They were expecting you to jump at the chance to run again. I'm sure it was quite the shock to her that you said no."

I tilted my head in her direction and smiled. "Very much so."

"On that note, you're being unusually quiet about this, Your Majesty." My cousin Tej Naidu was seated on the left side of the table several people down from me. There wasn't a single noble family untouched by Wilson's madness, but Tej had seen her sister executed for betraying the empire and then her mother shot for staying loyal.

I suspected, like me, she had buried her grief as deep as it would go so she could get up every morning.

Hooking an arm over the back of my chair, I surveyed the room for several heartbeats before I spoke. "Something about the Shen terrifies the Farians, but there's more to it than that. It's not just a matter of the Shen hiring mercenaries. Military estimates from the Farians say they outnumber the Shen ten to one. Their tech is better and they've got trade agreements or alliances with other human governments, including the Solarian Conglomerate. Though as Inana pointed out, ours is the oldest." I shook my head. "But the Solarians are in a far better position to fight a war with the Farians, and their alliance has the same defense clause in it. So why come to us?"

"The Shen are a threat," General Triskan said. "In number or a tech breakthrough. Javez seemed like an unimportant footnote in the military histories the Farians have given us access to. His children are already causing the Farians a great deal of trouble."

I smiled at the army general. Someone had done his research since getting the notice about the meeting last night. "The Shen are growing their numbers; Caspel has been able to confirm that much. Though we don't have any firm totals yet. And mercenaries can be bought for the right price, but you don't trust them to win a war for you."

"Why bring them in at all, then?" Inana asked.

I glanced in Hao's direction. I knew the answer to this question, but I was curious if my brother did. I knew Po-Sin had to be considering the Shen's offer. It was foolish to think otherwise. The Cevallas weren't amateurs and if the credits were enough Po-Sin would join them.

Which would leave my brother and me on opposite sides of a war.

"We all know the Farians don't fly with criminals," Hao said with a shrug that only I recognized as a shade too nonchalant. "The Shen have to know this. My guess is they've waited until now to take advantage of some of the better technology and the larger mercenary outfits. They've translated this weakness of the Farians' into a fighting strategy their opponent won't be able to defend against. Judging from the recent skirmishes, they were right to gamble. Not to be too blunt about it, but it's fucking brilliant."

I bit my cheek to stop the smile, wondering if Hao was deliberately being more like a gunrunner than necessary just to see some of the people around the table wince. "Hao and I have discussed the possible factions who would be willing take on such a job."

Hao nodded. "To go up against the Farians, the Shen have to be paying them well. I'd be more curious where the Shen are getting that money." He blew out a breath and shook his head. "That's a lot of credits."

"I'm looking into it," Caspel replied. "We know the Shen look enough like humans that they can blend in. I'd hazard a guess they're using that to set up businesses—legal and illegal—to fund this war against the Farians. I've been compiling what information we've been able to gather, and I'll send that out to all of you after the meeting. If you wouldn't mind speaking with me after this, Captain Cheng? Perhaps if we pool our resources we will get further."

Hao's smile was surprisingly hesitant as though he expected someone to object, but no one did.

I waited a beat before speaking. "Indrana has valued our particular alliance with the Farians for a very long time, but they are asking for more than I'm willing to give. I am slated to leave Pashati soon, and Alice will have her hands full here." I looked around the table, pausing a second longer at the seats Heela and Shivali occupied. "And I fully expect everyone to give her and Taz your full support.

"As it was pointed out, that much money would save Indrana. That much money would put us forever in debt to the Farians. It's a higher price than I'm willing to pay, and I suspect most, if not all, of you agree with me. I cannot leave the empire to play advisor in someone else's war." I wasn't going to go into the fact that my gut was still screaming that it was a bad idea to get involved in this. There were a few people here who would understand, but the others needed more logical reasoning.

"Unless Indrana is directly threatened, or attacked, I say we cannot authorize any involvement in this conflict," Inana said, and heads nodded in agreement around the table.

"Agreed," Caterina said. "We could send an ambassador of our own to Faria, but not you, Majesty. No matter how much the Farians may dislike the suggestion."

"I will inform Ambassador Notaras of the council's decision." I tapped a hand on the table and stood.

Everyone followed and as they filtered from the room, stopping to say their good-byes to me and Alice, I noticed that Inana and the rest of the Raksha had gathered in discussion on the far side of the room.

I exchanged a look with Alice, and she intercepted Matriarch Tobin before Masami could reach me. A second look at Emmory had him taking up a stone-faced position no one would dare to cross.

"How bad is it?" I kept my voice low, even though my Body-Guards and Alice's were now quietly ushering the remaining people from the room.

"If we get hit by either side?" Inana made a face. "It's hard to say, Majesty. We don't have hard data on the Shen or the Farians. Just a lot of hearsay and estimates. We wouldn't know where they were attacking or how big a force they would bring. I doubt they could be so foolish as to make a play for Pashati, or even Canafey with the bulk of the *Vajrayana* ships back there."

"I am less concerned about the possibility of us getting involved on the military side of things, Majesty." This came from Caspel. "We have a tenuous grip on peace here. The empire is on solid, if slightly shaky, ground. We could survive the loss of the Farian alliance, though it would hurt." He exhaled and shook his head. "We are isolated here in this arm of the galaxy and it has been to our benefit." He shook his head, the frown marring his hawklike face. "However, if something happens to unbalance peace in the Solarian sector? I don't know what the result will be."

I tapped my fingers against my lips with a frown of my own. "If two alien races want to go to war, I'm not sure anything can stop them."

Caspel sent me a sympathetic smile. "My fear is that you're right on both counts, Majesty."

I laid a hand on Inana's arm before the admiral could follow the others as the meeting broke up. "Where's Colonel Morri stationed?"

"Dio?" Hassan's eyes unfocused for a moment as she checked

her *smati*. "She's slated to be commander of the palace Marines. I recommended her myself. She's assigned to General Carter at the Academy until the palace construction is completed."

The Royal Marine had been a member of Inana's own ship when they'd fled Pashati during the coup, but her promotion after our victory meant she'd moved to a new posting.

"Will you let General Carter know I'd like to see her and Dio at their earliest convenience? Have her get with Alba about my schedule."

"May I ask why?"

"She was with Ambassador Notaras." I shrugged one shoulder. "I'd like the chance to talk with her more about what's going on."

"I'll pass it along, ma'am. Am I correct in assuming you'd rather Colonel Morri not know you're coming?"

"That would be preferred." I nodded. "Thanks, Inana, I appreciate it."

"You going to tell me what that thing with the prime minister was?" she asked with a smile.

I glanced around, making sure we were alone in the room. "She said some concerning things about Taz and the *Upjas* the other day. Caterina is taking care of it, but I figured a little push from me couldn't hurt."

"I'm glad to see you've learned how to delegate."

"You're just saying that because I want to punch her in the nose." I rubbed at my neck. "All joking aside, Inana, keep an eye on her and Heela. I don't mind them objecting to the reforms, but I swear to the Dark Mother that if you so much as get a whiff of them planning a revolt while I'm gone, you put your boot on them and do it hard."

"With a great deal of pleasure, Your Majesty," Inana replied.

14

N_{o.}"

"I'm sure that we could—excuse me, Majesty?" Adora stammered, her gold eyes filled with stunned confusion.

"I said we cannot help you, Ambassador. I'm very sorry, but the Matriarch Council has confirmed my original decision. This is not a good time for us to leave the empire. My heir has enough on her schedule and I have plans for necessary visits to various planets in my empire."

"Majesty—"

"We value our relationship with Faria and trust that the Pedalion will understand Indrana's needs. However, we are willing to provide whatever military assistance you may require within our means, and the offer to send an ambassador is still open—"

"That's not good enough!" Adora snapped.

My BodyGuards stiffened. Emmory took a step around my chair so that he was between me and the Farian. I stopped him with a hand.

"You forget yourself, Ambassador." I stood slowly, letting my reputation carry the menace in my words through the air. Adora took a step back and I smiled.

"The Farians have been our friends for a long time, but do not think for one second that I will put the well-being of my citizens, of my empire, to the side just to please the Pedalion. We are not your subjects, and if you wish for our alliance to continue you will remember that. I have no reason to travel across the galaxy, and you certainly have not given me anything worth making such a trip. I know the parameters of the treaty and will gladly follow it; however, Indrana is not beholden to you and I am not your servant to be ordered about. Are we quite understood?"

"I see." Adora's bow was stiff, sharp as a knife's edge. "Thank you for your time, Majesty. I hope you have a pleasant day."

She turned and left the room before I could reply, leaving me staring at the door.

"*Uff*, that went well," I muttered, rubbing a hand over the back of my neck.

"The only answer she wanted was the one you couldn't give her, Majesty," Emmory said.

"I know." I sighed. "She's not going to just let this go, I'd put a lot of credits down on that."

"You don't think the Pedalion will understand Indrana's need to look after their own affairs first before committing to something as serious as another conflict."

"I think they're not used to anyone telling them no." I couldn't shake the unease in my gut even as I forced a smile in Emmory's direction.

"Majesty, what if something happens?"

"Like the Farians or the Shen attacking?" I spread my hands wide and shook my head. "I don't know. We'll handle it. I trust you," I said. "And the others. We're enough if—Shiva forbid—things go sideways. We've all weathered that storm once before. I have faith we can do it again."

"I would rather keep you here where it's easier and safer," he replied.

"If you wanted easier and safer you shouldn't have dragged me home in the first place."

"Hush, Majesty."

Winking at him, I headed for the door. "We should get moving, I'm hungry."

"Majesty."

I glanced back, curious at the tone of voice. He'd started to follow me, but was stopped with a hand up and a frown on his face. "What is it?"

"Message from Trackers Peche and Winston. Elsa Khatri has been apprehended on Solas."

"Solas?" I whistled. "That's rough territory. We have an extradition treaty with them, though, don't we?" I pulled up the planet on my map. "Huh, she got farther than I thought she would." Exhaling, I started for the door again. "Tell them good job, Emmory, and to bring her home. She's already been tried. She'll be executed once her feet hit Pashati again."

"Yes, ma'am."

Former matriarch Elsa Khatri had conspired with Wilson to murder my sisters, poison my mother, and put my cousin on the throne. When her daughter had discovered the treachery, she'd reported it; and when Wilson's attempt to kill me had failed, Elsa had fled the empire.

She couldn't run fast enough or far enough away to escape me.

"I hate this part." Cueing up my *smati*, I commed Zaran Khatri and put her call up on the wall. I spotted Alba slipping into the room and waved a hand at her even as Emmory bent to give her the news.

"Good afternoon, Your Majesty," Zaran said, smiling. "What can I do for you?"

"They found your mother." There wasn't any easier way to say it, but I still hated the way the smile fell off Zaran's face.

"Good." The blank expression was in place, hiding any pain the young matriarch might have been feeling. "I'm assuming they'll bring her home?"

"We will. I've already instructed the Trackers to head back."

"We'll have nothing to say to her, Your Majesty. Nor will we attend her execution. I'll send a maid to witness if I can find one willing."

"We'll make sure the judge is notified," I replied.

"I appreciate it very much."

"Have a good day, Zaran."

"You, too, Your Majesty." She nodded, and I disconnected the call, returning my attention fully to my surroundings.

"I need a minute," I whispered, heading for the balcony. The wind ripped the tears from my eyes before they could fall down my cheeks. "You vain, selfish woman." I cursed Elsa's name, the wind catching that also and sending it flying.

Zaran had done a good job hiding the pain, but I could still see it. I always saw it in the eyes of the families of all the people I'd sent to die.

All the traitors, my mother's voice reminded me.

"They're still people and it still hurts."

Of course it does. That means you're human. You don't realize how often I cried on your father's shoulder. But you're the empress, Haili, it's part of what you do.

"This is a shit job," I muttered, staring up at the sky as I suddenly, desperately missed my mother. "I know you're gonna tell me to stop whining and get on with it. I won't lie, I wish you were here to do that in person."

The voice in my head was silent and I sighed, wiping my face as I went back into my rooms. "Alba, will you call Judge Claremont—"

"It's already done, Majesty." She reached out with a smile and brushed away a tear that was still clinging to my cheek.

"I don't know what I'd do without you." I touched her elbow. "I'm off to lunch with Hao and Dailun. I'll see you when I get back."

Alba smiled. "Have a nice time, Your Majesty."

*　　*　　*

A warm summer breeze blew through Garuda Square and in through the open storefront of the café, carrying with it scents of candy, *covan* smoke, and sounds of children playing in the fountain.

The square had recovered from the Pratimas blast and remarkably escaped damage from the battles in the capital during Wilson's coup. From my seat I could see the undisturbed ring of flowers someone laid out frequently for the victims of the explosion.

I loved these stolen quiet moments. Eating in my rooms wasn't the same, and nearly every meal out was with someone about imperial business. But the last few weeks I'd managed to sneak away to the square and sit in silence while I ate and caught up on work. It didn't matter that I was surrounded by BodyGuards, the café had been cleared out, and only Dailun sat by my side.

He was reading something on his *zhù*, his eyes flicking back and forth across the pages loaded into his *smati* only he could see.

I'd waved Hao off a few minutes before, his restless foot-tapping having finally gotten on my nerves, and I was scrolling through the day's news when a hand closed around my wrist.

"Empress Hailimi, could I have a moment?"

I looked up into the warm brown eyes of Aiz Cevalla as the sound of Emmory's shouted warning went to war with the whining sound of Hessian 45s powering up.

"Let. Her. Go."

Aiz's eyes flicked away from me for just a second and a smile curved his mouth. "You and I both know, *Ekam*, that you will not shoot me. You know my death will kill your empress as surely as if you'd shot her yourself. I do not want to hurt anyone, I only want to talk, and I believe that is why Her Majesty commed me in the first place." He was speaking in Galactic Standard, his words heavily accented but understandable.

"You could have commed back." I didn't know why the smart

comment was the first thing out of my mouth with a Shen's hand on my skin.

Aiz's grin flashed, transforming his stern face into something more boyishly handsome. "I like face-to-face meetings, and I confess, the chance to see the legendary gunrunner empress in person was enough to justify the risk."

"Have a seat. We'll talk." I gestured at the empty one next to Dailun. "I'll even give you my word you won't be harmed and can walk back out of here once we're done."

"Not here, it's a bit distracting with guns. You'll come with me alone. You need to hear what I have to say. Tell your people to stand down. I promise you won't be hurt."

"You're not going anywhere with her." Emmory's snarl was enough to scare me, but Aiz didn't even flinch at the menace.

"*Ekam*, this is a clear choice—you let us go or you kill both of us. There are no other options. I am not particularly interested in dying today, but I will if I have to. The Shen will continue without me for a time because they must, and then I will return. However, do you think Indrana can survive the loss of their star so soon after that ugly civil war?"

Choices. We were back to choices and trusting when I had no reason to do so. If Aiz had wanted me dead it would already be done. "Emmory." I reached my free hand out and laid it on my *Ekam*'s forearm. "Tell everyone to stand down. I'll go with him."

Emmory didn't look at me and his gun didn't waver.

"*Ekam*, that was an order. As is this: If he kills me, you tell Alice to take the full might of Indrana and help the Farians wipe the Shen from the fabric of the universe." I looked back at Aiz. "There is nowhere you can run, nowhere you can hide, no one who will protect your people if you harm me, Aiz Cevalla."

"Your terms are agreeable." Aiz nodded. "I want to talk, nothing more. What say you, *Ekam*? Are you going to kill us all, or trust me?"

Something about Aiz's tone made me realize he meant the entirety of the galaxy would suffer if we died, and I tightened my fingers on Emmory's arm just a fraction.

"I trust the empress," Emmory replied, holstering his gun. "All teams stand down. Clear the exits."

I squeezed his forearm as I got to my feet, Aiz's hand still wrapped around my right wrist. A thousand possibilities raged through my head. Was I fast enough to use this movement as a distraction and get free before he grabbed me again and killed me?

My bet was a hundred to one, which wasn't anywhere close to odds I liked. Indrana could survive without me. I wasn't so arrogant to think that I was somehow the beginning and the ending of this empire. But at what cost? Would my death reignite the war, giving those planets who'd defected to Wilson's side an excuse to break with the empire for good? The thought of Alice trying to fight another war instead of focusing on the empire and the future we were creating kept me from wrenching my wrist free of Aiz's grip even before Dailun spoke up.

"*Jiejie*, less violence, not more."

I nodded at him, forcing a smile, and then looked at Aiz with a raised eyebrow.

"This way, Empress." The Shen led me toward the back of the café, into the now-empty kitchen. I spotted the knife, tossed hastily to the side as the cook had fled. Aiz's attention was fixed on the door at the back of the kitchen, and I knew I'd have one chance.

Snagging the knife off the counter on our way by, I tossed a silent blessing Stasia's way for the sari I was wearing as I hid it beneath the deep green fabric. Aiz shouldered through the back door out into the shadowed alley.

The electric shock of his hand on my face took me by surprise and I nearly dropped my weapon. "Bugger me!"

15

orry." Aiz's grin, however, was unrepentant. "You'll find your *smati* useless for a little while, Majesty. It is not permanent, though."

"You'd better hope Emmory doesn't think you just killed me."

"A risk worth taking. This way." He led me down the alley and through another door into an empty building.

My stomach clenched, and I used all my willpower to not balk as we went down a set of stairs into the basement and then into a tunnel. The tunnel was old but showed signs of recent use, and as we took turn after turn, I realized I was about to be thoroughly lost beneath the city.

"You are testing my patience, Mr. Cevalla." I struggled to keep the quavering of my voice to a minimum but couldn't hide the way my feet automatically dug in to keep me from going deeper into the ground.

"You do well with that imperial voice. It's hard to believe you were a gunrunner for twenty years." His voice carried enough disdain in the word *gunrunner* to distract me from my panic.

"Just a little farther, Empress, and I promise the room is wide enough to keep your claustrophobia at bay." He smiled at me over his shoulder. "I hope you'll forgive me for this discomfort; it seemed safer to have you slightly off balance."

I tightened my grip on the knife. "You know an awful lot about me."

"I am a quick study when the occasion calls for it, and you are something of a celebrity. We have watched every documentary about you, and the live feed of your death." Aiz ducked through a dark opening on his left, practically dragging me through while my brain screamed in protest.

We entered a brightly lit room scattered with desks and couches coated in dust. A woman stood by one of the couches, and she turned as we entered. Aiz released me, backing away with his hands up and a smile peeking through his dark beard.

"Your Majesty, may I present my sister. Mia Cevalla."

Mia dipped her head, brown hair swinging forward to hide her face. She was even more distracting in person, and I stepped hard on the desire suddenly crowding out my panic. "Star of Indrana, it is a great honor to be in your presence." Her Indranan was halting and heavily accented.

"Your brother kidnapped me and threatened me, so it's hard to say the same," I replied. "Where are we?"

"Old *Upjas* hideout," Aiz replied. "Very handy. First, before you take off back the way we came, you'll get lost and none of us want that. Just listen to what we have to say, and I'll give you a map out of here and turn your *smati* back on so your people can find you."

"Aiz," Mia sighed. "Did you really threaten her?"

He shrugged. "I was mostly stating a fact. If her *Ekam* had shot me, it would have killed her."

I leaned against the closest desk, laying the knife down on the dusty surface. "You've got five minutes. Start talking. If I don't like what you have to say, I'm going to bury this in at least one of your throats."

Some of the smug certainty drained from his face, and I allowed myself a smile as his eyes flickered to the knife. "Kitchen?"

I nodded once.

"I didn't even hear you grab it," he murmured to himself with a smile. "I promised myself I wouldn't underestimate you, but it appears I have already done so." He dipped his head. "Why didn't you just stab me in the back?"

"Because I actually want to hear what you have to say, but I don't trust you. Not after that stunt." Crossing my arms over my chest and trying to ignore the hammering of my heart or the way the walls were pressing down on me, I stared him down and then looked at Mia. "A com link would have been a whole lot less fuss and wouldn't have earned Aiz the enmity of my BodyGuards or my annoyance. How did he get past them into the café?"

"If I've only got five minutes I'd rather not waste it." Mia's teeth flashed white against her tan skin as she smiled. "You are in danger, Empress. The Farians are trying to involve not only you but your empire in a war they cannot hope to win."

"I already told them no."

"They will not listen." Mia shook her head. "They will not stop. They will keep asking, and if you keep refusing they will find a way to make you involve yourself."

I raised an eyebrow. "Are you suggesting the Farians would actually attack us?"

"They are more ruthless than you can imagine, but they will not attack you outright. They will kill your friends, your heir, the fetus that carries the hopes of Indrana. They can and will make it look as though we were responsible. The Farians do not care about humans beyond what you can give them," Aiz said.

"And what is that, exactly?"

"A place for them to dispose of the energy they hoard because their gods refuse to let them use it on themselves."

That was not the answer I was expecting, and I stared at the pair for a long moment as my brain scrambled to wrap itself around the concept. The Farians had always said that helping humans was a pilgrimage to keep the gods' fire from burning them up inside.

The best lie is always at least a partial truth, Portis whispered in my head. "You stole their ships, burned down their colonies," I said.

Mia smiled, and the gray of her eyes warmed into a smoky haze. "We did steal those ships, but it was not the Shen who burned down those Farian colonies."

"Excuse me?" I dropped my hands, standing up straight from the desk. "Do you have proof?"

"I could provide all the proof in the universe, and it would still be my word versus the Farians, and because they have spent millennia on a disinformation campaign against my people, no one would believe me." The bitterness was clear on her face. "The victor writes the history, as you well know, Majesty."

"What do you want from me?"

"Join us. Help us win this fight. It is the only way the rest of the galaxy is safe." Mia held her hands out and took a step toward me, stopping when I automatically shifted back against the desk and grabbed for the knife. "Abdicate your throne to the capable hands of your heir. We will keep Indrana safe from the Farians."

"You're asking me to violate an alliance that is centuries old without any proof or justification beyond your word. I have zero reason to do that."

"The winds have shifted in this war, Majesty; you and I both know it. It will continue to escalate and it may take us another thousand years, but we will win." Mia's smile was soft, but I recognized the plasteel beneath the surface of it. "I don't want to fight you, I don't want to fight Indrana, but I will if I have to and I will lay waste to everything you hold dear. It would be better for everyone if you left now."

The passion in her words was true; whatever else was going on, Mia believed what she was saying. People with conviction and a cause were predictable, but they were dangerous. They'd give anything, do anything, sacrifice themselves and anyone else on the altar of their mission.

A year ago I might have jumped at the chance, but just like the Farians, the Shen had misjudged me. They thought the gunrunner was still staring longingly at the black just waiting for a chance to escape.

I wasn't. I was the Empress of Indrana and would be until my dying breath. "You probably shouldn't have picked a fight with the Farians, then," I said baring my teeth in a smile of my own. "We are Faria's allies. At some point I will have no choice but to help them, and I promise you Indrana will make you pay dearly if you come after us."

"By the time they are willing to beg for or try to force your empire's help, it will be too late." Aiz's smile had no warmth to it, and it chilled me to the bone. "For the good of the galaxy, join us."

"I can't," I whispered. "None of you seem to understand I'm not a gunrunner anymore. I am the Empress of Indrana, and Indrana doesn't want to be involved in your war. We are done with war. It is my responsibility to keep us out of this. I won't help you. I won't help them."

Mia held up a hand before her brother could reply. "I'm sorry to hear that. We had hoped to avoid this, but it seems the path is to be a violent one." She sighed and then smiled, and my gut churned with the way the word *violent* rolled off her tongue. "But such is life, we will go on. I appreciate your willingness to at least listen."

I tightened my hand on the knife handle, my panic over the closed-in space beaten back; as the adrenaline of an impending fight flooded me, I studied the pair. If they were smart they would attack me together. One of them would be able to get their hands on my exposed skin and kill me. The best I could hope for was to take one of them with me.

Instead, Aiz nodded, then folded his hands together and bowed. "Thank you for listening, Empress. We have kept you long enough. If you'll permit me to reactivate your *smati*, I'll show you the way out."

"You're an idiot if you think I'm just going to let you walk up and kill me."

They both froze. The shock was written clear across their faces and I tightened my grip on the knife until my fingers hurt.

"Your Majesty, I promised your—I promised I would not hurt you. I am no liar." Aiz held his hands up, but I shook my head.

"If you're telling the truth, just go. I'll find my own way out."

"You won't, and your BodyGuards won't be able to find you either." Mia shoved her hands into the pockets of her pants and crossed the room to me, ignoring her brother's protest when I brought the knife up between us. "I don't wish us to part as enemies, and leaving you down here would do just that." She leaned in, the blade at her throat, and for a second we stared at each other.

"Mia." Aiz's voice was little more than a gust of air, and I watched his sister smile.

"You'll have time to kill me if he does anything more than turn your *smati* back on," she said. "Neither of us wants to die, Majesty, so trust me this once." She pulled one hand free and held out a data chip to me. "Information and a way for you to contact us when you change your mind."

"I won't," I said, but I held the knife steady against her throat as I pulled the chip from her fingers without touching her.

Aiz approached us. He was pale under his dark beard, and there was a surprising tremble to his fingers as he reached out to me.

He brushed fingers along my jaw, pulling away in a fluid movement and knocking my knife hand away from Mia's throat. My recoil was part automatic, part from the jolt of electricity that lanced through me at the contact. My head filled with the rapid-fire orders on the com link as my *smati* came back online.

"... *sector by sector sweep. Gita reports they pursued underground. I want all exits in a ten-block radius covered by Marines.*"

"*Ekam, I have the empress's signal!*"

Aiz winked, bravado back now that he was firmly between me and his sister. "The map is on the walls, just follow the marks to the surface." He turned his back on me and ushered Mia through the door.

I followed them, but the blackness of the tunnel and the sound of water running slammed into me with a vicious fury, bringing with it images of water rising over my chest in the cold tomb of Wilson's coffin. I stumbled away from the doorway with a sob, back to the relative safety of the wide room and bright light.

"Hail, can you hear me?" Emmory's voice was in my ear, even over the com link bringing with it enough reassurance that I could piece together some sanity.

"I'm in an old *Upjas* hideout. Aiz and Mia are gone. He said there's a way out. A map on the walls, but it's dark. I'm sorry. There's water—I can't—"

"We're headed for you now. It's all right, Majesty, I'll be right there."

The knife clattered against the stone floor and I followed it to the ground, both arms wrapped around my waist, shaking.

"Hail!" It was Hao, not Emmory, who came through the door minutes later. "Are you hurt?" He cupped my face in his hands and then wrapped his arms around me. "Emmory, I found her. You got a lock? Okay, we'll meet you there."

"There's a map," I whispered. "I couldn't—there was water, in the dark." I knew it wasn't there, but I could see the inside of the box, the light shining in my eyes. I squeezed them shut and fisted my hands in Hao's shirtfront.

"You're okay. I'm here, little sister. It's okay."

Hao got me to my feet with an amazing amount of patience, his words soft, floating easily between Cheng and Indranan as he coaxed me out into the tunnel. He kept an arm around me, anchoring me to his side as he walked me through the darkness.

The light stung my eyes and I turned my head away, squeezing them shut again and hating the whimper that crawled its way out of my throat.

"Is she hurt?" Emmory's gloved hand was solid against my cheek.

"I don't think so. But she's having a bad flashback. She's talking about Wilson and water."

"Get her in the aircar." The rest of Emmory's words were lost in a blur of movement, and I followed along without protest as Hao ushered me into the aircar.

The door closed behind Emmory and we lurched into the air.

"No." My breath caught; the iron band that had suddenly locked itself around my chest was squeezing out all my air.

Hao released me and brought an arm up, but not fast enough. My swinging elbow caught him in the throat as I scrambled into the corner of the aircar. He doubled over with a choked sound, and Emmory put his hands up.

"It's all right. We have to get you back to the hotel. It's only for a few minutes."

"I can't be in here. There's no air. I'll drown."

"You won't," Emmory said. "I'm sorry, but you have to be in here. You're safe. Hail, look at me."

I pressed my hands to my eyes instead and folded forward, fighting the urge to bolt for the door. I knew it wouldn't open. I knew even if I could somehow get it open, Emmory would never let me out—and with good reason, as we were several hundred meters in the air.

"I'm sorry."

"You don't have to be sorry."

I heard the creak of the leather seat as Emmory shifted forward, and a moment later his hand settled gently on the back of my head. "You don't have to be sorry," he repeated. "Just breathe for me, and we'll be out of here shortly. What do you need?"

"I don't know." But the weight of Emmory's hand was grounding, and I felt some of the panic recede. I dragged in a breath, forcing it past the tightness of my chest, and then another until I could sit upright. Emmory shifted with me, his hand moving to my shoulder.

"I'm sorry," I said again, this time to Hao, who smiled and reached for my hand.

"It's all right, *sha zhu*." He laced his fingers through mine and rubbed at his throat with his other hand. "Did he hurt you?"

The carefully controlled menace in his voice almost sent me back over the edge. Shaking my head, I took a deep breath. "No. Mia was waiting. They just wanted to talk."

"What did they want?" That question came from Emmory.

"I'll send you the—" I frowned. "There's no video. He shorted out my *smati*."

"It's working fine," Emmory said. "We figured he'd jammed it once you left the café."

"No. Bugger me. Emmory, he *touched me* and it deactivated my *smati*, and then he just turned it back on like it was nothing."

I watched the thoughts chase across my *Ekam*'s face before he muttered a curse. "Zin, are you headed back to the hotel with Gita?" he asked over the com link.

"I am. What's up?"

"I need you to run a full diagnostic on the empress's *smati*. I'll explain more in person."

"Understood, sir."

Emmory took my free hand. "Tell me everything," he said. "From the beginning."

16

An argument raged around me the next morning as I picked at my breakfast, restlessly flipping the chip from Mia between the fingers of my left hand. Alice and Caterina were going head to head with Caspel and Inana.

I'd slept poorly, waking up almost as soon as I drifted off to sleep gasping for breath and drenched in so much sweat it was difficult to realize I wasn't wet from drowning. There was whiskey in the glass in front of me, even though it was 08:00 and even though it had earned me dark looks from both Zin and Gita. The burn was the only thing strong enough to chase away the chilling reminder of the tunnels.

"All I'm saying is maybe we need to rethink the Farians' offer." Caterina shook her dark head. "If the Shen are just going to stroll in here and take the empress hostage—"

"We should do exactly what we've all been saying is a bad idea?" Inana interrupted her. "No, Caterina. That's the opposite of what we should do. We can't afford to react without thinking."

"What Admiral Hassan said," Caspel replied with a nod. "We need to improve security for Her Majesty and for the rest of the councils. It's worrisome that he was able to just walk right up to her."

"How did you not know they were on the planet, Caspel?" Alice's question wasn't quite hostile, but there was enough bite in her words that I glanced up briefly before going back to pushing food around my plate.

"Your Highness, despite rumors to the contrary I am not omniscient. I only know the things my operatives tell me, and since this Shen can apparently walk by royal BodyGuards without being flagged, it doesn't surprise me we didn't see him until he wanted to be seen."

"He dragged Hail underground," Alice hissed. "He could have killed her!"

My vision fogged, the smell of water-wet metal crowding out the whiskey taste in my mouth, and my throat closed up. It only took a heartbeat and I was back in that damned box, the water crawling up my thighs. The argument around me faded away.

"Never did I do fire sacrifice. Chanting millions of mantras," I murmured.

"Majesty?"

I blinked at Caspel, spying Dailun standing behind him by the window. My brother was watching me with sad eyes. "Sorry, what?"

"Ah, if it is all right with you, the four of us are going to put our heads together and come up with a better plan here. We'll have to tighten up security for the hotel, and I want a complete overview of the plans for the tour."

"That's fine." I returned my attention to my still-full plate as the others said their good-byes. An uneasy silence filled the room as soon as the door closed. I picked up my glass and drained it, shoved my chair back, and crossed the room to get more.

"I think you've had enough, *jiejie.*" Dailun intercepted me, blocking my access to the liquor cabinet.

"You're not in a position to lecture me, little brother. Step aside."

Dailun's smile was in that vicinity of patient, and his next words were careful, though I suspected that was only because of Gita. "I'm not going to fight with you, honored sister, it's the last thing you need. So stop trying to pick one."

"He's right, Majesty," Gita said from behind me, and I turned to face her. "And before you say it, I sort of am in a position to lecture you about it."

I stared at her, calculating my odds in a fight against my brother and my *Dve* until Dailun stole the glass out of my hand. I bared my teeth at him and for a moment was tempted to just grab the bottle and take a drink. But the likelihood that Dailun would tackle me to take it away was high, and my nerves were jumbled enough without getting into a fistfight.

"Did you have another flashback just then?" He gestured at the table with the glass still in his hand.

"I—" I shoved both hands into my hair and muttered a curse. "I guess? I don't know."

"You were praying, Majesty," Gita said gently. "And that particular prayer, I believe, is now burned into all our brains."

Dropping onto the couch, I pressed my forehead against my knees and fought down the nausea that threatened to crawl up my throat. I felt the couch shift and the cool touch of Dailun's fingers on my neck just before he whispered in my ear.

"It's all right, honored sister. You're going to be all right. This was expected. It just took you a little longer than anyone guessed."

I sat up. "You were all waiting for me to lose my shit?"

"Majesty." Gita sat in the chair across from us. "Most people struggle to cope with one major trauma. You've been through no fewer than four, including dying, in the last year. It was going to happen."

"And Aiz made sure it happened while I was down there so everyone would be focused on me and not bother to look for them as they escaped. Fuck." I pressed a hand to my mouth and then dropped it into my lap. "He played us. He—did you figure out how he got past everyone in the deli?"

Gita shook her head. "We've been over the footage, every millisecond. He really does just appear out of thin air, but that's not possible."

"The kitchen was empty when we went out the back."

"I cleared it when Emmory gave the order to stand down," she said. "I was around the corner with Indula when he took you into the cellar. We tried to follow, but he moved too fast. I'm sorry."

I reached a hand out and closed it around her wrist. "He knew exactly what he was doing. Don't beat yourself up over it."

"The bigger question is, how do we keep him from doing it again?" Dailun asked.

"That I don't have an answer for." I released Gita and stood. "I can tell you I'm not going anywhere unarmed until this whole mess is over."

"You're not going anywhere until we get a handle on this, Majesty," Emmory said as he came into the room.

"If he'd wanted me dead I would be, Emmy." I saw Zin wince as he followed behind his partner, and I felt a stab of guilt for my words. "They really just wanted to talk."

"Gita," Emmory said and she turned to him. "Indula and Iza are going over the digital recordings from everyone's *smatis* again; go help them. I want to know how he got through our security. Dailun, find somewhere else to be; I need to talk to Hail alone."

It was extremely rare for my *Ekam* to use my first name in front of others and historically he'd only done it when I was in danger. I watched as the others, with the exception of his husband, scattered at his orders.

I felt stupidly fragile, like the slightest tap would shatter me to pieces. I'd survived so much. This couldn't be the thing that finally broke me.

"You didn't eat your breakfast," Zin said, resting his hands on the windowsill. "Stasia is going to have words for you when Emmory finally lets her in here."

"I don't suppose I could talk you into eating it for me and saving me from the lecture?"

A smile curved Zin's mouth, but he shook his head. "You're on your own there, Hail. The only person I'm more afraid of crossing than your maid is Emmory."

"He's lying," Emmory said from behind me. "Zin is not the slightest bit afraid of me. He ignores me on a pretty regular basis."

"This must be bad. You're both calling me by name," I said. "What's going on?"

"Do we really need to say it?" It was Zin who asked the question, though when I turned it was easy to see the echo of it on Emmory's face, and I reached for both of them. I wrapped an arm around Emmory's neck and dragged Zin in close with my free hand, squeezing them tight for a heartbeat.

How I had hated these Trackers who dragged me out of the wreckage of my ship and away from my life to sit on a throne I'd never wanted, but now their solid presence was the only thing keeping me from screaming.

"Aiz went to a lot of trouble so his sister could talk to me in person. Why?" I released my BodyGuards and tossed my hands up in the air. "And why in the fires of Naraka are the Shen and the Farians so damn interested in me?"

Emmory sighed. "I don't know, Majesty, and it makes me nervous."

"Join the club," I shot back. Feeling the need to move, I started pacing the confines of the room. "Let's be realistic. I'm nothing special, whatever the newslines like to say. And Indrana's reputation is mighty, but her current state doesn't put her on any playing field with most of the major governments in the galaxy. We're better off than the Saxons, obviously, and most of the smaller alliances, but if the Solarians wanted to come after us right now they'd crush us. To say nothing of the tough time we'd have keeping the XiXu, the Parisian Alliance, or the Hampton Planetary Consortium off our backs. The Farians could have gone to any one of them for help, but they didn't. Why?"

"I don't know about legendary, but Cressen Stone had a very impressive reputation," Zin said, and I snorted.

"I have told you not to believe every rumor you hear."

"The Farians might," Emmory said. "So might the Shen. And they're not entirely wrong, Majesty. You are a legend, like it or not. But that's not the point here and to be fair, this is way out of either Zin's or my area of expertise. It's really something you should discuss with Caterina or the other matriarchs."

"Don't you start." Spinning around, I stalked back across the room and poked Emmory in the chest. "I trust you. I value your opinion more than anyone out there, except maybe Hao, and I am tired of everyone trying to make me into something I'm not!"

"Majesty, I just—"

"I am the Empress of Indrana. I have given myself body and soul to this, and Shiva damn them for putting me here in the first place. I don't care if they don't like that I ask my BodyGuards or my brother for advice. I've fought with you at my back. I know you. The rest of them, they could betray me at any point and we all know it." I dropped back onto the couch, stunned by my breaking voice and the tears on my face. I wiped them away, cursing under my breath, so frustrated at myself for this ugly tangle of emotions that my interaction with the Shen seemed to have dragged to the surface.

"Hail." Emmory knelt at my side. "You don't mean that. The matriarchs are loyal to Indrana. They're loyal to you."

"I'm not saying they aren't," I snapped. "You know what I mean, Emmory. We've fought together, bled for each other. I—there isn't anyone—" I couldn't find the words I needed, but thankfully Emmory seemed to understand.

"I know," he said.

The door slammed open, and the commotion from outside spilled into the room along with Ikeki. Emmory and Zin both drew their guns, bringing the whole situation to an almost comical freeze-frame.

I was halfway to my feet, grasping at the empty spot on my hip where a gun should have been, and when I spotted Adora in the hallway with Kisah's gun in her face, my sharp laughter cut through the air, startling everyone even more.

"Majesty—" Ikeki broke off when I raised my hand.

"Let her in, Kisah." I watched my BodyGuard lower her Hessian, but not holster it, and the others moved from the door to allow her into my room. Crossing my arms over my chest, I shook my head. "Ambassador Notaras, it's never a good idea to try to burst into my rooms without approval," I said. "But you've picked an especially poor time to do so. Is there a reason I shouldn't have my Body-Guards shoot you and send a nicely worded apology to the Pedalion along with your body?"

Adora seemed surprised, though I wasn't quite sure if it was from the guns or my words. "Your Majesty, I wanted to see if you were all right. We heard about the Shen attack."

"I wasn't attacked." It annoyed me that the words even left my mouth, but it was too late to stop them. Now it sounded like I was defending the Shen, and I bit the inside of my cheek to keep from screaming. "We had a run-in with the Cevallas, but I am fine. They merely wanted to talk."

"To talk? About what? He touched you, Your Majesty. You are unclean. I can make sure he—"

"Ambassador Notaras! If you take another step toward me I won't even bother with an apology to the Pedalion. You are violating my space, and you are making my Guards uneasy. I have been thoroughly checked out by my doctor and my *Ekam*. I am fine. I have no need of your assistance."

Adora's face went blank. "My apologies, Your Majesty. I am concerned for your health. Despite our recent disagreement, Faria does value its relationship with Indrana and we would mourn should anything happen to you."

"I am fine," I repeated. "It was my understanding you were headed back to Faria."

"I was."

"I suggest you be on your way, then." It wasn't *quite* an order, but Adora stiffened all the same before she gave me a sharp nod and left the room.

Emmory and Zin lowered their weapons at the same time and shared a look. "Stay here," Emmory ordered, holstering his weapon. He grabbed Ikeki by the arm. "What were you thinking coming in here? You don't ever open the door if the empress's life is in danger."

"Sir, I—what was I supposed to do?"

"Shoot her."

"The ambassador? But, *Ekam*—" Ikeki's shocked voice vanished into the hallway with the pair.

"Is it just me or was the ambassador not quite herself?" I mused and Zin frowned.

"What do you mean?"

"She was practically frothing at the mouth about the fact that Aiz touched me, and I'm not entirely convinced it was out of a concern for my safety." I rolled my eyes. "She said I was unclean." I shuddered. "That's got all sorts of connotations and most of them bring to mind a host of religious dogma."

"She seemed very out of sorts."

"That's a nice way of putting it." I rubbed a hand against the back of my neck, suddenly exhausted. "Something about Aiz in particular seems to put our ambassador off her diplomatic game, bet you ten credits."

"No thank you on that one," Zin replied. "To be fair, she's not the only one concerned. Are you all right?"

"You know I'm not." I patted Zin on the arm with a wan smile. "But we'll go on regardless. I have had more than enough excitement for this morning. I'm going to go get dressed and finish going over some reports. Tell Stasia I promise I'll eat my lunch."

"Chicken," he murmured, and I chuckled under my breath as I headed for my room. As soon as his back was turned, my smile vanished and I headed immediately for my wardrobe. The shaking in my hands only dissipated once I had my holster buckled and the heavy weight of my SColt 45 pressing comfortingly against my leg.

17

G eneral Carter."

"Your Majesty." Jula Carter braced to attention behind her desk and saluted me.

"At ease, General." I wiggled my fingers, gripping her by the fore-arm when the older woman extended her arm. "It's nice to meet you. Admiral Hassan filled you in?"

"She did, ma'am." Jula smiled. "You didn't have to come over to the base, though. I could have made it easier on you and brought Colonel Morri to the hotel."

"You could have, but this way she doesn't realize I'm here until she's in your office." I winked. "And I hear you have an excellent firing range, which my *Ekam* has agreed to let me use. With your permission, of course."

Jula smiled again, dark eyes darting to Emmory standing by the door. "Of course, Majesty."

I took a seat away from the door, crossing one black-clad leg over the other and resting my hands on my knee. There was a knock at the door.

"Come in," Jula called, leaning against her desk.

"You wanted to see me, General?" Dio noticed Emmory first and then looked around and braced to attention when she saw me. "Your Majesty."

"At ease, Colonel Morri," I said.

Dio shifted, so clearly nervous I almost took pity on her until I reminded myself what was at stake.

"Colonel Morri." General Carter cleared her throat. "The empress has some questions for you. I expect your full cooperation."

"Of course, ma'am."

I brushed an imaginary piece of lint off my knee and then looked up at her with a smile. "Tell me about the Shen."

"Majesty?"

"Tell me about the Shen."

She looked at her commanding officer, a worried frown digging into the space between her red eyebrows. "Majesty, I don't understand—"

"Colonel Morri, you are an officer in the Indranan military. Per our alliance with Faria, that means as long as you hold rank, you are subject to the laws of Indrana and to me as empress. I asked General Carter to bring you here today both to remind you of that fact and to bear witness if you chose to hand over your commission."

"Hand over my commission? Majesty, why would I—"

"I'm asking you a very simple question, Dio. Tell me about the Shen. If you don't want to follow that order, General Carter will accept your resignation."

Panic flashed in Dio's platinum eyes, and they darted around looking for somewhere to land before she inhaled, straightened her shoulders, and fixed her gaze to the spot behind me on the wall. "What would Your Majesty prefer, for me to tell you the story of the Shen or answer any questions you may have?"

"Start with the story. If I have questions, I'll ask."

"Long before I was born, Majesty, the Shen came to Faria. They claimed to worship our gods, said they were our distant cousins returning from a sacred voyage through the stars. It made sense. The gods often sent us away from Faria to see the universe, to spread our message and light.

"A celebration was planned; the gods were called. We were all there to welcome our kin back home." Dio closed her eyes, reddish lashes catching the unshed tears and scattering them through the air when she opened them again. "The Shen betrayed us, Majesty. They were heretics, liars. They were not Farians. When they came face-to-face with our gods, they spat vicious lies. They claimed the gods lied to us. They had been sent into the black as sacrifices and had returned to claim their vengeance. They slaughtered our gods, drank their blood in the streets. Only two survived the attack."

"This was not something I was taught in school," I murmured. I wasn't sure I believed gods really existed and had blown off the Farian stories about their gods as some inexplicable metaphor rather than reality. But if the Shen could truly kill gods—Farian gods at that—they could be a more dangerous enemy than any of us had guessed.

If the Shen could kill gods, why was Aiz convinced he needed help from a human?

"I could be excommunicated by the Pedalion for telling you this, Majesty," Dio replied. "It is one of our most sacred stories, not something for those who do not believe."

"I'll deal with the Pedalion," I said. "What happened to the Shen who killed your gods?"

"They escaped. We were not an aggressive people, Majesty; we still aren't. Our faith prohibits using our gifts to kill or injure, gifts we received from the gods themselves. We were unprepared for such an unprovoked assault, but we have been at war ever since."

"And did you find out who the Shen really were?" I asked.

Dio looked down at the floor. "The gods said they were parasites, wastrels who scavenged the universe stealing anything they could get their hands on. They stole our gods' power, but it's corrupted, twisted. It's why they kill, Majesty. They have no souls, no sense of right or wrong, only the desire to take what they want—and that they take by force."

A shudder forced through me at her words, carrying with it the memory of Aiz's carefully planned kidnapping. Except he hadn't been interested in anything but talking to me, trying to get me to see their side. He'd had plenty of chances to kill me, and even I could see the logic behind his cruelty—I'd want me off-balance, too, when it came down to it. There was a much better chance of him getting out alive because of that.

Dio's words rang with religious fervor, and that made me even more uneasy than the memory of those tunnels.

"How much of a danger to Faria do you think the Shen are?"

I watched her hesitate. "We outnumber them ten to one, Majesty. They are rabble, disjointed and just as prone to fighting among themselves as coming after us for these past millennia. However, I have not been home for some time, and if the Pedalion thought it important enough to send *Ite*—Ambassador Notaras to speak with you and ask for your help, it must have been for a very good reason."

Dio made it sound very reasonable, and part of me believed she was convinced of the truth of her words. If I hadn't spoken to Aiz and Mia, I'd probably agree with her assessment of the Shen based on what we knew so far. But they'd offered to protect Indrana from the Farians, and that didn't sound like something a disorganized pack of guerilla fighters would be capable of doing.

"I'm sure," I replied. "Unfortunately for both the Pedalion and the ambassador, I am extremely busy and the council doesn't think it's wise to send me all the way to Faria. Thank you for your help, Dio. I appreciate it."

"Yes, Majesty." Dio braced to attention and saluted.

I exchanged a nod with General Carter, and the pair headed for the door.

"Colonel Morri," I called as they reached the door and crossed the room to her, Emmory on my heels.

"Yes, ma'am?"

"The next time a Farian ambassador, or any other visitor to my empire for that matter, comes to you and asks you to circumvent my chamberlain and bring them to my rooms…" I leaned in until our noses were almost touching. "I expect you to either report to the general and resign, or send Alba a message requesting a moment of my time. Is that understood?"

"Yes, ma'am."

"Good. Don't fucking do it again."

Dio swallowed. "Yes, Your Majesty."

Jula closed the door behind her and blew out a breath. "With respect, ma'am, I'd thought the rumors about you were mostly that. I was wrong."

"It really depends on the rumor." I grinned, but sobered quickly. "That was a nice piece of propaganda."

Jula nodded, her own expression equally grim. "I haven't known the colonel for very long, but her jacket is filled with commendations, and every officer she's served with says she's honest to a fault."

"It's easy to be honest when you don't know you're repeating lies, Majesty," Emmory murmured.

"I have a feeling both of you know something I don't," Jula replied.

"True," I said with a tiny smile. We hadn't released any information about the conversation with the Cevallas beyond my inner circle, in part because we had no digital records to back up my memory of it but also because my gut told me it was better the Farians didn't know what we'd discussed. I mulled over my next words. "I've had more interactions with Farians in the last week than I had in the previous thirty years. Before and after I left home the interactions were brief, and after I returned?" I gave a little laugh. "I suspect everyone knows by now that Fasé doesn't exactly fall into typical anything category. Either way, the more we poke at their reasons for being our allies and their version of the fight with the Shen, the more holes I find."

"Fasé would be one of the bigger rumors," Jula admitted. She glanced Emmory's way again. "If I'm out of bounds here, tell me please, but did she really bring you back from the dead?"

"She did," I said, before Emmory could answer. "Admiral Hassan also. It's something we'd prefer to keep as a rumor, though."

"Of course, Majesty." Jula nodded. "My aide is telling me that the range is open for your use. I can escort you over there?"

"Emmory knows where it is. I've taken up enough of your time, General. Thank you for your help today."

"Of course, Majesty, anytime."

I said my good-byes to General Carter's aide and then headed out of the building and across the deserted central lawn with two teams of BodyGuards splayed out around us. They were two of the newest teams, with faces and names I was still getting used to.

"I'm surprised you let me out of the house," I said to Emmory, squinting at him in the bright afternoon sun. "And with a bunch of newbies, no less."

"It's good practice for them. Zin and the others are available as backup should we need it." Emmory's shoulders were relaxed, but he still scanned the area and his new Guards with a rhythmic sweep of his eyes.

He wasn't wrong. The Academy's fall session didn't start for another few months, so only a handful of staff and other assorted visitors were on campus. The ones we'd crossed paths with steered clear with quick salutes once they realized who I was.

"Are you worried Aiz will come after me again?"

That made Emmory's shoulders tense, and I winced internally, but he relaxed again and shook his head.

"Not here. He planned it perfectly and he's long gone. He knows you're leaving Pashati for the tour; it's not a secret. But we're going to be out in the black and anything can happen. Just like the Farians, they weren't happy with your refusal to help them, and if I can't figure out how he slipped by us..." Emmory muttered a curse.

"I've been over every scrap of those digitals. We all have. Nobody can figure it out."

"I haven't looked at them," I said, amused when he glanced at me in surprise. "Already thinking of me as a useless noble, *Ekam?*"

"It will never happen, Majesty. It just didn't occur to me to ask you to do my job for me."

I punched Emmory in the arm, startling the young Guard closest to us. "Get used to it, Lathan," I told him with a wink. "I'll punch you, too, if you get smart with me like Emmory here."

"Yes, ma'am."

"Seriously though, Emmory. Send me the files. I'll take a look at them and see if I can spot anything."

He nodded. "I will. Speaking of digitals, I spoke with Fenna again about her recording."

"Did you now?" I asked, pausing as we reached the door of the range and Emmory sent four Guards in to sweep the place. "I thought you weren't supposed to involve yourself in politics?" It was supposed to be a tease, but I winced at how bitter I sounded.

"It has to do with your safety, Majesty."

"I'm sorry. That was uncalled-for. What did she have to say?"

"She did some digging into the two Farians. Put together more detailed profiles on them. They're both sons of what appear to be higher-ranking members of the Farian government."

"Interesting."

"Very much so," Emmory agreed. "It's hard to get good intel beyond what she can dig up there, obviously, but on the surface it looks as though Fasé's faction is actively recruiting people like Lucca and Miles."

"Doesn't that sound like they're looking to destabilize the Farians from within?" I hated that I hesitated in asking the question, that I was already wondering if I was crossing some unseen line, but Emmory merely shrugged.

"It's a possibility. Or they just want more people who can move about freely in human space."

"It seemed like they're moving extremely freely now," I replied.

"I know, Majesty. That's what makes me nervous." Emmory put a hand on my back and escorted me into the building.

I let the conversation die, smiling as the range master checked us in. The man babbled a bit nervously as he ran through his safety protocols and checked our weapons with us. I took my SColt back from him and followed Emmory into the range, sighing a bit when the door closed behind the range master and left us in silence.

Lathan stood by the door; the other BodyGuards were at the outer doors and running patrol around the building.

"So the Shen are recruiting, and they're looking to do it from a pool of highly ranked Farian children."

"As you said, if you want to destabilize a government, Majesty..." Emmory trailed off.

"Good point. You know, I've never actually tried to take down a whole government. Did a few gangs that way, though." I checked over my gun a second time. "Emmory, do you remember Fasé telling us the Pedalion thought about wiping humanity out when they first saw us?"

"I do. The only reason they didn't was because of whatever the future-seers told them." He shook his head and focused downrange. "They changed their minds once, they could change them again."

"I was afraid you were going to say that. I need to talk to Fasé," I admitted with a sigh. "Can we get back out to the estate?"

"It'd be easier to bring her to the hotel, Majesty. Especially now that the Farians are gone. I'd feel better if she were somewhere closer," Emmory replied.

"True. They're going to find out she's here sooner or later. Once the asylum request is processed, those go onto the public record.

They'll demand we hand her over." I sighed. "I should probably talk to Caterina to make sure we can legally say no."

"Legal or not it might not make a difference if they come and take her."

"I really hope they don't, but I also won't stand by and let them hurt her," I said. "Best three out of five?"

"Fine, but just for fun. I'm still getting snide remarks from Zin about the money I had to pay you last time."

"It's not my fault you shoot like a cross-eyed old man." I slid my ear protection on and picked up my SColt, settling into an easy stance and bringing the gun up to fire.

"Hao's late." I pushed away from the window and made a face at the time in the corner of my *smati*.

"Didn't he tell you?" Johar asked.

"Tell me what?"

"He had something to take care of, said he'd meet us at Shivan's." Johar held her hands up at the look I shot her. "Don't get mad at me, I thought he would have told you, not expect me to be the messenger."

I hissed in annoyance. Hao had been acting strangely since my kidnapping. I'd only seen him once, twice if one counted the brief wave from across the hotel the other day, and my coms had been answered with terse, one-word replies. "*Dhatt*, we've been sitting around for twenty minutes for no reason?"

"Apparently." Johar clapped me on the shoulder. "Let's go eat, I'm starving."

The narrow three-story restaurant in the heart of the capital's warehouse district had survived Wilson's coup with little damage. Shivan's was an icon, made even more so by the current proprietor's friendship with one gunrunner empress.

"Where's your fan club?" Johar murmured when we slipped from the aircar into the quiet night.

"Alice and Taz are at a fund-raising gala," I replied, following Emmory up the stairs to the entrance of the restaurant. "The press enjoys following them around a lot more these days."

I did not miss the constant attention I'd suffered for the first few months after stopping Wilson. And after a while the whole "gun-runner empress" angle started to die down. The new royal couple made for better press, especially with the occasional controversial pieces about Taz's *Upjas* past and the baby on the way. They were a much better public face of the empire anyway; I still had a habit of saying things to the reporters that set off all sorts of alarms in the public relations office.

"Good evening, Your Majesty." The young man at the wide reception desk smiled at me as we came through the doors. Behind him the first-floor dining room bustled in quiet symphony as waiters in gray and black *salwar kameez* served the few diners who were here this evening. "Avan wanted me to extend his condolences. He was sorry to have missed you."

"It is fine, Burno. As I told Avan. I knew he was looking forward to the gala." I winked. "In fact, I believe I threatened him if he dared miss it on my account."

Burno smiled back at me. "He may have mentioned that, Majesty. Your room upstairs is ready, have a wonderful dinner."

"I always do. Send Hao up when he gets here?"

"Of course, Majesty."

"I love this place," Johar murmured as we made our way past a display of bright orange and yellow orchids toward the towering glass elevator. "I have eaten at my share of amazing restaurants in the galaxy, but this is one of the top."

The contentment in the gunrunner's voice made me chuckle, but I knew exactly what Johar meant. Shivan's was a haven, specifically designed as such by Avan's grandfather, and I'd taken full advantage of Avan's kindness, hiding in the kitchens of this great restaurant as a teen.

The members of Team Two stationed themselves outside the elevator; Jagana was the third BodyGuard along with Kisah and Ikeki. She was quiet but thankfully took her cues from the veterans as to how to respond to me, and she was warming up faster than the others.

I sent Hao a quick note with my *smati* telling him we weren't holding dinner and to hurry his ass up.

His snappish reply, *"I'm on my way,"* came back almost immediately.

Zin and the other members of Team One were already in the room, Indula and Iza smiling at me as they left. Johar made a beeline for the waiter and had drinks ordered before I'd even finished saying hello to Zin.

We were settled at the table enjoying our drinks when Hao walked in. Emmory caught him by the arm.

"Thank you," he said. "For being there for her the other day."

Hao answered him with a sharp nod. "She is my sister, *Ekam*, I would move the heavens for her."

"Where have you been?" I raised an eyebrow at the bottle of vodka and glass already in Hao's hands.

"I had something to do." Hao tossed back what little was left in his glass. "Johar was supposed to tell you."

"Don't get snarly with me," Johar countered. "I'd figured you told her you were going to be late. I'm not your damn messenger."

Hao threw a hand in the air and refilled his drink. Vodka splashed into the glass, but I kept my mouth shut at the way his hand shook and the tense set of his shoulders under the dark blue of his long-sleeved shirt. Whatever it was, he wasn't going to talk about it now, not in front of an audience.

Johar seemed unconcerned by Hao's behavior, and I let her take the lead on the conversation by telling us all about her trip to the islands. She hadn't gone so far as to start dressing like an Indranan, instead still in her customary black pants and sleeveless top, but from the sounds of it Johar's little vacation was turning into something more long-term.

"You've settled in well," I said with a wink, lifting a bite of the lemon dessert to my mouth. "Is Rai going to be angry with me for stealing you?"

Johar's partner, Bakara Rai, was the head of a criminal syndicate that rivaled Po-Sin's. Their on-again, off-again relationship had been going for as long as I'd known them. Rai could be a touch possessive, but Johar frequently did her own thing.

Shrugging, Johar rolled her glass between her long fingers. "I think he's angrier with me at the moment, to be honest. I told him yesterday I was staying in Indrana."

Hao fumbled, the clatter of his silverware on the plate breaking through my own surprise. "You told him you were staying here? Are you sure—"

"I know my own heart, Cheng Hao." Johar cut him off, her face serious.

"Staying as in, moving permanently?" I asked, breaking up the staring contest that had unexpectedly started between them. "I knew you were looking at property, but I thought—"

"Staying as in retiring from my life of crime and settling down." Her laughter bounced around the room like bubbles, and the joy in her words was even more surprising to me. "However, yes, I like it here. I put in my citizenship request yesterday; I'm surprised someone didn't tell you. I have enough money to survive for quite a while, and Indrana has a lot of options for me to make more." Johar winked. "In more legitimate ways than I have traditionally participated in. Plus, I am too old to continue to go running around in space getting shot at. That used to be fun. Now it's more fun to have dinner with people I know for a fact aren't going to try to kill me."

"You're going to make me cry." I threw my arms around her neck and hugged her.

"Aren't I kind for waiting to tell you until we're in private?" Johar squeezed me tight and then released me.

"You are." My smile was a bit watery, but I managed to keep my tears under control. "This explains a lot, actually. I'd wondered why Emmory was okay with you hanging out with the BodyGuards so much and why nothing had been said about you coming with us on this trip."

"It'll be a fine chance to see the whole of your empire." Johar shrugged again. "Or at least a decent chunk of it."

"I'm glad. I really am." I raised my glass in her direction and drank, the wordless toast more fitting than anything I could think up on the fly.

"Besides, it sounds like interesting times ahead."

"Gods help us," I murmured. "I haven't recovered from the last round."

Johar tossed her drink back with enthusiasm, but Hao didn't drink. My mentor stared morosely into his half-empty glass, his eyes shadowed with a sorrow I didn't understand.

18

The small temple on the palace grounds that contained the massive statue of Ganesh had been undamaged by the explosion of the main building. It was a small mercy that the statue I loved as a child, and the one I swore an oath on to stay and help Indrana as an adult, had survived Wilson's trap. I'd been here repeatedly over the last six months, and my BodyGuards were well used to my one-sided conversations with the elephant-headed god.

It was early; shadows still gathered in the corners and the cool night air lingered, heavy with moisture, within the structure.

I wrapped my blue-gray sari closer around myself and leaned forward to press my forehead against Ganesh's foot. *"Om Gam Ganapataye Namaha.*

"Om Gam Salutations to the Lord of Hosts," I whispered, sitting back on my heels and folding my hands at my heart. *"Gajaananam Bhoota Ganaadhi Sevitam. Kapitta Jamboophaala Saara Bhakshitam. Umaasutam Shoka Vinaasha Kaaranam. Namaami Vighneswara Paada Pankajam.*

"Grant us safe passage, Lord Ganesh, as we set out on this journey around my empire. Grant us peace and open the minds of those who are closed to us both at home and out in the black. Help me settle our empire firmly into peace so that the ones who come after me will not have to suffer heartache and loss."

Ganesh stared down at me with that unchanging mix of amusement and pity on his face that had always been there.

"I am here," I said. "And I will remain here until the empire no longer needs me. That is the duty we agreed upon; I know now what I was meant for and I will do my best."

The sigh slipped out of me and I bent forward again, the smell of durva grass filling my nose as I rested my head against the edge of the dais. "Open my brother's heart, Father. Open his damned stubborn mouth. I want to help him, but I don't know what's wrong."

Hao had taken off shortly after dinner last night, a move that didn't entirely surprise me but frustrated me nonetheless because it meant I hadn't been able to corner him about just what in the fires of Naraka was wrong.

"Majesty." Emmory's voice was low, but I could hear the urgency running underneath it.

"What is it?"

He tilted his head to the side and I caught a glimpse of Caspel standing just beyond the columns. Emmory held his hand out and I took it, touching Ganesh's foot one last time with my free hand before I rose and walked away.

"Caspel."

"Your Majesty, I'm sorry for bothering you." Caspel's bow was perfunctory, the kind he gave me when he was distracted.

"What's happened?"

"The Shen hit another Farian outpost. About an hour ago just outside of the Persuor system."

"Same as the others? How many Farians?"

"Yes, ma'am. Several thousand. There was also a group of Solarians visiting, and we think possibly an Indranan citizen."

I muttered a curse in Cheng that made my *Ekam*'s eyebrow shoot upward. "When can we get confirmation, Caspel?"

"I'm working on it now. We think it was this young woman." He put her photo up on the nearest column, the image wavy with the textured marble. "Gatani Tsai, a graduate student at the Persuor Fudan University."

"Why would she have been at the outpost?"

"That I don't know, Majesty." Caspel shook his head, his mouth pulled into a frown. "The Solarians are understandably furious. There's been no response from the Shen, and the Farian fleet presence has already tripled in the Solarian arm of the galaxy the last six months. I don't like the idea of it increasing even more, but it's almost guaranteed with this latest attack. How long before the attacks start closer to home?"

I rubbed at the bridge of my nose and sighed. "Get me a confirmation of Gatani's death before we go public with any kind of statement. I'll find Alba—"

"I've already messaged her, Majesty," Emmory said. "She's at the hotel waiting for us."

"Let's head back, then. We'll need to draft a statement in response. Caspel, do we know where Gatani's parents are?"

"They're on the third planet in the Persuor system, Majesty. I have someone headed to their house now."

"I'll want to speak with them as soon as possible."

"Yes, ma'am." Caspel bowed and moved away at my nod.

"I hope it's not true," I whispered to Emmory.

"I know, Majesty," he replied, and put his hand on my back as we headed for the aircar.

That afternoon we sat in my main room at the hotel. Dailun and Johar were there. It didn't surprise me that Hao was not. He'd nearly killed Fasé after Cas's death, and it was probably better they weren't in the same room.

Emmory had called Iza just after Caspel's news, and she brought the two Farians back to the hotel. I hadn't told my maid that Fasé was on planet, but it was worth it to watch Stasia's greeting die in her mouth when I stepped aside to reveal Fasé, and the way my maid had launched herself through the doorway into the Farian's arms gave my heart a happy little ache.

"You are, if it is at all possible, more sentimental than my honored cousin, *jiejie*," Dailun had whispered. I'd touched my temple to his and hit the panel, closing the door and giving them a few precious moments alone.

Now Stasia was back to her duties while Fasé and Sybil sat together on a pair of chairs near the fireplace as we waited for the others. Caterina came through the door, followed by Zaya Prajapati, the head of the Ancillary Council. She had a round, dark face and wide eyes much like her mother's, and I knew from experience she was extremely intelligent and could argue a point to death. Which was decidedly not like her quieter mother.

Caterina raised a black eyebrow as she took in the assembled group, but didn't say a word and took a seat next to Alice with a murmured greeting.

"I appreciate you all coming at such short notice," I said. "Recording of the following conversation is not allowed, so if you will all switch off your *smatis* I would appreciate it." I waited a beat and then continued. "Two things. First, the Shen hit an outpost in the Persuor system. An Indranan student from Persuor Fudan University, Gatani Tsai, was killed. We received confirmation from the Solarians approximately two hours after the attack. I have already spoken to her parents."

Alice folded her hands together and touched her fingertips to her heart, lips, and forehead. The gesture was echoed by the other Indranans in the room.

"The second is, in about an hour, the request for political asylum made by Fasé and Sybil here will become public record. I expect a furious com link from the Farians within thirty-two hours after that." I looked at Caterina and Zaya. "I also expect the councils to approve the request before I get that com."

Caterina frowned. "Majesty, we just finished telling the Farians we didn't want to involve ourselves in their business. Now you—"

I held a hand up, cutting her off. "I'm not going to deny that I have some personal reasons for that request, but there are other things at work here. It's in Indrana's best interests to allow Fasé her freedom, and our long-established precedent of welcoming political refugees is well-known."

"Will it cause problems with the Farians?" Alice asked.

"I don't know." I shook my head. "They have bigger issues facing them, as we all know. Fasé has done this empire a great service. She's not a criminal, according to Ambassador Notaras, and I see no reason why the Farians would push the issue. But if they do I will handle it."

"Your Majesty," Zaya said. "You could have easily messaged us about this matter. What is the real reason we are here?"

"We don't know enough about the Farians, and what we do know is what they've told us. Almost none of that involves their dispute with the Shen," I replied. "Fasé is going to fill us in about the history between the Farians and the Shen and about just why the Farians have been so friendly to Indrana all these years."

Fasé stood, her hands folded at her waist, and recounted the same story I'd heard from Dio until she got to the part where the Shen had come to Faria.

"Fasé? Did you just call them 'my ancestors'?"

"Yes, Majesty, why?"

"Colonel Morri said that the Shen came to your world and murdered your gods. That they lied about being long-lost kin? She didn't say they were actually Farians."

Fasé's smile was sad. "She's not entirely wrong, Majesty, and she wasn't lying to you. She just doesn't understand the whole story because she's been lied to all her life. We all were. She believes that the story she told you is true."

"You believed it once," I said.

"I did. Then I met you and snatched him from the edge of the underworld." She gestured at Emmory standing by the door. "And everything changed."

Fasé paused, searching for words, and said something to Sybil in Farian. Sybil sat beside her, her hands in her lap and her pale gaze locked on the floor. She replied to Fasé's question with a nod, and Fasé looked back at me.

"It was terrifying to see and not understand. Worse still to come home to Faria, where everyone looked on me as an abomination. I realize now that my return home was necessary. I wouldn't have understood what had happened and what is happening without Sybil."

"Fasé's choice to save your *Ekam* resulted in a shift in the energy inside her." Sybil picked up the narrative with such ease that I wondered how many times they'd practiced this conversation. "This is the gift from our gods for our devotion, but it is a gift with strings attached. We are not to spend the energy uselessly. We are not to use it on ourselves or other Farians, not without express permission. When we use it on humans we are only supposed to heal with it, never kill, and never interfere in the natural order of things."

"You mean bring people back to life," I said.

"Yes, or extend their life."

"Sybil, we've been told the Farians come to humanity as a mission. That you are called to share your energy with us or it will consume you?" Caterina asked.

"Yes, this is true. It was commanded by the gods."

"What happened before humanity existed?" I asked, picking up on the direction the matriarch was headed. "Wouldn't you all have burned up from the energy before us?"

"Oh no, Majesty." Sybil smiled. "We gave it back to the gods; we still do that for the gods who are left."

"I didn't mean to start a rebellion," Fasé said, suddenly looking sad. She mustered up a smile and straightened her shoulders, a gesture I was intimately familiar with when I wanted to shore up my failing confidence. "I just wanted to share what I had seen. Bringing Emmory back was like ripping a screen away from the universe. I— it still gets tangled at times, but I can feel it here that the only hope for all of us is to put aside this ancient conflict and face the storm together." She pressed a hand to her heart.

"Pulling us back to the original discussion for the moment." I cleared my throat, my own heart beating a little quicker at Fasé's words. Intentional or not, it was easy to see why people were following her if she'd been speaking with that sort of conviction back on Faria. She reminded me of Cire in that moment, as gentle as my sister and yet still a leader. "The Shen are Farians."

"They were, Majesty, but not anymore. When those first Shen returned to us, they weren't Farians any longer."

"Fasé, you're back to not making sense."

Fasé laughed. "I can always count on you, Majesty. Promise me you will never stop calling me out. If things continue on their present path, I will be surrounded by people who will think everything I say and do is priceless and precious. I don't trust myself not to let that go to my head. But you, you will never lie to me."

"I won't," I promised, surprised to realize I meant it. "The story she told me is true?"

"Yes, it's just missing details."

"Such as?"

"The Shen weren't some strange travelers who lied about being our distant cousins. They didn't randomly attack our gods to steal their power. They had that power. They were our kin. They were sacrificed into space, left to die by the gods themselves.

"They returned for vengeance for those who did not survive. Those who returned killed the gods to claim their revenge and to take their blood. Then they left again. They evolved, changed from what you are familiar with as Farians. They bore children with

185

humans, taught them how to use the gifts, strengthened themselves with your resilience and—" Fasé grinned at me. "Your somewhat stubborn nature. They rejected the dogma and strictures of Farian law and faith. They believe in the chaos of the universe."

"The Shen are part human?" Caterina asked.

"Some of them yes, and part Farian. The others are technically Farian, but they have chosen to be something different. They are Shen."

"But how?"

"The normal way, I would assume. Though I suppose with the kinds of technology lately—"

"Not how do they make babies, Fasé, I'm relatively aware of how that process works," I said, and waved a hand in Alice's direction.

Emmory choked, and I threw a wink at Zin as he slapped his husband on the back. Alice covered her mouth, but her giggle slipped between her fingers and Caterina sighed heavily.

"Oh, good," Fasé sighed. "Because honestly, that's not really my area of expertise."

It was Gita's turn to choke, my *Dve* making a noise that sounded like she was fighting back laughter, and I shot her a look first before glancing past Fasé at Caspel.

He grinned at me, but it faded as he turned to Fasé. "I didn't think Farians and humans could have children."

Fasé snorted. "That's what the Pedalion has always said, but it's not a biological thing, it's just anathema. All Farians who go off-world are temporarily sterilized to prevent such a thing from happening. They knew it would be too hard to prevent us from having relationships with humans, so they just made reproduction impossible."

"Not 'impossible' if the Shen found a way around it," Emmory said.

"True," Fasé admitted, shaking a finger at him over her shoulder. "I suspect the Shen's return home had something to do with it, but

Aiz has been less than forthcoming about it. They came back to Faria for revenge and to undo what had been done to them."

"Fasé, what's going on with the Farians?" Zin asked. "You mentioned a civil war back at the estate, and I'm reasonably sure you didn't mean the fight between the Farians and the Shen."

"Yes and no. The fight between the Farians and the Shen is so old. But at home, it is worse than just a war; the division is religious in nature. There are some who will choose to follow the Shen. Some will follow the Pedalion. And others will follow me because of what I represent."

"Which is what?" I asked.

"A healing," she replied. "An end to this conflict. An end to the hate."

"People are always going to hate."

Fasé smile was almost apologetic. "We are not people. We are Farian. Our faith is so interwoven into our society that there is virtually no separating it, but the reappearance of the Shen now, when the future that the Council of Eyes has spoken of seems to be coming to pass, will rip it out by the root." She sighed. "I am not blameless in the chaos to come. There are those who will follow me because of what I see. Ours is a third faction that is not welcomed by either the Farians or the Shen, though at present the Shen seem much more receptive to the idea. There are still some on both sides who will try to erase me."

"As futile as that endeavor may be," Sybil said. "The box once opened can be closed again, but the world will never be the same."

"Is this because of what happened on Red Cliff, Fasé?" Alba asked.

"Yes," Fasé said, turning her golden gaze to Emmory. "I started something when I saved you, and whether for good or ill, there's no stopping it now. We would have lost both of you that day."

"Can we trust Aiz?" I asked, trying to ignore the pressure that the thought of losing both Emmory and Zin put on my chest.

Fasé's laughter floated into the solemn silence that had filled the room. "Not in the slightest, Majesty. But he has his uses and does occasionally tell the truth. The trick is figuring out which is which."

"I'll keep that in mind."

"You'll need to."

I stared at Fasé for several heartbeats, but she didn't elaborate on her ominous statement and I finally surrendered with a sigh.

"Fasé, what is this future you are talking about?" Caterina asked.

"Yes, sorry." Fasé held up a hand and made a curious gesture, thumb and middle finger touching as she brought her index finger to her left eye, then her right, to her mouth and then to the center of her forehead. "Better to have Sybil tell you."

Sybil made the same gesture with her left hand and said in halting Indranan. "I am Sybil Delis, third future-seer of the Council of Eyes. I was the one who saw this future."

19

"oly Shiva, what?" Alice's exclamation rang through the stunned silence. I sighed and rolled my eyes at the ceiling, counting to ten before I looked down at Fasé.

"More than your jailer, Fasé. Bringing one of your sacred future-seers to my empire and applying for asylum with her is a piece of need-to-know information."

She smiled at me, unrepentant. "Now you know."

Everyone started talking at once as I pressed the heel of my right hand between my eyes, and I snorted in amused laughter as I heard Caterina say, "it gives me a little comfort that you are as shocked as the rest of us, Majesty."

"Quiet." I didn't raise my voice as I dropped my hand into my lap. Silence fell once more. "Sybil, forgive me for the rude question. Are you here of your own free will?"

"I am, Your Majesty."

I nodded, privately pleased that I could manage to keep such a stoic expression while my brain grappled with the idea that the two Farians in front of me were thousands of years old, if not older.

"Fasé, how old are you?" I asked before I could stop myself.

"Six, maybe seven thousand years, Your Majesty." She waved a hand. "Like Sybil said, we tend to lose track."

"You don't look a day over twenty-two."

Her laughter danced out into the air, and Sybil said something in Farian that made Fasé laugh harder. I cleared my throat and the pair sobered.

"I am sorry, Your Majesty," Sybil said. "Fasé's current body is only twenty-two, so it's not too far of a stretch."

"You're immortal?" This question came from Zin and carried with it an awe I'd yet to hear from him.

"I suppose that's the easiest way for humans to understand it. Our physical bodies age—though significantly slower than yours even with your medical advancements—but our souls remain. We are born and we die. When we are born again, we remember the time before. We keep our names from one body to the next because it pleases the gods for us to do so," Sybil replied. "That's the official line anyway; honestly I think it's just because it would get really confusing if we kept changing names."

"How much trouble are we going to be in for granting you political asylum?"

Sybil shook her head. "None, Your Majesty. Adora will bluster and threaten you, but she will do nothing. The Pedalion will do nothing."

"How can you know that?" Caterina asked. "You're putting us in a very dangerous position here." She held up her hand before anyone could protest. "I'm not saying we will turn you away, but we need to consider the consequences here before we make a decision that could throw us into a war with one of our oldest allies."

"They will not go to war with you right now," Sybil replied. "The Pedalion cannot risk driving Indrana into supporting the Shen. In all honesty, the war with the Shen is a blessing for us. I will not downplay the threat Fasé's message represents to the Pedalion and their grip on power. We are risking a lot making this move now and asking you to do the same. But move we must because the time is fast approaching when there will be no choices left.

"The Pedalion will be very unhappy about you sheltering us, Your Majesty, and no war will prevent Adora from issuing threats in the hope that you will capitulate. I would advise you to watch your temper with her. If you untie her hands by engaging in hostilities against Faria, they will feel justified in responding to them."

"Duly noted." I waved a hand. "We've gotten rather far from the topic, though. Sybil, the future you saw?"

"Yes, my apologies." Sybil spoke to Fasé for several minutes in Farian, then inhaled, and for a moment the world seemed to freeze around her.

"I saw a Star in the cold, empty black of space. A blue-green jewel of a planet. Home to warriors capable of shattering worlds. There would be no hiding for virtuous monsters or unjust gods from the accelerated—" She frowned, then spoke to Fasé while still looking at me.

"What do you humans call the birth again?" Fasé asked.

"Childbirth?"

"No, of the universe," she replied.

"The Big Bang?"

"Yes." Fasé nodded. "But not that." She was frowning and moving her hands outward from each other while Sybil waited patiently. "This. *Spread* is an incorrect word."

"Expansion," Johar said, and everyone turned to look at where she was leaning against the mantel.

"That!" Fasé nodded.

"There would be no hiding for virtuous monsters or unjust gods from the accelerated expansion," Sybil continued. "I saw a light that is not light spreading. We all fight—we will all die. We surrender—we will die. There is no true shelter for sides that will collapse without each other to lean on."

"I have a feeling that loses something in the translation," I muttered into the silence that followed, and an uneasy laughter met my remark.

"How can you know the planet you saw is Pashati?" Caterina asked the question, and I shared a look with Alice over the suspicion in the matriarch's voice.

"It was seen," Sybil replied. "I have seen many futures, Matriarch Saito, but none so clear as this one. None with the enduring power to shape the whole galaxy as this one does."

"How do you know that for sure?" Caterina pressed, waving a hand. "There are billions of stars, plenty of governments that use stars in their iconography. That's a leap of faith to claim this applies to us."

I was grateful for her skepticism. Caterina was grounded. Her first and only thought was for the well-being of Indrana. According to Alice, being out in the black had given Caterina a clarity she was lacking before, and while she could worry a subject to death, I wasn't the least bit sorry about her focus where this was concerned.

"Caterina, we Farians live and die by the futures our seers bring to us," Fasé said. "It is what shapes policy. What has shaped our interactions with all humanity since the first time we made contact." She smiled. "It is all right if you don't believe it, but what you must believe is that both the Farians and the Shen believe in this future. They will do everything they can in service to it."

Sybil nodded. "These are old words, Matriarch. I saw the future that would come to pass well before the Shen broke from us. Before Indrana even existed. Before humanity existed. We waited for you. We made sure we were the first to greet you. We have solidified our place in your empire—as helpers, as warriors, as healers, and as watchers."

"You invaded us without firing a shot," Caspel said, horrified, and my heart thudded in my chest.

"I suppose you are not wrong," Fasé replied after considering his words for a moment. "We did weave ourselves into the fabric of all humanity and especially Indranan society. Though we didn't seek—still don't, I'd imagine—to conquer you. Would you still be Indrana if you were under our rule?"

"Fair point," I said. "What about the Saxons? Or Wilson? If

Indrana is so damned important to you, why didn't Faria step in when my family was being slaughtered?"

Silence dropped like a rock in high gravity and I pressed my lips together, as surprised as anyone over my sudden anger. Fasé and Sybil both stared at their laps, but finally the older Farian lifted her head to look at me.

"It had to be you, Majesty," she said. "I'm sorry. We didn't intervene because I saw all of this—the wars, the dead. And you—on the throne of Indrana."

"I—I need a minute." I got to my feet and walked blindly to the balcony, closing off the voices echoing through the room as I pushed the door shut behind me.

Anger screamed through me, ugly and sharp enough to cut through a bulkhead. They'd seen all of this and done nothing to stop it. Everyone I loved could still be alive.

You'd never have met my brother, or Zin and the others, Portis whispered.

"You're asking me to choose between you. That's cruel."

It's just life, Hail. I could so easily picture him winking at me. *Everything we do is a choice between one thing and another.*

"Hail?" Alice's voice accompanied the sound of the door opening and closing again. My heir came to stand at the balcony next to me.

"They let my family die. They're supposed to be our allies, but they just stood by and watched as this empire was nearly destroyed. For what? To put my inexperienced ass on this throne? They could have stopped all this."

"They're not gods, Hail." Alice put a hand over mine where it gripped the railing. "Don't give them that kind of power. Whatever they see, or know. I don't believe they could have stopped what happened. Wilson was responsible. He killed your family. You've put him down and let that anger go. Don't resurrect it now."

"It's not that easy."

"I know." Alice pulled me around to face her, reaching up to cup my face in her hands. It was so forward of her, even in private, that her next words washed away my anger like a wave. "I know it makes you angry to hear that they saw this coming and didn't do anything to stop it, but hear me out. I'm grateful you're here. I grieve every day for those who were lost to Wilson's madness, but I am equally and eternally thankful for you and Taz and this baby and the fact that Indrana never would have made the kinds of changes she's headed for if you hadn't shown up and knocked us all on our ears."

I pulled her into a hug. "I was doing really well not crying until that."

"You've got about fifteen more seconds before one of our Body-Guards knocks on that door, so get it out of your system."

I laughed and released her, dragging in a breath and exhaling. "Thank you."

"Of course," Alice winked at me when someone knocked on the glass. "Told you."

I opened the door, answering Emmory's searching look with a quick nod.

"Majesty, I am sorry." Fasé held her hands out to me as we came back into the room. "That could have been handled better."

"Yes, it could have." I squeezed her hands and then sat back down.

"So, I have a question," Johar said, and all eyes in the room turned to her a second time. "As vague as that future is, it doesn't sound very cheery. Why wouldn't the Pedalion be doing everything in their power to keep it from happening?"

"Because they can't. It would end everything." It was Sybil, not Fasé, who answered the question. "Billions of years of expansion snapped back to the starting point in a blink of an eye. This was the best future I could see. It's not always a choice between good and bad outcomes." She smiled softly, and her next words echoed Dailun's from earlier. "Sometimes we have to make the best of a bad situation. Make our choices and ride out the wave. Survival is paramount, no matter the cost."

The room fell into an uneasy silence and I let it linger for a moment. We were trapped between battling *asuras*, and anyone who'd read a single ancient text born of our homeland on Earth knew that mortals frequently came out on the losing end of those encounters. I'd seen my share of religious fights over the years and knew with bone-deep certainty that Fasé was right. Logical reasons mattered very little when the fight was about faith.

I rubbed a hand over my bare arm, trying to still the gooseflesh that had risen up, but there was no antidote for the chill in my soul. Religious fights were messy, and Indranan had landed right in the middle of what was possibly the oldest one in the galaxy. I remembered again what Fasé had told us while we were fighting to get my throne back about the Farians and humanity. It wasn't a question I wanted to ask in front of everyone, so I stood. "Does anyone else have any questions of immediate concern, or can we wrap this up?" I asked, looking around the room.

"I have plenty, Majesty," Caspel said, also getting to his feet. "But they can wait until we get our guests settled and everyone else has had a chance to think about the information we've just received."

I glanced Emmory's way. *"I need to talk to Fasé alone,"* I subvocalized over our private com link, and he nodded. The other Guards in the room started ushering people out as the conversations continued. I caught Fasé by the arm. "Fasé, do you remember when you told us the Pedalion was going to wipe out humanity, but that the future-seers stopped them?"

"Yes, why?"

"Is this—" I swallowed. "Is this why?"

She stared at me, her golden eyes wide and her expression so alien it ran shivers down my spine. "What do you think, Majesty?"

"Bugger me. Fasé, what am I being dropped into the middle of?"

"Not dropped, Majesty. You were born to do this. As much as

Sybil is convinced this is a future that will come to pass, there is still a measure of doubt. No future is set in stone; that defies the very laws of the universe. But you—I have a great deal of hope now that I am back with you." She patted my arm. "I will see you in the morning when you need me."

"Those two make my skin—" Johar shuddered as a finish to the sentence and I turned from Fasé's retreating back with a sigh.

"It doesn't get any less creepy—that's for sure."

"So, what did I do to piss Caterina off?" Johar passed her glass to me and I took a sip of the Hyku vodka, grimacing a little as the alcohol burned on the way down.

"Nothing, why?"

"She kept looking at me."

"Oh." I laughed and handed the glass back over. "That's not you. That's me. They all think I should be more discerning about who I talk politics with, but you're practically family, you'll be an Indranan citizen soon—" I winked. "And I'm in a mood."

"You were having a royal temper tantrum and decided to use me for it?" She grinned at me from behind the rim of her glass, and I didn't even try to stop the laughter that burst into the air.

"I hate you. And yes."

Johar sobered. "She's not wrong, Hail. I know you trust Hao and me, and Dailun; but, well—" Lifting a shoulder as she took a drink, Johar swallowed before she spoke again. "You're going to have to move on from your previous life. Really move on, not just claim to have done so while you're still acting like a gunrunner."

"I am a gunrunner." The reply was automatic and Johar laughed at me.

"That's just reflex. You *were* a gunrunner and you were very good at it, even if your morals got in the way. You and I both know that life is over for you." Johar tipped her glass at me. "Now you're an empress and you are surrounded by some very intelligent people

who know a shit-ton more than we do about empires and econo-
mies and the like."

"You're a smart woman, Jo, don't try to pretend otherwise."

"If you need to know how to cut limbs off and keep a guy from
dying of shock in the process, I'm your girl. But I know jack about
running an empire," she replied.

"You asked good questions, though."

"Eh, someone else would have. Don't dodge the point, Hail.
We're still here for you, we always will be. But you've got a different
life now, time to start living it."

"Yes, ma'am."

She shoved me, grinning at Emmory when I squawked in protest.

"When you're done laughing at me," I said, "please stop Sybil
and ask her if she'd go down to the beach with me. I'd like to speak
with her in private."

Emmory's chuckle followed him out of the room.

"I appreciate you taking the time to speak with me, Sybil—" I
frowned. "Is there a title I should be calling you?"

"No." Sybil smiled and shook her head. "It is nice to hear my
name after so long, Your Majesty. And of course, I have the time.
It is the least I could do after all you are doing for us." She gestured
with a gloved hand at the beach stretching in front of us and the
quiet waves lapping at the shoreline. "This is lovely and a welcome
peace."

We walked along in silence, Zin and Indula behind us, Iza and
Emmory a meter in front. I put my feet into the prints Emmory left
behind for several steps before I realized I looked a bit like a child
trailing after her father.

Sybil's laughter ghosted through the air. "Fasé often spoke of you
with a great deal of delight, Majesty, and now I see why."

"I'm afraid she probably exaggerated. I am new at this empress business. Most of the time I seem to be managing it, but sometimes I am more the gunrunner than the royal." I offered up a wry smile before I stared up at the pale shadow of Dasra, where it hovered above the water. The second sun in our system was closer to Ashva than Pashati but moved on an elliptic that sent it past us during its eighty-year orbit.

"If it eases your worry, I can tell you that you are one of the better ones," Sybil replied. "And will remain one of the most loved not only in Indrana but throughout the galaxy for a very long time."

I caught my boot in the hem of my sari and stumbled, swearing. Sybil, mindful of my Guards, did not try to stop me from falling.

"Majesty?" Zin reached me first, helping me back to my feet and brushing the sand from the green silk.

"I'm fine," I replied with a sigh, squeezing his hand and inspecting the torn hem with a second sigh. "That's the third one this month, and Stasia wonders why I'd rather wear pants." I pointed a finger at Sybil. "I'm blaming this one on you."

"You can. Stasia likes me." She lifted a shoulder and started walking again. "What was it you wanted to talk to me about, Your Majesty?"

"You don't know?"

"Why would I—oh." Smiling, she looked out over the water and then shook her head. "I have learned to quiet things. Also, it's rude to poke like that. Fasé has a tendency to be too interested. In time she'll learn." Sybil laughed softly. "Maybe."

"Can you answer some questions for me?"

"I might be able to. I confess I'm curious why you're asking me instead of Fasé." She tipped her head back to me, pale eyes searching.

"We did not part on the best of terms, and though I am trying to overcome that past," I said, swallowing, "I feel like a different perspective is important here."

"What do you want to know, Your Majesty?"

"The civil war, how bad is it?"

"At the moment it's more like a rebellion, but it is growing. Our escape will have fueled the fire even more," Sybil replied. "Honestly, I don't know which way it will go in the end. There are too many variables. Too many important players whose lives are wrapped up in it for the path to be clear even to someone like myself."

"So it's bad?"

Sybil laughed. "Any war is bad, Your Majesty, you know that. Unless you're on the winning side." She gave me a sideways look. "And even then? To give you the answer you seek: Things are not good at home. Faria will be divided and it will weaken us further in the fight with the Shen and the danger coming."

"What danger?"

Sybil shook her head. "I can't tell you that. Not only because I don't know, but I think even if I did I couldn't tell you for fear of impacting your choices. You need a clear head, Majesty, for the days ahead of you. They are going to be tough and filled with pain. I am sorry for that. You deserve happiness and peace."

I worked my jaw for a moment before replying. The feelings rolling around in me were a mess of resigned acceptance and sorrow. It seemed no matter what I did, I wasn't going to get a moment's rest. Not as Cressen Stone. Not as Empress Hail Bristol. "Why did you help Fasé escape?"

"Because it was necessary." Sybil laughed softly, as though she hadn't considered anything other than the outcome that had happened. "To leave her where she was would have killed her eventually, possibly killed all of us. There are things I can't see. I am not omniscient. All I can do is read the possibilities and hope that the choice I make is the right one." A smile flickered across her face before she sobered. "I just happen to have a little more information about it than you do, is all."

"Why did you say I would be remembered?"

"You are the great peacemaker." Sybil stared into the distance. "Or the one who brings about the destruction of so many lives."

"No pressure," I muttered.

"No more than this life, or the one you had before. I know it sounds dire, Your Majesty, but you won't be presented with the choice in such an obvious fashion. It won't be as simple as *choose peace or choose war*." She smiled. "Fasé told you to pay attention to the little things, didn't she? Every single choice we make is important. Every single choice changes the trajectory of our lives in ways we can't even fathom. But we make the choices, because to do otherwise is an even worse fate—that of letting the universe drag us along like a swimmer caught in a riptide."

20

The expected angry com link came from Adora the next morning.

"Is she mad?" I asked Alba.

"Very much so, ma'am."

"All right, put her through to my desk screen." I was reasonably sure Adora was going to be yelling and I didn't need the accompanying headache that answering her com in my *smati* would offer. "*Itegas* Notaras, good morning," I said.

"Your Majesty. I demand you return the fugitive Fasé Terass and her kidnapping victim immediately."

Bolstered by Sybil's promise that nothing bad would happen to Indrana, I was possibly a tad more flippant than I should have been. "Kidnapping? I spoke with Sybil myself and she assured me that she was here of her own free will."

"You spoke with her?" Adora's eyes were saucers in her pale face.

"At great length." I smiled. "As for Fasé, she and Sybil both have requested and been granted political asylum. I'm afraid I couldn't turn them over even if I wanted to."

"You wouldn't dare."

"I have dared. Though it wasn't me. Both councils approved the request unanimously."

"You'd dissolve Indrana's treaty with Faria? Wipe away thousands of years of friendship and peace for this?"

"I'm not wiping away anything, *Itegas*, and I'd like you to mind your tone. Nowhere does our treaty prevent either side from welcoming any requests for asylum except by proven criminals."

Adora smiled triumphantly. "There you have it. Fasé is a criminal. You will return them both at once. I will have a ship sent and Colonel Morri can accompany them back to Faria."

"When I first met you, you told me specifically that Fasé wasn't a criminal and I had that conversation entered into the record," I replied, and watched Adora's mouth thin. "Were you lying to me then or now, *Itegas*?"

There was a sharply indrawn breath from somewhere off-screen and Adora's mouth tightened even further.

"I'm going to be blunt and say it doesn't matter," I said, not waiting for an answer. "My side of things has been duly processed and is legally binding. If you'd like to try to explain to the rest of the galaxy in detail why you dissolved our treaty, you go right ahead." I pinned her with a don't-fuck-with-me look. "But I'll warn you now, *Itegas* Notaras, if you put my empire at risk over this, I'll happily accept the Shen's very gracious offer to join them in their fight against you."

"You wouldn't dare."

"You said that already, and yes, I would. Try me." I disconnected the com link and leaned back in my chair with a muttered curse.

If Fasé and Sybil were wrong about that, I'd just royally fucked over my empire in the space of two minutes.

They've yet to be wrong about anything, though, haven't they? Cas whispered in my ear and I frowned. But he wasn't wrong.

"Damn you, Cas." I got to my feet with an exasperated exhalation and paced the room for a minute before returning to my chair. Spread across the desk were a handful of paper books and a tablet that had half a dozen more opened on it.

I'd been reading from *A History of Indranan/Farian Relations* when Adora commed, and I picked up the book again only to set it down with a sigh. "This is all cowshit."

I knew the information in all our history was suspect. The Farians had fed us whatever stories worked to further their goal of ingratiating themselves with my ancestors. I couldn't blame them; had I been in my ancestor-grandmother's place when an advanced alien race came calling I probably would have made the same call.

There was a knock on the door, and at my "come in," Jagana stuck her head into the room.

"Morning, Majesty."

"Morning." I got up from my seat. "How did your brother's baller game go?"

"They did really well, ma'am. Made it to the semis but lost in the final quarter. I think they'll take the championship next year."

"Tell him I'll come watch if they make it all the way to the championship next year," I replied with a grin. "What do you need?"

"Oh he'd love that. They'd all love that." Jagana beamed. "Fasé is here to see you, ma'am. I didn't know if you were busy."

"Send her in."

Jagana opened the door the rest of the way and came into the room, closing the door behind Fasé and stationing herself beside it. I briefly considered and then rejected telling her to leave. Emmory would fuss at her if she left me alone. Fasé was technically no longer ITS, no longer subject to the empire—and by extension me—and not entirely back in my good graces.

Though I was working on it.

"Good morning, Your Majesty."

"I've been wrestling with a problem," I said by way of greeting. "Which I suspect is why you're here. All this is crap." Gesturing at the books strewn across my desk, I sat down in my chair and watched her as she leaned over and grabbed the history I'd just tossed down moments before.

Fasé read for a moment, laughing softly as she put the book back down. "It is, Majesty, though you obviously don't need me to tell you that."

"I—" I exhaled and shoved a hand into my hair. "Indrana knows next to nothing about a race we've been allies with for hundreds of years."

"Everything you know was fed through specifically chosen channels." Fasé nodded as she sat in the chair across from me. "You, and the rest of humanity, have seen of the Farians what we wanted you to see. No more, no less."

"Tell me the rest of it."

Fasé shook her head. "You'll see it first person, Majesty, and I think it's best if you learn some things on your own."

"Firsthand? You're telling me I'll end up on Faria despite all I'm doing to avoid that."

"It's a possibility, Majesty." Fasé bit her lower lip and sighed, staring at a point past my left shoulder. "I try—Sybil cautions me to be careful, and I know I should be. It is so hard to know and not be able to speak. Especially, to keep those I care about from pain." She shook her head and focused on me, and again I was struck with just how much she'd changed in the last six months. "The Shen think you will be unbiased against them because of your history in the black and that your distrust of the Farians will grow the longer this plays out. The Farians want to nudge you in the direction of the outcome that best suits them. The one future they have seen and have worked so hard to make true all these years. They think it means their victory over the Shen, but they are only focused on the outcome, not the choice, and every push at you has the opposite of their intended effect."

"You mean I dig my heels in and resist the more they try to manipulate me?" I asked with a laugh that Fasé didn't echo.

"Yes, Majesty, but the Farians don't know subtlety. If they cannot convince you, they will force you."

"Aiz and Mia said something very similar, you know?"

Fasé lifted a shoulder in a noncommittal gesture. "They know what the Farians are capable of doing, Majesty. My goals may not be aligned exactly with theirs, but they are certainly closer than that of the Pedalion's. I would be lying if I said otherwise. But Aiz is lost in his hate and at the moment would see all that I love destroyed. I won't stand by and let him do that, even as I cannot remain silent about the Pedalion's continued abuse of our faith. He and I want the war over, but we have very different ideas of how to accomplish that. I want a shift from the Pedalion's religious rule over my people to something much more open and secular."

"Fasé?" I tapped a finger on the desktop while I searched for the words to the question I wanted to ask, even knowing she'd likely refuse to answer. "Tell me one thing, if you can? Sybil said I would be remembered; does that mean Indrana will survive?"

"Of all the questions you could ask me," Fasé said with a smile. "It's never about you, about what happens to you, but always about Indrana. Yes, Majesty. Indrana will survive."

I leaned back in my chair and released the breath I'd been holding. "Good. That's good," I murmured.

Fasé smiled as she got to her feet. "I'll get going," she said. "You've got another visitor on the way." As soon as the words had left her mouth, Jagana answered the knock at the door and spoke quietly with Kisah before turning back to us.

"Majesty, Matriarch Saito is here to see you."

"Let her in, Fasé was just leaving," I replied, waving a hand to Fasé as she headed for the door. "Caterina, good morning."

"Does Johar know how to skin someone alive?" Caterina asked, and I couldn't stop my surprised laugh. "I'm serious, Hail, that seems like the sort of thing she'd know how to do."

"I have never asked her, and I'd advise against you doing it unless you want an extremely detailed story. Sit down and tell me what's wrong."

"Shivali," Caterina replied, her jaw tight.

"Ah." I laughed. "Last night's news interview with our esteemed prime minister?"

"You saw it. How are you not angry? Did you already talk to Jo?" Her dark eyes went wide and she held up her hands. "I was kidding about the skinning alive. Mostly kidding."

I laughed again. "I can't stop her from going on interviews, Caterina, and if she doesn't think I made the right call allowing asylum to 'renegade Farians' and feels my judgment is clouded by my friendship with Fasé?" I lifted my hands in the air. "That's her opinion."

"She cited your friendship with Taz as a further example of your personal feelings for people crowding out your duty to Indrana."

"I know. I watched the whole thing." I shook my head. "So did Matriarch Maxwell, who called me in the middle of the interview to apologize for bringing Shivali to the meeting about the Farians because, and I quote, 'if I'd known she'd pop her mouth off on imperial TV about sensitive information, I'd never have given her the time of day.'"

"You're kidding."

"No." I shook my head. "Shivali misjudged the people's feelings about me, about Taz, and about the reforms. Never mind managing to piss off Heela. You didn't see the morning shows, did you? Three different shows called her out for 'crossing a line.'" I didn't bother to stop the grin that spread across my face, and Caterina chuckled in response. "We haven't heard the last of it from the prime minister, but she may have been forced to rethink her strategy."

Caterina sobered and was silent for a minute. "Did we make a mistake here, Hail? Did we push too hard and too fast with the reforms?"

I shook my head. "Traditions aren't meant to be stagnant. They always change. People try to convince themselves otherwise, but nothing stays the same indefinitely. Taz and the other men aren't the problem. We're the problem. Stuck in our ways, comfortable in our power. If we don't speak up, who will?"

*　　*　　*

My own words stuck with me throughout the day and as I sat in a meeting next to Taz later that afternoon, listening to him patiently explain for what felt like the fourth time why we needed to do more than just encourage young men to enter certain woman-dominated fields, but that it was also necessary to look into the attrition rates and make plans for ways to keep them in those fields.

"If you look at the studies, Prime Minister—"

"I have read the studies," Shivali replied.

I looked up from the tabletop, raising a single eyebrow at the tone of her voice. Several people around the table swallowed, but Taz didn't miss a beat.

"The primary dropout points happen the further along students get into their studies. It's not hard to see an equal split among, say, first-year astrophysicists at all the major universities, but by the time they hit graduate student level or even first-year interns? The numbers of male versus female candidates are drastically different."

"Possibly because they can't keep up with the pressure; studies have also shown men just aren't able to handle that kind of environment." Shivali's smile was so smug it took all of my self-control to keep my expression unchanged.

"I've read those studies also, Prime Minister. I believe they specifically mentioned that dealing with the pressure of their education and the sexism of their fellow students and co-workers makes men burn out a lot faster," Taz replied with his own smile.

"You don't have to be snide—"

"That's quite enough," I said, cutting Shivali off and getting to my feet. Everyone else followed suit and I looked around the room. "The universities have already agreed to work on this problem. I want to see an integration program planned out before the start of the fall semester for all Pashati universities. We'll do a test run there and then see what, if anything, needs to be fixed and improved upon before we pass it to the other universities in the empire. Make it happen, people." I tapped a fist on the tabletop and turned away.

Taz shook his head at me and for just a second I considered letting it go, but then I heard Shivali laughing and turned back around. "Prime Minister, if you'll wait a moment?" I called and crossed the room, Emmory right behind me.

The women around her scattered like leaves in a breeze. I managed to keep from getting in Shivali's face, though I could feel the steady pressure of Emmory's hand on my arm, hidden from sight, my *Ekam* not quite pulling me away from the smaller woman. "A word to the wise, Prime Minister. Speak to the prince with respect. I don't care if you feel it or not, but you will demonstrate it if you wish to remain a representative of my government."

"You don't want to deal with the fallout if you try to remove me." She didn't even blink. "I am not afraid of you, Your Majesty."

"You should be." I smiled at her until she dropped her eyes. "You may go." I watched her leave the room, pleased at the final, furtive glance over her shoulder at me before she left the room. Shivali Tesla wasn't a fool; she was afraid of me, she was just slightly better at hiding it than the others.

"Thanks," Taz said.

"I'll be honest." I turned on him with a frown. "I expected you to tear into her."

His smile was weary. "You know I can't. I'm accused of mocking her just for pointing out that the research she cited proves her wrong. Can you imagine what would happen if I lost my temper at them?"

"Fair point." I sighed and rubbed at my face with one hand. "Are you going to be okay without me around to not-so-subtly threaten people on your behalf?"

Taz chuckled. "I'm reasonably sure I'll be all right." He bumped his shoulder into mine. "Besides, you have a whole empire of people out there for you to threaten; it'd be selfish of me to ask you to stay home."

"Just remember," I replied with a laugh. "I'm a com link away, and Admiral Hassan has permission to step on anyone who gets too far out of line. Get to work on that proposal. I want something in my inbox within the month, and we'll go over it until they can't find a single thing to complain about."

"When did you become such an optimist?" he asked with a grin.

I shook my head. "I honestly don't know, but to tell the truth it feels nice."

"I'm going to miss you, Hail." Taz exchanged a look with Emmory and then held his arms open for a hug. "If I don't see you again before you leave, take care of yourself out there and come home soon."

I hugged him tight. "I will. I promise."

The days passed quickly. Preparations for the trip took over my daily routine as the intelligence briefings grew more and more dire. My head was filled with the latest reports from Caspel as I stepped out of the aircar into the warmth of the late-summer sun. Alice stood on the front steps of her family's country estate, the smile on her face echoed by the bright yellow sari wrapped around her.

"That color suits you." I held a hand out and laughed. "Plus, I like seeing you defy people's expectations."

"You're a horrible influence in that regard. Hail, you look better." She tilted her head, her eyes narrowing critically. "A little worse for wear around the edges?"

"Rough night and morning." I pressed my cheek to hers. "The Farians and Shen seem bent on war. If I thought they were going to keep it in their own backyard I wouldn't care."

"But they may not," she agreed, taking my arm and leading me into the house. "I read Caspel's reports just a bit ago."

There had been another skirmish in Solarian space a week ago, and this morning Caspel had laid out all the details his agents had acquired. According to him, Mia was the one in charge of the Shen fleet and the ships were like nothing we'd seen before.

"I'm surprised President Hudson hasn't commed me yet," I replied. "How are you doing?"

"A bit tired. She kept me up last night." Alice rubbed a hand over her stomach. "Otherwise good, Dr. Yanla is pleased."

"I'm glad to hear it. You will have plenty of help from Caterina and the others, so make sure not to push yourself while I'm gone."

Alice smiled as we headed through the arched doorway of her home. "You are no less than the thirtieth person to remind me of that. In fact, I'm reasonably sure Taz thinks you'll kill him if anything happens to me while you're gone."

"I may have insinuated as much," I replied. "What's the use of having a reputation like mine if I can't use it?"

"You mean like with the Matriarch Council? Yes, I heard about that," Alice said, snorting at my innocent look.

"Honestly, Heela did most of the work. To hear her tell it I'm some bloodthirsty renegade."

"And the prime minister?" Alice asked with a smile.

"How'd you hear about that?"

"Better question, why didn't you tell me?"

I took the tall glass Gita passed on from a servant as I sat on a comfortable blue couch in a room filled with photos of the Gohil family. "I didn't want to bother you with it."

"I'm not made of glass, Hail. Taz and I don't need you to fight our battles for us."

I smiled, swirling the drink around. The ice clattered against the sides. "It gives me something to do. What's this?"

"Hua is trying out a new iced chai. She's terribly nervous, so if you hate it tell me and I'll lie to her," Alice replied after a moment, letting me change the subject.

"It's perfect," I said, laughing at the idea of anyone caring if I liked a drink or not. "I'm partial to it hot, but this is very nice." I sipped it again; the chai was less spicy than my preferred blue chai, but the softer vanilla flavor worked well with the ice.

"I don't understand how you could drink anything hot in this weather."

Making a face, I glanced up at the ceiling, imagining the sky above, and beyond that the endless expanse of space. "Twenty years spent mostly in space?"

"I suppose that would do it." Alice stared at the window for a long moment. "I've never been, you know."

Blinking at her in surprise was about all I could manage, and my heir smiled at me.

"There was a significantly greater percentage of Shakti dementia in the Gohil family than most of the other noble families. It led to us being cautious about space travel."

Exposure to radiation in the early days of space travel had triggered a genetic mutation that resulted in a new form of dementia none of the known cures could touch. My own ancestors had also been "touched by the Mother Destroyer," and initially everyone thought the same thing happened to my mother.

Until we'd discovered she was being poisoned.

"Alice, I—"

"It's all right, Hail. If things had gone normally around here, Clara probably would have used the objection to keep me off the throne. As it stands, I am willing to take the risk for Indrana and hopefully she will be stronger." She rubbed at her belly with a smile. "Taz's family has never suffered a case. We may not be able to determine the risk factor, but we do know that will help her odds."

My *smati* pinged and I pulled up the message from Alba with a sigh. "Well, the break is over. I am reminded that I have a magazine interview in an hour and time is required to make me presentable."

Alice grinned at me as I helped her to her feet. "You deserve this victory lap. Take it and enjoy yourself."

It was my turn to grin. "It's not a victory lap, Alice."

"It is when the cameras aren't on us."

I hugged her, pressing my cheek into her hair. "Take care of yourself and don't work too hard."

"I'm reasonably sure that Uli has been taking lessons from your chamberlain on how to make me do what she wants without me realizing it." Alice squeezed me once more and then stepped away. "And whatever she misses, that husband you foisted off on me picks up on."

"I don't see how you can claim that I was at all involved. I wasn't even on the planet."

"I haven't figured it out yet, but I'm blaming you regardless," she replied.

"I can't hold you responsible for his decision, Fasé." I sighed. "I want to, but I know—I remember Cas and his determination to make Emmory proud. No one could have talked him out of it."

Fasé dropped red lashes over her golden eyes for a moment and then smiled up at me. An aching smile of loss and sorrow, it was heavier than the heart of a star and sharper than a nanoblade's edge. "I know, Majesty. He wanted to make you proud, too. I cannot apologize for what I did: I would do it again in an instant, so would Cas, and so would you.

"What I am sorry for is the hurt I've caused you. I wish it hadn't been necessary. Believe me when I say it is all right if you never fully forgive me. All I hope is that you'll someday forgive yourself. That moment. That choice. It has changed the very universe. Like when I brought Emmory back from the dead." She squeezed my fingers and released me.

I swallowed, the memory of Emmory dead on the floor of Hao's ship flashing in my vision. Zin's terrible cry, the sound of a heart ripping in two, filled my ears and my breath stuck in my throat. I pushed off the couch and wandered to the window.

"I know it's painful, Majesty." Fasé joined me. "And I don't remind you of such things to cause you pain. We are walking on the edge of a knife. I must be careful what I say to you." She shook her head. "I can't risk influencing your moment."

"Isn't that the whole point of you being here?" I asked with a laugh.

"No, Majesty." She fixed those wide eyes at me in surprise. "I am here to support you. It is right that I am at your side." A smile flickered to life on her lips. "And on a selfish note I am happy to be with Stasia again."

The suns had set and lights were coming on all around the city. My inhale dragged the humid air into my lungs; the taste of the sea was unsurprising. But the peculiar spice of Rama's Noodles somehow beat out its competitors to find its way to my nose, and my stomach gave an appreciative growl.

"Stasia, I know Yun Li has something prepared for this evening, but would it be an awful trouble to send someone to Rama's Noodles?" I subvocalized the request over my com link with my maid.

"For your usual, ma'am?" There was laughter in her voice.

"Please, my regular order. I'll share with Fasé, though, and I'll still eat dinner, I promise."

"It's no trouble, Majesty." Now Stasia's laughter was alive in my ear. *"We'll have someone up with it in twenty minutes."*

"I appreciate it. Thank you."

"She was not very cooperative with taking that time off," I said out loud.

"It's true." Fasé grinned. "She got rather sulky that you wouldn't let her do her job. I appreciate the time, though, and so does she. We were separated for too long; I was worried..." Fasé trailed off and gave me a small apologetic smile as so many people did when they caught themselves complaining about their relationships to me.

"She still snuck in here to do her job." I waved a hand at my clothing. "This was all laid out on my bed every day, and I'm reasonably sure it wasn't elves."

Fasé's grin spread. "I am not the least bit surprised by this. We went for a lovely walk on the beach this afternoon while you were at your interview."

The door opened and Iza came in. "Majesty, Hao is here."

"Let him in." I turned from the window with a smile.

"Hey." Hao came in behind Iza, stopping when he spotted Fasé. He seemed to consider walking back out again before he exhaled and looked at me. "Do you have a minute?"

"Sure. Come on." I waved him the rest of the way into the room. "What's up?"

"I'm going to borrow the *War Bastard* again."

"Tonight?" I pushed away from the window, Fasé following in my wake. "We're leaving for the tour tomorrow. I thought you were coming with me."

"No offense, little sister, but unlike Johar I'm not interested in a getting-to-know-you tour of your little empire. I'm not planning on settling down here."

I was offended, but damned if I'd give him the satisfaction of knowing it. "I'm sorry it's so boring around here. What do you need the ship for?"

"I have a few things that need to be taken care of," he said. "I do still have a business of my own to run, *sha zhu*."

"Is that what you're calling it these days, Cheng Hao?" Fasé asked, putting a curious emphasis on his last name.

I raised an eyebrow when my brother winced, but he recovered quickly enough and leveled a stare at Fasé that I'd seen spell trouble for far too many people.

"Some of us work for a living, Farian. We don't just run our mouths about things that get people killed."

"What's the matter?" Fasé smiled slowly. "Afraid I'll say too much if I run my mouth?"

"All right, that's enough," I said when I saw Hao's hand twitch toward his gun, and I put a hand in the middle of his chest. "Fasé, don't antagonize him, you just got back. Give me a few minutes before you two start sniping at each other. You're both adults. Try to act like it."

"Can I take the ship or not?"

"Oh, were you asking permission?" I dropped back onto the couch and crossed my arms over my chest, all too aware of the fact that I looked like I was sulking. "I guess. Don't damage it."

"Fine." He looked as though he wanted to say something more, but shoved his hands into his pockets and headed for the door.

"Fine," I snapped, and stuck my tongue out at his back as he left the room.

21

I t's not my place to talk about it, *jiejie*." Dailun shook his head. His pink hair had grown out from when we first met, and now it flopped about his face. "He will talk with you when he is ready. Not before."

"How am I supposed to talk to him when he takes off with you and the *War Bastard* instead of coming on this tour with me and refuses to take my coms?"

We were more than a month out from Pashati, headed toward the HCL system, our fifth stop on the tour. The first four had been inner worlds, easy stops at planets that'd never wavered from supporting the throne. The trip had given me time to speak with Fasé and Sybil, who'd joined us on the *Hailimi Bristol*, about their plans and the continued problems between the Farians and the Shen.

Alba was proving to be a master at knowing just how much interaction I could endure before my empress persona started to slip back into gunrunner annoyance, and when she had to get me away from the crowds. The fawning and flattery was unnecessary, but it didn't stop some members of my empire from engaging in it nonetheless.

Dailun gave me an earnest smile. "I cannot make my honored cousin talk to you and I cannot tell you why he won't." He shook his head, still smiling before I could protest. "I am Traveling with you, Sister, but it does not mean I will involve myself needlessly in things that are better done between the two of you."

"You're not Traveling with me," I replied. "You're out running around with him."

Dailun grinned. "Semantics, honored sister. With you or with him, it makes little difference at the moment and he needs me. We'll be back with you soon. I promise."

"Sometimes you sound like Fasé, you know that?"

I'd taken Po-Sin's great-grandchild on as a pilot while we were on the run from Wilson's forces. Dailun was Svatir on his mother's side, and his rite of passage known as the Traveling allowed him to break from Po-Sin's family without any harmful repercussions. He was free to do as he wished, and he'd asked me if he could travel the stars with me.

I still didn't quite know what to do with this young man who was part counsel, part companion, part BodyGuard—not that I'd ever say that around Emmory—and part free spirit. Dailun seemed happy with his choice and happy with the freedom to come and go as he pleased. I was sure he was happier now that we were back in space; it showed in the glittering of his black eyes, and the silver chasing his pupils was brighter out here in the dark.

"I will take that as a compliment," he said.

"You are so little help. Why am I letting you fly my ship?"

His grin flashed, followed by laughter. "Because they won't let you fly it, *jiejie*."

"I hate you," I said with no heat, because he was right. Before I'd lent it to Hao, I'd floated the idea early that I take the *War Bastard* out for our trip. That idea had been shot down by a dozen people, my *Ekam* included. Instead I was safe in a *Vajrayana* ship obnoxiously named the *Hailimi Bristol*.

"No, you don't." Dailun sobered, his face taking on that serious look that made him seem far older than his nineteen years. "Hao will sort through this, honored sister, if you let him tend to his business. He must do so on his own; it is not something you can help him with." He glanced away, worrying at his lip with his teeth.

"Keep trying to speak with him; it is helpful for him to know that you care. That is all I can say."

Exhaling, I rubbed at the back of my neck with a hand. "I will. Thanks."

"Anything for you." Dailun nodded once and disconnected the com.

I stared for a moment at the blank screen and then slid it away with a sigh and a muttered curse. Whatever was going on with Hao would have to wait. Hopefully Dailun was right and he would work himself out of this funk without my help.

I'd already had my daily com with Alice. Things were quiet around the empire and especially at home. Caterina seemed to have found an ally in Heela as far as dealing with Prime Minister Tesla was concerned, and the number of news stations that wanted to speak with the PM had dwindled dramatically since my departure. Bringing up the information packet on our next stop, I settled back in my chair to read.

The HCL system had a G-class star and five planets: A large gas giant orbited the star at the outer edge of the system, while three rocky planets inhabited the interior and one ice giant swung in a wide loop through the Oort cloud and back into the system. The second and third planets were habitable, but only barely, and all the planets along with the gas giant were constantly bombarded with comets. One of the empire's major science outposts occupied an underground complex on the second world.

It was a primarily research-focused system, with some copper mining on the inner planet. Those sites were automated with minimal human staff. The Earth-based mining corporation Hindi Copper Limited had changed as they left Earth with the other colonists, but their mission always stayed focused on copper to some extent. Their annual payment of the mining rights for the system allowed for the research on the other worlds.

We were here to see the scientists, though I knew from Alba's schedule that there was going to be a virtual tour of the mining facilities on the innermost planet also. This system hadn't had a reason to waver from the empire during the turmoil, which had made it a perfect stop on the tour. Besides, I found the whole thing fascinating and decided early in the tour planning that I was going to get at least one or two stops that I truly enjoyed.

I flipped through the digital pages, skimming over the history of the system until I got to the research section.

The scientists were split between the study of early stellar behavior and the formation of Earth-like planets. The influx of comets increased the chances of the two closer planets potentially hosting life-forms, and for the last few years the focus had been on allowing specifically selected comets to pass through the net and strike the planets in the hope of encouraging the formation of more habitable terrain.

"Majesty?" The knock at the door accompanied Gita's call, and I blinked away the report.

"Come in."

She slipped through the cracked open door. "I can come back if you're busy."

"No, come in." I waved her in. "I was just reading about silicon-based organic compounds, and I confess my eyes were starting to cross."

Gita laughed. "Coming from someone who's read a lot of dry things, Majesty, you have my sympathies."

"You mean there's a subject Gita Desai doesn't know forward and backward?" I asked in mock shock. I'd come to learn that my *Dve* was something of a prodigy: Her linguistic skills and natural talent at mechanics of all kinds were coupled with an impressive array of military postings that only added to her experience.

"Astronomy and organic chemistry were some of my worst subjects at the Academy."

"Yes, I saw those horrible B-minus scores." I folded my hands one over the other and rested my chin on them. "That's not why you're here, though. What's up?"

Gita looked at the floor and I felt an eyebrow crawl upward at her hesitation.

"I need to confess something to you, Majesty."

"Okay." I sat up in my chair. "If this is about Hao, I don't—"

"I was a member of the Galactic Intelligence Security." She gaped at me. "What?"

"Excuse me?"

Gita's eyes went wide and I closed mine briefly, trying to get a handle on the amusement that had suddenly gone to war with my shock.

"That was not what I thought you were going to say," I said after a moment. "Let's start over. You're what?"

"Was, Majesty. I was a member of the GIS, the military branch. Director Britlen recruited me when I was still in the Academy. I was in deep cover. Not even my mother knew."

"Does Emmory know?"

"I told him the day I applied to be your Guard, ma'am," Gita replied.

"Emmory, my rooms, now," I said over the com link.

"Majesty, about Hao? I broke it off. I know it was an inappropriate relationship. I just—didn't know if we could trust him and—" She dragged in a breath. "Once he recovered, Emmory didn't discourage it because we figured it was the easiest way to keep an eye on him."

It was a trade-off as to who was more surprised by both the snarl of rage that clawed its way out of my throat and the fact that I came up out of my chair. Gita took half a step back, her hands raised, and I dropped back into my seat, struggling to get my anger under control.

"Hao is not just some gunrunner. He has feelings. He cares about you, Gita, and you were just keeping an eye on him?" The fury in my voice made my BodyGuard flinch back a second step, and I grappled with my anger, finally bringing it to heel before I did something I would regret. This was not how I'd thought this conversation would go.

"No, Majesty, I—" Gita looked miserable as Emmory came through the door, closing it behind him. He paused, one eyebrow arched at the obvious tension in the room.

"I know he's more than just a gunrunner," Gita continued, dropping her hands at her sides. "I do care about him. I didn't realize it would sneak up on me like that, but he's . . . not predictable."

"No argument there." I sighed heavily and pinched at the bridge of my nose. "*Uff.* I wonder if this is what's been needling at him. Hao is complicated, but whatever else he is, he's loyal to me, Gita. I know that like I know the beating of my own heart. I'm not second-guessing your decision where he's concerned. I understand the position you're in and it was the right thing to do. I wish—" Words failed me and silence dropped onto the room. It lingered for several heartbeats.

"Majesty?"

I dropped my hand. Emmory stood with his hands folded in front of him, his face blank.

"Gita was GIS, and I'm just now finding out about it. Is there any particular reason you didn't tell me?" It made several things that had happened while we were on the run a lot clearer.

Emmory lifted a shoulder. "You didn't really need to know, to be honest."

"So why do I need to know now?"

"You haven't told her?" Emmory looked at Gita, who gestured weakly with her hands.

"We got sidetracked. Majesty, there's not just mining and research at the HCL system. The GIS has two agents there doing long-range reconnaissance of a Farian colony."

"Why?" I drew the word out, noticing that the wrist of Emmory's glove was flashing green lights. "Are you jamming surveillance?"

"Precautionary," he said. "And to answer your question, the GIS is watching a Farian colony because it's one of the few ways we can get any intelligence about the Farians."

"You're not wrong about that, I guess." I sighed. "We didn't know about the Farians' recent problems until after the schedule had been finalized, so was this just a weird coincidence?"

"As much as it surprises me, yes, Majesty," Emmory replied. "Gita and I thought it best you have a chat with the agents while you're down there, and since she knows them we also thought it was time to let you in on her previous job."

"I'm guessing your relative fluency in Farian has something to do with your previous job?"

"Yes, ma'am. I was attached to the Farian consulate as a guard for several years."

"They would flip their shit if they knew that."

Gita smiled. "That's why we go to great lengths to keep it a secret."

"We are so happy for your visit, Your Majesty." Dr. Lore Zellin was a stately older woman who easily kept pace with me and Johar as we walked through the quiet hallways of the HCL Research Facility. "Our people have been doing great work on exoplanetary evolution."

"Yes, I read up on it somewhat on our way over. I confess a lot of it went over my head."

"All of it went over my head," Johar announced.

Dr. Zellin laughed. "You're not alone in that. Hopefully by the time we're done with our tour, you'll understand it a little better. We're in here." She gestured at the door ahead of us. "*Ekam* Tresk, I believe your people cleared the room; however, if you would like to go in first?"

"Yes, thank you." Emmory nodded and moved forward to speak with the Marine who appeared at the doorway. Zin stayed at my side, but Iza and Indula followed him.

Moments later Zin was ushering Johar and me into the large briefing room, and Dr. Zellin introduced me to the cluster of scientists who looked understandably nervous about not only meeting the Empress of Indrana but all the BodyGuards surrounding them.

I settled into a seat with Dr. Zellin on one side of me and Zin on the other. Emmory had vanished somewhere in the back. A young man with a round face and bright eyes stepped up to the front of the room and cleared his throat.

"Your Imperial Majesty and other assembled guests, thank you all so much for coming." He folded slender brown hands in front of him as he bowed. "We are most pleased to welcome you to our facility and beyond excited for a chance to share with you our work. I am Rupja Singh, and I will be facilitating this presentation. If you could hold all questions until we reach the specific departments, it would be most appreciated. Despite what my colleagues think, I am not all-knowing."

There was a ripple of laughter behind me at the inside joke, and I grinned.

"The HCL Research Facility is made possible by a generous grant from Her Majesty's government and from Hindi Copper Limited." Rupja waved his hand and a massive hologram appeared on his left. The planets of the HCL system spun around the yellow dwarf star. "Our mission here is to observe the development of HCL Three as it relates to the early development of Earth using established science-based methods. We are comparing and contrasting a number of factors, including the influence of the comets that HCL Five drags into the system with her orbit through the Oort cloud."

I watched as the ice giant looped out of the system into the Oort cloud and the hologram zoomed in to show the comets she dragged in her wake as her orbit brought her back into the system.

"We have three major departments, Your Majesty," Rupja continued. "They focus on the planet's geological development, on observing the comets that impact HCL Three and the resulting changes to terrain and makeup of the planet's surface, and on the chemical composition of the comets themselves as well as early star development. I would now like to introduce the department heads." He gestured at the two women and one man standing off to the side.

"Our major questions, Your Majesty, deal with whether HCL Three will end up looking like Earth." Dr. P. J. Yánez was a petite woman who was a full thirty centimeters shorter than me with black hair and light blue eyes. Dr. Yánez was the head of the geological department and she moved with a speed even I was hard-pressed to keep up with. "It's obviously of great interest not only to the empire but to humanity as a whole. Terraforming science has come a long way, but planets that naturally evolve not only hold the promise of new life, which we're legally obligated to protect, but tend to be a better fit for humanity as far as settlements go."

"I would imagine so," I replied with a smile. "Though obviously I couldn't tell you exactly why that is."

Dr. Yánez shared my smile. "That's why you're the empress and I'm the geologist, Majesty."

"True enough. So, tell me about the planet."

"The good news is that Three has a heavy iron core similar to Earth's, and that has resulted in the development of a magnetic field that is also similar. Both HCL Two and Three have atmospheres, and while they are not quite tolerable for humans, the situation may improve over the life of the system."

"Interesting. So can we be on the surface at all?"

"Yes, ma'am. It's not immediately toxic, but long-term exposure would kill us. Dr. Petra Giosan is our geophysicist, and her major focus is plate movement." Dr. Yánez gestured at the woman standing very straight by a workstation. I resisted the urge to tell her to relax.

"Majesty." Dr. Giosan dipped her head. She barely contained her anxiety behind a stiff smile. Her braids were pulled back from her face at the base of her head and hung down over one slender shoulder. "We look at both the comet impact–caused disruptions and the more naturally occurring plate tectonics. So far what we've seen closely resembles events that we suspect happened at the end of the Archean period on Earth."

"And you know this, how?"

"Observations of the plate tectonics, Majesty. Along with various hot spots and volcanic activity. The rock samples we've retrieved have a similar composition to metamorphic rocks like gneiss back on Earth."

"And you only send robots down to the surface?"

"Yes, ma'am. We're required to preserve the environment. There may already be prokaryotes on the surface or in the oceans, so we—"

"I'm not familiar with that term."

Petra ducked her head. "Sorry, ma'am. Unicellular organisms, no membrane-bound nucleus." She smiled. "Though that's really all K.K.'s arena rather than mine, and she'll be horrified if I steal her moment in the spotlight."

There were chuckles from the assembled scientists, and the conversation flowed into the next series of questions as Alba took over for me and I fell into step with Emmory on our way to the next department.

"Having fun, Majesty?"

"It's actually quite interesting. Everything quiet?"

Emmory nodded, returning his attention to the pair of Trackers waiting for us at the end of the hall. Another round of room clearing, another pause in the action before I was allowed into the lab and swept up in the energy of one Dr. Khala Kuryay.

22

After lunch, Johar and Alba headed back to the ship while I headed for the section of the facility devoted to the 5th Space Recon Group. The classified-research side of the HCL facility was heavily shielded, and my *smati* cut out as we passed through the first of several locked and guarded doors. It made me twitch a bit, my claustrophobia flaring up as the final door closed behind us with a sinister hiss.

Gita stepped forward to greet the GIS agents, giving me the moment I needed to compose myself.

"The Farians set up a colony on a world right on the outer edge of the Solarian Conglomerate, Your Majesty." Agent Has Dougan was a pale man with wild red hair. He'd bowed solemnly in greeting, but I'd spotted the complicated handshake he'd shared with Gita. Their interaction had been playful and familiar, not at all like his formal demeanor now.

"With the telescope power available here, we've gathered a decent amount of data, not only on the colony itself but on the Farian ships," Agent Luis Paez, the other man on-site, picked up where Has left off. "There's been a lot of movement lately that we suspect has something to do with the recent Shen attacks. Most of the outer colonies would have to be nervous that they're next on the list."

"I don't blame them." I'd gone over the reports on the attacks before leaving Pashati, trying to make sense of an adversary that would burn a colony to the ground on one hand but steal ships without killing a single person on the other. Meeting Aiz in person and hearing his proposition threw that further into doubt. What if he was telling the truth about the Farians?

"Luis, you don't have eyes on any of the colonies that were hit, do you?" I asked.

His eyes unfocused as he consulted his *smati*. "Three of them are on the other side of the Solarian Conglomerate, closer to where we think Faria is located, so they're completely out of range for us. The outpost that was hit was a little closer to home." He trailed off and then crossed the room to the bank of screens set against the far wall. I followed, holding in my questions as he brought up a menu on one of the screens and began swiping through files.

Has leaned in, apparently understanding exactly where his partner was headed. "That one," he said, pointing.

"That's two days prior."

"I know, but it was on this side and we were moving the telescope. There might be a chance we caught the tail end of it before it fell off screen."

"Hmmm." Luis nodded. "It's possible. Majesty, we'll have to do some looking. Anything we find will need to be enhanced anyway; it's not something I can just pull up for you." He smiled in apology. "I can't even guarantee we'll find something, but we'll do our best."

"That's all I need. Send Gita anything you find." I clapped him on the shoulder and he looked up at me with a grim smile.

"Yes, ma'am."

"What else have you got to show me?" I asked, rubbing my hands together. Has and Luis took the cue and for the next hour showed me around their area and explained the other projects they had going. In addition to being GIS agents the two were excellent astrophysicists and were studying the effects of colliding stellar remnants on interstellar travel.

By the time we left the locked-down site, I had two messages from Caspel, and one from Alice. I sent the encrypted one from Caspel to Zin as we headed to the *Vajrayana*.

Back on the *Hailimi* and safely in my rooms, I fed the messages from Caspel through to the screen and leaned against the wall next to Emmory. Gita hitched a hip onto the desk and crossed her arms.

"Aiz Cevalla has sent you a message, Majesty. It didn't come through official channels but was passed along to me through an operative. I thought you would want to see it before I inform the council. I've attached the video." Caspel gave me a quick nod and the screen went blank for a moment.

Then Aiz appeared. He stood outside, a blue sky and snow-capped mountains in the background. He was alone, his sister Mia nowhere to be seen, at least not in the frame of the video.

"Empress, I am comming you as requested." He winked. The wind teased at the ends of his brown hair but the audio was unaffected by the breeze. "I hope you are no longer angry with me over the rather improper tone of our first meeting."

"No, but I'm angry at you for killing one of my people," I murmured.

"I have a request for you." Aiz folded his hands together, his intense gaze focused on the camera. "We had hoped you would join us in this righteous fight, but at Mia's urging I tried to respect your desire to keep your empire out of it. However, as you well know, things are escalating and I know they will only continue to get worse. Through forces outside my control, you may already be too tangled in this situation." The smile twisted the corner of his mouth.

"It looks as though the one thing I want is the one thing I cannot have."

I tried to ignore the way my skin crawled down my arms at his words.

"The Solarians have contacted me with an offer. They wish to host a peace summit between the Farians and ourselves. The unfortunate casualties in our last few encounters have resulted in the

Solarians' involvement in our conflict. I am in reluctant agreement and have told the Solarians we will come to the table, but only if you are the one to lead the negotiations."

I heard Emmory's indrawn breath beside me.

"I suspect you will hear from the Solarians shortly, but I wanted to ask you personally. I will be honest with you: I do not think that anything will come of this summit—the hatred between my people and the Farians is old and full of teeth. But I will not let it be said that the Shen are unwilling to at least listen, even if all the Farians will do is spout lies.

"You can send a reply to the Solarians directly. And if you wish to message me back, you know how to contact us." He smiled, and this time it was weary, clinging to the edge of hope. "I look forward to speaking with you."

The screen blacked out and I whistled, rubbing a hand over my face. "Bugger me, Emmory. Thoughts?"

"He's not lying, but that doesn't make him safe," Emmory said. "The second message from Caspel is a priority message from the Indranan ambassador on Earth."

"Put it through." I frowned. "I'd bet good credits that it's something about this peace summit. I'm in agreement with you about Aiz. He may not be lying, but he's not telling me everything."

"He's telling you enough to get your attention, same as the Farians." Gita shook her head. "Trusting him is a bad idea."

Emmory rubbed a hand over his face. "But his claim that the Farians have killed their own people is more than a little worrisome."

Dhatt. I shared a look with them both. "We're caught in a battle between *asuras*."

"Adityas and Danavas," Emmory murmured in agreement. "This is going to be ugly."

"We're going to get trampled unless we can stop them," Gita added. "If this fight truly spills over into our arms of the galaxy? It's humanity who will pay the price."

"Do we even know which side to back if it comes to that?" Emmory's question was soft, but it cut through me like a knife.

I stared at him as my brain tried to catch up. The question was so simple, and yet—we had no way of knowing if the Farians were the good ones here. All we had were their assurances that the Shen were bad.

Heretics.

Dangerous.

I swallowed. All we knew about the Shen were what the Farians had told us, and I already knew I couldn't trust any of that as the full truth. "They have been our allies for thousands of years, Emmory," I whispered, the words raw in my throat. "Am I supposed to believe they've been lying to us all this time?"

"I don't know, Majesty."

"As odd as it sounds, you know who I'd back right now if they demanded an answer?" I waited a beat for Emmory to raise an eyebrow. "Fasé, Emmory. She wants peace. These others. They just want more war."

Emmory smiled softly. "You're not wrong," he admitted.

"What kind of chaos am I going to cause if I show up at this supposed summit at the request of the Shen?"

"Technically it's the Solarians doing the asking."

"You know what I mean."

Emmory closed his eyes, his breath hissing out. "I was afraid you were going to say that. They are not safe. I can't condone you going into a meeting with two alien races who could kill you just by touching you, even if one side is supposedly prohibited from doing so."

"It's no more dangerous than anything else we've done, but that's not what I'm talking about. I'm just saying, what if I send them a reply? Tell them I'm willing to listen to their request for my presence at this summit?"

"Best-case scenario? This entire thing ends up as a full-blown war between the Farians and the Shen."

"That's your best case?" I couldn't stop the laugh from bursting out into the air.

"Worst case is Indrana and the rest of humanity get dragged into the war as well," Emmory said, and I muttered a curse under my breath as I cued up the message from the ambassador.

"Your Majesty, I am Heyai Zellin. It is a great pleasure to serve as the empire's ambassador to the Solarian Conglomerate. This morning I received a message from the president and I have attached for you an invitation to a summit that is being held on Earth in two standard months. Your presence has been requested by both parties involved."

"Oh, well, that solves that problem." I rolled my eyes. "Apparently the Farians want me there, too." It was more than interesting that only the Shen had sent me a direct message about it.

Gita muttered a curse.

"If you could provide me with a reply at your earliest convenience, I will pass it along to President Hudson." Heyai smiled and folded her hands together, touching them to heart, lips, and forehead. "Shiva's blessings on you, Star of Indrana."

It was my turn to curse as I rubbed at my face. I held up a hand and started the recording. "Ambassador Zellin, thank you for your message. If you would, please let President Hudson know I need to speak with my people at home before I agree to any requests of this magnitude." I sent it along and then reached into my pocket for the data chip I'd been carrying since that day on Pashati.

23

That evening, Alba paced my room until I stepped into her path and steered her toward a chair. "We've got a three-day trip to Desira. There's plenty of time to sort out any problems. You don't have to do it right now."

"Sorry, Majesty." She smiled sheepishly at me.

I frowned. "What is it? What's bothering you?"

"I don't know, ma'am. I feel—" Alba paused, searching for words. "Everything feels heavy—or maybe *weighted* is a better word. Like we're right on the edge of something big. Have you ever been through a hurricane?"

"Not a lot of those in space," I said, smiling. "And when I was young, we were moved to the summer home in the country several times for safety. I never stayed in the palace through one."

"There's so much preparation, ma'am. So many things to do. Everyone is a flurry of activity. Once that's done, there's this moment before it hits…you don't have anything to do except wait. There's nothing you can do, even though you know this massive thing is bearing down on you." Alba made a face. "Ever since the Farians arrived with that request, I don't know why, but I've felt like that. It didn't go away when the Shen took you, it only got worse. And now they both want you to sit in on a peace summit? Why?"

"I can't blame you," I replied, my voice low. Alba had just given voice to the feeling rolling around in my own gut. It grew worse with every passing day and every new piece of information that landed in my lap. The conflict between the Farians and the Shen would continue to escalate, and I knew that the efforts of the Solarians to bring them to the table would fail.

Forcing a reassuring smile, I patted her on the back. "We'll get through it."

"I know, ma'am." Her shoulders relaxed with my touch. "That's what we do."

The door opened, and Zin came in as Alba got to her feet.

"Let me know immediately if Ambassador Zellin messages again."

"Yes, ma'am."

The door closed behind her. Zin passed over the address to contact Aiz without comment, and I waited a beat before raising an eyebrow in his direction.

"You don't think I should do this?"

"I—don't know, Majesty." Zin made a sound of frustration I was all too familiar with since normally it was directed my way. I bumped my shoulder into his with a chuckle. "I promise not to tell anyone I asked for your opinion if you won't. Alba is nervous about all this. What's your take?"

"All this meaning the Farians and the Shen?"

"If you want you can weigh in on this gunrunner-turned-empress mess, too, I'll just remind you that you're the reason she's in charge to begin with."

"That's colder than space, ma'am."

It was a relief that even after six months of peace, my *Ekam*'s husband hadn't gone back to his painfully formal behavior from when we'd first met. The jokes came mostly in private, but there was still the occasional one where others could hear.

Zin was the perfect complement to Emmory. My *Ekam* could bust his way through a bar fight without breaking a sweat, but Zin could walk into any fancy restaurant in the galaxy and get us a table for twelve, no matter that they were booked six months out. He was kind and thoughtful, a calming influence with just his presence alone. Zin could decode anything, was an amazing cook, and seemed to have a bottomless well of patience—not only for his husband but for me.

To say I adored him was something of an understatement.

"I think we're all waiting for something to happen," Zin said carefully after a moment's silence. "I hope I'm wrong, but it's hard to trust that the peace will last."

"We're looking for something to go wrong because we think it will eventually anyway?"

"Basically." He lifted a shoulder and went back to staring at the message on the wall. "Things like this or the Farians' strange request for you to visit their homeworld are bad enough. But Aiz waltzing in and dragging you underground? Both the Shen and the Farians wanting you to head this summit? Those things don't help settle my nerves."

I leaned into him again. "Stop blaming yourself for what happened in the café, would you? I know you all are. The man is a Shiva-damned ghost. I've been over the recordings and can't figure out how he got in either."

"Emmory mentioned that he let you have them." Zin sighed. "I guess it was too much to hope that we'd get lucky and you'd spot something we all missed."

"Maybe; I'm still looking at it, though. We could still get lucky. So you think we're overreacting?"

Zin shook his head. "I didn't say that. You spent twenty years out there in the black, ma'am, you know what people are capable of. Emmory and I . . . we've seen the dark, hunted it, been kissed by it. We always expect the worst because we're so rarely disappointed.

"Alba, though." He rubbed a hand over his dreadlocks. They'd grown out since I first met him and were gathered in a neat ponytail at the back of his head. "She grew up outside the capital on the coast. Her parents weren't nobility, but they are well-off. She went to university, got a good job in Clara Desai's household. Until we ended up on the run at Red Cliff the most trouble she'd probably ever been in was the time she got drunk with a bunch of college friends and almost got a citation from the local PD."

My laughter slipped out. "I wasn't aware of that."

"He let her off with a warning." Zin smiled. "My point, Majesty, is that I could discount it to a certain degree if it were just us jumping at shadows and being suspicious. That's nearly impossible to train out of a person; but to train *into* one? It would take lot of effort and a lot of time. Alba being worried worries me."

"You think she saw something and just doesn't realize it?"

"It's possible. I'll talk with her, see if I can get her to name what's bothering her beyond a vague feeling."

"I'd appreciate it. I know you're good enough to figure out where it's coming from."

"Found you," he replied with a grin.

"You had help, that doesn't count." The thought of Portis wasn't sharp. Instead it was just a sadness, an emptiness in my heart, and I knew I'd carry that hole for the rest of my life.

The ping of an incoming com on my private address jerked me back to the present before I could fully sink into missing Portis once more.

"It's Alice," I said to Zin, waving him toward the door as I answered it.

It wasn't just Alice, I realized as I put the com up on the wall, but Caterina also.

"We just finished talking to Ambassador Zellin," Alice said without preamble. "You need to go to Earth."

I crossed my arms over my chest and stared at my heir. "Excuse me?"

"Majesty," Caterina said, the word heavily laced with a sigh. "What Her Highness meant to say was that the Matriarch Council believes very strongly that averting a war between the Farians and the Shen will be in the best interests of all. Because both factions have asked for you to head this summit, it seems fairly obvious that you should go. You can pick up your tour after you are finished on Earth."

"Caterina, that still sounds suspiciously like an order."

"It is in the best interests of Indrana," she replied.

"I don't know that I agree with you." I crossed my arms over my chest. "What happened to our 'Indrana is not going to involve herself in this' stance?"

The two women glanced at each other, but it was Alice who answered. "None of us like the idea of Indrana stuck between two warring human forces right now, let alone two alien ones. I don't see how averting a war could be a bad thing. The Solarians want this to happen; both sides are willing to come to the table."

"We don't jump just because the Solarians want us to, Alice."

"You sound like your mother," Caterina replied, and I bit down on my tongue. "I'm sorry, Majesty. That was unkind. My point is, Indrana has a chance to have a real impact on the galactic stage. We haven't been in a position to be this involved for several decades. This will also show them our stability. If we can afford to send you to Earth in the middle of a tour, no one will question that you're secure in your position. Peace between the Farians and the Shen, brokered by the Empress of Indrana—it's not only something for the history pages, but the economic repercussions will benefit us all."

I shook my head with a sigh. "The more I hear about it, the more I'm certain the Farians and Shen have been at war since before there were humans. While I understand the Solarians' concerns with these latest attacks and I certainly share them, I do have to take my own empire into consideration. This conflict between the Farians and Shen is a bigger issue than anyone can guess at." Waving a hand at myself, I pinned the women with a challenging glare. "Yet everyone thinks I'm going to be able to make them agree."

"You are very good at being diplomatic, Majesty."

"Oh hush." I shot Caterina a look. "You were there the last time I was in a negotiation. Did you forget the part about a building coming down on our heads?"

"That wasn't through any fault of your own. You were, in fact, doing very well with things before that happened," Caterina replied, unsuccessfully holding back a smile. "Hail, this might be our only chance to get out of this without war breaking out in our arm of the galaxy."

"I know." I was unwilling to give words to the unease growing spiked thorns into my chest and snapped my fingers as an idea struck me. "I will agree to lead the negotiations on one condition— that the Shen and the Farians agree to Fasé and her faction taking part."

My words surprised me almost as much as they did Caterina and Alice; however, I was much better at hiding it. But my conversation with Sybil about Fasé's importance floated back into my brain, and I suddenly knew it was the right thing to do. Fasé needed to be part of these negotiations for them to have any hope of succeeding. Her faction was growing in power every day, which meant with every day that passed the Pedalion was having to devote more resources to trying to contain her message rather than fighting against the Shen.

"Majesty?"

"I'd have gotten a less shocked reaction asking for someone's head," I muttered, and Gita choked on a laugh. "I didn't stutter, Alice. I'll do it, but only if they agree to this."

"May I ask why, Majesty?" Caterina asked. "We can't afford to have a war break out on any scale, but the amount of destruction the Farians and Shen could rain down on us if you propose something they object to—"

"Fasé's return to Faria is vital to their stability. The more the Pedalion focuses on this schism with her instead of the war with the Shen, the less they're focused on the fight out there. The Shen will defeat Faria if that happens, I've seen this play out so many times before with other governments." I found the explanation easily, as my conversation with Sybil on the beach suddenly made perfect sense. "I don't know about you, but I don't particularly trust the Shen to stop after they roll over the top of the Farians. If we have any chance at preventing a civil war on Faria, it will happen at the negotiation table."

"Yes, ma'am." Both women dipped their heads.

"I'll send my reply to Ambassador Zellin and we'll see what they say. In the meantime, we're going on to Desira, and I'll continue with this Shiva-damned tour as planned until we hear otherwise."

"We'll talk later," Caterina replied.

I disconnected the com after a nod, shoved both hands into my hair, and folded over with a long sigh. "Adityas and Danavas." I inhaled. "We are going to get fucking trampled."

"Maybe not, Majesty," Emmory said. "Maybe having Fasé there will help. I hadn't thought of it, but I don't think the Shen see her in the same light as the Farians do. Maybe her presence will force the Farians to be more open about the changes happening?"

"Either way, it takes the pressure off Indrana," Gita agreed. "If they say no to your requirements, it's on them, not on us."

24

I sent my message to Ambassador Zellin and we continued the tour, passing through Desira and what even I had to admit was a delightful visit with a group of schoolchildren. Taz and Alice joined us via the com for a question-and-answer session. The kids' questions were insightful and thoughtful and at times made their teachers stammer and apologize but made Johar and me laugh.

"Your Majesty." Fasé met us at the *Hailimi*'s boarding door that evening. "What were you thinking demanding I be included in the peace talks?" she asked, reaching for the arm Emmory had just released.

I avoided her hand by dancing back a step. "I was thinking it was a good way to make sure the Shen didn't roll over the top of you all while you were busy fighting with each other."

"Adora will never agree to it," she replied, her brow knotted together in a worried frown. "I appreciate what you are trying to do, but it will backfire on you. You're risking the negotiations for me."

"Have you seen this backfire?"

The question got me a narrow-eyed look that preceded a rather sulky, "No. I'm speaking from experience. I know Adora."

"They asked for me. If they want me involved, this is the cost. You are not omniscient. I managed just fine without you whispering in my ear for the last six months; I think I can handle this."

"Majesty, I—"

"We appreciate your input, Fasé, but you are here as our guest, not as an advisor. I will decide what is best for Indrana. If I want or need your assistance I will ask for it."

"Yes, ma'am." Something of her Imperial Tactical Squad training kicked in and Fasé braced to attention, stopping just short of saluting.

It would seem you haven't entirely forgiven her after all, a voice whispered in the back of my head, but I ignored it as I headed down the corridor.

From Desira, we traveled to Leucht, and I made a special point of requesting to meet Gunnery Sergeant Jasa Runji's daughter, Hannah. The Royal Marine had been on my detail back on Canafey when Emmory was scraping for personnel to fill in the gaps of my dwindling BodyGuard ranks, and she'd acquitted herself quite well in the days that followed.

The fact that Gunny happened to be on my Marine detail that day was simply coincidental, and I certainly didn't manufacture the whole thing so Jasa could see her brand-new grandchild on the empire's dime.

Or no one was going to call me on it if I had. If I was going to be empress I'd use the perks of the position how I damn well pleased.

While I'd been on Leucht, I'd received a reply from Mia, filtered through Ambassador Zellin. Her simple "we will be there" reply hadn't really surprised me. If anything, it felt like Fasé's faction and the Shen had more in common with each other than they did with the Farians of the Pedalion faction.

Now we were headed to Kurma and the Farians still hadn't replied to my demands.

We'd been in space for a week, in warp for most of it, and we would have to refuel in Kurma. I was looking forward to standing on solid ground and breathing open air.

"Bugger me." Staggering away from Johar's punch in the ship's gym, I shot her a disgusted look and shook my head to dispel the ringing before I dabbed at the blood oozing out of my split lip. "Really?"

"You dropped your guard again," Johar said, lifting her chin and winking.

"I have to be in public in two days."

"Don't drop your guard." She grinned at me and I leveled a stare at her that only made her laugh. "Please, you don't scare me just because you ended up with your ass on a throne. I've known you for too long. I still remember that wide-eyed girl on her first job. You were trailing after Hao like a shadow."

I'd met Johar shortly after she'd hooked up with Rai, but long before I ever met Rai in person. My very first job with Hao's crew, officially his crew, not just tagging along, had been to pick up a shipment of expensive paintings from the then-freelancing Johar.

She'd been different then, a man as massive as a Solarian tank with a scowl barely contained by a bushy black beard. Johar's fascination with me had put both Hao and Portis on edge, but I'd found her delightful, and we'd bonded over the local sushi.

The job offer the next morning had been met with a snarled "She's mine" from Hao and my own profuse apology.

"We're a long way from that wide-eyed girl," I replied, putting my hands up again and gesturing for her to come at me.

"Tell me about it, all grown up and ruling an empire." Johar moved in, and I dropped an elbow on her foot when she made a play for my ribs. It barely slowed her down, but I stepped inside her guard and my two quick punches to her gut did the trick.

"You know," Johar wheezed, staggering back a step. "You would have ended up at Hao's right hand when he took over the Cheng if you'd stayed, so I guess either way you slice it, you'd have ended up in charge of an empire."

"Po-Sin's never going to retire," I said, avoiding Johar's next strike with Zin's favorite move.

She stumbled past me, swearing something about damned ghosts, and I laughed.

"Not now he isn't. There was talk of it twenty years ago, though. He was all set to step aside and let Hao take over."

This was the first I'd ever heard of it and I frowned at her, blocking her trio of punches and pivoting to the side to land another strike to her ribs. "What happened?"

"Are you joking?" Johar stopped and dropped her hands while still within my reach, staring at me in shock. I punched her in the face and she staggered back with a pained "Fuck!"

"Don't drop your guard," I suggested.

"Did you say that just to confuse me?" She demanded.

"No. What happened that made Po-Sin decide to not retire? I haven't ever heard anything about it."

"Holy shit, you are serious. No one ever told you." Spinning in a circle with both hands on her head, she laughed at me. "*You* happened, Hail. God-damned green-haired orphan stole Po-Sin's nephew right out from under his nose. That's almost a direct quote, rumor has it."

"I what?" Johar took advantage of my confusion, darting forward and delivering another shot to my face. Stars exploded in my eyes. I stumbled back, too stunned to care much about the pain.

"Hao met you on that cruise ship, invited you to join his crew, and then quietly told his uncle he wasn't interested in taking over the gang and he'd rather be out in the black than trapped behind a desk. He suggested Dailun's father as the replacement. Po-Sin refused. Told Hao to take whatever time he needed to think it over." She pointed at me, backing away and shaking her arms out. "He'd probably deny that it had anything to do with you, but Po-Sin obviously thought you were somehow responsible because Hao did an about-face when you showed. I can't believe that story's been floating around for twenty years and you never heard a thing about it."

"Jo, I—Hao and I, it's not like that. It never has been."

"I know that." She shrugged. "Hell, everyone does. I'll admit early on there was a lot of speculation about you two. When Hao snarled at me for offering you that job, I was convinced he had his eye on you. Thought for sure Portis would die mysteriously during some run before the year was out."

I stared at her, stunned. "Hao would never—"

"Pfft." Johar waved her hand, cutting me off. "It was all wild rumor at the time. It's more than clear now. You're his little sister, Hail, and that man would walk through fire for you. However, he's also trapped, you know that. Hao owes his uncle his loyalty. It's probably why he's been so salty these last few months." Johar grabbed a towel hanging off the ropes and tossed it at me. "Wipe your face, you're bleeding on the mat."

I caught the towel and dabbed at my bloody nose and split lip as I ducked through the ropes. Johar's words shouldn't have been such a revelation. I knew Hao cared about me, I just never thought—I didn't understand why he'd walked away from command of one of the largest gunrunning syndicates and what reason there could have been for it. I didn't believe for a second it was because of me. It wasn't a right Hao had been given because of his birth. He'd earned it. Fought and clawed and worked his way into Po-Sin's trust and his inner circle.

Why had he really refused to take over all these years? And why did everyone—including Po-Sin—think it was because of me?

I didn't sit on the bench along the wall but went down on a knee next to it and then sank the rest of the way to the floor, resting my head on the edge. My face was throbbing now, and Emmory was going to give me a disapproving look right before he marched me to Fasé and made the Farian heal me.

"Have you talked to Rai?" I asked, changing the subject.

Johar's lover controlled one of the largest reaches of space on the tail end of the Orion-Cygnus arm. His smuggling operation was nearly the size of Cheng Po-Sin's, though somehow Rai had kept himself on good terms with Hao's uncle all these years.

I liked Rai, even though I knew better than to trust him to do anything that didn't serve his own interests. We'd worked well together a number of times, most recently after the Saxons failed to kill me on Red Cliff. I'd paid him generously for the assistance and we'd parted on good terms.

"Not since I told him I was staying. Why?" Johar dropped onto the bench and unwrapped her hands.

Putting the towel aside, I peeled off one of my wrappings. I rolled it methodically before I started taking off the other. "Curious. Before he got mad at you, did he say whether the Shen had approached him with an offer about this conflict?"

Johar smiled at me and shook her head. "No, but they will. They'd be stupid not to. Before you ask, I don't know if he's going to say yes. If the money is good?" She wiggled a hand, lips pursed in a moue of thought. "He'll do almost anything if the money is good."

"It's always about money with him."

"He learned early not to trust anything but the numbers." She laughed. "If you want him out of it, your best bet is to make him an offer you know they can't top."

"I don't have that kind of money," I replied with a sigh, and rested my head against the bench.

"Me neither." Johar grinned at me. "But Rai owes me a favor or eight. He wouldn't give it to me, though, at least not while he's sulking."

"Jo, I can't ask you to burn favors on me."

She sat on the floor next to me and put a hand on my knee. "I know. Proper behavior and gunrunners and all that. *Ni modo.*" She shrugged and pursed her lips. "You know I have cared little for proper. That's why I am who I am. If I decide to help I will do it and tell you after. You can't refuse a gift from an old friend, and Caterina at least knows how insulted I will be."

The door slid open as Emmory and Alba came into the quiet

gym, and I swallowed back my laughter as Johar helped me to my feet.

"Do I need to revoke your privileges?" Emmory asked her after a look at my blood-streaked face.

"You can. She's the one who dropped her guard, though." Johar gestured at the bruise spreading around the pale skin of her eye. "She got me back."

"What's going on?" I asked.

"Ambassador Notaras is on the com for you," Alba replied. "Should I call Fasé to—"

"I'll answer it." I waved a hand around the empty gym and then grinned. "I know she hates being kept waiting."

Emmory gave me the Look, and my grin widened until the cut in my lip stung and I felt the blood well again. Dabbing at it with a towel, I headed for the far wall and tapped on the embedded screen.

"*Itegas* Notaras."

Adora brought a hand to her mouth. "Your Majesty, are you all right?"

"I'm fine. You caught me in the middle of a sparring session. What can I do for you?"

The Farian was so clearly thrown for a loss that it took her several seconds to remember why she'd commed in the first place. "Your Majesty, we cannot agree to your ridiculous demands for these peace talks. We have not pursued the impropriety of you harboring the fugitives Sybil and Fasé; however, we will not sit down at a table with them and speak as though they have anything more than heresy to say."

I resisted the urge to comment on how Sybil's status seemed to have shifted from victim to active participant in the Farians' eyes.

"The Shen agreed to my request that Fasé be allowed to join the peace talks, as she represents an integral part of Farian society that deserves a voice."

Adora muttered what I was certain was a curse in Farian and I made note of the word to ask Fasé about. "The Shen will agree to anything that will further conceal the fact that they are also heretics and furthermore, murderers. The Cevallas only agreed because they knew it would anger us."

"Sounds like you should consider not letting it get to you," I replied, and Adora's mouth pulled into a thin line of disapproval. "This isn't a negotiation, Adora. You want me to head the peace talks, those are my terms."

"I will not stand here and let a human involve herself in our politics!"

"Are you fucking kidding me?" I asked with a laugh, and heard Alba's indrawn breath behind me before my chamberlain was able to muffle her surprise. "You asked me for help! You want me to head peace talks between you and the Shen. What's the difference?"

"The difference is that Fasé's transgressions are an internal matter to be handled by the Pedalion," Adora hissed. "You want to bring that all into a public setting and give her even more ears for her insanity. Majesty, you must realize she is sick. Worse, she has infected Sybil with her foolishness."

I knew that everyone around me had stiffened at the insinuation that Fasé was ill; given how little we knew of Farian physiology it had even worried me for a second. But then Adora slipped up—the use of the word *foolishness* told me the only infection in question was Fasé refusing to kowtow to the Pedalion. I cleared my throat.

"*Itegas* Notaras, we have been asked to head this summit by both you and the Shen. One can only assume that is because everyone agreed on it. If you change your mind now, that's on your head. Fasé's presence there is necessary for long-term peace in your region and you know it. Tell the Solarians why you refuse to come to the table and see how they like it." I disconnected the com link and rubbed a hand over my face before I remembered my injuries. The pain was fierce, spiking through my head and down the back of my neck with such strength I almost threw up. "Bugger me."

"Majesty." Emmory closed a gloved hand around my upper arm. "Fasé will meet us at your quarters."

"I'm all right," I protested, but my *Ekam* wasn't listening and I had to start walking with him or be dragged along in his wake.

Fasé stood at the door of my quarters in quiet conversation with Kisah and gave the Guard's arm a squeeze as she turned to us with a smile. "Majesty."

"Dropped my guard," I said, walking through the open door.

"So I see. Have a seat." She cupped my face in her hands after I sat and stared at me for a long moment. Her golden eyes were filled with unasked questions and endless futures.

My eyes fluttered closed as the energy filled me, wrapping around my limbs and my battered face like a soft blanket. I could hear Fasé's soft murmured benediction, most of the Farian still alien and unknown to me, but the tail end of it was familiar.

"You're sorry? Sorry for what?"

Fasé released me. "Your Farian is getting better, Majesty. I should probably remember that."

"You're dodging the question."

"I am." Fasé turned to Johar and held a hand out, but the woman shook her head.

"I'm good. It'll fade on its own and no one cares if I'm all bruised up." Johar grinned, throwing me a salute on her way out the door. "Keep your guard up, Hail."

"I'm trying," I murmured.

25

The massive O-class blue giant star of the Kurma system loomed large in the viewscreen as the *Hailimi* made her approach to the single planet. Previously owned by BreadBasket Enterprises, the terraformed world had applied for imperial annexation almost a hundred years ago when the corporation filed for bankruptcy.

Indrana renamed the system Kurma, because the bright star was the eye of the constellation by the same name you could see from Pashati and a number of other planets in the empire. Kurma, the second avatar of Vishnu, appeared at a time of great crisis for the gods, helping to save their immortality and preventing the *asuras* from drinking the nectar that would allow evil to live forever.

The planet didn't have much choice about their loyalty to the empire when you got right down to it. They were too far from the Solarian Conglomerate for membership; the distance had been part of the reason for BBE's downfall. A hundred years ago, the shipping costs to and from the SC had been too much for the floundering farming corporation to bear. Even now the costs were still prohibitive.

Which made their unwavering and extremely vocal support of me during Wilson's coup even more impressive. Unlike their neighbors on Hothmein, Kurma's people would be happy to see me.

They were shocked to receive royal attention, if the conversations between Alba and Anju Chaturvedi, the person responsible for organizing the trip schedule, were any indication, but happy.

I blew out a quiet breath. Emmory glanced in my direction. "Majesty?" He kept his voice pitched low.

"Part of me wishes someone would take a shot at me, just to break up this tension." I shot a wry smile at him. We both knew I was lying, but it was the best description I could find for what I was feeling.

"We'll deal with it, Majesty. I know..." He hesitated for a moment before looking at me. "I know you have been worried about making the right choices. For what it's worth, I think you have."

A warmth bloomed in my chest at his praise. "Thanks," I said, not looking away from the viewscreen where the planet glowed green in the black. I braced myself on the railing and leaned into Emmory as we started our descent through the atmosphere. My *Ekam*'s solid presence eased my nerves somewhat and I watched the rippling shift of the shields as the crew of the *Hailimi* brought us in with cool precision.

"Nicely done, Ensign," Captain Isabelle Saito said as Ensign Kohli landed the *Vajrayana* with an ease she hadn't displayed when first helming the ship. It appeared I wasn't the only one settling into a new job.

Captain Saito had been part of the skeleton crews scraped together from Admiral Hassan's fleet to pilot the *Vajrayanas* after we'd captured the system of Canafey.

"Commander Nejem, you have the conn."

"Aye, aye, ma'am."

Shaking out my pale lavender sari, I let Emmory lead me off the bridge, Isabelle following behind. The rest of my BodyGuards were waiting in the cargo bay, resplendent in their black uniforms with the twisted crimson star of Indrana above the left breast.

"Majesty?"

I let Stasia do one final check as Emmory issued orders over the com link and shared a half smile with Fasé. The doors were already open, Zin and his team running a sweep with the Marines from the

Hailimi's detachment and the advance team who'd landed a few days before us.

Then a nod from my *Ekam* indicated we were ready to go and I headed for the ramp, Alba falling into step beside me, Emmory just in front.

I regretted my earlier comment about someone taking a shot at me. After all this time it still slipped by me some days that the man in front of me would die for me, without question or hesitation.

Bugger me, Hail, now is not the time to be thinking about this. I hissed the thought at myself, straightened my shoulders, and walked out into the sunshine.

"We thought you would prefer something with a more intimate feel, Your Majesty." Anju gestured at the room, a smile on their darkly handsome face. "But if you dislike this we can move elsewhere."

"No, this is fine, Anju, thank you." Even had I disliked the venue, I wouldn't have requested a move. Emmory and the advance team had already cased out the place and knew all the exits, all the blind spots, anything that would potentially be an issue.

And the venue itself was stunning anyway; we'd taken a short aircar ride to the local university and were now in a brightly lit community room dedicated to agricultural education. The high ceilings should have given an uncomfortable echo to the place, but the wooden tables and comfortable chairs set on either side of the aisle Anju's people had laid out muffled the sound enough that the acoustics were actually gorgeous.

Anju relaxed, their thin shoulders loosening under the carefully pressed white *salwar kameez*. They folded their hands and bowed. "I am going to go check and see how close we are to being ready, Your Majesty."

I murmured a reply and waved a hand, studying the mural painted on the wall behind the chair they'd set up for me. Men were dropping their swords into a river of fire that flowed over a cliff, a waterfall of fury dumping itself into a cauldron. From there the scene shifted: more men bathed in sweat, slaving against the fire as they worked the molten metal into curious shapes.

"They shall beat their swords into plowshares, and their spears into pruning hooks; nation shall not lift up sword against nation, neither shall they learn war anymore."

I glanced at Hao. He stood with his hands clasped behind his back, a long-sleeved black shirt covering him from wrist to neck.

"What are you doing here?"

"I finished early," he replied.

"Plowshares?"

"Farming," he replied, pointing at the next scene further along the wall. "It's from the Christian Bible. An admonition against war Christians never seem to listen to."

"Do any of us?"

Hao shrugged. "War is inevitable. The strong prey on the weak. Those with power only covet more. All you have to do is crack open a history file to see the truth of it."

As depressing as it was, I couldn't disagree with him. Everywhere we'd been in the galaxy, more often than not, that was what we ran into. Naraka, I'd encouraged it because it had been good for business.

"I didn't expect you," I said, turning from the mural to face the room. A room that would soon be filled with numerous citizens of Kurma anxious for a look at the infamous gunrunner empress.

"Like I said, I finished early," he replied. "And I decided it was more fun to explore than stay on the stuffy ship."

"Watch what you say about my ship."

Golden eyes that didn't give away a hint of his emotions fixed themselves on me. "It's stuffy and too small."

"Maybe you should let me buy you a new one like I said I would." Hao's ship had been destroyed by the Saxons, and I'd been so relieved he wasn't dead that I'd promised to buy him a new ship. An offer he kept turning down, though I couldn't quite figure out if it was because of Indrana's financial problems or something else. A single light craft wasn't going to put my government into chaos and he knew it.

That earned me a flicker of emotion, but it was gone so fast I couldn't identify it.

"It would just gather dust at this point." Hao lifted a slender shoulder in a shrug that almost fooled me with its calculated nonchalance.

"Are you ready to tell me what's wrong, honored brother?" I asked in Cheng.

Hao looked back at the mural; a sigh that was little more than an exhalation passed his lips. "This is the wrong place for it, little sister. A discussion of *Yuánfèn* should be—"

"Majesty, we're almost ready." Gita interrupted us and I bit back a curse, watching as Hao retreated, the carefully created mask of Cheng Hao, gunrunner, falling into place.

"BodyGuard Desai," he said with a nod.

My *Dve* was less practiced at hiding her emotions, and the flicker of hurt that appeared on her face with Hao's sneered greeting made me want to reach out and smack my brother so bad that my hand twitched in that direction before I stopped myself.

"Ready," I said, and instead smiled at Gita.

The crowd filed into the room, vibrating with barely contained excitement. I kept the pleasant smile on my face and touched palms with those Jagana led forward. The line continued for more than an hour, with smiles and curious eyes, presents and blessings.

"Your Majesty, this is Askansha and her father, Rahul Bhinder." I took the box from Jagana as the old man dropped into a low bow, the woman at his side awkwardly curtsying.

"Askansha and Rahul, it's a pleasure to meet you." Flipping the catch of the box over with a smile, I lifted the lid and froze.

Gita's curse when she looked into the box sliced through the air, and the BodyGuards on either side of us reacted to it as though it were an order, whipping their guns up and training them on the pair in front of me. Screams echoed in the hall, quickly stifled as people dropped out of the line of fire.

"I scanned it." Jagana's whisper carried through the stunned silence. She reached for the box.

"Don't touch it!" Hao ordered. "It could be trapped."

"Father, what have you done?" Askansha looked from her father to me and back again, panicked eyes wide.

"What was necessary," he replied, standing calmly amid the chaos. "You killed my son, Your Majesty. I felt it right to bring you a token to remember him by. I would have come alone, but my daughter insisted. I would ask you not to hold her responsible for my actions. She had no knowledge of my plans."

The ruined gun lying in the box was no danger to anyone, but I wasn't the least bit surprised Gita had interpreted it as a possible threat. The Grendel UT47 had taken considerable damage in an explosion of some kind and was little more than a twisted hunk of polymer resin. It was an older model of a now-defunct company, something I would have come across early in my years as a gunrunner. There was no way of knowing what shipment this was from, who I'd sold it to, or even when the transaction took place.

"It's clean," Hao said as he finished his scan.

"There's no explosive," Gita murmured almost at the same time, reaching out to me. "Majesty, may I take it?"

I shook my head and shifted away from her before she could grab the box. "No, I'll keep it. This is a conversation better had in private, though. Anju, is there a room nearby that would suit?"

Anju shook themselves out of their shock. "Yes, Majesty. Just this way." They headed for a door to the left side of the room as my BodyGuards herded people toward the exits.

Hao nipped the box out of my hand as I stood, closing a hand around my upper arm before I could take it back. "I want to look at it closer."

"I suspect Emmory will want to as well," I said as my *Ekam* made his way up the aisle. His expression was that stone mask he wore when he was well and truly angry. "I am all right."

Emmory barely spared me a glance. "Jagana, move your ass."

She jerked and followed him toward the doorway Anju was waiting by. I headed in the same direction, exchanging a look with Gita on my way past. Indula and Iza stood on either side of the old man and his daughter. "Stay here with them. We'll let you know when we're ready."

"You're going to talk to them?" Hao kept his voice low.

"Of course I am."

"You didn't kill his son, Hail."

"I sold a gun that may have killed him. Is there a difference?" I held up a hand before Hao could reply. "Not out here, wait until we're inside."

"You didn't look in the box." Emmory was quiet, calm, but in Jagana's face when I came through the doorway. It didn't bode well for the BodyGuard.

"No, sir. He had it in his hands. I assumed you and Zin had checked it at the front. I scanned it before I handed it to the empress. It was clean." Jagana's back was straight, her eyes locked on the wall behind Emmory's head.

Emmory's hand flashed out and I winced. The slap to the side of Jagana's head wasn't designed to do more than ring her bell, but I knew it wasn't the physical discomfort that hurt.

"You've got two working eyes. You should have used them. And assuming things gets people killed." Emmory shifted as though he were going to slap her again, thought better of it, and dropped his hand, fisting it against his thigh. "You were lucky. You only put the empress in an extremely embarrassing situation. You could have just as easily gotten her killed. Either way, I have zero patience for that kind of failure."

"Sir?"

"I'm discharging you from your duties. We'll see about putting you on the first ship headed back to Pashati."

"No, please." Tears filled Jagana's hazel eyes as her composure broke. "It won't happen again, sir, I promise. I'm sorry."

I kept my face blank when Emmory looked in my direction. No matter how much I wanted to argue to give her a second chance, I'd promised my *Ekam* I'd never interfere with his job, and it was a promise I wanted to keep.

I especially wasn't going to interfere with something so serious. We were a long way from Pashati, and even though he could likely task a Marine replacement like Gunny Runji, who knew my Body-Guards from her time with us on Ashva and knew how the Guards ran, it was risky. Jagana had been training with Kisah and Ikeki for six months. Sending her home would put a hole in my Guards, and I knew as well as Emmory did that that could prove more dangerous than this current incident.

"Get out," Emmory said finally, jerking his head toward the door. "Tell the rest of your team you are all off-duty, and I'll see you at oh two hundred hours in front of the empress's quarters."

"Yes, sir." Jagana scrambled for the door. Emmory watched her go, a sigh hovering on his lips.

"Why didn't you look in the box?" I was the only one who could ask the question of my *Ekam* without getting shot.

Emmory jerked, closed his eyes, and muttered a low curse. "He was hiding it in his coat when he came through the doors. None of us saw it, and these damn guns never did set off any weapon detectors. I'm sorry, Majesty. We should have been patting everyone down, but I don't have enough people for that kind of security sweep."

I hummed in sympathy and patted my *Ekam* on the arm. "Don't beat yourself up over it—and don't try to fire yourself, I won't stand for it."

"I thought you said you wouldn't interfere in my BodyGuard decisions."

"I believe I said I'd try my best not to." I glanced at the door Jagana had closed carefully behind herself on her way out. "She made a mistake, Emmory; she's a good Guard."

"He could have killed you."

"Maybe. Had it been an explosive or a live gun, you would have caught it. Had it been something else—" I tried not to smile but failed. "If I lose a fight against a hundred-and-thirty-three-year-old man, I probably deserve whatever happens."

Emmory's muttered curse was extremely uncomplimentary and I laughed as I crossed the room to Hao. He'd set the box on the table and opened the lid. Reaching past him, I pulled out the ruined Grendel and turned it over in my hands. "Explosion, you think?"

Hao took it and made a face. "Almost had to have been. If it had taken a hit from a grenade launcher or something bigger, it would be in pieces." He passed it back to me and shook his head. "They weren't very well made, probably why they didn't stick around all that long once the UT90s came on the market."

"And then Grendel went under two years later. Do you remember when we sold them?"

"Are you serious?" He muttered an ugly curse in Cheng when I stared implacably at him. "This is a load of shit. You can't possibly plan to be responsible for the decisions of every person who bought a weapon from us?"

"I just got done executing no fewer than two dozen people who weren't directly responsible for my family's deaths. They only helped Wilson. How is that any different from what happened here?" I set the gun back in the box and crossed my arms over my chest.

"They were plotting against your empire, against you." Hao stared at me, his golden eyes narrowed. "What is going on? Are you suddenly ashamed of being a gunrunner?"

Emmory stiffened at Hao's tone.

"I am not," I replied, shooting Hao a warning look. "I am, however, capable of taking responsibility for the choices I've made. When did we sell them?"

"When did I sell them, you mean?" he countered.

"You know what I mean, Hao. When did we sell these?"

Hao hissed at me in frustration and shoved a hand into his hair as he started searching through the files on his *smati*. I knew he kept records of every sale he'd ever made and that even if he hadn't, he'd be able to recall it just on memory alone given enough time. However, I let him stall, as he obviously needed the time to wrestle with whatever it was that bothered him about this.

"Three sales," Hao said finally. "Two were on the outer edge; there's no way it would impact a citizen of Indrana unless they were a very long way from home. The third deal was with the Losties in the Solarian Conglomerate, do you remember?"

I did. The Losties were a bunch of mercenaries, little more than a gang of unhappy young people who collected other unhappy young people and did stupid things like knock over transport ships. I'd disliked them immediately; their arrogance and entitlement were eclipsed by only their reckless disregard for the lives of anyone they encountered.

I'd gotten into a fight with one of them on our first meeting, breaking the asshole's nose for a muttered comment about my chest, and Hao had restricted me to the ship for the rest of our stay in port.

"Maybe I should have ignored your order about staying on the ship?"

Hao rolled his eyes. "I would have kicked your ass off right then and we wouldn't be here now." He reached across me and picked up the gun again. "There is no way to prove this came from that shipment, and even if it did, if this dead kid made the choice to run with the Losties? That was his doing. Why is any of that our responsibility?"

"I don't know, Hao." I sighed. "Maybe I won't take responsibility for every single person I ever sold a gun to, but this man is a citizen of my empire, and his son was a citizen of my empire. I owe them an explanation at the very least."

"It wasn't your empire when this happened." Hao tossed the gun on the table with a look of disgust. "We made that SC run less than a year after you officially joined my crew. It was your mother's empire then."

"Bugger me." I shoved a hand into my hair. "I don't know how you can untangle these two things so easily. I may not have been the Empress of Indrana then, Hao, but I am now. Why are you pushing so hard on this? I'm not asking *you* to take responsibility for it."

Hao cleared his throat but didn't respond, and my temper slipped free.

"I am the Empress of Indrana, Cheng Hao, and I will not flinch from my responsibilities." It wasn't meant to be a stab at him, but Hao jerked as if my words hurt, and I sighed. "I think we're talking in circles at this point. I at least owe it to his father to hear him out, to give him peace." Holding up a hand before Hao could say anything else, I continued. "That's enough. We put the gun in his hand, Hao."

"If we hadn't done it, someone else would have. He made the choice to use it."

"I said enough." I don't know if it was my tone or the look that finally shocked Hao into silence, but one of the two things did the trick. "Emmory, is Zin finished searching them?"

Emmory nodded and opened the door at my gesture.

26

Zin and Gita escorted the Indranans into the room as Hao moved away from me and stood on the far side, his arms crossed over his chest.

Askansha dropped to her knees, prostrating herself at my feet with her palms up before anyone could stop her. "Your Imperial Majesty, please, I beg you not to harm my father. His grief has been eating away at his mind for so many years, he doesn't realize what he's done." Her words were muffled against the floor and I waved Zin off before he could pull her away from me.

"Askansha, look at me." I crouched down, laying a hand in one of her upturned ones. "I'm not going to hurt your father. I'll admit there was probably a better way to do that; however, what's done is done. We should have a talk, though, and this conversation is difficult enough to have without you doing it facedown on the floor. Get up and have a seat."

Rahul was already sitting when I helped Askansha to her feet and pressed her into the chair next to her father. I hitched a hip onto the table behind me and folded my hands together.

"Let's start at the beginning. What was your son's name?"

"Tamil, Your Majesty."

"Tell me about him."

For the next hour, I listened to a tale of a young man searching for some way to prove himself and a father who wanted him to do better with his life than he had. There wasn't anything particularly new about the tale, nor was I at all surprised when it ended with Tamil taking off against his father's wishes and ending up in the clutches of the Losties.

"He was killed aboard a Solarian freighter. The only reason they were able to identify his body was because of a vid Askansha had sent him the week before asking him to come home for my birthday." Tears stood in Rahul's dark eyes and he dropped his head into his shaking hands. "The gun was in his pack also. I have held on to it for all these years. When I heard about you I just assumed—you were a gunrunner. You could have sold him the gun." He lifted his head, the expression pleading with me to tell him that hadn't happened.

Putting a gentle hand on his shoulder, I crouched so I could look Rahul in the eyes. "The truth of the matter is, you're right; I could have sold that gun to the Losties who in turn gave it to Tamil. We'll never know for sure. I'll own up to that, even knowing there's nothing I can do to replace your son or relieve you of the grief you've carried for all these years.

"Here's the harder part of this. Your son chose to use that gun. He chose to run with the Losties. His choice, not mine or yours, but his. It cost him his life."

Tears filled the old man's eyes. "I drove him there. I was too hard on him."

"You made your choices, same as the rest of us, and you get to live with them. I face it every day." I folded my hands and shook them in his direction. "I have perhaps gotten too good at hiding that fact, but I can promise you that not a day goes by since I came home that I don't ask the gods for clarity and wisdom in dealing with my past. May I keep the gun?"

Rahul hesitated and for a moment I thought he would refuse. However, he finally nodded. "I think perhaps it will better serve you as a reminder of the lives you are now responsible for, Your Majesty, and better serve me as only a memory."

Nodding, I gripped his shoulder briefly and smiled. "Shiva's blessings on you, Rahul."

"And on you, Majesty."

"Thank you, Majesty," Askansha said, as her father moved off to speak with Emmory. "He has been holding on to this grief for so long. I think, maybe now, he'll let it go and live the rest of his days playing with his grandchildren."

"Maybe." I reached out and squeezed her hand. "Your father needs help, and I will gladly provide the money."

"Majesty, we don't want your money."

"It's not an offer, it's an order." I tempered the words with a smile. "Grief is a funny thing, it sneaks up and sinks its teeth into us and never really releases us. I can see it in your eyes, too, even though you've pushed it aside for his sake."

A tear slipped free, sliding down her cheek, and she brushed it away. "I loved my brother, Majesty, but I'm still so angry at him. He threw his life away. He was selfish and spoiled and didn't care that he hurt the people who loved him. My father has painted over his memory with this varnish of sainthood and it infuriates me. He's wasted all these years grieving and these past months obsessing over you. I needed him, and he wasn't there." She glanced over her shoulder at her father. "I would be as selfish as Tamil if I told him all this. So I don't." Straightening her shoulders and forcing out a smile that broke my heart, she curtsied again, smoother this time. "You have carried your share of grief, Majesty. I hope you find some rest from it all. Thank you."

I watched her join her father, wrapping her arm around his waist and escorting him from the room. Emmory looked in my direction, and I waved a hand. He nodded and left Hao and me alone. Hao didn't move when the door closed, but his shoulders tensed.

Staring down at the warped and twisted Grendel sitting in its little box, I took a deep breath and dove into the conversation my brother had been trying to avoid for months.

Yuánfèn could be translated as *fate*, but I knew there was so much more weight to the word than that and I suspected whatever it was had to do with this odd orbit Hao and I had found ourselves in for the last twenty years.

"Gita interrupted us earlier. Now we are alone. Are you going to tell me what's going on with you?"

"It doesn't concern you, *sha zhu*."

I took the ruined gun out of the box and rolled it over in my hands. "You concern me, big brother," I replied in Cheng. "You have not been yourself lately. I can see it clear as sunshine through glass. You used to trust me enough to confide in me; but now it seems I am not worthy enough to share a burden you carry." I crossed the room and dropped to a knee behind him. "What must I do to regain the faith you once had in me?"

"Hail." My name was followed by a curse, and Hao turned, yanking me to my feet. "Don't. You can't do things like that. You are the bloody empress of Indrana, not a member of my crew."

"As we have established, but I am your sister, am I not? Or have we been lying to each other all these years?"

His hands flexed on my upper arms, tightening to the point of pain as my words stabbed at the demon Hao was wrestling with.

"I don't understand what is bothering you." I pushed further. "What is going on, Hao? Why you won't just tell me what the fuck is going on so I can help you?"

"There is nothing you can do. You are the *problem*, not the solution. My life would have been easier if you'd been the orphan you claimed to be!" He shoved me away, the muscles of his jaw tightening as he closed his eyes and jammed both hands into his hair.

Shock and hurt coursed through me, a thousand cuts opening up all at once from the sharp edges of his words. I was the problem, or rather the Empress of Indrana was the problem. I felt the tears building in the back of my eyes as I struggled to keep this last little piece of my past from slipping away. It was an awful choice—Hao or the empire—but one I'd already made, and obviously one that had split us in ways I'd never even considered.

Hao opened his eyes, visibly getting his temper under control before he reached for me. "Hail, I didn't mean that."

I backed away. "No. Fine." Putting my hands up between us and fighting off the tears I didn't dare let fall, instead I grabbed onto the anger and held it up like a shield. "That's fine. If I'm the problem, I will just—I'll get out of your fucking way. Go back to your life. Leave my ship here, I'll have Alba help you find something to buy or transport off—"

"Would you listen to me?"

"No, I have obviously been wrong about us. We aren't—" The words stuck in my throat so I pushed open the door, ruined gun still clutched in my hand, startling my BodyGuards. No one said a word out loud, though I'm sure the conversation over the com link was fast and furious as they scrambled to catch up with me when I strode from the room. I kept my eyes locked on a spot several meters ahead of me while I chanted, *Don't fucking cry* in my head to the rhythm of my shoes on the tile.

"Straight to the aircar, Majesty?" Emmory murmured the question near my ear after he matched his steps to mine.

"Yes, just you and Zin, please. Everyone else can follow. And give my apologies to Anju if you would for not staying longer."

"I will, Majesty." Emmory peeled off, Zin taking his place without comment. Gita and the others were in front of me when we cleared the door.

I pasted a smile on my face and held up my free hand to the crowd gathered several meters away from the entrance. Scanning the blur of faces more out of habit than anything, my eyes caught on a pair of warm brown eyes in a round, wrinkled face. The old woman smiled, folding her hands together and pressing them to heart, lips, and head. I nodded in acknowledgment and then let Zin usher me into the aircar.

Emmory joined us and I curled into a ball on the opposite seat as the aircar took off, staring dry-eyed at the scenery as it sped by.

The sticky *sindoor* on my forehead had dried, and it flaked against my fingers as I touched them to my heart, lips, and head before pressing them to Hanuman's foot.

"Durgaam kaj jagat ke jete sugam anugraha tumhre tete."
The burden of all difficult tasks of the world become light with your kind grace.

It had been a very long time since I'd heard a priest recite the devotional hymn to Lord Hanuman, though the words tripped through my brain, recalling moments when Iza and Indula had murmured one phrase or another to each other.

Now it was my turn, though the words in my throat were as thick as the paste the young priest had swiped down my forehead with a gentle smile.

My faith had always been a mutable thing, shattered when my father died and lost during my time in the black despite Portis's best efforts. I'd thought that maybe I'd found it again when I came home, but the statue Zin had bought me became part of the rubble of the palace, and I think my faith had gone with it.

It was a silly thing, but as the days stretched on and my hours were filled with more practical things, I couldn't find it in myself to believe again. I did my appearances as expected, but other than that conversation with Ganesh right before we'd left Pashati I couldn't bring myself to believe overmuch.

Life was too capricious. If I believed in the gods, I had to believe they were equally capricious. That only made me angry, so I'd discarded the whole train of thought time and again when it floated to the front of my brain.

The celebration of Hanuman Jayanti on Kurma was our last day on planet, and so I played the dutiful empress and went through the motions, no small part of me waiting for the gods themselves to strike me down for my lack of devotion.

I got to my feet, the folds of the gorgeous blue sari that had been a gift from the president of the local university and her wife floating around me like falling leaves. Pressing my hands together, I bowed low and then turned from the statue. My BodyGuards formed up around me and we headed from the temple.

A week had passed since the fight and I'd settled into numbness. I'd attended several more functions and a wholly boring party hosted by the same university president and her wife where I was relieved to have a panic attack over an accidental broken wineglass that required me to leave earlier than planned.

I'd received four messages from Hao so far that I'd been ignoring, partly because I couldn't bring myself to read them but also because I had moved from sad to furious back to sad and I wasn't sure my heart could take any more.

"Are we staying at the hotel tonight?" I asked Gita as we got into the aircar.

"Yes, ma'am. Unless you'd rather go back to the *Hailimi*?"

"No," I said. "I'll sleep in a regular bed while I still have the chance."

"They are more comfortable, aren't they?"

I turned away from the window to offer a small smile and then looked back at the fields of newly sprouted wheat stretching out across the open space. Wrapping my arms around myself, I pressed my head to the window and stared at my reflection.

"Majesty, are you all right?"

"I'm fine."

"I know I may be overstepping here, but if you need someone to talk with? I am here."

I reached for her hand, squeezed it, and then released her with a sigh. "If I knew what I had done, I could talk about it." My reflection in the window blurred as the tears gathered and then slipped free. "But I don't even know that. I only know my brother is angry with me because I am me and there is nothing I can do to fix that, is there? I made my choice to stay with the empire and he has made his."

"Hail." Dropping the formality of her job, Gita slid across the car seat and pulled me into her arms. "It's not you. Whatever issue has crawled up that man's ass and died there is not your fault. Please believe that."

Part of me knew it and the laughter tangled with my tears. "I wish things had been different between you two. Watching you kick his ass for this would be the highlight of my year."

"I still might, Majesty," Gita said, releasing me. "I won't lie."

"Watch out for his sweeps if you do, he's damn tricky with them." I rubbed my hands over my face. "I'm sorry I've been rather difficult to deal with on this stop."

"You don't have anything to apologize for."

"I know; I still will, though." I mustered up a small smile as the aircar dipped down to the front of the hotel. It disappeared when I spotted Hao and Dailun standing on the wide steps.

Dailun smiled, dropping into a bow as I climbed the steps. Hao remained upright and I let my eyes settle on his for a moment before I looked down at Dailun with a smile.

"How was temple, *jiejie*?" he asked, coming up out of the bow with a smile of his own.

"It was nice." I leaned in to kiss his cheek. "Are you headed out?" I couldn't bring myself to ask if Dailun was going with Hao or staying with me. Alba had already reported Hao's refusal to either purchase a new ship or allow her to transfer credits into his account.

"I believe we are traveling the rest of the way with you. I can find someone to take the *War Bastard* back to Pashati if you'd rather avoid the wear and tear on her."

"No," I said, quickly enough that Hao raised an eyebrow. "You're enjoying flying her, go ahead. I'll see you on our next stop."

Dailun dipped his head. "Of course."

I started for the door, Gita at my side, stopping when Hao spoke.

"Your Majesty, may I have a moment?"

"You may not," I said, not turning around.

"Hail—"

"Her Majesty doesn't wish to speak with you." Gita did turn, her hand on her Hessian.

"How am I supposed to apologize if she won't talk to me?"

"That is not our problem, Cheng Hao." Gita's voice was ice. "It's yours, as is the fact that you have five seconds to step away before I shoot you."

"You wouldn't dare—"

The hissing whine of her Hessian 45 powering up was enough to shock Hao into silence. I heard Dailun whisper something and the echo of their footsteps moving away before Gita rejoined me.

"You wouldn't have shot him," I murmured.

"Not anywhere important. He is your brother, after all," she replied, and it was enough to drag a laugh out of me.

27

Still nothing from the Farians?" Alice sighed at my head shake. "You'd think the Solarians would lean on them as least as hard as they did the whole time Indrana was fighting with the Saxons."

"The Solarians leaned on us because it was disrupting their shipping opportunities, nothing more."

"Listen to you, sounding like a bitter old politician," Alice teased, and I chuckled.

"I was bitter before I ever left home, believe me. What's new at home?"

"Taz got the proposal approved by the university committee. Despite the prime minister's attempts to block him, the university presidents all voted in favor of his plan." Alice smiled. "I'm proud of him. You should have seen how happy he was."

"I'll bet. He worked hard on that." We'd made him rewrite the proposal four times until he'd been cursing at me, but according to Alice's keen eye the final draft had hit all the right points. "It's a great first step and I'm looking forward to it doing so well on Pashati that they move the program to the other universities in the empire."

"So am I." Alice shifted on her couch with a muttered curse. "I will also be relieved when this little girl decides to make her appearance."

"Soon?" I'd lost track of time on Pashati, which was common out in the black.

"A few weeks, hopefully no more than that. Even money is on her showing up before the Farians finally agree to the peace talks."

I snorted with laughter. "Shiva will show up before they agree to it, from the sounds of things."

I'd gotten several messages from Ambassador Zellin and from Mia; even Fasé had eventually calmed down to the idea of being involved in the peace talks—likely because of Sybil's interference. Everyone was on board for the talks.

Everyone except for the Farians, who were silently stonewalling the Solarians, and the tension in my gut had only gotten worse with every day that passed without a reply.

"I'll admit I was unsure at first about your plan, but I have spoken with Sybil and she put me in touch with Farians here on Pashati who support Fasé's cause." Alice shook her head. "I think Fasé—and by extension, Indrana—is on the right path here. Faria has been isolated for a long time; their people are growing tired of it when they know there is a whole galaxy waiting for them."

"Did they give you a sense of how many Farians back home support Fasé?"

"Not specifically," Alice replied. "They are still having to be very cautious because of the Pedalion's enforcers. I get the impression there are a lot, and their numbers are growing every day. It could be enough to overthrow the Pedalion even without peace with the Shen."

"We still need that," I said, shaking my head. "The Shen aren't going to stop just because Faria has a change in management."

"True." Alice nodded. "I don't trust the Shen; I don't care how easily they accepted these peace talks or your insistence on Fasé joining them."

"Don't worry." I laughed. "I don't either. They are arrogant, especially Aiz, strolling into my café like he owned it. Both of them expecting me to just up and leave because I couldn't possibly be happy as the empress."

"I think we've all misjudged you," Alice replied with a smile. "Have you had a chance to read any of the reports I've sent you on the councils?"

"Not yet, but I will. We've got a decent stretch of time in the black once we leave Hothmein." The contested stop on the tour was also the smallest stop on the tour, I'd be meeting with even fewer people than at the HCL research facility, but I was especially looking forward to seeing the new governor, Jia, and her husband, Nakula.

The pair had been inseparable since the former intelligence agent had rescued Jia from the Saxon attack on Canafey. Before that though, I'd known Nakula as a gunrunner, when his deep-cover missions had put us on the same deal for some brand-new plasma cannons from the Solarians.

"Do it," Alice said. "The short version is integration is going really well. There've been some obvious difficulties, but people are starting to come around to the idea that this really is what's best for Indrana."

"Good," I replied. "It's nice something is going smoothly."

"Are you okay?" Alice asked. "You seem sad."

"I—" The answer got stuck in my throat and I closed my eyes for a moment. When I opened them again, Alice's frown had deepened. "Hao and I—I'm all right." Talking to Alice about Hao just felt like it would rip the rift between my brother and me even wider. I'd already decided to talk to him on Hothmein; maybe with Nakula there Hao would finally admit what was bothering him.

"You're not," she said. "But it's okay if you don't want to talk about it. I'm here if you need to."

"I appreciate it." I put a hand up on the screen. "Thank you, Alice, for caring."

"Get used to it." She smiled and brushed away a tear. "I'd better go. If I ruin my eye makeup and Yina has to fix it, I'll be late and Taz will never let me hear the end of it."

"Tell him hi for me, and congrats on the proposal. I'll talk to you tomorrow."

"Of course, Majesty. Have a good evening."

I was curled up in my bed on the *Hailimi* that evening, absently scrolling through the reports Alba had filtered out for me, when the conversation with Alice floated back into my head.

Strolling into my café like he owned it.

Aiz hadn't strolled into the café. There'd been no video of him coming through the door. Nothing we could find of him sneaking in through somewhere else, but a horrible thought lodged itself in my mind and I scrambled upright.

"Fuck me," I muttered, and brought up the video of Aiz in the café. I scrolled through the footage until I found what I was looking for. It was a piece from Zin's recording, just before the incident. "Stop." I cued up Iza's recording from her spot by the front door and watched as Hao came back into the café. Only it wasn't Hao. The walk was wrong.

I went back to Emmory's recording, watching as Hao said goodbye with a brush of his hand over my shoulder after I'd shooed him away from the table. He left the café, turned the corner and then someone who looked like Hao but wasn't reappeared with a smiling apology, first to Iza and then to Zin, as he came back in the door.

"No. Please no. Tell me you didn't, Hao." I muttered the useless prayer as I kept watching. My gut clenched in misery as not-Hao vanished from Zin's sight behind a display, and a second later Emmory finished his sweep of the café and realized that Aiz had a hold of my wrist.

I pulled surveillance of the building, easily finding the corner Hao had gone around, and I watched as he went into an alleyway only to come right back out several heartbeats later.

"He wouldn't have. Oh, Dark Mother, he wouldn't have." I tried to tell myself the lie. Aiz could have been hiding in that alleyway.

He could have slipped out after Hao had passed him by. He could have—

"How did he know I'd be there unless Hao—? Bugger me."

The door slid open and Emmory came in. "Majesty, are you all right? Your readings are all over the place."

Shaking my head, I swallowed down the grief and got up from my bed to put the recordings onto the screen. "I found it," I said, my voice raw as though I'd been screaming. "I know how Aiz got past you in the deli."

"Gita, Zin, get in here," Emmory said over the com link as he watched the recordings and I showed him what I'd found. "How could he have pulled this off?"

"There are black market masking programs by the bushel. We used one when we took Canafey, remember?" I said. "We used to use them all the time for small jobs. They won't stand up to most scanners, but they're enough to fool *smatis* on the first glance—" I gestured at the screen as Gita and Zin came in the room. "It works perfectly on simple con jobs where people are expecting to see exactly what they see."

Gita's curse was ugly and I swiped at the tear that leaked down my face. My brain kept scrambling for an explanation that didn't involve Hao betraying me even as all the times I'd insisted on his loyalty slapped me in the face.

"Maybe Hao didn't know?" I said, grasping for anything to prove my eyes wrong. "Maybe Aiz just saw the chance and took it?"

"No," Zin said, shaking his head. "I'm sorry, Majesty, but this was planned out, every detail. Aiz Cevalla isn't the kind to leave things to chance."

"We're going to have to scan anyone who comes within a meter of her," Emmory said, his mind already whirling with plans on how to protect me from this new threat.

Zin nodded. "I'll get to work on something right away."

"I am going to cut him into pieces," Gita swore.

I pressed a hand to my mouth and sank back against my desk. "I asked him if Po-Sin had been approached by the Shen, and he didn't give me an answer. I am a fucking gullible idiot. I thought—" I couldn't stop the tears, could barely keep myself from screaming.

"Majesty, I'm sorry." She apologized, reaching for my hand.

"Why? Why would he do this? It doesn't make any sense."

"I don't know." Gita squeezed my hand and then released it, wrapping an arm around my shoulders instead. "The latest report from Caspel said there are more indicators every day that Po-Sin is going to declare the Cheng as allies of the Shen. Hao is his second-in-command. It's not a position you just walk away from."

"I thought we were family." The whisper was loud in the silence. "Bugger me. Where's the *War Bastard*?" I pushed away from the desk, dislodging Gita with my sudden movement.

"A day ahead of us, ma'am. They'll be at Hothmein in about seventeen standard hours," Zin replied.

"I don't want a word of this to leave this room, is that understood?"

"What are you planning?" Emmory asked.

"I don't know yet, but I'm going to have a talk with my brother." I bared my teeth at my *Ekam* as my anger fed upon my grief. "And possibly put my foot up his ass in the process."

"Majesty, you're sure you want to wear one?" My maid shook the pair of delicate crowns with a hesitant smile on her face.

"I'm sure," I said, and reached for the silver one. Had I been in a better mood, I would have teased her about the way she held it out of my reach, but my discovery of Hao's betrayal lingered in my mouth like poison even twenty-four hours later.

Without a doubt, at least part of her concern was that for what was probably the first time I was wearing a crown with my traditional black uniform. It was a deliberate choice, a reminder of who I was, both to myself and to anyone who saw me.

Stasia slid the crown into place, fussing for far less time than she would have spent had my mood been better, and then stepped back with a second smile and a nod.

I returned the nod, too weary to even try for a reassuring smile, and headed out of the bedroom into the main room of my suite aboard the *Hailimi*. Emmory and the others came to attention, a precise line of black in the center of the room.

"Ready, *Ekam*?"

"Yes, Majesty."

I'd debated wearing a sari and discarded the idea in much the same way I'd had to give up on the desire to march down the ramp and kick Hao's ass the second we landed.

The crown was enough. There was still a risk that something could go sideways here, and if I had to get into a fight I'd rather not be wearing something ridiculously formal.

"You look imperial," Johar said, one black eyebrow arched as we exited my rooms and headed for the cargo bay. "What's the occasion?"

"Part of the point of this tour is to remind people who I am," I said with a smile that got lost before it hit my eyes. Johar noticed, but didn't comment. "This seemed as good a time as any."

"Fair enough."

Johar was relaxed, all loose limbs and easy smile. I hated that I distrusted her now, because if I couldn't trust Hao, how could I trust her? I wondered if she was reporting back to Rai while lying to me about moving to my empire. I hated that it bothered me at all, that'd I'd grown so attached to her presence.

And I hated Hao for planting the seed in the first place.

The door opened, revealing the spotless interior of the main hangar for the 101st Division. To the left I spotted Hao and Dailun, deep in conversation. Directly ahead of us stood a small group of military personnel and civilians. General Prajapati came to attention, the others following suit while the civilians looked on.

I put a little more warmth in my smile, straightened my shoulders, and headed off the ship.

"Your Imperial Majesty." Maya Prajapati dropped her salute at my nod. "Welcome to Hothmein."

"General. Everything under control here?" I glanced past her to where Colonel Lou Nyr stood, and the smaller woman gave me a nod. General Maya Prajapati had disgraced herself by throwing her support to my cousin upon my return home, but her redemption seemed to be going well.

There had been protests over my decision to move her from Basalt IV to Hothmein for obvious reasons. Putting someone whose loyalty was in question on a planet that had been in full support of Wilson's coup was questionable at best. However, I'd understood Maya's reasons for going up against me upon my return—she hadn't been the only person happy about a former gunrunner sitting on the throne. The fact that Wilson had been careful to keep her out of the loop on the real reasons for their power grab told me a lot about Maya's loyalty to Indrana.

Colonel Nyr was the general's keeper, with orders to shoot her if Prajapati so much as hinted at taking a stand against me again. Because of that, and the general's ferocious stand on Basalt IV, I'd felt she was the perfect choice to send here.

"Yes, ma'am," General Prajapati replied. "As requested, your arrival wasn't announced until just after you touched down. Governor Ashwari was unhappy about it, but that's life." She gestured over her shoulder at the tiny civilian waiting just behind her.

"Jia," I said, extending both my hands and crossing over to the former governor of Canafey Minor. She was the other reason I wasn't the least bit concerned about Prajapati.

"Your Majesty." Jia took my hands and I bent down to press my cheek to hers, throwing a wink to the lean man standing next to her. "You gave us no advance notice."

"I know. You can have Nakula shout at me later; I'm sure he

wants to." I squeezed her hands once and then let her go. "This is a shitty reward for all your assistance, but I am deeply grateful you agreed to it."

"It's not so bad," Jia replied, her smile twisting her cupid's-bow mouth upward. Jia Li Ashwari had been instrumental in our success at Canafey. The governor, with help from Nakula, had escaped Saxon custody and fled with the lock codes for the brand-new *Vajrayana* ships that were being built in the shipyards around Canafey Major. Ships that had been useless thanks to the Saxon attack. Because of her, we'd been able to retrieve the ships, take back the Canafey system, and eventually use those *Vajrayanas* in the fight for Pashati.

"Majesty." Nakula Ashwari bowed, gray eyes narrowing slightly as he came up.

I stepped forward and embraced him, pressing my cheek to his with a smile.

"You're upset." His voice was pitched low against my ear, and I kept my expression neutral as I pulled away, a tiny hum in the back of my throat.

When I'd met Nakula, I'd known him as Vasha, a fellow gunrunner and smuggler. We'd worked several jobs together over the years. But only after he appeared in Santa Pirata with Jia had I discovered he was a GIS agent whom Caspel had tasked with rescuing my governor from the hands of the Saxons.

"How's married life?" I asked, and watched his mouth tighten in amused annoyance.

"It's good," he replied. "Even if I think it was an abuse of your powers to suggest you were going to order me to get married."

"You were being extremely obstinate about the two of you coming from different worlds," I said with a smile and a wink. "The only reason I didn't order you is because I knew Jia would wear you down eventually."

Jia slipped her arm through Nakula's with a wink of her own. "I didn't even have to do that much, Majesty. He finally realized that just because my family is established doesn't mean they were going to hate him for growing up poor. My offices are this way and my staff is waiting. I know Emmory will feel better once you're not out in the open, though I promise things have calmed down a lot here in the last few months."

I followed the pair, Alba slipping into the open spot at my side as we headed through the hangar and into a long, brightly lit corridor.

"Major Gill." I held a hand out to the broad ITS officer and she took it, a smile creasing her weathered face. "Good to see you again."

"Majesty." Ilyia nodded to me and then to Emmory. The ITS officer had been in charge of the original squad who'd brought me home. Several of her people had been killed during an explosion set by a more violent sect of the *Upjas* and Lieutenant Aashi Saito had been promoted to captain a month ago and assigned her own squad. Ilyia's squad was composed of all new faces, but I trusted her and that was enough.

"The way is clear," she said. "Things are quiet. We'll keep an eye out though for trouble once the news spreads that you're here."

"Do we honestly think there will be trouble?"

Ilyia shook her head. "It's hard to say, ma'am. The majority of the population doesn't seem to care about the empire one way or the other. It was the former governor and the military command who were in Wilson's pocket. But we get paid to think there will be trouble, so it doesn't catch us flat-footed when it happens."

"Fair enough." I patted her on the shoulder and continued down the hall. Emmory stayed behind and Gita slipped easily into the empty space.

I fell back half a step, letting Alba chat with Jia as we headed down the hallway so that Dailun and Hao could catch up.

"How was your trip?" Dailun asked.

"It was good enough."

"Are you going to let me apologize? Or are you still mad at me?"

Hao said without preamble, putting a hand on my arm. He kept his voice low, but I was still surprised when Gita snarled at him.

"Get your hand off the empress. Now."

Hao took in my *Dve*'s hand on her gun and carefully removed his own off my arm. His eyes slid up to the crown on my head and then back to the floor. "My apologies for the familiarity, Your Majesty. I was out of line the other day and my words were hurtful."

I reached out and put a hand on his shoulder, the material of his long-sleeved shirt smooth under my fingers. "They were, and I forgive you. I trust you," I lied, and felt him tense, almost imperceptibly, under my hand only because I was waiting for it. "Whatever the problem you have with me, when you're ready to talk to me about it, I'm here."

Hao looked up at me, an unidentifiable tangled pain washing over his face. I stepped hard on the sympathy that blossomed in my chest, all too aware that Nakula's intense gray gaze was settled on us. Even now, here I was being a sentimental fool when Hao was still a gunrunner to the bone.

"Jia, tell me more about Hothmein. I did some reading on the way over." I gave Hao a little push in Nakula's direction and slipped my arm through Jia's as we reached her offices. The twins were already in place, and I exchanged a smile with my BodyGuards before turning my attention to the civilians standing behind them.

"Your first meeting is with some of the salt miners, Majesty. I'd hate to steal their moment," Jia replied. "Let me introduce you to my staff."

Thanks to the incident in Kurma, and Emmory's general distrust of the citizens of Hothmein, the pre-meeting screenings were far more thorough.

I disliked it immensely because it cast a pall of nervous energy over the entire proceedings, but at the same time I wasn't about to protest. Emmory would pack my ass back up on the *Hailimi* and we'd be on our way.

I stood outside the main offices for Indranan Salt Limited, one of the top three companies mining salt in our corner of the galaxy, surrounded by Guards, Marines, and ITS troops; plus Hao was on my left, Nakula and Jia were behind me, and the young man who'd been chosen to take us on the tour looked as though he was going to pass out from sheer fright.

My *smati* identified him as Pablo Zatrevie, though he'd been introduced to me as Zat. "Relax," I whispered. "I promise I won't do anything awful if you won't."

"Yes, ma'am, uh, Your Majesty."

"*Ma'am* is fine. How'd you end up here, Zat?"

"The pay is good?" Zat looked at the floor and sighed. "I probably should have said something a little more inspirational, huh?"

"It's a justifiable reason for taking a job," I replied with a smile. "How did you hear about it?"

"There was a recruiter for the company at Krishan University. I'd just started my second semester, but I wasn't—" He made a face and glanced up at me before returning his eyes to the floor. "I wasn't doing all that well. I went to college because my parents expected it. This seemed like a steady paycheck."

"You're from Pashati?"

"Yes, ma'am. My parents live in the Bilmont Province. I got to see them last year."

"Majesty, room's clear."

I smiled at Zat and gestured for him to lead the way into the control room as he began his practiced spiel about how the mining operation worked.

"Salt is extremely important," I said, and looped my arm through Hao's, trying to act as though I didn't want to punch him then and there. "Humans can't survive without it."

"Correct, Majesty," Zat said when he heard me. "Lucky for us it's plentiful in the universe. The other three planets in this system were once all oceans. The climates shifted and the oceans evaporated.

279

"Everything is automated," he said, gesturing at the bank of screens behind him as he wrapped up his script. "There are personnel on the planets and we do also occasionally go down into the tunnels themselves to do equipment maintenance and for tunnel checks."

I couldn't suppress the shudder that ripped through me, and it didn't go unnoticed. Hao's jaw flexed, the muscle ticking away by his ear, and he swallowed but didn't look at me.

"I am not a huge fan of tunnels." I looked over at Hao for just a moment as I said it and watched Nakula's eyebrows furrow with curiosity. "This part isn't so bad, but if you put me in a dark tunnel? Things get a little ugly."

Hao looked away.

We moved through the tour, with me asking questions and various members of the mining crew speaking up to answer. Lunch was in the tiny mess hall, and Johar entertained the miners with a long-forgotten—and heavily edited—story about the first time Portis and I had met Bakara Rai.

"She's having too much fun." I elbowed Hao. "You should take lessons."

"Chatting it up with miners isn't really my bailiwick," he replied.

"Why are you so grumpy?" I knew very well what the answer was. I also knew I hadn't been helping matters with my carefully placed barbs.

"What's with Gita? I thought she was going to shoot me for touching you earlier."

The question surprised me. "Maybe she's mad at you."

"What for? She dumped me," Hao hissed.

"Doesn't mean you didn't break her heart," I replied, and went back to my food.

28

Are you going to clue me in on what's going on?" Nakula asked later that afternoon as we stood shoulder to shoulder at the wide window that dominated the southern wall of Jia's waiting room.

"I'm so busy with being empress these days you'll have to be more specific."

Nakula ran his tongue over his teeth and subvocalized his next thought over a private com link. *"Hail, what the fuck is going on with you and Hao? You keep looking at him like you want to punch him in the throat and he's wound tighter than a sparse-coil."*

I slid a sideways glance to where Hao was in conversation with Johar and Dailun on the other side of the room before I answered. *"It is the worst sort of feeling to not know who you can trust."*

"He's a complicated man, Hail, but he—"

I looked back at the window, my reflection on the reinforced glass overlaid on the bustling streets below us. For just a moment I let the sorrow I'd gone to such great lengths to hide show on my face. *"He's been working for his uncle this whole time. I assume you heard about Aiz's showing up in Krishan and kidnapping me. He only got close to me because Hao gave him access."*

"Hail, he wouldn't."

"I have video proof, Vasha."

The grief on his face was identical to mine, swallowed just as quickly by fury. I snapped my hand out, closing it around Nakula's before he could pull his gun free, and gave a silent shake of my head. *"Do not. I'll handle this."*

Nakula took a breath and made his expression impassive, but the fury in his eyes was painfully clear and I squeezed his hand once before I let go.

"I should be less surprised," he said finally, grief sliding back into the empty space when the anger drained out of him. *"There has been an enormous amount of chatter about Po-Sin lately. I just assumed."* He sighed out loud, too quiet for anyone but me to hear. *"I assumed that with all the talk you would show up here with him in tow. Just under better circumstances."*

"Why is that? Po-Sin's about to announce his partnership with the Shen and my brother will go where he is ordered."

"I don't think it's as simple as all that, Hail. Yes, we've caught wind of Po-Sin and the Shen. The Shen are buying up mercenaries faster than a casino winner buying shots for the bar. But there's more than that. Lately there's been a whole lot of chatter that sounded like Hao was about to break with Po-Sin."

"What?" My question slipped out in the open air before I could stop it, and I could feel everyone's eyes on me.

Thankfully Jia broke the awkward silence by coming out of her office. "Majesty, do you have a moment?"

I followed Nakula into her office, closing the door behind me after a quick look at Emmory.

"Everything is set," Jia said. "I've got Caspel on the com link. He's got more news about the unrest between the Farians and the Shen." She gestured at her chair.

I sat and the screen flickered to life.

"Majesty." Caspel nodded, his gaze taking in Jia and Nakula, both standing behind me. "We've received confirmation that Po-Sin will publicly announce a partnership with the Shen sometime in the next thirty-six standard hours. This news is bound to make the Farians nervous, but I don't know if it will be enough to push them to the table. The Cheng gang controls most of the smuggling activities in the Solarian sector, and they are the largest criminal syndicate operating out of the Cygnus arm. I anticipate the Solies will start putting serious pressure on the Farians to come to the table, and if that doesn't work they'll turn their eye to us."

"I'm not changing my mind about Fasé's involvement, Director. It's necessary."

"I understand, Majesty." Caspel gave me a sharp nod. "And for what it's worth I agree with you. My assessment of the current situation is changing by the hour, but the Farians embroiled in a civil war in addition to a fight with the Shen ends badly for everyone in the galaxy."

I exhaled and smiled. "I'm glad to hear it. We are set up here to take care of this"—the words stuck in my throat for a moment— "security issue." I'd messaged Caspel before we hit the ground at Hothmein with the news of Hao's betrayal, as much as it had hurt to admit how wrong I'd been. I'd known that I needed my intelligence director's expertise.

"I understand." Caspel nodded, his face solemn. "You have my hope that it goes better than any of us are expecting."

"Thank you. Is there anything else?"

"No, Majesty."

"I'll have Nakula message you after to let you know how it went," I said, and disconnected the link.

I turned as I got out of my chair and spotted Jia and Nakula sharing a look, that kind of silent communication people who loved each other shared. For a moment I ached for the loss of that connection.

Welcome to your new life, Hail, Portis whispered in my ear. *Empresses rule alone.*

"I won't stay in my office, Vasha, so don't even suggest it," Jia said, and I had to muffle a smile not only at her use of his other name but the defiance in her voice. "I'm not any safer in here and if anything, maybe there will be less chance of violence if I am out there."

"Everything will be fine," I said, patting him on the arm.

"He's armed, Hail."

"He won't be for long." I headed to the door and opened it with a smile. Alba was standing by the door, talking with Emmory, and she looked up as we came out into the main room. I nodded to them both and she swallowed.

"Majesty, dinner's almost ready."

The door opened and Gita came in, followed by Fasé and Sybil. Major Gill and her team were just outside the door if we needed them, though I truly hoped it wouldn't come to that.

Strolling across the room to the bar, I touched Hao on the arm on the way by and gave him a smile. "Drink?"

"Sure." He got up from his seat and followed me.

"I'm understanding better why Wilson went to a lot of trouble to secure this planet. The amount of money that's funneled through here is incredible. Your uncle has some mining concerns at the outer edge of Solarian space, doesn't he?" I asked, leaning past him to grab the bottle on the far side of the bar with my right hand. Hao's preferred weapon, a Type 883 pistol, was in a holster at his hip and it came free easily in my left.

I slipped it into the waistband of my pants, the metal cold against my lower back through the material of my shirt, and poured our drinks with a smile.

"Probably," Hao replied. "I haven't paid all that much attention to his various businesses over the last few years."

"I would have thought that was a requirement of your position." I looked up; Dailun was perched on the arm of the couch next to Johar, and he'd distracted her at the exact moment I'd lifted Hao's weapon.

I leaned a shoulder against the wall and sipped at my drink.

"Po-Sin might want to hold off on a decision about backing the Shen."

Hao froze and turned away from the bar. "What?"

I lifted a hand, hoping that my façade of carelessness wasn't completely see-through, though my heart was steady in a way that Fasé would be proud of. "I said Po-Sin might want to hold off on backing the Shen. I suspect even with the latest round of posturing by the Farians we'll still end up at the table, especially if the Solarians refuse to back down. The Solies will get their way in the end. They did with us and the Saxons after all.

"I'm not holding out a lot of hope it'll accomplish anything in the long run, but it's their time to waste, I guess. I'm surprised Po-Sin didn't tell you; you are his right-hand man, after all."

"Is there any particular reason you've mentioned my uncle multiple times in the last two minutes?"

Setting my drink back down on the bar, I crossed my arms over my chest. "I suppose I'm just curious when you're going to go back to being a gunrunner instead of staying here pretending to care about me."

"Excuse me?" He stiffened, finally noticing my *Ekam* and *Dve*, stone-faced on either side of the only exit and the others in the room staring at us. His hand dropped to his holster, and his jaw clenched when he found it empty. "What is this?"

Oh, brother, you are slipping, I thought, allowing myself a tiny smile. *You never used to be this slow.*

"You heard me." I struck him in the chest with the palm of my hand, sending him back a step. "I saw you. Saw Aiz wearing your fucking face and walking past my Guards. You helped him kidnap me. You've been working for the Shen this whole time."

Johar went from relaxed against the couch to on her feet in the blink of an eye. "You did what?" She gaped at Hao.

Something inside me wept with relief at the incredulous note in her voice. Hao betraying me was soul-shattering enough on its own, and if Johar had also been involved I wasn't sure I would have survived it. But that kind of shock and fury couldn't be feigned, not without warning of what was going to happen.

Dailun urged Johar back down into her seat.

Hao took a step toward me. "Hail—"

"I may not understand just why I'm a problem for the Farians, and the Shen, and your uncle, and *you*. However, it's clear that I am. What you should know is I'm not just going to go away. You of all people should know that. I'll play the long game on this. The odds are in my favor anyway."

"You don't understand."

"What don't I understand?" I shoved him again. He knocked my hands away with a curse, and everyone in the room tensed, bracing for a fight. I shook my head, anger filling the cold smile that spread across my face. "I understand we're not family, despite everything you've said to me. I understand you fucked me over when I, like an idiot, proclaimed your loyalty to me over and over again. I understand that you've been lying this whole time."

"You stop right there, Hail. I have *never* lied to you." Hao held up a hand, his face hard. "I haven't told you everything and I haven't answered questions you never should have asked in the first place. That much is true, but I—"

"I just want to know why, after all this time, you'd sell me out like this."

"I don't have a good answer for you," Hao said, his eyes locked on the floor. "I thought—I should have known avoiding the choice was only going to make it worse."

"Avoiding the choice? You didn't avoid anything. You sold me out. You let a man who could have killed me walk right up and put his hands on me."

"He just wanted to talk to you, Hail. It seemed like the easiest way to make it happen. I should have—He was never going to hurt you. That would have escalated the very war he's trying so desperately to avoid. I have never lied to you. You *are* my family, Hail. This would have been so much easier if you weren't."

"You are so full of shit," I replied, curling my hands into fists. The urge to pull Hao's gun and shoot him was a copper tang in my throat. "You talk about easier? How was any of this easy? No, it's fine." I sliced a hand through the air before he could respond. "It's not like you betrayed me, put my life at risk, let a fucking madman drag me down into the dark where you know I am terrified of going.

"Except you did." I fed my grief into my rage, keeping the words even and as cold as I could make them. Watching him flinch when they landed gave me surprisingly little satisfaction. "He dragged me into the dark!" I grabbed Hao by the shirtfront and slammed him back against the wall. Emmory didn't move, but Gita jumped at the impact. "Shiva damn you for all eternity."

He bowed his head, his hands hanging limply at his sides this time when I hit him. He made no attempt to defend himself. This new, broken Hao was an unfamiliar and unwelcome sight that only fueled my anger.

"I have stood for you. Stood with you. Taken gunshots and beatings for you. Put my life at risk time and again for *you*. Because I thought you were my brother. Do you know how many times I told them that I trusted you more than anyone?" I took a step away, unable to keep the disgust off my face as I flung a hand at Emmory and Gita. "After everything we meant to each other. How could you?"

"I was trying to get clear! My uncle—" Hao dragged his hands through his hair. "Damn it, Hail. I saw. I saw what it did to you. Aiz said he just wanted to talk to you and that he wouldn't hurt you. I thought I knew him well enough. I thought he'd do it right there in the café and I had no idea Mia was there also. It never occurred to me he'd take you, especially not underground. And the second I heard what he'd done I knew I fucked up. I went looking for you."

"You went looking for me." I reached back, pulling Hao's gun free and hitting the button to power it up. "You should have run the other direction."

"Majesty, don't."

The look I shot Emmory could have melted steel, and my *Ekam* put a hand up in surrender. "You don't want to do this," he said, his voice low.

"This is what we do, right?" I said to Hao, his gun heavy in my hand. Hao didn't move. No one else breathed. "All those rules about loyalty and honor that you drilled into me. All those speeches. How you hammered it into me that just because we did illegal shit, we didn't have to behave like criminals. How many times did I watch you execute someone for your uncle because they had been disloyal?" I pressed the gun to his chest. "At least I'll give you the respect of looking you in the eyes when I blow your heart to pieces."

29

Hao didn't move, didn't beg. He just stared back at me with resigned sorrow etched on his face, and I felt my finger start to contract around the trigger.

It was Gita's indrawn breath that stopped me. The almost silent sob that I wouldn't have heard if she'd been a half step farther away looped a chain around my fury and dragged me back from the brink before I could tighten my finger on the trigger. I powered the gun down and tossed it aside.

It slid across the wooden floor, coming to a stop near her boot.

"I am the Empress of Indrana, as you have so sneeringly pointed out, Cheng Hao. I am no longer a gunrunner. I don't execute people in my governor's offices. Consider that a small mercy. I should have listened to everyone who told me you were a risk. That whatever our history together, you would—if the payday was large enough—betray me." It took all my strength to keep my voice even. "I should kill you, make no mistake and be thankful that I let you out of here with your life."

There was a heartbeat of silence, and then Hao dragged in a breath.

"Yes, you should have listened, but I know why you didn't. I know why you stood by my side for all those years and even after. Don't think I am not both endlessly grateful and ashamed of your loyalty to me." Hao's voice was raw as he slid down the wall to the floor, his hands in his hair. "Believe what you want about me. I never would have let Aiz get that close had I known." His words were muffled by his arms, but the pain was clear enough.

I backed up. The desire to hurt him was still acid in my veins, and I didn't trust myself to not grab for the gun still in my own holster. I looked away. Dailun watched us, relief tinged with sorrow sliding over his face. He met my eyes and nodded, a silent confirmation of Hao's words.

"I have no right to ask you for forgiveness," Hao said, lifting his head as I looked back at him. "My cowardice and indecision have been far more than I would have tolerated from anyone, and I would not blame you if you kicked my ass and then dumped me into the black to crawl back to my uncle in dishonor."

Hao dragged in a breath and then exhaled, the sound loud in the sudden stillness. "I have something I need to show you and something more that needs to be said. Even if your answer to me is no, I would ask for the mercy."

"Say your piece, then," I replied, shoving my shaking hands into the pockets of my pants.

Getting to his feet, Hao reached up behind his head and dragged off his shirt.

My inhale was automatic. My stomach clenched. I stared at him in shock.

Somewhere through the stunned silence I heard Dailun whisper: "So the legend grows, by casting aside our chains we make our way closer to the light of the star."

"Holy shit." Johar whispered almost inaudibly, "I don't fucking believe it."

Hao's arms were bare. Gone were the tattoos that once proudly proclaimed him a member of Po-Sin's family. Gone were all the tallies and stories of his escapades as a Cheng gunrunner. Gone was the ink that declared him trusted and honored among his people. There were only two tattoos now, the rose over his heart, white petals scattering across his chest as if caught by a breeze, and a new tattoo on the back of his right hand.

My crest, the Bristol family emblem, an elephant head overlaid on the Indranan star. The motto of my family ran just below his knuckles: *Satark ke liye, nidraadheen ke liye nahin.*

For the vigilant, not for the sleeping.

Hao pressed his hand to his heart, covering the rose with the crest, and bowed low. Then he came up and met my eyes. "I am sorry it took me so long. Sorry it gave you just cause to doubt in me. Sorry for the choices I made because I could not admit to myself what needed to be done. I have always known this day was coming, and I was a fool to ignore it, a fool to try to walk the middle road between right and wrong. You are and have always been—my family. I beg your forgiveness for my injury of you, knowing all the while I do not deserve it."

"What have you done?" I whispered, already knowing the answer to my question. It was as clear as the new tattoo.

Hao's smile was tentative, shadows of pain still lurking in the gold depths of his eyes. "I chose a side, *sha zhu*." He held up his bare arms. "I chose you."

"Hao." The magnitude of what he'd done for me was a hot weight of lead in my chest.

"It may have come too late, and that's fine. I'll own it. It took me far too long to admit to myself where I needed to be. Dailun can tell you, if you wish, that I stripped away myself shortly after I betrayed you and allowed you to come to harm." He gestured at his bare arms. "The ritual isn't yet complete; I still have to tell my uncle, and I will regardless of what you say. I hope you will accept my apology, but you have every right to send me into the black alone and shamed." He bowed his head.

My face was wet with tears; they streamed down my cheeks as I stared at my brother. "You've signed your own death warrant. He will never stop hunting you for walking away from him like this."

"It was unavoidable and, in truth, something I should have done years ago. You came into my life and changed everything. I should have told Po-Sin no and just made the break then with my ship and my crew." Hao sighed and raised his head. "Instead I put him off, telling him I wasn't ready to take over the gang and digging myself ever deeper into a miserable hole. Maybe had I not been a coward then, I could have avoided the consequences."

"Why me?"

"I have known from the first moment I saw you that you were going to change my life, little sister, and you have. You have never let me down. You have always been at my back even when I didn't ask for it. I have not shown my love as I should have, and I have let you down time and again. I am so sorry for that failure."

My sob caught in my throat, and I heard Nakula's low curse when Hao went to his knees. I spotted Fasé sitting quietly in the corner with Sybil, small smiles pulling at both of their faces. Johar was still staring at us with wide eyes. My *Ekam* was expressionless as was Zin, though of the two I could see the shock better in the set of Zin's broad shoulders.

"I am tired, little sister. Tired of being on the outside of this family you have created, tired of being pulled to pieces between where I should be and where I am required. I am tired of being in a place where you cannot trust me. I know where my loyalties lie." He thumped his fist to his chest. "Where they have always been: with you."

There were tears standing in Gita's eyes that my *Dve* wouldn't let fall, and her hands were balled into fists, screaming her conflicting feelings for everyone in the room to see. I knew those feelings; they were rolling around in my own chest. But no one was paying attention to us. Everyone was focused on Hao.

"Your Imperial Majesty, Hailimi Mercedes Jaya Bristol. Star of Indrana. My sister. I pledge my loyalty to you, my life and limb, with all the honor I have garnered over the years and all the breath left to me in my lungs." He held his hands out, palms up, and bowed his head fully to the ground.

I took his hands in mine and urged him to his feet. "Look at me," I demanded, and when Hao raised his head I leaned in and pressed my forehead to his, staring into his eyes, and whispered too low for anyone else to hear. "You are mine, *gege*, and I forgive you for your stupidity. But I am still so angry at you."

"You have every right to be," he murmured back.

The next words rose up in my throat, not of any Indranan oath, but the very same words Hao had spoken to me when I'd pledged myself to him so many years ago. These I said loud enough for the whole room to hear. "We are lucky to see such loyalty offered from such an honorable name. Your life and limbs we will use as we see fit for as long as the breath stays in your lungs."

Hao let go of the breath he'd been holding, and it seemed like the rest of the room followed suit. I stepped away toward the window, feeling the solid warmth of Emmory's gloved hand on my back almost immediately.

"Are you all right?" He pitched the question low and I nodded, gripping the windowsill with both hands in an effort to keep myself from sagging against it as the relief flooded through me.

The quiet sounds of my BodyGuards ushering people from the room filtered to my ears past the thumping of my heart, and I was grateful for Emmory's ability to recognize when the public empress was no longer on duty.

Finally, only my BodyGuards, Dailun, and the two Farians remained. I turned from the window and looked at Fasé.

"That went down differently than I expected," she said.

"You sound surprised." I stared down at her. "A heads-up about that would have been nice."

"You're the one who said you got on just fine without my help."

"Fasé, your manners," Sybil said sharply.

"I dislike him." Fasé shrugged. The tiny gesture reminded me painfully that she was still picking and choosing and playing god with our lives.

Dailun muttered something in Svatir that earned him a sharp look from Fasé. Then she laughed, the amusement reluctant as she shook her head.

"I couldn't interfere, though, not in this. Not with everything between the three of us. I won't lie to you, Majesty. I was sort of hoping you'd kill him, or that he'd choose Po-Sin. He is a reminder of your past and your poor choices. He is unpredictable. It's hard to see the choices he will make, and by extension harder to see the choices you will make when you're with him."

"I could say the exact same thing about you, you know." I couldn't keep the frost from my voice.

"I do." She nodded slowly, dropping her gaze to the floor for a moment. "I am still learning, still trying to find a balance between where I must intervene and where I must not. I know it makes me seem cruel. I swear to you all the things I do are with the full weight on my shoulders. I know this. I take the weight seriously. The consequences are mine to bear, and I do not make such choices thoughtlessly.

"Hao's heart was twisted up, as divided as his loyalties. When I say I was hoping you'd kill him it was because I—"

"Fasé." Sybil's warning tone was clear.

"I am sorry. See, still learning." Fasé offered up an apologetic smile. "He made this choice almost the moment he met you, but it took him so long to finally admit it to himself, and more importantly, to you." Her mouth curved into a sly smile. "It makes him slightly less unpredictable. He is yours now, and that is not a choice that will change. It may lead him to his death—or not. As I said, it's hard to see and even harder to speak."

Her words ran a chill finger up my spine, and I couldn't stop myself from closing my free hand around my SColt 45, still in its holster. Fasé, of course, saw the movement, and a smile curved her mouth.

"I know no one understands what this is between us, but I won't let anyone kill him, Fasé."

Dailun reached a hand out, closing it gently around my wrist and pulling my hand from my gun. "Less violence, honored sister, not more, is always an option."

"So very rarely," I replied, but I smiled when I said it.

"You and Hao are the most interesting puzzle," Fasé said. "Your lives are entangled like lovers but without the slightest attraction to give it reason. At first, I thought it was just because Portis was in the way, but—" She shook her head. "Even with Portis gone, neither of you is interested in moving from your chosen orbit. Instead you just circle." She rolled her hand through the air. "Dancing around each other like a pair of neutron stars."

Po-Sin's com came late the next morning, and we took it on the bridge of the *Hailimi* as we headed for Draupadi Station and the Pandava Shipyards.

I'd wanted to be there with Hao, so several of Captain Saito's crew were flying the *War Bastard* and Hao and Dailun had moved onto my ship.

My brother was back in his long-sleeved shirt, with Dailun on his left and me on his right. Po-Sin looked between us, taking in the others on the bridge, and his dark eyes narrowed. Dailun's father, Heng, stood next to Po-Sin, his lean face unreadable.

"This is a conversation better had in private, I would think," Po-Sin said.

"No, Uncle. We will have it here."

"Very well. I am done with this disobedience, nephew." Po-Sin's face was blank, his words calm. "It is time you stop playing pretend with this woman who is not your family. You will come home and take your rightful place at my side. It is your duty. You have denied it for long enough."

Even knowing it was coming, the words he chose made my stomach clench. I didn't dare a glance at Hao, standing there with his hands folded together. Dailun was equally calm and I willed myself to be the same unmoving face of resistance.

Hao shook his head and straightened his spine even further, taking a deep breath. "No, I am done. While I will remain endlessly grateful for your support over the years, I am no longer yours to command, Uncle. I have sworn my loyalty to the Empress of Indrana."

He reached behind his head and pulled his shirt off. The bridge was silent, all my people as still as statues, ordered not to react or intervene. Po-Sin's eyes widened a fraction, a reaction that on him was the same as a shouted denial.

"Witnessed by Cheng Dailun and now by you, Cheng Po-Sin. I renounce my loyalty to the family—"

"Hao, think of what you are doing."

Hao ignored Po-Sin's plea. "—and any benefits of protection I may have enjoyed as well as any riches due me from this point forward. I am no longer your family. I have no loyalty to you, nor am I owed any by you or any connected to you."

"Nephew—" It was shocking and a sign of his affection that Po-Sin tried one more time to dissuade Hao from his choice, even though everyone could see it was long past the point of turning Hao from his path. "You cannot turn from your blood."

"There are few things in the black stronger than blood." Hao acknowledged his uncle's protest with a nod. "However, this loyalty was chosen from the moment she and I shared the same air," he continued. "It is a choice stronger than blood and means more to me than my own life. I know you do not understand, but this is what is meant to be. My destiny does not lie along the same path as yours and hasn't for some time. I would have no honor at all if I turned my back on it." He smiled, a brief flicker of emotion. "It is already done. I have sworn my allegiance to the Empress of Indrana. The only thing that will change it now is my death."

Po-Sin's sharp gaze snapped to me. "I will never forgive you for this theft."

"I have stolen nothing. You do not own him, Cheng Po-Sin." I met his challenging look and veiled threat calmly, giving Po-Sin a small smile in return. Heng's hissed protest at my lack of respect filled the air. "My brother makes his own choices."

Po-Sin snarled a curse in Cheng that made Emmory tense. A frown carved itself deep into the old man's weathered face, and he heaved a sigh. "Cheng Hao. Outcast is what I am forced to name you. You are Cheng no longer; you are no longer my nephew. The next time we meet, I will kill you for your betrayal."

Hao bowed, his eyes never leaving Po-Sin's face. "Good-bye, Uncle."

The screen went blank and silence settled onto the bridge like a heavy layer of snow.

30

It's not every day you witness someone severing ties with what's quite possibly the most powerful gang in the galaxy," Johar muttered from behind us, breaking the tension, and Hao's laugh snapped through the air.

Dailun patted Hao on the back. "It was a mighty hurdle, cousin, one well-handled once you pulled your head from your ass."

"Shut up," Hao muttered without any heat.

"Majesty, are we going to have a problem with Po-Sin?" Emmory asked.

"Unlikely," I replied, still staring at the blank screen. "That was required posturing. He'll put a bounty on Hao's head, but most people won't be stupid enough to try to cash in on it."

"And he won't pick a fight with Indrana," Johar volunteered. "No matter how mad he is—and he was pretty angry there—picking a fight with your empire would be like declaring war on every government out in the black."

I nodded in agreement. "No one could stand by while a criminal organization attacked us. It would open up all sorts of problems. Indrana wouldn't even have to do anything. The Solarians would come down on Po-Sin like a bag of bricks."

"What if someone takes a shot at him and hits you?" That question was from Gita, who, by her tone, had clearly still not forgiven Hao for his part in Aiz's kidnapping.

"It's the same thing," I replied with a soft laugh. "Accidentally killing me means Indrana goes to war with Po-Sin."

"No one will be stupid enough to try to kill me anyway," Hao said softly.

Gita snorted. "You aren't that good."

I laughed. "That's not what he means, Gita, though the point is debatable."

She frowned at us.

Sharing a look with me, Hao shrugged a shoulder. "The most anyone would do is try to take me alive, but they would have to try it without hurting her. No one will kill me—that duty is reserved for Po-Sin. When he gets his hands on me, he'll make good on his promise."

"Your Majesty, may I speak with you in private?"

I raised an eyebrow at Gita's formal words but nodded in agreement, and after squeezing Hao by the upper arm and gesturing at Emmory, I headed for the hallway.

Gita didn't say a word until we were back in my quarters, but the second the door closed, the words spilled out of her mouth. "Majesty, I am not trying to be forward, but you are making a mistake."

"What, by standing up to Po-Sin?" I laughed, shaking my head. "Gita, he really won't come after us. There's no profit in it and far more loss than he—"

"I am not talking about Po-Sin, at least not in those terms." Gita interrupted me, and I exchanged a look with Emmory. "They are playing you, Majesty. This whole ridiculous show from yesterday up to now looks like something out of a bad drama. I understand that you love Hao and have a history with him, but you are letting it blind you to the truth."

"Excuse me?"

I wasn't sure what it was that had Gita so upset that she either missed or flat-out ignored my freezing tone of voice.

"He betrayed you once, and he will do it again."

"*Dve* Desai, you will watch your mouth."

"Emmory, you can't possibly back her on this. These gunrunners are criminals. You can't—"

"Think very carefully about your next words." Emmory stepped between us, as imposing as a thunderstorm. Gita stared at him, her mouth open.

"Sir, I—" She looked past him to me, her eyes wide, and swallowed hard at the anger on my face I didn't bother to hide.

"Sit. Down," I said, jerking my chin at the nearest seat.

"Yes, ma'am." Her scramble for the couch would have been amusing but for the situation. Emmory backed out of my way, his own shoulders still tight with anger, but he didn't say anything else and for that I was grateful.

I folded my hands together as I took a breath and slowly let it out. "A few things, *Dve*. While I take no issue with you questioning my decisions, and I appreciate that you had the sense to do it in private, it is excruciatingly clear that not only are you missing some important pieces of information but that your own feelings for my brother are tangled up in all this.

"First, I do love Hao. He is my brother. He has watched my back for longer than anyone alive, and I once trusted him more than anyone alive. That trust is damaged after his stupid fucking decision back on Pashati, but it is mine to rebuild as I see fit.

"I would have continued to love him even had he not done what he just did, the import of which you *clearly* do not understand." She jerked when my voice sharpened, and I took a second breath. "I would have loved him even after I killed him. As luck would have it, I don't have to."

"Majesty, how can you just trust him after what he did? How do you know that the whole performance, the removal of the tattoos, wasn't just part of their plan?"

I closed my eyes, fighting back the shocked laughter that wanted to burst into the air. "You should have stayed a spy, Gita. I think it would have served you better. Though how you can be so fucking naïve having been a spy is beyond me," I said finally. "Look at me." I held a hand up when she winced. "I don't mean that as a condemnation, just an observation. I suppose the suspicion has its uses as a Guard, but a little trust in my judgment would be nice."

"Majesty, I don't—"

"For Shiva's sake, don't interrupt me again." I stared at her until she nodded. "How do I explain to you the importance of what he has done?" I asked, "When you have no basis for comparison? The weight of this gesture is—" Linking my hands behind my head, I searched for the right words.

"Hao didn't just remove ink from his skin, something he could easily replace when this ruse you think he's perpetuating was over. He erased everything he was, everything he's done in service to Po-Sin. It is all gone. Forty-eight years wiped away as though it never existed. It was witnessed. It cannot be reclaimed. That is not something they would have done just to keep him close to me, even if I thought he was capable of that depth of betrayal." I shook my head. "Empress of Indrana is not a title I earned. I'm not important enough to justify that kind of unheard-of sacrifice. Cressen Stone held more esteem than me, but she is gone, and even she was not ranked high enough among them to be worthy of such a gesture.

"Cheng Hao? He was Po-Sin's favored son, in a manner of speaking. He was the trusted. The enforcer. The honored. It was all written there in his skin—everything he was. And now? It is all gone."

Sitting next to her on the couch, I reached for her hand. "He gave up the one thing in his life that had any meaning for him, the one place he was respected and valued, and he did it not to make me trust him—because I already do, even when he's being an idiot—but as a promise." I smiled. "He's never broken a promise to me, and I don't expect he'll start now when I am surrounded by people willing to kill him if he fucks up."

"I wish I had your faith, Majesty. I'm sorry."

"I don't blame you for your doubts. I have known him a long time. You may come to know him better, Shiva help you." I shuddered and squeezed her fingers. "For now, do something for me."

"Anything, Majesty."

"Watch the com channels on the criminal side. There will be a flurry of news about what Hao has done for about thirty standard hours, and then it will be as if he never existed. If I'm wrong about that, let me know."

Gita bowed her head. "Yes, ma'am."

"And think about accepting Hao's inevitable apology. He had his reasons for what he did. I accept them because I understand being torn between your duty and your desire. I'm not going to tell you when to accept his apology. Just try not to hurt him too much in the interim."

"This doesn't put you in line for the throne, so don't get any ideas."

Hao choked on his drink and Johar laughed so hard she fell out of her seat. I grinned, feeling better than I had in months now that this weight was off my chest.

It didn't matter that Po-Sin had announced that the entire Cheng organization was officially providing support to the Shen in their fight against the Farians less than an hour after his conversation with us. That had been expected and I knew Hao's defection hadn't impacted Po-Sin's decision on the matter.

It also didn't matter that the fighting between the Shen and Farians had escalated: The Shen had taken five more Farian ships with the help of a joint mercenary force the size of which I hadn't ever seen. The other governments were in a panic over the cooperation, with messages flying thick and fast across the com links.

Everyone was in a holding pattern while the Solarians tried to convince the Farians to come to the table, and I expected any day for the demand to come that I agree to participate without Fasé's presence.

After two weeks in warp with a quick stop at a refueling station on a tiny moon, we'd dropped out of the bubble and were on a long approach to Draupadi Station, home of 8th Fleet. The station and the shipyards were in the Pandav system, a K-class orange dwarf star with four planets. None of the planets were classified for human life, so the station and the yard were the only things there. It was on the border between Indranan and Solarian space, looking out over a yawning expanse of nothing.

But our path in would take us past a white dwarf binary system, and it was well worth dropping out of warp to see such a sight.

Johar thumped the arm of the couch and got to her feet. "That's it for me, I'm going to bed."

"Night." I stole her spot, curled my feet up underneath me, and rested my cheek on the back of the couch. "Can I ask you something?"

Hao gestured at me with a smile.

"What's your read on Aiz?"

His smile faded, replaced by guilt, and I reached out, threading my fingers through his.

"I'm sorry. I—you met him, didn't you? You talked like you knew him better than just a brief interaction in the alley. I need a second opinion." I dragged in a breath past the tightness in my chest. "I couldn't think very well underground and I don't have anything but the memory to go on."

Hao called up the file, though he hesitated before sending it to me. "I was the go-between for my—for Po-Sin. Aiz and I met several times over the last eight months. He is dedicated, Hail—fiercely loyal to his people and his sister and this cause. As odd as it is to say it, he's a lot like you." He sent the file with a sad smile. "Don't watch that right now. I can't be here when you see me betray you."

"Hao—"

"It is the truth. I won't hide from it. Not that Gita would let me even if I tried." He touched my face with a gentle hand. "I will spend the rest of my life trying to make it up to you."

"I've already forgiven you," I whispered. Hao lifted a shoulder and I put the file with all the others I'd collected on the Shen leader. "Why does everyone seem to want something from me?"

Now Hao laughed. "Isn't it obvious? You're the linchpin in their plan. The Farians believe that if they have you on their side they'll win this war, and the fact that they've seen a future where it happens just makes them all the more determined to get you on board. Same with the Shen."

"Who told you that?"

Hao gave me a look. "Please," he said. "I may not like Fasé, but it doesn't mean I haven't been paying attention. We're talking about religions and belief here, Hail. Don't expect reason and logic to play a big part in their decision making."

"So you're saying they're only picking me because they're delusional?"

He laughed. "You know my feelings on religion, but that's not what I'm saying. I'm saying they believe in you. The reason why matters a hell of a lot less than the fact that they believe it. Now me? I know where I want you to be in a fight and it's not on the field across from me. Because I've seen the damage you can do."

Making a face at him, I untangled my fingers from his. "Apologize to Gita. She might accept it."

"You're changing the subject, and I tried earlier. She almost shot me." He got up, waving a hand at me before I could say anything. "And don't you dare do something like order her to forgive me, Hail." His exhalation was as shaky as his smile. "I fucked this up. I'll figure out a way to fix it on my own."

"All right." I pushed to my own feet and kissed his cheek. "I'll stay out of it... for now, but you should remember what happened with Emmory and Zin. I won't stay out of it forever. Grovel, beg, promise. Do whatever you have to, so I don't need to get involved."

"You're an insufferable brat."

"I'm also your empress," I reminded him with a broad grin as I opened the door.

"I'm already regretting that oath."

"No, you're not." I gave him a gentle shove out the door and then stepped aside so Stasia could come in. "Good night, *gege*."

"Good night, little sister." Hao smiled at Stasia on his way by and nodded to Emmory in the hallway. My *Ekam* returned the nod, his face still expertly hiding whatever personal feelings he had about Hao.

"I don't expect the rest of you to trust him—you know that, right?" I said after Hao had disappeared down the corridor, and my *Ekam* smiled.

"I would be disappointed in you if you did, Majesty," he replied. "I understand. My job is to keep you safe, no matter what."

"You've done an excellent job up to this point." I tapped him on the shoulder. "I'm going to bed. See you in the morning."

"Good night, Majesty."

"Are you going to want anything else?" Stasia asked as I came into the bedroom.

"No," I said, and impulsively hugged her to my side as I walked her to the door.

"What's that for?"

"I'm feeling sentimental. Thank you for everything you do for me."

"Of course, Majesty. It's a pleasure. I am glad that things turned out all right with Hao." Her smile was soft. "You deserve some happiness, even if you don't believe that you do."

"Now who's sentimental?" I laughed, ignoring the sting of tears at the back of my eyes. "Go get some sleep."

"Yes, ma'am."

With Stasia gone, I settled into bed and pulled up the recording Hao had sent me. I wrapped my arms around my knees and watched every painful second of my brother betraying me. When it was over, I watched it again, and this time I was able to focus on Aiz's face, see the lies and the truth.

He'd promised Hao he wouldn't hurt me and he'd meant it; I wasn't sure why Aiz had made such a promise and kept it. Killing me would have thrown Indrana into chaos—maybe not enough to cripple her, but it would have kept us from offering any help to the Farians. It also would have made the Shen a primary target for Indrana's rage, and surely Aiz had realized that.

My *smati* pinged with an incoming call from Taz, a direct call, not routed through Alba, and my heart gave a painful lurch as I answered it.

"Taz, what's wrong?" I saw the sterile white background of a hospital room and my heart thumped a second painful time before my childhood friend stepped aside with a wink to reveal Alice.

"Your Majesty, if I may introduce our daughter—Ravalina Hailimi Alice Gohil, Crown Princess of Indrana."

The tears slipped free before I could stop them, and I pressed a hand to my mouth as Alice tugged down the blanket's edge to reveal the sleeping face of the future of the empire.

"She's perfect. You almost gave me a heart attack." I shot a glare in Taz's direction, but he merely grinned.

"I wanted to get to you before Caspel or one of the others sent you the notice," he replied. "And she is perfect, Hail. Thank you."

"I didn't do anything." I wiped the tears off my face. "Alice, she's lovely."

"Thank you, Hail." Alice looked down at her daughter. "For everything and for securing a peaceful future for her."

We chatted for a few more minutes before I signed off. I curled up on my side, fingertips pressed to my mouth as the feelings rolled through me. If something happened to me, the empire was secure. It would be in Alice's safe hands and then the hands of her daughter.

The pressure of negotiating a peace between the Farians and Shen welled up in my chest. I owed it to Ravalina, to all the other children of Indrana, to make sure this fight never touched our shores. To make sure it never stole another life away like it had Gatani's.

The question was how to do it. How did I force the proud Farians to swallow their pride and sit down to talk about peace with their enemies—both old and new?

31

The klaxon yanked me out of my sleep, followed by Captain Saito's voice rolling over the intercom. "All hands, brace for impact. I repeat. Brace for impact." There was time for me to stick one foot against the wall and grab for the bar above my head before the *Hailimi* shuddered with the force of whatever had just hit us.

I rolled out of bed, cursing the lights on and fumbling for clothes. The door opened, and Gita stuck her head into the bedroom as I was jerking on a pair of uniform pants.

"I'm up," I said, unnecessarily, dragging a shirt over my head and buckling on my holster. "What's going on?"

"We don't have all the details yet, ma'am," she replied. "We dropped out of warp near the white dwarfs when the maydays started and the debris field appeared. There's a split open freighter directly in front of us. Captain Saito is on the com with Vice Admiral Tobin. Emmory sent me to get you."

"Bugger me," I muttered, and stepped into my boots, fastening them quickly, then followed her out of my rooms. "Do we know what hit them?"

"Not yet, ma'am. Whatever it was, there's still incoming fire." Gita grabbed for my arm and a roll bar to brace us when a second warning blared over the intercom and the ship shifted again. "We are too close," she murmured half to herself.

When we hit the bridge, we saw the reason for the jolting and I covered my mouth with a hand. "Dark Mother preserve us."

The stern of the freighter had broken in two, then exploded as Ensign Kohli tried to maneuver out of the way. Her quick thinking and the *Hailimi*'s shields had kept us from getting nailed head-on by the debris but led to the somewhat rocky contact down the *Hailimi*'s port side.

"Emmory, what's the situation?"

My *Ekam*'s face was grim. "As near as we can figure from the chatter, someone shot at the Chennai Pharma freighter group. Seven freighters total in the group. That was the wreckage of the *Blue Diamond* we just flew through."

"Who would shoot at us this close to Indranan space?"

Emmory's look was grim. "It's worse than that, Majesty. There's a passenger liner out there also."

"How many people on the liner?" An awful sense of dread sank into my bones. Losing the two-hundred-plus souls aboard the freighters was bad enough, but passenger liners carried several thousand people—families, children.

"It's a midsized Star liner, Majesty, with Calcutta Galactic Tours," Emmory said. "It runs from Earth to Pashati. We're still trying to get an ID on it, but they can carry a passenger list of twenty-three hundred plus another two hundred crew if they're fully booked."

Bridge officers wrangled with the chaos. Captain Saito was on the com link with Vice Admiral Li Tobin.

Masami's fifth daughter oversaw our task group: fifteen ships including her Jarita battlecruiser the *Light of All*, three Sarama destroyers, five smaller Jal fighters, and six *Vajrayana*.

"Stay on task," I said to Commander Nejem before she could announce me. "There are lives at stake."

"Yes, ma'am."

"Captain Saito, report."

Isabelle looked up, her mouth in a hard line. "Majesty, approximately fifteen minutes ago we came out of warp into the debris field left by the freighter *Blue Diamond*. According to reports, the group came under fire shortly after they dropped out of warp to view the same binary white dwarf system we were planning on viewing. They are still under fire; the passenger liner appears to have gotten clear but their warp engines are damaged.

"The vice admiral is currently headed for the freighter group and the passenger liner with the bulk of our task group. She just ordered me to warp to the safety of the station. The freighters who can follow will do so." Isabelle looked unhappy with the order and I sympathized, but neither of us was going to argue.

"Do we know who's firing?" Part of me wondered if Po-Sin was responsible. Despite my earlier insistence that he wouldn't start a war with us, I couldn't discount the possibility, though I wasn't about to say it out loud.

"Not yet, Majesty," Li replied with a shake of her head. "But your safety is our primary mission. We'll do what we can to help these people. I want you out of the line of fire. Please don't argue with me."

I hadn't been planning on it, as much as it bothered me. My desire to stay and fight was equal to Isabelle's, but we were both keenly aware of our duty compelling us otherwise.

I nodded to Li and put my hand on Isabelle's shoulder, squeezing lightly. "Understood, Admiral. Take out whoever is firing on our people, and Shiva watch over you."

Li nodded in return. "For Indrana and the Star that shines over us all."

The com link clicked off, leaving the bridge in silence.

"Get us out of here, Captain."

"Aye, aye, ma'am."

Draupadi Station was a less than ten-minute warp from the binary system, but it was ten tense minutes filled with silence.

We were in Isabelle's ready room bent over the console when we came out of warp, and the coms came alive with traffic.

"Yes, out in the border gap. I was told there were a total of seven freighters. One was destroyed at location. The other six are inbound. I've got two coming out of warp now."

"Yes, ma'am. We have dispatched ships to the last known location of the *Light of All*."

"We have the *Hailimi Bristol* inbound to the station now, Admiral. She just came out of warp."

"Freighter *Lightning Crashes*, please proceed to docking bay ninety-four. Medics will be standing by."

"How many people?"

"A few hundred."

"Was it really the Farians?"

The last bit of chatter ripped me out of my daze. "What?"

"Captain Saito, I have Admiral Bolio on the com."

"Put her on, Commander," Isabelle said.

"Your Majesty." Kartia Bolio appeared on the screen in front of us and snapped into a salute. The older woman's bright green eyes stood out against her tan skin and her gray hair was twisted into a knot at the base of her skull.

"At ease, Admiral. Are you in contact with Vice Admiral Tobin?"

"No, ma'am. My people just arrived. They're off-loading passengers and crew from the damaged ships now, and we've got some engineering crews with them to see if they can fix the damage to the *Utalia* enough for a warp back to Earth. Are you injured?"

"We weren't in the fight, Admiral," Captain Saito answered. "The *Hailimi* suffered minimal damage from the debris of one of the freighters before Admiral Tobin ordered us to bug out for the station. Is the rest of the task group okay?"

"Vice Admiral Tobin engaged the unknown hostiles several minutes after you warped out." Admiral Bolio looked to the side, and my stomach clenched. "They destroyed the targets, Majesty.

311

The *Light of All* was severely damaged but she can warp; I'm told Li is in critical condition. Three of the five Jal fighters were lost in the battle and one of the Sarama destroyers, the *Rising Tide*, was lost."

"Lost?"

"All hands, ma'am. Direct hit to the reactor." Admiral Bolio swallowed. "I'm told they put themselves in between the passenger liner and the hostiles as they were fleeing."

I put a hand to my mouth. Captain Khalifa had just taken over the command of the *Rising Tide* after his promotion from the Battle for Pashati. I could call up his bright smile with ease, and it was a punch in the gut.

"Why am I hearing chatter that it was the Farians who fired on us?"

Kartia shook her head. "Because we think it was, ma'am. I'm getting sensor confirmation once the undamaged ships return to station. I've got a carrier group who should be at the location now to keep the damaged ships safe."

"We'll be on station in a few minutes," I replied. "I want Admiral Hassan on the line and up to speed by the time I get there. I want to know who's responsible for this. Tell whoever you sent out there to give us some answers and do it fast."

"Yes, ma'am." The screen went blank.

"Fuck." I slammed a fist into the console. "Emmory, get the teams ready to disembark as soon as we're docked."

"Majesty—"

I could see all the reasons why he should say no to me scroll through Emmory's eyes and come up against his own feeling of helplessness.

"I'll be on a naval station, Emmory. My naval station."

"We have no idea what the situation is, and most of my support was on those ships."

"Major Gill is on the station, isn't she?"

"Yes, ma'am."

"Get her on the com now and tell her to meet us in the hangar. I'd be surprised if she's not there already helping out with the incoming wounded. I'm heading off this ship for answers as soon as we dock." I checked my *smati*. "You've got five minutes."

Emmory nodded once and turned his attention to his *Dve*. "Gita, get teams One through Three ready to disembark. I'll let Admiral Bolio know we're coming on board."

"Tell her no fuss," I said. "That's an order. She's not to interrupt search-and-rescue protocol for me."

The scene in Draupadi Station's docking bay was one of organized chaos as I came off the *Hailimi* with my BodyGuards around me.

"Your Majesty. Commander Bisley." The naval officer snapped to attention, dropping her salute when I nodded. "I'm Admiral Bolio's aide, if you'll follow me."

The forward momentum of my BodyGuards facilitated the ease with which people moved from our path, and I acknowledged the greetings as best as I could.

"We're on board the War Bastard, *Hail, headed back out,"* Johar said over the com link. She and Hao, along with Gita and Muna, were going back to the attack site to gather as much data as they could.

"Tell Gita to be nice," I replied.

"I can hear you, Majesty."

"Good. Behave yourself, both of you."

Johar chuckled. "I'll keep them in line. We'll see you in a while."

I took a deep breath and then followed Commander Bisley into the lift, grateful for Iza's fingers curling around mine as the door closed.

Was this all my fault? Had the Farians hit us deliberately because I'd pushed about Fasé? Or were they panicking about Po-Sin? The sick certainty that I had messed up twisted itself in my gut.

"Her Imperial Majesty, Empress Hailimi Bristol."

The entire bridge came to attention as I stepped off the lift and the announcement rang out into the air. I forced a smile, extending my hand to Admiral Bolio.

"Welcome aboard, Your Majesty. My ready room is over here. Several of the freighter captains have joined us, and Admiral Hassan will be on the com shortly."

I followed her across the bridge, waiting by the door with Iza as Emmory and Zin went into the ready room and then gave the all clear.

"Your Majesty, this is Captain Rushi and Captain Hando of the Chennai Pharma Freighters *Lightning Crashes* and *Opa's Revenge*."

"Your Majesty." The pair bowed. One was soot-covered; the other much cleaner, though her uniform bore several smudges. They both saluted.

The man cleared his throat. "Apologies for my appearance, Majesty. I was—"

"In the middle of a firefight." I interrupted him with a soft smile. "I don't need an apology, Captain. Are you injured?" I asked.

"No, Your Majesty."

"What happened?"

"We were making our normal run from Bismouth to Mathura and had dropped out to see the white dwarf binary because it's such a big draw. It's a regular part of our route. I don't know if they were waiting for us or what. We never even saw the ships."

"Bugger me." I muttered the curse into my hand.

The screen in front of me flickered, and Admiral Hassan appeared. "Your Majesty, Admiral," Inana said. "Apologies for my clothes." She gestured at her gray sweater.

"Why does everyone suddenly think I care what they're wearing? We woke you up, Inana," I replied. "It's fine. Except it's not. Are you up to speed here? Someone destroyed at least one of Chennai Pharma's freighters, one of my Samaras, and possibly damaged *Light of All* beyond repair. We also lost three of our five Jal fighters in the engagement." There was a second burst of pain in my chest. I'd met with all those pilots before we started off and now I couldn't recall any of their faces or names. "I'll need you to scramble some replacements and send them our way."

"Yes, ma'am. I've already got another task group underway. We'll have an ETA for you shortly. Did you lose any *Vajrayanas*?"

I glanced in Admiral Bolio's direction and the woman shook her head in reply. "No. Inana, we think it was the Farians."

She muttered a curse and rubbed a hand over her face. "Do we have confirmation?"

"Not yet, ma'am," Admiral Bolio replied. "The freighters couldn't get a reading before they bugged out, and the *Light of All*'s bridge took a direct hit." She held up a hand. "I'm getting a com from Commander Fitz, I'll patch her in."

The screen split and a dark-haired woman appeared, whiskey-brown eyes taking in the details before Admiral Bolio could fill her in. "Your Majesty," she said with a dip of her head. "Admiral Hassan."

"Commander Fitz, what's your status?"

"No additional hostiles spotted. We are headed back home, ma'am. Passenger liner is damaged, but we patched her enough to form a warp bubble back to the station. That seemed safer than making the long haul to Earth. I have the other two freighters intact and able to warp out. We're leaving four ships here to watch out for *Light of All*." She looked away from Admiral Hassan to me. "They were Farian, Your Majesty."

The curses of the officers around me were drowned out by the rush of blood thumping through my ears. "You are sure?" I asked, and Commander Fitz nodded.

"Yes, ma'am. I had the crew go back into the bridge and pull what sensor data they could. Between the data from our sweep as well as reports that Captain Khalifa transmitted before impact, it's solid they were Farian ships. We've finished collecting the crews of the three freighters." She gestured, and the screen widened slightly to show a slight, dark man at her side and two taller women behind him.

I heard the muffled sob Captain Rushi tried unsuccessfully to hold in and glanced in her direction. Her blue eyes were locked on one of the women, who caught her eye and gave her a little nod.

"Commander Fitz," I said. "I sent the *War Bastard* back to collect more data. It's got my *Dve* and my brother on it. I'd appreciate it if you wouldn't blow them out of the black when they arrive."

"Yes, ma'am."

"We'll see you in a few hours, Commander." Admiral Bolio cut the com link and shared a nod with Inana. "Anything else, Admiral?"

"I want a full report as soon as you have something," she replied. "I'll talk with the others here, get them filled in."

"Have Alice com me after. I want her on the line when I speak to the Farians. And Inana?"

"Yes, ma'am?"

"Meet with the Raksha, tell them to prepare for war."

Inana met my grim smile with one of her own and nodded in acknowledgment before disconnecting the link. A chill had settled into the room along with the silence.

"Are you all right?" I asked Captain Rushi, putting my hand on her shoulder as she leaned on the console.

"Yes, Majesty." She swiped away an escaping tear. "Captain Lewis of the *Blue Diamond* is my wife. I thought—I thought I'd lost her when her ship blew." The slender woman exhaled and rubbed a hand over her face. "We've been together almost forty-five years. We went to school together on Leucht, got jobs with Chennai Pharma, and worked our way up to captain. We've been doing this run for damn near twenty years. I've never seen anything like this, not even during the Saxon War."

These shipping lanes were too heavily traveled by non-Indranan interests for the Saxons to have outright attacked anything in the area. There had been some merchant raiders out here during the war that Mother suspected were being paid by the Saxons to harass our freighters, but she never could get proof.

Now there was a bigger problem than the Saxons lurking in the black. And my arrogance might have dragged us right into the middle of this fight that I'd been trying so hard to avoid.

32

Your Majesty, I am terribly sorry, I can't—"

"I don't care about what you can or can't do," I said, making the poor Farian who'd answered Ambassador Notaras's com link swallow nervously. "You will get her on the link, and you will do it now."

"Your Majesty," he tried again. "The *Itegas* is not avail—"

"Enough!" I slammed my palm down on my desk. "She will *make* herself available. My people have been killed by Farian missiles and I want to know why. If you don't want to be responsible for the severing of an alliance that is hundreds of years old, then get her on the com. Now."

"Yes, Your Majesty."

The screen flipped to the normally soothing blue of the hold image and I dragged in a breath.

"Hail, are you all right?" Alice's face on the right side of the wall was etched with worry. Caterina was in the screen to her left. And above them Admiral Hassan was in her home office. It was still early morning back on Pashati, but despite my attempts to get them all to go back to sleep, these three women insisted on being there for my call to the Farians.

Given Alice's hesitant question, it was probably to try to mitigate any potential incident I was about to cause.

"No, I am not," I said finally, dragging in a deep breath. My eyes still locked on the blank screen of the com link with the Farians. "People are dead. A good man sacrificed himself so we didn't lose even more. If the Farians targeted us deliberately, we're about to dissolve our treaty with them and go to war. If it was an accident, I—"

Shaking my head, I closed my eyes for a moment and replayed Captain Khalifa's last message from the *Rising Tide*.

"This is Captain Khalifa of the Rising Tide. *Our shields are nearly depleted; however, we have incoming Farian missiles headed for the unarmed passenger liner* Utalia. *We will do what we can to stop them. Better our lives than others."* He nodded once. *"May the Star of Indrana shine bright in the black."*

"Not better your lives. Better no one's lives," I whispered. "If it was an accident, I need to know *exactly* how it happened, Inana."

The screen flickered back to life. Adora stood in front of a white wall. She was wearing a high-collared gray dress, but other than that I couldn't get any sense of where she was or what time of day it was on Faria.

"Your Majesty, I must ask you not to shout at my assistant. He was under orders not to put any calls through."

The stray thought that Alba would have just hung up on me wandered through my head, but I wasn't about to give that suggestion to Ambassador Notaras.

"I would think you'd train your people to understand when breaking instructions is necessary," I said instead. "We need to talk."

"Your Majesty, this is highly improper, I am in the middle of—"

"Fuck your propriety," I said calmly, and watched with some satisfaction as Adora gasped at me. "I have Indranans dead, *Itegas*

Notaras. I have scans from my naval vessels confirming that Farian missile strikes destroyed three civilian freighters and damaged three others. I have a civilian passenger liner with wounded Indranan and Solarian nationals on board. So you tell me what kind of propriety I should follow when you've caused the deaths of my people?"

Adora seemed shaken by the news, and judging from the rise in the noise level she wasn't alone in whatever room she'd answered my com in. "Your Majesty, I—I am truly sorry for the loss of your people. I will need to make some inquiries and get back to you before I can say anything more."

"I'll send you the data I have and the location of the incident. You have seventy-two standard hours, Adora. If I don't have an answer I'm happy with at that time, then the first thing I'll do is speak with the Matriarch Council about dissolving the treaty between Indrana and Faria."

"Majesty—"

"And if I find out this was an attack on my empire authorized by the Farian government, things will get much worse from there." I disconnected the com link, crossed my arms over my chest, and looked at Alice.

"Tell the others to start going over our options. Keep the names of the freighters and the ships out of the press for now. I want a chance for Chennai Pharma to notify the families. I'll call Captain Khalifa's family myself."

Alice nodded. "Yes, Majesty."

Caterina echoed her nod and both women's screens went blank. Inana stayed on the link, her mouth pulled into a grim line.

"Majesty, we can't go to war with the Farians."

"I know." I sighed. "We can't go to war with anyone right now. I'm hoping it won't come to that, or if it does, the Solarians will back us. They lost people in this attack also and they can't afford to let the Farians run wild like this."

"What if it was the Shen?" Inana asked. "They've stolen Farian ships. There could have been a battle."

"I know, and the thought occurred to me, but Aiz has been fighting to keep us out of this. It doesn't make any sense for him to make a move that would drag us right into it now." I rubbed both hands over my face. "Go over the data on your end. We'll send you more as we get it. Gita is back from looking over the incident site, and they brought back the wreckage of one of the Jal fighters. I'll let you know if we find anything new."

"Yes, ma'am." Inana saluted and then cut the connection.

"Okay," I said. "Emmory, get Zin and the others in here; let's look at this data and see what we can make of it."

There was a brief pause and then the door of my rooms slid open and Stasia came in with a tray, followed by Admiral Bolio's people, my BodyGuards, and Hao. I snagged a cup of chai and bent over the console to look at the sensor data from Commander Fitz's ship.

An hour later my BodyGuards had gone through a shift change and the members of Team Two were standing near the door in quiet conversation with Emmory while Hao and I continued to go through all the data.

"Johar and Dailun are crawling through that Jal wreckage with a few techs," Hao said. "We've also got sensor data from the *Light of All* on the battle itself. We know the fighters were taken out by other similar-sized craft, not the missiles or other larger weapons on the Farian ships, but look at this."

"This timing is impeccable," I said.

"Tell me about it." My brother raised a metallic eyebrow at me. "I don't think those fighters have pilots."

"You think they're automated?"

Hao nodded. "Watch the pattern. It's good, but—" He pointed at where one of my fighters juked at the last second and avoided the shot. "The only reason those two pilots survived is they figured it out and used the predictability of the computer against it."

"Where are they?" I waited as Admiral Bolio checked her *smati.*

"Docking bay, Majesty. They just came back with the Nadi carrier *Vishnu's Chariot.* Commander Resnik, leader of the freighter group, and Captain Mocki of the passenger liner *Utalia* are there also."

"Let's go down, then." I rubbed at my face and drank the last of my chai, grimacing at the cold dregs. "Where's Fasé?"

"She's still helping with the wounded," Emmory replied as we headed out the door.

"Majesty, a ship just dropped out of warp." Admiral Bolio's voice came over our private com link. "They're requesting permission to dock."

"Who does it belong to?" I took the SColt 45 Kisah passed over and checked it before I slid it into my holster.

"It's Farian, Majesty," Emmory replied as we headed down the corridor. "Fasé says they've been expecting it."

I ignored Hao's frown and nodded. "Tell them yes."

I kept one hand on my gun as we came into the docking bay a few minutes later, Emmory and Kisah at my side.

Fasé stood by a distinctly Farian ship; the angles and edges made it look like a cube folded in on itself. It was smooth and black, eating so much of the light around it that it looked like a hole in the fabric of reality. A pair of golden-haired Farians were bowing to her.

"This is a riot waiting to happen," Hao murmured, and I followed his gaze around the docking bay. People hadn't quite gathered in a circle around the new ship, but there were hard looks and harder words floating on the air.

I picked up my pace, reaching the trio in a few strides, and Fasé looked over her shoulder with a smile.

"Your ships were caught in a battle," Fasé said. "Specifically, between the Farians and the ships that Mia recently stole for the Shen."

"How do you know that?" Hao demanded.

"Mia stole those ships?" I asked in surprise. "I would have assumed Aiz was the one responsible."

Fasé's smile was a bare-toothed challenge. "Because I know everything, Cheng Hao—oh, I can't call you that anymore, can I?" She reached out and trailed a hand down his bare arm. Hao jerked away and hissed a curse at her.

"Fasé, focus." I glanced over my shoulder. "And while we're at it, let's take this conversation into the hallway before you three end up on the wrong end of an angry crowd. Hao, go find those pilots and talk to them; then meet us back on the bridge. I want to know how they figured out the Farian fighters were on autopilot."

"My siblings," Fasé said as I took her by the arm and propelled her toward the exit. "Of a sort. May I introduce Veeha and Volen Riantin."

"Star of Indrana." The twin Farians, one male and one female, bowed in unison and then followed us out of the docking bay. "We are honored to be in your presence."

"I don't mean to be rude, but why are you here?"

"They are here for the peace talks," Fasé replied with a smile. "I figured it should be more than just me and Sybil if we were to be a proper delegation.

"This attack was not your fault, Majesty," she continued, looping her arm through mine as we headed down the corridor. "I know you must think so, but demanding that Adora allow me to the table was the right course of action. For whatever my opinion is worth to you these days."

"I'm not sure what it's worth at the moment, honestly. But I do need something more than you saying this was the Shen and the Farians shooting at each other. Do you have proof?"

"The pilots you sent Hao to find will have it." She squeezed my arm with a smile. "Go on back to the bridge; your answers will be there. I will be safe with my family. Do you mind if I steal Stasia? I'd very much like for her to meet them."

"Go ahead." I nodded and shoved my hands in my pockets as Fasé headed away from me with the other Farians in tow.

"Are we going to have a problem there?"

Emmory shook his head. "I don't think so, Majesty. Fasé spent the last several hours healing the wounded, as have the other Farians, but I'll let the admiral know to keep an eye on it."

"Come on, we need to go back to the bridge."

Emmory led the way, the members of Team Two arrayed out around us as we made our way back through the chaos of the station.

"Your Majesty, Admiral Bolio is in her ready room." Commander Nejem informed me. "She's waiting for you."

"Thank you, Commander."

Hao leaned over the display, shoulder to shoulder with the admiral, as he pointed out the ships on the scan and I allowed myself a soft smile before I cleared my throat.

"Hail," he said, and Admiral Bolio raised an eyebrow at the easy familiarity. "Not only did those pilots have info on the auto-fighters but they got scans from both sides of the fight. Come look."

I joined them, following the path of Hao's finger as he traced the battle out on the display.

"Two sets of Farian ships. One here. The other there on the far side of the binary stars."

"And the freighter convoy in the middle. Bugger me," I cursed. "Do we know which group fired first?"

"Based on the damage reports: the ones hidden behind the stars. Their opening salvo is what damaged the ships at the back of the convoy. It was the closer fleet that destroyed Commander Resnik's barricade."

"Can I say what everyone is thinking?" I asked, and heads nodded around the room. "One of those fleets is the Shen in the stolen Farian ships."

"Without a doubt," Admiral Bolio replied, her face grim. "They were shooting at each other, didn't see us until it was too late."

"No. They knew." Hao crossed his arms over his chest and shook his head. "At least one of those captains knew, or worse, both of them did."

"They just didn't care that we were in the cross-fire," I agreed. "I'd put credits on that one. This is two giants fighting on top of an ant pile. They'll crush us without thinking twice about it."

33

Over the next several days I met with wounded freighter crews and tourists from the passenger liner. I was part of endless meetings with the Matriarch Council via com links as we waited for the Farians to report back to us.

"It doesn't make me feel any better. My gut is still screaming at me," I said, leaning on the console in Admiral Bolio's ready room.

"It also doesn't answer the question of whether Shen forces were involved or just Farians," Captain Saito replied. "It may make perfect sense that the two forces are Farians and Shen, but until we have confirmation we can't rule out the possibility it was just the Farians. Shooting at each other, or at us—the end result is the same."

"Unfortunately, you're right," I said with a sigh. "Fasé claims her people haven't been anywhere near this sector, but we can't discount it as an option. I'm waiting on a message to see if we can get any confirmation." The look I shot Caspel's screen had the GIS director wincing.

"It's a lot of data and only two men, Majesty; you're asking me to piece together ship IDs from only sensor data in the middle of a firefight," he said over our private com link.

I checked the timer in the corner of my vision. *"You've got less than three hours left. I want an answer before the Farians get back in touch with me so I know if they're lying to my face."*

"I'll see what I can do, ma'am."

"Don't see. Get it done, Caspel, or you're not going to have the budget for anyone over there next year because I'm going to have to spend it all on this war."

"Majesty, I'll be right back," Caspel said out loud, and I waved a hand in reply as his screen clicked off.

I tapped a hand on the console and glanced up at Alice's screen; Fasé's earlier warning about things backfiring on me was raging in my head. "I'll say it if no one else is going to. I fucked up. If I hadn't pushed for Fasé's faction to be included in the negotiations, we wouldn't be here."

"Hail," Alice protested. "You can't know that for certain. The Farians have refused to even deal with the Shen up to this point; there's no reason to believe they'd have reacted any differently."

"Our people are dead, Alice. I am empress. It was my call. At least now if the Farians really did take a shot at our people, I can use it to force them into coming to the table." The very words made me sick to my stomach.

"Either way, we'll cancel the rest of the tour. As soon as repairs to the *Hailimi* are finished and the rest of Admiral Hassan's reinforcements are here, I'll head for Earth or for home." Several people swallowed nervously at the hard look on my face. "The Farians and Shen wanted me involved. I hope they like what they've called up."

There were grim looks all around, but no other protests as we wrapped the meeting up. I followed Admiral Bolio and Captain Saito to the door.

"How long until the repairs on the *Hailimi* are finished?" The damage to the *Vajrayana* had been mostly superficial, but a few of the hull plates had taken direct hits from the *Blue Diamond*'s debris and the shipyard had the ability to fix them, so we'd decided to stay with the ship rather than transfer my things over to another *Vajrayana*.

"Five more days, a standard week at the most, Majesty."

"See what you can do about shortening that. The replacement ships for our task group will be here tomorrow."

"Yes, ma'am." The pair saluted and moved down the hallway, leaving me alone with Emmory.

I sighed and leaned into him for a moment. "I'm sorry."

"For what, Majesty?" His gloved hand settled on my arm in a comforting gesture before I straightened.

Looking at him for a long moment, I shook my head and started down the hallway in the opposite direction from the naval officers. "I know you don't want to go to Earth; it's dangerous and nothing we've prepared for."

Emmory chuckled. "I also know it's necessary and you're not just being unduly reckless."

"When have I ever been reckless?"

"You punched an assassin, shot the king of the Saxons, jumped off the side of a canyon, hijacked a gunrunner's ship—"

"I did not hijack it," I murmured. "Hao was there because you told him to be, and he'd have given me the ship if I'd asked."

Emmory ignored me. "—flew into the stronghold of Bakara Rai, personally led an assault on an occupied station—"

"Shiva, stop," I said, laughing as I pushed him. Emmory caught my hand and stopped us in the hall.

"My point, Majesty," he said, smiling at me, "is that this is my job and you don't have to apologize for it. It was an unexpected twist to my life, but I wouldn't change it for anything in the universe."

"Are you trying to make me cry?"

"No, ma'am."

"In my initial letter to President Hudson I told him you got to have the final say in security decisions for the summit." I looped my arm through his and continued to my quarters. "If the Farians agree to this, I'm also going to insist that we all stay armed."

"That's a good idea."

"I occasionally come up with them," I replied with a grin that faded when I spotted Alba waiting for me outside my rooms.

She saw the look on my face and sighed. "You're going to send me home, aren't you?"

"The staff at the embassy can help me facilitate the peace talks if they happen," I said, reaching for her hand.

"I know what you're trying to do. You feel guilty about people dying and you're going to try to get as many of us out of harm's way as you can."

I blinked at her. "Excuse me?"

"You always do this." Alba's eyes were dry, but there was a surprising urgency in her voice. "I didn't fight you on Canafey when you made me stay there. I knew you were going into a war zone and I wasn't suited for it, but this is exactly why you hired me. The embassy staff on Earth doesn't know you as well as I do. Please don't send me back to Pashati, ma'am. I am of more use to you at your side than I am back home."

"Alba—"

"Majesty, she's not wrong," Emmory said, and I looked at him in surprise. "I know I agreed with you earlier on this, but it isn't more work for us to watch after Alba, especially since she is usually by your side. And a pair of critical eyes for a situation this politically charged can't be a bad thing."

"Traitor," I muttered, but it was with a laugh. "Wipe that smile off your face, Chamberlain, and I guess don't pack your bags."

We were fifteen minutes away from my deadline when Caspel commed me back. "You're cutting it close, Director."

"I know, Majesty. I'm sorry. We found it, though. Agent Paez was able to match IDs to one of the groups with the Farian ships that were stolen by the Shen. The other group appears to be regular Farian forces. We tagged their IDs coming through a port exchange near Sol."

"Who fired first?"

"The Farians, ma'am. It was their opening salvo that caught the *Blue Diamond*." Caspel frowned. It was a look I was starting to dread seeing on my intelligence director's face, because it meant he was worried. "Here's what's weird, Majesty, and I can't prove anything. Looking at the data, it looks as though someone was actively jamming the signal from the freighters and the passenger liner. The Farians shot as though they could clearly see the convoy, but the Shen?" He shook his head.

"They fired their answering salvo right into the middle of them. When our ships showed up it was too late."

"Yes, ma'am. It's why Captain Khalifa had to do what he did. Those missiles would have obliterated that passenger liner." Caspel rubbed a hand over his face, sighing in frustration. "I'm old enough to admit that maybe I'm overly paranoid, Your Majesty, but this looks—"

"Like the Farians were trying to set the Shen up and using us to do it." I finished his sentence and he nodded at me. "Bugger me. Tell Alice and Inana about the jammed signals, but no one else. I'll notify President Hudson that we're coming to Earth. We'll leave as soon as things are wrapped up here."

"Yes, Majesty." Caspel dipped his head. "Ma'am?"

I raised an eyebrow at the tone. "Go on."

"Be careful."

"I will," I replied with a smile, and disconnected the com.

The door to my rooms slid open and Stasia came through with a tray.

"Is Fasé's family settled?" I asked with a smile.

"Yes, Majesty." She nodded. "Do you need anything else?"

"No, I've got a com with the Farians in a few minutes, so it's probably best you're not in here anyway." I winked at her and waved my hand. "I'll serve myself; you go on and spend time with Fasé."

"Yes, ma'am." She disappeared back through the door and I poured myself a cup of chai. My com pinged, and I answered it. "*Itegas* Notaras."

Adora nodded. "Your Majesty, if I may introduce *Itegas* Rotem." The man at her side also nodded. He was tall for a Farian, with gray hair and the same piercing platinum eyes as Dio's. He offered up a gentle smile, one that was well practiced and a total lie.

"*Itegas.*"

Adora cleared her throat. "Your Majesty, I regret to inform you that the loss of your people was a result of an altercation between our ships and the Shen. I'm terribly sorry, our crew had orders to shoot on sight. It's no excuse, they should have been aware there were humans in the area."

"Yes, it's very curious their sensors didn't pick that up."

"We suspect the Shen were using our jamming technology." Rotem lied easily. "The return fire from the Shen did the larger amount of damage, but we fired the first shot, Your Majesty, and will take responsibility for it."

I kept my face blank. "We will speak with Chennai Pharma about the cost of replacing the freighters as well as the death benefits for their crews."

"Of course, Majesty. We deeply regret this whole incident and will do whatever is necessary to help ease the burden."

Had it not been such a precarious position, I'd be more impressed by the Farians' ability to wrap a lie in the truth and present that gift as though it was something I should be grateful to receive. As it was, all I could do was smile at the pair and deliver my own strike.

"I want you and whoever else from the Pedalion you need to join me on Earth in two standard months for this peace summit. Fasé and her people will be there. So will the Shen." I held up a hand before Adora could protest. "You asked for my help initially, *Itegas*, and thanks to your feud with the Shen my people have died, so

331

you'll deal with the fallout from that. You'll sit down and talk to each other and we'll figure out a way for everyone to live peacefully in this galaxy."

The pair of Farians shared a look, a silent decision not to argue passing between them, and I kept in the breath I wanted to release. This wasn't going to be easy, even with their cooperation, but at least the first step could go smoothly.

Smoothly. All it had required was the deaths of my people.

The slow burn of fury in my gut was alive and well, flaring brighter with Adora's nod of agreement.

"Very well, Your Majesty. It's not an easy task in front of you, but I wish you the gods' blessing in your attempt."

"I'll see you soon."

Disconnecting the com, I muttered a curse into the empty air and grabbed for my chai. "They weren't the least bit upset about the fact that we destroyed their ships," I muttered.

It didn't take a genius to figure out that the Farians had somehow engineered what everyone was now calling the Chennai Incident with the kind of cold precision I normally admired.

The question was: why?

I could assume it was because they wanted me mad at the Shen, that they wanted an excuse to get Indrana to back them in this conflict. I just still couldn't figure out why. The Shen might have the tactical advantage if it was true the Farians couldn't wrap their heads around mercenary tactics, but the Farians had the numbers and an obvious technological advantage if they could fool the Shen into shooting at a bunch of civilian ships that easily.

Muttering another string of curses in Cheng that would have shocked even my *Ekam*, I checked the time on Earth and cued up Ambassador Zellin's com.

"Your Majesty." Heyai's assistant was a bright-eyed young man with long brown dreadlocks.

"Good afternoon, Jinga. I'd like to speak with Ambassador Zellin if she's available?"

"She is, Majesty. Please hold."

I drank the last of my chai while I waited and then smiled when the screen switched and Heyai shook her folded hands at me. "Your Majesty, it's a great pleasure to speak with you."

"Good afternoon, Heyai." I returned the gesture. "I will start with an apology for making your life more difficult. I have a new message for President Hudson. Due to the incident that has occurred with freighters from Chennai Pharma, I have issued an ultimatum to the Farians and they have agreed. I will preside over the peace talks, which will involve two factions of Farians and the Shen. We will be there just as soon as we finish repairs on my ship and our reinforcements arrive from home. I've included a copy of the letter for you, and so you are up to speed I will be sending along a list of non-negotiable items we will require not only from the Solarians but from both the Farians and the Shen for these negotiations to proceed. I suspect more will be added onto that during our journey to Earth, so keep that list to yourself until I tell you otherwise."

"Yes, Majesty."

"My *Ekam* will contact you soon about appropriate lodgings, and I assume we will be sending several teams to you early both to scope out a good location and to run point on security. Any suggestions you will have for them is appreciated."

"I'll get my staff on it right away, ma'am."

"Good," I said and smiled. "I'll see you soon, Heyai."

"Safe journey, Your Majesty."

I disconnected the com and had time to take a breath before Alba poked her head in through the doorway.

"What is it?"

"I just received a message from Aiz Cevalla requesting a moment of your time."

"Is he live?"

She nodded. "He's holding, ma'am."

"Put him through," I said. "And come on in here, I want your take on his reaction."

The screen shifted as Alba sent the com link through, and she sat in the chair on the opposite side of my desk.

Aiz dipped his head at me. There were hints of dark circles under his eyes, and his hair was barely presentable. The background in my vision was conspicuously blank, leaving me to wonder again just where he was. "Empress Hailimi," he said formally. "Thank you for taking my com."

"Took you long enough to get in touch." I gave Aiz a steady look. "A little too long."

"I am sorry, Your Majesty. We've been rather busy."

"Yes, shooting up my people."

Aiz blanched. "Empress, that wasn't—" He stopped, closing his eyes as he drew in a deep breath. "It was us, but it was not supposed to happen. You have my deepest apologies for the deaths and injuries to your people. If we had realized there were civilians in the way we never would have engaged the Farian forces. And when I realized you were there as well?" He bowed his head and shook folded hands at me. "It was too late to do anything but watch. I am sorry."

"I appreciate the apology," I said. "And your honesty, which I have to say is refreshing."

"You already knew we didn't know your people were there." His warm brown eyes narrowed slightly. "How?"

"I'm sorry, you're going to have to drag me into at least one more basement before I start telling you my secrets."

The Shen's grin was sharp as a blade. "I'll keep that in mind."

Hail, you are dancing on the edge of a fire, and you don't need to get burned. The abrupt warning—in Portis's voice, no less—startled me enough I almost gasped.

"Keep in mind you'll also have to kill me first," I said. "The Farians have accepted responsibility because they fired the opening shot and will be the ones responsible for reparations."

"The Shen are more than prepared to do what is necessary for our part in this."

I bit the inside of my cheek, pleased with finally getting a handle on what made Aiz tick. His pride was something I could use. "Your reparations will be to show up at Earth in two standard months willing to listen and open to finding a solution that will bring peace."

"I thought—" He paused. "I thought the Farians refused to agree to your terms."

"It would seem they have little choice now. If left to your own devices you and the Farians will murder the rest of us just to satisfy this feud of yours. I will not allow that to continue." I kept my voice even, the cold chill of my clipped words sliding across the link to slip between Aiz's ribs.

He winced and, for just an instant, looked ashamed.

"I will be on Earth. You and your sister will meet me there. You will follow my requirements for the peace summit when they are presented to you. And you will do so without complaint. Is that clear?"

"Absolutely, Your Majesty."

"Good. I will see you on Earth." I moved to disconnect and noticed Aiz's expression. "What?"

"I've misjudged you again, Empress," he replied, his lips curving into a smile. He winked. "See you on Earth."

The screen vanished. I pressed fingers to my lips and shared a look with Alba.

"He acts like this is a game," she whispered. "But the intensity behind his words makes it all a lie."

"Yes," I replied. "That's precisely it. He doesn't seem to care that we can see through that façade. I wonder sometimes if I'm not missing something else because of it, though."

"How so, ma'am?"

"He's been more honest than the Farians. They looked me in the face and lied to me about the incident. He at least admitted he was at fault." I gestured at the empty wall where the screen had been and got to my feet with a muttered "Bugger me."

"Ma'am? May I say something that might offend you?" She smiled sheepishly at my raised eyebrow. "Aiz scares you, doesn't he? He beat you before you even realized you'd been dragged into this mess."

"Should I not be afraid of a man who can kill me with a touch of his hand? I like to think I'm not nearly as reckless as the stories say."

Alba got to her feet, brow furrowed in thought as she searched for the right words to say. "You've been trying very hard to be an empress, and succeeding at it. It would be normal for an empress to be afraid of a man who refuses to play by the rules. In your pursuit of your duty, you've forgotten who you are."

I hooked my hands behind my neck and stared at my chamberlain. "Go on."

"Ma'am, you are not just an empress. You are not some empty-headed noble raised in pampered seclusion." Alba squared her shoulders and faced me. "You are Cressen Stone. You are the Star of Indrana. Neither of those people would be afraid of someone like Aiz Cevalla."

"You have an enormous amount of faith in me, Alba," I said, dropping my hands with a sigh.

"I have seen you, Majesty." She reached a hand out, linking her fingers through mine when I took it. "We all watched you face death with such composure. I know you are struggling with it now. I know it is not easy. Don't forget who you are in your pursuit of your duty."

"You're telling me I should behave more like a gunrunner and less like an empress?"

A smile peeked through Alba's anxiety. "Yes, ma'am. Though I'll deny it if Emmory asks."

My laughter filled the room and I wrapped my arms around Alba, hugging her tight. "A secret just between the two of us," I said. "Emmory would probably agree with you."

34

I finished off the last of my saag paneer, humming in contented delight as I ran the final piece of roti around my plate and shoved it into my mouth. The mess hall aboard the *Hailimi* was mostly quiet, the sounds of my BodyGuards eating and the staff cleaning up in the back of the kitchen the only noises wafting through the air.

Hao pushed his plate away with a sigh and rubbed at the back of his neck. Dailun and Alba sat opposite us in quiet conversation.

Nursing the cup of chai Stasia had somehow managed to shove into my hands before I could grab a cup of regular tea on the line, I leaned back in my chair and looked around the room. Emmory had finished before me. Johar was still eating. Zin, Indula, and Iza were by the door; they were technically on duty and had eaten earlier, but I wanted them in the room for the discussion that was about to happen.

"Majesty?"

I smiled at Emmory. "I think we're close enough, *Ekam*. If we wait for Johar to stop eating, we'll be here another hour."

It was impressive the way she flipped me off without slowing at all, and several Guards chuckled.

"Ladies, gentlemen, and enbies," I said. "We are headed for Earth, as you all have no doubt heard, to facilitate peace talks between the Farians and the Shen. Since I am going to be in the thick of it, we're here to discuss some basic rules I can require the participants to follow that will make your lives easier."

"Call 'em out, people," Emmory said. "Don't stand on any ceremony here, but try to keep it from getting too chaotic."

"If we use the embassy for the negotiations," Indula said from the doorway, "it's going to make controlling the situation a lot easier. Just the delegates on the property, no one else except for us."

"That's not a bad idea." I saluted him. "I don't know why Iza keeps saying you're an idiot."

"She's jealous." Indula grinned when Iza kicked him.

"Limit the participants," Johar said around a mouthful of food. "Four each with the warning that they need to be unanimous in their decisions. It keeps the numbers low, but if you require a unanimous vote you don't have to worry about an even split deadlocking things."

Heads nodded around the room.

"I would be firm with anything we propose," Dailun said. "Do not offer it as a suggestion, but make it mandatory if they want the negotiations to proceed."

"No weapons would be an obvious one, but I'll say it anyway." Kisah had her knees tucked up under her chin, her blond hair obscuring part of her face. "Except for us. We'll have our weapons, right?" She looked Emmory's way and he smiled.

"It's going to be an extremely short negotiation if they say no," he replied.

"Majesty?"

Holding up a hand until the laughter from Emmory's comment had receded, I gave Jagana an encouraging nod.

"The Farians have to have skin-on-skin contact, don't they? What about the Shen?"

"They both do," Fasé confirmed from her spot across the table.

"Why don't we make them cover up? Long sleeves and gloves, or...?" She wiggled her hands. "I know it seems silly, and it wouldn't stop them if they were determined, but it would be enough of a hindrance, wouldn't it?"

There was a moment of stunned silence.

"That is fucking brilliant," Hao said, and saluted Jagana with his mug. She ducked her head at the praise.

"It actually is," Fasé said, smiling. "Plus it's going to piss the other Farians off something fierce. Only prisoners are required to cover their hands."

"How will the Shen react?" I watched the other BodyGuards voice their approval for Jagana's suggestion, pleased she'd found her way back after her mistake on Kurma.

"They should be fine with it. The Shen don't have the same bias in regard to covering their hands," Fasé replied. "If they're not, it's not like they have much of a choice when you get right down to it."

I chuckled. "We're going to Earth for peace negotiations, Fasé, not to start another war."

The Farian lifted a shoulder, a study in casual nonchalance that chilled my blood as much as her words. "Sometimes wars start no matter what actions we take to try to stop them."

It was more than a week later, the *Hailimi* speeding her way through the endless black of the space between the galactic arms containing the Indranan Empire and the Solarian Conglomerate, when I sat down with Fasé in my rooms to talk. At full warp, with three stops to refuel, it would take us six more standard weeks to reach Earth and I was trying to make the most of the downtime, piecing together as much of the Farian/Shen history as I could.

"Aiz and his father were there when the gods were killed?"

"Yes," Fasé replied, her knees tucked up under her chin as she sat in the corner of the couch in my quarters. She was wearing a white dress with long sleeves that hid her hands. "They were the ones who killed most of the gods, though some of the others fell beneath their companions' weapons. None of those Shen survived the fight."

"How old is Aiz?"

"Older than me, Majesty. Possibly older than Sybil."

Sybil was on the Farian ship with Fasé's siblings. The trio had chosen to ride in their own vessel rather than with us, while Fasé had stayed aboard the *Hailimi*.

"Do you have any concept of how staggering that is?"

"I don't suppose I can, Majesty," she replied with a tiny smile. "It is just life for us. If anything it's staggering to me how fast your lives go by." She sighed. "In so many ways I envy you, though."

"How so?"

"This conflict is endless, and it will remain so because those who started it are still alive. They still have all those old hurts and hatreds burning them up inside. We cling to those grudges because we know we have the time to see the revenge through. You humans—" She sighed. "You hate and you kill, but you forget, and you forgive also, and I think you do it because your lives are so fleeting." She lifted her cheek off her knees and smiled sadly. "It's why you forgave Hao, isn't it?"

"I—"

The question stunned me into silence and I stared down at my hands. I'd explained the reasons to Gita as to the significance of his sacrifice, but none of those really said anything about my forgiveness.

But I had forgiven Hao. I'd done it without even really thinking about it, between one breath and the next.

"He's my brother, Fasé. How could I not?"

"I know," she said. "But Aiz is Adora's brother by blood and I fear she will not forgive him even after the universe snaps itself back into place. It is not something you can just teach; but oh, if you could? Imagine the wars you could stop before they even started. Imagine all the lives you could save."

Fasé's eyes were glowing with the possibilities, and I felt my own heart beat faster in response. "I wouldn't even know where to start," I said with a soft laugh.

"Everyone starts with a choice, Majesty."

The door slid open before I could reply, and Emmory came

through. "Are you ready for this briefing, Majesty, or should I hold off a while longer?"

"No, we're ready," I replied after a moment, and waved a hand. "Bring everyone in." I got up from the couch and wandered across the room as the others filed in, shaking my hands at my sides to dispel the restless anxiety forming from having so many bodies in my space.

"Emmory, you want to give us the rundown on the plans?" I said, and my *Ekam* gave me an understanding nod as I settled by the open door.

"The peace talks are going to be held at the Indranan Embassy in the Interstellar Swiss Complex. We decided it was the safest space and the easiest to control given the short notice. There's already a squad of Royal Marines on the ground, but they will be supplemented by the contingent aboard the *Hailimi* and Major Gill's team.

"All participants in the peace talks will be unarmed except the empress and her Guards. All Farians and Shen, including Fasé and her companions, will be gloved at all times."

Fasé nodded. "It's not a perfect solution, Emmory, but preferable to the alternative and essential to your protection. While I doubt things will devolve to the level of the Farians and Shen trying to kill each other with their bare hands, it's always a possibility."

"Is that even possible?" It was Indula who asked the question from his spot on the couch. Iza nodded in concert as did several other BodyGuards.

"For us to kill each other?" Fasé asked. "Certainly. It is—think of it as a battle of wills rather than a physical contest. The Shen have an edge in this. They have committed to their fight and committed to the idea of killing with their power." She shook her head. "There are many Farians who will never be able to make that decision, even in defense of their own lives."

"We're not taking the chance. Uniform will be long sleeves and gloves," Emmory said, looking around the room. "I want everyone painfully aware of how fast these people can kill any of us and leave the empress undefended. You are to keep yourselves armed and in between any Farians or Shen and the empress at all times, is that clear?"

The echoes of agreement bounced along the walls.

"I'm included in that, everyone, just in case you were wondering. I don't want to risk someone coming for me and Hail being injured or killed instead," Fasé said with a nod.

"The talks will start with Her Majesty meeting each group separately to get an idea of the complaints and how to proceed. From there it will be her call on how the talks continue and in what format." Emmory pulled up schematics for the Indranan Embassy from the console on my desk. "Here's what we're dealing with as far as security goes. There will be eight teams of..."

I looked around the room as Emmory detailed the layout and security for the embassy, my mind flashing back to the number of times I'd done this with Hao or Portis for jobs that were far less aboveboard. My BodyGuards watched Emmory intently. I could tell that the Gupta twins were both taking notes on their *smatis* while Muna and Jagana busily picked out faults in the security net and pointed them out to Emmory.

Kisah was leaning against Zin's knee. Iza whispered something to Indula that made the man smile and tap her shin with the back of his hand. Ikeki was frowning and spoke quietly in Gita's ear when my *Dve* prodded her.

Everyone seemed relaxed, but the undercurrent of tension hummed in the room like a live wire. The awareness that we were going to sit down with three groups of deadly aliens—all of whom hated each other to some degree—was there just below the surface of what looked like a regular briefing. We could plan all we wanted, but I knew it would take less than a heartbeat for anyone—Farian or Shen—to slip off a glove and put their hands on my people.

My people. I had come to terms with the notion that all the citizens of Indrana were my people, but it was still a faceless mass of humanity, and nothing compared to the swell of love in my chest when I looked over my BodyGuards. These women and men had agreed to give their lives for me. There were holes, spaces left for the ones who already had, and I felt each loss so keenly at times.

However, Cas had been right. I couldn't prevent them from choosing their path. All I could do—should do—was be grateful that they'd chosen to spend it with me.

35

"How long has it been since you've been to Earth?" Johar asked as we walked out of the *Hailimi*'s cargo bay into the twilight.

"More than a decade, I think," I said, blowing out a breath in surprise and pulling my jacket tighter around myself. It was the height of summer in Geneva, supposedly, but still far cooler than Pashati, and it appeared I'd acclimated from all those years in space back to my home planet's climate a lot faster than I'd thought I would. "You?"

"Not very long ago," she said after a moment's thought. "I did a job for Rai a few standard months before you showed up in Santa Pirata. Brooklyn space port is not nearly as pretty as here."

The mountains surrounding the landing pad for the Interstellar Swiss Complex were drenched in purple from the sun settling down behind them. The occasional streak of gold cut through mountain and cloud, running the length of the landing pad and casting our shadows onto the buildings on the far side. It was late by local time, and my *smati* automatically reset itself to match.

"Your Imperial Majesty." Ambassador Heyai Zellin dropped into a curtsy, the members of her staff following suit as they greeted me. "Welcome to Earth."

"Everyone up. Thank you, Heyai; I wish I were here under better circumstances, but it's nice to meet you."

My ambassador was a round-cheeked woman with curly black

hair and wide-set amber eyes who jumped a little when I embraced her but recovered and smiled up at me.

"We have your rooms ready. Your advance team has already secured the area if you'd like to head in that direction."

I knew by the movement around us that Emmory had already issued an order to several of the BodyGuard teams as we headed to the embassy vehicles.

"I'm surprised there wasn't anyone from the Solarians here," I said to Heyai as we settled in the back of the car.

"They wanted a larger welcoming party, Majesty, but your *Ekam* and I thought it would be better for just your own people to be here tonight."

I glanced at the driver's seat and the back of Emmory's head with a smile. "Ah, well, I try to stay out of Emmory's way where those things are concerned. And I'm not going to lie, it's more than a little amusing to think of the blustering confusion that happened as a result."

Heyai chuckled. "There was some, though I think they're getting used to you. It wasn't nearly the fuss that they made after you kicked their people off Canafey."

"Heyai, I removed them from an active war zone for their own safety."

"Oh, of course, Your Majesty." She grinned at me.

Zin looked over his shoulder at Emmory. "I think we're in trouble here putting these two together."

"It's fine," I said. "Not like I'm doing some delicate negotiation between two mortal enemies that could plunge the galaxy into war if I fail."

That earned me the Look from Emmory in the rearview mirror.

The first full day on Earth I had completely to myself as we waited for the delegations to arrive, and after my check-in via com link with Indrana, Emmory allowed me to leave the Indranan compound and wander the shops of the nearby outdoor mall.

It was a shade on the touristy side but also surrounded by the various compounds of the other galactic governments, which explained my *Ekam's* willingness to send only two BodyGuard teams and Major Ilyia Gill's squad with me.

Gita strolled at my side, while Kisah and Riddhi's teams covered us front and back.

A young woman crossed the street in front of us, stopped, and bowed low to Sergeant Biem Rose.

"Majesty," Gita said, holding an arm out. "Wait."

"*Dve*, the young woman says her grandfather owns a restaurant nearby. She would like to invite the empress to have a meal," Ilyia said over the com link. "Should we check it out?"

Gita glanced my way, but I merely smiled. "You are in charge," I reminded her.

"Would you like to go, Majesty?"

"You know I would, but I'm not going to push it if you don't think we should."

"Major, head on over and check it out. We'll hold here."

"Yes, ma'am."

Ilyia and the rest of her squad followed the young woman down the sidewalk and turned down a street on their left.

I turned my face to the sunshine with a hum of contentment and heard Alba's poorly concealed amusement.

"Hush," I said, opening my eyes with a smile. "It's a new feeling."

"What is, Majesty?"

"I'm a bit invisible." I smiled and gestured around us. The other people out and about spared us a few glances but otherwise went about their day. "No one really cares who we are. Other than the young lady who recognized me, it's like no one knows me. It feels a bit like old times, I guess."

"Cressen Stone!"

The man who emerged from the crowd shouting my name never had a chance. Gita caught him by the throat and slammed him to the ground. People scattered when my other BodyGuards pulled their guns free.

"So much for that," I muttered, looking down at where Alba had stepped in front of me, her fists raised. I peeked through my wall of BodyGuards and laughed. "Gita, at ease."

"Majesty?"

"I know him." Patting Alba and stepping around her, I stopped just behind Gita. "Ahmed, that's a good way to get yourself killed."

The man on the ground had dark eyes and close-cropped hair, and was dressed in an outfit I'd charitably call well-worn. He grinned up at me, apparently unfazed by the body slam, but then Ahmed Hasigan had always had a strangely high pain tolerance.

"This is a far more protective crew than the last time I saw you, and that's saying something." He eyed Gita. "Prettier, though. Who's this?"

"You are addressing the Empress of Indrana," Gita growled.

"The what? Was I really that drunk the last time I saw you, or did I miss something?" He demanded. Ahmed had a baby face that was excellent at looking innocent, but I wondered if he was really surprised or just pretending. I'd been expecting to see some old faces around here. The Shen would be foolish not to count on some mercenary backup for the negotiations, and others would be looking to cash in on the bounty on Hao.

"Have you had your head buried in a rock?" I asked, laughing despite my suspicions.

"I've been in the outer rim for the last five years. We just got back into port today. Thought it was my good luck when I spotted you." He glanced in Gita's direction, and then back at me. "Can I get up now, Your Highnessness?"

Kisah choked on her laughter, barely managing to smother it before it burst free.

"Ikeki?" Gita said.

"Scans clean, ma'am, Sergeant Ahmed Hasigan, Hyperion Royal

Marines, honorably discharged. He's done some black market runs, a few jobs for Po-Sin. One for Jamison. A handful of lower-level criminals, nothing of consequence."

"You did a run for Jamison, really?"

Ahmed spread his hands after shooting Ikeki an impressed look. "He paid really well, Cress, give me a break."

"I should break your arm," I countered, but waved a hand. "Gita, let him up. He's mostly harmless."

"It's 'Your Majesty,'" Gita said as she lifted Ahmed to his feet. "And I shoot you if you touch her, understood?"

"Yes, ma'am!" Ahmed braced to attention but didn't salute.

"I'm going to hug him, Gita, so don't shoot him." I stepped around Kisah and wrapped my arms around the lanky man. "Honorable discharge, huh?"

"Yes, Cressen—uh, Your Majesty," he said, shaking his head. "Got out a few years back. I've been freelancing supply runs since then."

"Where's S.T.?"

Ahmed's face fell. "Killed in action on Indigo XIII not six months after we met you."

"I'm sorry to hear that." S.T. Toulous could have charmed a saint into her bed if her morals hadn't prevented her from such underhanded tricks. She'd sung like a chorus of Adityas and I'd had more fun than I probably should have coaxing smiles out of her and getting her ass drunk the last time I saw her.

"You and me both," Ahmed said with a shrug that masked the pain in his dark eyes. "Where's Portis?"

As expected as the question was, it still hurt and I closed my eyes a moment, struggling for the words as Ahmed muttered a curse.

"He was killed about a year ago," I said, opening my eyes and trying to smile. "My navigator, Memz, and part of my crew mutinied. She'd been paid by—" I stopped and shook my head. "It's a very long story."

"I'm sorry about Portis. I always liked him." Ahmed's answering smile was sad.

"Majesty, Major Gill says the restaurant checks out. We can go." Gita put a hand on my back, her eyes scanning the area around us.

"Of course. Ahmed, do you have somewhere to be? Or do you have time for some food?"

"All the time in the world, Your Majesty." He offered his arm and I took it as we headed down the street.

Twenty minutes later I found myself at a table in a quiet corner of the Grand Nepal restaurant, sipping one of the best cups of chai I'd had in my whole life. I'd whispered a little prayer of thanks for the pants I was wearing, because sitting on the floor in a sari would have been awkward. Though Alba had shed her heels and tucked her feet up under her skirt with a grace I could never hope to match.

The establishment was owned and operated by one Rajesh Thapa, a wiry old man with no hair and gorgeous dark eyes. His parents had moved from India to Switzerland when he was fifteen to pursue their political careers. Rajesh had fallen in love with Geneva but never lost touch with the food of his homeland. Now, his granddaughter Esha had come to stay with him while she attended a nearby university; she had recognized me from the news and invited me to eat.

They were Solarian, not Indranan, but so much of it didn't seem to matter. The few times I'd been to Earth I hadn't had the opportunity to visit the land of my ancestors, but the stories were strong connecting us across the black.

Bright paintings of the gods decorated the walls, and equally bright statues had lined the entrance to the restaurant. I reached a hand out, touching my fingers to the dancing Ganesh's foot as we'd passed.

Rajesh and Esha came out of the kitchen, bearing two trays of food. Gita followed behind them, a smile on her face.

"We're going to have to cart Major Gill and her team back to the embassy," she said as Rajesh passed plates and bowls of food, both familiar and not, onto the table.

"What's wrong with them?"

"Nothing, Majesty. They volunteered to taste everything. Rajesh is quite the chef."

"You are very kind, *Dve* Desai."

Gita smiled down at him and nodded. "Emmory and Team One are headed this way with some Marines so Ilyia can take her team back."

"You messaged him, didn't you?"

Her smile was brief, and her eyes flicked to Ahmed, who was talking with Alba, before she answered. "Of course."

"It's a fascinating coincidence, him showing up, isn't it?" I asked over our com link, and had to hide my grin behind my chai mug as I watched the surprise flare in her eyes. *"Do you think I've gone soft, Gita?"*

"No, Majesty, of course not. It's just—"

"I'm teasing, mostly." Rajesh was wrapping up his speech about the food and with it our window for this conversation. *"It's fine, Gita, you made the right call. I'll find out what Ahmed is up to before we're done eating."*

"Can I eat, *Dve*?" I asked aloud.

"Yes, Majesty."

"Cress—" Ahmed cleared his throat at Gita's stare. "Sorry, Your Majesty. How on earth did you end up here?"

"On Earth? Hitched a ride." I laughed, digging into the food with my fingers, when he leveled me with a glare. "I told you it was a long story."

"We got time." He gestured at the food.

"True. I was born Hailimi Mercedes Jaya Bristol, second daughter of the Empress of Indrana..."

36

Emmory came in through the front door of the Grand Nepal just as I'd finished my story, and Ahmed blew out a breath.

"That one is going down in the history pages." He saluted me with his glass.

"Most likely already has, at least back home. Emmory."

"Majesty. How was lunch?"

"Amazing. Alba, go see if there's enough leftovers for us to bring back so the Guards can enjoy it once we're at the embassy."

"Yes, ma'am." She scooted out of her spot, taking Emmory's offered hand before she slipped her shoes back on her feet.

I leaned in as soon as Alba was gone. "Why are you here?"

Ahmed smiled at me and then at my grim-faced BodyGuards, who stood arrayed around the room so that every exit was covered. "I just ran into you on the street. It was a happy coincidence?"

"I don't believe in those."

"I don't blame you," he said, placing his hands carefully on the tabletop. "It's mostly true. I heard Hao was in town; I was looking for him. When I saw you, I figured you'd know where he was."

I sighed, disappointment settling into my chest like a stone. "Ahmed, I will give you this one chance because you are—were—a friend of mine. Anyone who goes after Hao will answer to me. He is mine and I will not tolerate anyone who seeks to harm him."

"Oh." Ahmed shoved a hand into his hair. "Oh, no. That all

makes sense now. All I heard was Po-Sin put a bounty on him, but you—oh." He pointed at me with a grin. "I'm not—sorry. I'm not here to try to get you to turn on him. I have a warning for him. I figured you could pass it on." His laugh was sheepish. "I didn't even realize that you—he turned his back on Po-Sin for you? Wow, I didn't put any of that together."

He was cute but not all that bright. "A warning?" I asked, snapping my fingers. "Focus, Ahmed."

"Yes. There are a ton of mercenaries converging on Geneva. This is the biggest payday in the history of paydays. Everyone wants in on this action."

I couldn't figure out if Ahmed was trying to muddy the issue by focusing on the bounty or if he really didn't know about everything that was going down with the Shen. I was leaning toward the latter. He'd never been the brightest star in the black and most of his mercenary associations had been secondhand. The run for Jamison had been well before this whole mess started. Given that he was trying to warn Hao, I decided to give him the benefit of the doubt.

"Do they have any idea what's going on here starting tomorrow? The amount of security there's going to be?"

"It's an extra challenge, according to some," Ahmed said with an apologetic smile.

"Why the sudden desire to help Hao?" Emmory asked, breaking his silence.

"We worked together on a job right after I got out of the service. He didn't have to help me, I owe him," Ahmed replied, and then he smiled at me. "Plus, I got a chance to catch up with you."

I returned it, cautiously. "I'll pass the warning along. He'll appreciate it, Ahmed, and so do I."

"Are we still friends?" he asked.

"At the moment." I hoped my smile eased the sting of my words. "Emmory, you want to see Ahmed out while I say good-bye to our host?"

"It was good to see you," Ahmed said, getting to his feet and giving me an exaggerated bow. "Your Majesty."

"Get out of here before someone spots you," I replied with a smile.

Emmory led Ahmed to the door. Alba returned, Rajesh in tow, and I got up from my spot.

"Thank you again for the food, Mr. Thapa," I said to the elderly man, folding my hands together and bowing.

"You enjoyed it?"

"Very much so. I never realized how much our cuisine changed over the years. It was a delight to taste the original dishes. Please tell your daughter thank you again for thinking of us."

"I will, Your Majesty. Thank you. I wish you luck with your negotiations."

Back in the embassy, I settled onto my couch and shared a look with Emmory. "That's another hurdle to deal with," I said. "I'd like to think they'll all be smart enough to follow Po-Sin's example and the fact that there are not one, but two alien races here and keep their guns in their holsters."

"Mercenaries aren't always known for their common sense, Majesty."

"I'll pretend like that comment doesn't include me anymore," I said, reaching for my glass.

"Why would Ahmed go out of his way to warn Hao?"

I stared at the ice in my whiskey for a long moment before I replied. "It's complicated. Hao is—he's always been good at engendering loyalty from people. I don't know that there's really any explanation for it."

"Sounds familiar," Emmory murmured, a smile tugging on his lips.

"I didn't learn it in the palace," I replied with a laugh, but then I sobered. "Emmory, Hao will try to leave because of this. To keep me out of danger. I don't want him to."

"I know, Majesty."

I got up from my seat with a sigh of frustration. "Our lives were so—" I broke off as I passed the cracked-open door, hearing Johar's voice in the hallway, and waved a hand at Emmory to keep him quiet.

"I'm not saying he's not an ass, Gita, because he is, and you have every right to keep hating him. I'm just saying it means something when the great Cheng Hao admits he was wrong."

Gita's sigh was heavy with frustration. "He could have gotten her killed, Jo."

"We all know that. Hao knows it. He'll carry that regret for the rest of his life, no matter what kind of absolution Hail gave him. Think on that, though, Hail forgave him. Be mad at him for betraying you, if he did, but don't take on his betrayal of her as well. It's not your place, and you know it."

"Why are you so fucking smart?"

Johar chuckled. "So many reasons, my friend." She kissed Gita loudly on the cheek. "Have a good night. I'm going out. Rai is in town and he wants to apologize."

I crept back to the couch, whiskey forgotten, and Emmory gave me the Look. "Do you always eavesdrop on your Guards?"

"Sometimes it's the only way anyone tells you anything when you're the empress," I replied.

"You could just ask."

"How's Zin?" I grinned at the way Emmory's dark lashes fell over his eyes when he rolled them upward and picked up my whiskey. "See? You should ask Hao, I did this shit all the time out in the black."

"You need a hobby," my *Ekam* countered.

"I had one, and then you all dragged me home and made me be empress."

"Gunrunning is not a hobby."

"True." I carried my whiskey over to the window. "I am concerned about Ahmed's news, Emmory," I said, pulling us back to our original conversation. "And Rai's in town."

"Will he come after Hao?"

"I doubt it." I knew I didn't sound particularly reassuring, but with Bakara Rai you never could tell. "He knows the payoff is really good, but he also knows that the cost-benefit ratio going up against Hao is going to be high. My brother has people besides me who are loyal to him. They will come to his defense." My exhalation was shaky, and I gave Emmory a poor attempt at a smile. "This could turn into a massive gang war on top of everything else."

"Want to go three for three and see if we can start something with the Solarians?" Emmory replied with a wicked grin.

"Who are you and what have you done with my *Ekam*?" I gaped at him.

He leaned on the windowsill next to me. "Trying to get you to see the ridiculousness of worrying about things we can't control, Hail. Focus on the negotiations. Whatever your doubts, I know you can do this. You were born to do this."

"You sound like Fasé, you know. Please tell me you're not seeing the future now, too?"

He chuckled, putting a hand over my free one and squeezing it. "I have faith in your ability to make them see reason."

"Did you ever think you'd say such a thing to me a year ago?" I asked, leaning my head against his shoulder.

"No, Majesty," he replied with a rumbling laugh. "But you have proven me wrong time and again, and I am both humbled and grateful to be able to say it to you now."

My *smati* pinged. "Caspel's on the com," I said, reluctantly pushing away from the window and heading to the desk in the corner.

"Majesty, *Ekam*," Caspel said as he came onto the screen. "I have several updates for you I thought you should know about. Sending the files over now. I spoke with my Solarian counterparts and they are increasingly concerned about the mercenary uptick over the last few days."

"It's because of Hao," I said. "There's nothing we can do about it except hope that they don't want to piss off the Solarians by starting something in their territory."

"We could have him go elsewhere, Majesty."

I pinned my intelligence director with a flat look. "He goes nowhere, Caspel. He's mine now and if someone wants to try to bring him to Po-Sin they'll have to come through me to do it." I knew even as I said it that I was committing Indrana to the same course, but I'd already done something similar with Fasé and I owed Hao just as much, if not more.

"That's what I'm afraid of, Majesty." Caspel cleared his throat and shot Emmory a pleading look past my shoulder. "This situation is an Alcubierre/White Drive about to explode as it is."

"If I could tell them all to go away I would, Director."

"I realize you're in a rather delicate position, Majesty. Just be careful."

I snorted. "Everyone keeps saying that to me as if I haven't been extremely careful, and *Ekam*, if you laugh I will shoot you."

That made Caspel chuckle and shake his head. "I made some progress on the money trail for the confirmed mercenaries the Shen have hired, ma'am, including Po-Sin. There are several banks there on Earth that we think have been used to send out payments. I recommend you have Gita follow those leads if you can spare her. If not, I can put you in touch with an operative."

"I'll see what we can do. I realize you may not trust him, but Hao and Dailun might get further on something like that."

"I understand, ma'am," Caspel replied. "I know you are quite capable of handling yourself and you are surrounded by the best Indrana has to offer, but, Majesty?"

"Yes?"

"I don't have a good feeling about this. Be careful."

"I will. I promise."

I met with President Hudson late the next morning. It was a formal event at the Indranan Embassy, filled with news cameras and an awkward handshake that pushed the boundaries of even my tolerance for not-so-subtle displays of power.

I squeezed his hand back, a pleasant smile on my face as I wondered who'd forgotten to tell their Earth-born president that Pashati's gravity was slightly higher than Earth's and I wasn't exactly what one would call delicate.

Regardless, it wasn't my issue, and I kept smiling as the immaculately tailored and polished man hid his wince and untangled his grip from mine.

"Your Imperial Majesty, it's a great pleasure to have you here. Allow me to express my condolences for the attack on your empire's ships. The Solarian Conglomerate shares in your grief with our own dead and hopes we can use this tragedy as a bridge toward peace between the Farians and the Shen."

"I sincerely hope that is the case, Mr. President."

"Your Majesty, is it true you've accepted the loyalty of Po-Sin's nephew Cheng Hao?" A reporter at the back of the room shouted out.

President Hudson sighed. "Joseph, we talked about appropriate questions."

The reporter grinned, unrepentant.

"The answer is yes," I replied. "But that's all I'm going to say about it."

"What's the response at home over the attack on your ships?"

"Is it true you're going to force the Shen and the Farians to wear gloves at all times?"

"Do you have a plan for getting the Farians and Shen to come to a peace agreement?"

The questions were yelled on top of each other as my reply to the first reporter opened up the floodgates. I folded my hands at my waist and waited patiently for them to realize I wasn't going to say anything until they fell silent.

"I dislike being shouted at," I said. "One at a time. You first."

37

confess I've never seen someone handle the press quite so well, Your Majesty," President Hudson said later when we were settled into the quiet study of the embassy eating lunch.

"They were not much louder than home. Still, my people have come to expect I will walk out of a press conference if they get out of hand."

Hudson smiled and passed a hand over his gray hair. "I'd ask you for pointers but I suspect your history has a great deal to do with it. My press would not let me walk out of anything. No one fears a former banker."

"They would if they were smart." I let the backhanded compliment slide on by and instead sipped at the wine. It was cloyingly sweet with a bitter aftertaste that would have made me concerned about poison if Emmory hadn't tested the glass himself before setting it in front of me.

"We appreciate your assistance with this situation, President Hudson. I suppose we will see if the Farians and Shen can come to some agreement."

"Certainly. I have received coms from a number of other governments with some requests. Primarily we think it would be of paramount importance to have you inform all sides that we require an immediate cessation of military activities in our sectors." The Solarians had become the de facto voice for humanity in this arm of the galaxy, given Indrana's isolation and the long-running war with the Saxons, and with everything else going on both at home and here I wasn't looking to challenge him on that front.

At least as long as he was gracious enough to keep our diplomats in the loop, and last night Ambassador Zellin had assured me that was happening.

"Are you willing to back that with force if they don't agree?"

The president scratched at his scalp. "Indrana already has, Majesty, and without consequence it would seem. But yes, the Solarians and a fair number of others are willing to engage in a show of force should it be deemed necessary."

"Fair enough." I nodded. "Send me any additional coms that come your way. I'll bring up the issue during the negotiations and see what the response is."

"So, tell me, Your Majesty, just what was it like being a gunrunner?"

"Dreadfully boring," I replied.

For the better part of an hour I dodged, deflected, and otherwise avoided the president's repeated attempts to get me to talk about my past. I left the meal in a foul temper and strode for my rooms, leaving a startled Alba staring after me in the hallway.

Emmory handed me a pillow off the couch without comment. I stared at him and he shook it. Taking the blue velvet cushion, I buried my face in it and screamed.

"Better, Majesty?"

"Yes, thank you." I handed the pillow back to him and smoothed my hair away from my forehead. "The nerve of that man. I deserve a medal for not killing him."

"I'm very proud of you."

I rubbed at my temples. "At least he didn't try to insert himself into the negotiations, thank Shiva."

"I believe Ambassador Zellin had some very stern words with him about that before our arrival. It helps that the Farians and the Shen have been very clear that you and only you are the one leading the negotiations," Emmory said. "However, it's also why you didn't get to wear your guns to lunch." He handed my holsters over, passing the SColt 45s along once I'd gotten myself situated.

"I love that you trust me to not shoot a pair of warring alien races but not the president of the Solarian Conglomerate."

"You did eject the Solie ambassador and his staff from Canafey, Majesty."

"Removed them from a war zone for their own safety," I replied with an absent smile as I checked over my guns. "I swear it's like you're all conspiring against me to get me in trouble."

"You get in trouble enough on your own."

I laughed and shoved the SColts into my thigh holsters. "All right, *Ekam*, let's go try to make peace."

The Farians turned as a single unit when I came through the door with Emmory and Alba at my side. The first thing I noticed was that there were five of them, instead of the four-representative limit I'd laid out clearly in my terms for the negotiations. And the second thing—

"*Itegas* Notaras, where are your gloves?" I came to a stop before Emmory put his hand out.

"I didn't think you meant *me*." Adora smiled in a poor approximation of an innocent look, and I crossed my arms over my chest in response.

"I meant everyone, and I'm not sure if you think I can't count or I wasn't going to notice because of how short you all are."

The Farians gasped, again as one, which was getting decidedly creepy, but I threw up a hand before anyone could say anything. "You get four reps, Adora. Not five, or eight, or seventeen, but four.

And I guess since you are missing the proper attire for this affair you get to leave."

"Your Majesty!"

"Other option is I'm out of here and I tell the Shen you weren't interested in these talks because you couldn't follow the rules. We'll just sit down with them and Fasé instead."

"You wouldn't."

"Try me," I replied, and headed for the door. I had my hand on the handle before Adora folded.

"Your Majesty, wait. Tilla, give me your gloves and go back to our quarters."

I stepped aside so the young Farian could get past me on her way to the door without incurring Emmory's wrath and turned back around, waiting patiently as Adora pulled the gloves on. She held her hands up.

"Happy, Your Majesty?"

"Follow the rules. I won't give you a second warning."

Adora's mouth tightened. "Your Majesty, before we start I'd like to know when you're going to deliver Fasé and Sybil to us."

"I'm not. They are here as part of a legally recognized faction for these negotiations."

"Legally recognized by whom?"

"By Indrana and by the Solarians as of this morning. If I need to I'll have eight other human governments sign on to that by sundown. Again, you can take it or leave it. You killed my people. You have killed Solarians. You and the Shen brought this war to us through hubris or negligence, I really don't care which. You will pay the price for it one way or another."

"Your Majesty!"

I took a step forward, and a humorless smile curved over my face when the Farian closest to me took several scrambling steps in the other direction. "*Itegas* Notaras, if you truly wish to use your precious time here in an argument—which I promise you, you will lose—that is your choice. However, I would think very carefully about leaving this room without giving me any indication of what it is you want to negotiate with the Shen about, because then I am left with only their options to bring to the table."

For a moment I thought I had pushed Adora too far, but the Farian drew in a deep breath after fisting her hands at her sides and finally dipped her head in my direction. "We will proceed with the negotiations."

"Fantastic. Have a seat."

All four Farians moved around to the opposite end of the table and I settled into my chair. Both women were taller than Adora, one of them almost Zin's height with her hair cut short, almost militarily so. The other had curls like Fasé's, the whole mass done up in a knot at the base of her neck.

The man was stiff-shouldered and wide-eyed; his lighter silver eyes kept darting from me to my BodyGuards and back again. It was impossible to tell their ages, but I pegged him as the youngest of the group—at least now that Tilla was gone. If he wasn't the youngest, he was clearly the most inexperienced and I wondered why Adora had brought him along.

"A list of our demands, as you requested, Your Majesty." Adora slid the tablet across the table. "My companions and I would like the record to reflect that we are open to negotiations on all those points save the final one."

I scrolled to the bottom of the list and froze.

"Itegas—"

"Since there has been no discussion yet of reparations in the murders of our gods," Adora continued, "the Pedalion will accept one hundred Shen to be sacrificed for each god who was murdered by Javez and Aiz Cevalla."

I swallowed back the million protests that rose up in my throat and settled for the one most like a question. "You want me to negotiate for the deaths of five hundred Shen for a crime that was committed before they were even born?"

"Four hundred," Adora corrected, her businesslike nod so unnerving that I almost missed the fact that the number meant Colonel Morri's story had another inaccuracy. "And it's likely that some of them were, but that is immaterial. Blood will be spilled for blood, one way or another. They can do it to try to foster this useless peace, or they can do it when we go to war."

Fasé's contingent was made up of Sybil and the twins, their presence in the room a welcome respite for all of us. I could see the way my BodyGuards' shoulders relaxed, even if only minutely, as the foursome came into the room.

For a moment I didn't recognize my—could I call her my friend? Fasé was younger than Sybil and at times so inexperienced, but as she walked into the room it was clear she was in charge, and I caught a glimpse of the Farian who was inexplicably leading a revolution against the might of the Pedalion.

Over the last year Fasé's clothing had gone from her ITS uniform, to an approximation of a gray prison outfit, to the white dress she'd been wearing on Pashati. Now she was in all black, an outfit very close to my own chosen uniform. Her red curls were pulled back from her face, done up in an intricate braid that was no doubt the work of my maid. She and the others wore black gloves and I muffled the amused thought that they all looked a great deal like my own BodyGuards rather than Farians.

"Come have a seat," I said.

"Did you have any trouble with Adora?" Fasé asked as she settled into the chair closest to me, Sybil at her side. The twins sat on the opposite side of the table.

"Some." Taking a drink of the chai Stasia had slipped me during the break, I shot Fasé a smile over the rim. "She wasn't wearing gloves and had an extra person. I almost kicked her out of the proceedings."

Fasé's laughter bounced off the ceiling. "I don't suppose I could impose upon you for a recording of that exchange?"

"Maybe." My smile spread into a grin. "I'd rather not be accused of favoritism, though."

"It's probably too late for that, Majesty. However, we do appreciate your support." Sybil passed a tablet across the tabletop. "Here are our requests."

I took the tablet and read through it, looking up at Fasé. "You know how Adora's going to react about wanting the Pedalion disbanded?"

"We do." Fasé nodded. "But it is the driving force behind this revolution, Majesty. I can't not include it. We wish to open Faria up to humanity. We want to share our technology with you, our medical knowledge beyond just this." She waved her gloved hands with a rueful smile. "There is more we can teach you rather than just making you ever more dependent on us to fix what is wrong. In turn you can teach us how to live and how to die. We have all lived for so long we no longer truly understand what those things mean, and we must or this whole experience becomes pointless."

"Okay," I replied with a nod, surprised by the emotion Fasé's words had dragged up in my soul. "Everything else seems straightforward. Are the Shen in agreement with you over the Farians providing land for them to settle on Faria?"

"I believe it will be one of their requests." Fasé looked down at her gloved hands for a moment and then smiled as she stood. "We tried to keep things to the major issues. We will handle the issues past these on our own."

I wasn't entirely sure what she meant by that but didn't like the way my gut twisted, or the possibilities flooding my brain with her words.

*   *   *

I noticed Mia first as I came into the room. The Shen leader was dressed in a suit of pale green, dark buttons running the length of the long skirt on one side and her hands covered by a pair of darker green gloves that reminded me of the forests of Basalt IV. Her hair was loose, the curls spilling over one shoulder and down her back. "Your Majesty," she said, folding her hands together and bowing, all the while keeping her stone-gray gaze on me.

Portis had always teased me about being a sucker for a pretty face.

"Empress," Aiz said, pulling my gaze from his sister and executing an elegant bow of his own. He moved toward me, only to be brought up short by Emmory and Zin closing rank in his way. Alba immediately filled in the space Emmory had left at my side, and somehow my chamberlain reached out and squeezed my fingers without anyone seeing.

Her words about meeting Aiz like a gunrunner rang in my ears and I only just managed to keep from backing up even though the sound of rushing water filled my ears, and I had to bite the inside of my cheek until I tasted blood before it disappeared.

"I have an additional requirement for you, Aiz Cevalla," Emmory said. "You will stay a meter away from the empress at all times. If I see the slightest gesture that makes me think you're going to put a hand on her, I will kill you."

"There is no need for such hostility, *Ekam*," Mia replied, putting a gloved hand on her brother's arm. "We are here because we want peace."

The other two Shen stared, stone-faced, at my *Ekam*, but Aiz merely smiled as he allowed Mia to tug him back a step. It was a slow curving of his lips that made me think of a snake about to strike. He looked past Emmory and his smile grew.

"We are thankful you chose to assist us in these negotiations, Empress, and we will gladly follow any rules that are set forth. You know my sister. May I introduce my comrades?"

"Proceed," I said, heading for the front of the room, my movement breaking the standoff between my BodyGuards and the man who could kill them with a touch.

"I'm afraid we don't have fancy titles like our counterparts," Aiz said. "I present to you: Kag and Thiago."

The Shen were as varied as the Farians I'd met an hour ago were similar. The two men standing behind Aiz were both taller than him; Thiago had the same dark hair and eyes as most Shen I'd seen, while the other—Kag—had blond hair and pale blue eyes.

I realized that both Farian contingents had only one man in their group, while the opposite was true for the Shen, and I caught myself curious as to how much power Mia had in the Shen. I had no clue about the power distribution among either race, but thinking back on it almost all the Farians I'd had contact with were women.

Was that purely because of how much time they'd spent courting Indrana?

"Mia. Gentlemen." I inclined my head in their direction. "Have a seat."

Aiz seated his sister at the other end of the table and then took the seat on her right, the other two Shen pulling out chairs on the other side and sitting with the same easy grace I'd seen from the Farians earlier in the day.

"For the record, Empress, we are both here only because we trust Indrana to keep us safe. Should something happen—"

"Nothing will happen."

"The last time you were at a negotiation the Saxons blew a large hole in a planet."

"Not my fault," I muttered while Aiz grinned and held up his hands.

"I am teasing, please continue."

Folding my hands over the tablet in front of me, I threw out my carefully laid-out plans and looked at Mia. "Tell me a story," I said with a smile.

It threw them into confusion, this departure from what they expected of me.

"A story?" A frown appeared on Mia's lovely face.

"Tell me about the Shen. I've heard from the Farians how you came to be. I'd like to hear it from you."

Aiz crossed his arms over his chest and stared at me. "What did the Farians tell you?"

"It doesn't matter. I want to hear it from you."

"It's an unpleasant tale, Your Majesty." Mia shook her head. "One of oppression and sacrifice."

"I've heard a number of them," I replied. "Indulge me."

"We were Farians once," Aiz said after looking at his sister and then down at his gloved hands. "Their gods were cruel, capricious things. They liked to see us suffer. They liked to send us out into the black as sacrifices. Those sacrificed weren't reborn. They were lost forever. Our brothers and sisters thought it was a small price to pay for the protection and favor of the gods; but then, they were the ones with the protection, so why wouldn't they think that?"

"What changed?"

"A group of sacrifices came home—my father and mother and I—a handful of others. They pretended to be glad to see us. We pretended to be glad to be back, and lied about a glorious thing we had discovered."

"It wasn't a total lie," Kag spoke up.

"True. We did find something out in the black. Knowledge of how to manipulate this gift." Aiz snorted and held up his gloved hands. "This *gift* from the gods. A gift that they'd given us but throttled and constricted under layer after layer of laws and lies. It wasn't a true gift; it was just one more chain wrapped around our throats."

All of them vibrated with barely contained anger. Even Aiz, who'd been so controlled the few times I'd seen him, was tight-jawed, his eyes full of fire.

Then he smiled at me, a terrible, cold smile.

"They held a feast for us. I suspect the gods were planning to kill us in front of the others as a lesson to future sacrifices not to come home. Instead, we killed them. Slaughtered, the Farians would say, but to us it was a legal execution of war criminals, a justice meted out for eons of oppression."

"You and your father murdered them in the streets and drank their blood."

Aiz snorted a laugh. "A Farian story told to keep their people in line. Don't question, don't put a toe out of step, or the Shen will come and drink your blood." He waved his hands in the air in mock panic. "Please, Your Majesty. What possible reason could we have to drink the blood of the gods?"

His dismissal was too quick, too practiced, too smooth, and his sister didn't react at all. Why he'd just chosen to lie to me about something that happened so long ago I couldn't fathom, but he had, and it was enough to make me wonder why.

"Fine," I said with a dip of my head in his direction, my face carefully expressionless. "A Farian...fairy tale, as it were. But you did kill them."

"All but two," he confirmed, and I resisted the urge to tell him his numbers were wrong. The truth would come out once I presented the Farians' demands at the open session tomorrow. "Our aim was to save the Farians from the gods and from themselves, but we failed in that."

"Tell me," I asked, steepling my fingers in front of me. "What is it you want out of these negotiations?"

"That's easy, Your Majesty. I want my father's soul back."

"Excuse me?" I couldn't keep the shock out of my voice and off my face. After the Farians' demand earlier that afternoon, I'd thought nothing else about these negotiations could surprise me.

It looked like I was wrong.

"Aiz, ibkeito na perisperar," Mia said in Shen; judging from

the poorly restrained urgency in her voice, I wasn't the only one shocked.

"*Das,*" Aiz hissed back. "*Ya queríthel na perisperar. Tha syneguiré.*"

I cleared my throat and when the pair looked at me, I smiled. "There seems to be some disagreement? Do we need to take a break?"

"We do not, Your Majesty." Aiz answered me after a moment, and I wondered again just how even this joint leadership of the Shen was. At the present, it was clear Aiz was the one in command. "My apologies."

"So, you would like the return of your father's soul. Is that everything? Or—"

"We do have more, Your Majesty." Mia slid a tablet down the table. Emmory intercepted it and passed it to Zin. She did not shrink from my *Ekam*'s glare, nor the one coming from Aiz.

I chuckled and said, "Emmory will likely shoot you also, Mia. I would be careful."

Mia's smile was fleeting, vanishing into a solemn look. "Men are impatient creatures, are they not, Majesty? I sometimes wonder how much we could accomplish in this galaxy if all places were run as Indrana is."

"It does not seem to me that your main fight with the Farians was caused by a gender complaint," I replied.

"True." Mia lifted one slender shoulder and smiled. "But Fasé and I get along well enough, and I like you—"

"Mia." Aiz practically snarled his sister's name, and my Body-Guards tensed.

She slid a sideways look at her brother, briefly rolling her eyes upward before returning her gaze to me. "Read the list, Your Majesty. I think you'll find most of it quite reasonable. Even the return of our father's soul, though it may seem strange to you, is not going to surprise the Farians much.

"We are here because we love our people. I feel like you can understand that love. I carry it with me as a reminder of this burden and will do whatever is necessary to secure a future for them."

I couldn't look away from her. Whatever these new and tangled feelings for the woman across the table from me were, it hadn't escaped my attention that Mia said her people's *future*, not their *peace*, and the determined fire in her eyes made me certain these negotiations were going to be even more difficult than I'd feared.

38

It was well past sunset by the time I made it back to the quiet of my rooms. Emmory and Zin followed me in, my *Ekam* stopping at the doorway to speak with Indula for a moment before he closed it, leaving the three of us in private.

I wandered over to the bar. "Ooo, Yamazaki!" My coo of delight was met by a snicker from Zin. "Hush, you."

"My apologies, Majesty."

"This is rare shit," I said, pouring a drink and sipping at it with a sigh. "Alba, do you want a drink?"

"After that? Yes," she replied. "I'll get it myself, though; you go change."

"Call Ambassador Zellin also, will you? I'd like her input on this."

I set the glass on the ornate table on my way to the bedroom, kicking the door shut behind me, more so Zin wouldn't have to heave a beleaguered sigh and follow me to close it than out of any sense of propriety, and stripped out of my uniform. I smiled at the comfortable gray pants and top Stasia had laid out on the bed and pulled a heavy wrap of darker gray from the nearby chair before heading back into the main room.

"Look at this mess," I muttered, tapping several keys on the nearest console to bring up the demands from the Shen and from both

Farian groups side by side on the large screen on the wall. "It's like they *want* to keep fighting each other."

Zin came to stand at my side, passing me my drink and crossing his arms over his chest. "Even Fasé's request of the dismantling of the Pedalion is just this side of impossible. We're not going to make it through two days of these peace talks. They'll get stuck on those, I guarantee it."

"We won't open with those," Emmory said. "There will be some posturing tomorrow when the entire lists are read, but Her Majesty will be able to get through most of the demands."

"He's right. I'll save those for last. There's no point in setting ourselves up for failure. Maybe if I can get them to talk over these easier terms." I pointed at a few. "Especially something like land for the Shen, which Adora is outnumbered two to one on; I might be able to work them around to something on these last three points."

Alba joined my side. "The Solarians wanted these peace talks to happen, and once Indranan concerns were dragged into it, so did our government. That has to count for something."

"Indranan concerns." I sipped at the whiskey, letting the slight sting ease some of the bitter taste from my mouth. "Is that what we're calling it now?"

"The dead don't care what we call them, Majesty," Emmory replied. "And there will be a whole lot more of them if these two races go to war in our arms of the galaxy."

"Why can't they just go back to the other side of the galaxy? Have their little fight and whoever wins can come home. Or shit, even just go back to wherever they're hiding their homeworld. It's far enough away not to bother the rest of us." I wondered, scanning the lists of demands. Erasing the three most daunting ones did make the task seem easier, and I started sorting through them, letting my mind wander as I imagined what the various reactions would be to each group's requests.

Mia's easy smile slipped into my thoughts and I cleared my throat, earning a strange look from Emmory.

"I wish I had a good answer for you about that, Majesty. Something tells me they're content to have this fight right here." Emmory shook his head.

"That's what worries me," I replied. "I don't know. If you take away demanding that the Farians dismantle their government, the return of a soul, and wanting people killed; then the rest of this?" I gestured with my glass. "Isn't so bad. It looks an awful lot like the demands Mother went back and forth with the Saxons over during the war."

The door cracked open, Iza smiling in my direction as she escorted Heyai into the room.

"Majesty."

"Ambassador. I thought your expertise would be helpful here." I gestured at the wall. "We're discussing the likelihood of getting these three groups to agree on anything on their lists. Each group has made some rather outrageous demands; we've removed them for the moment." I put them back on the screen for Heyai to read and her eyes widened.

"A good choice to remove those for now, Majesty. It's possible they're just shock tactics to make their other requests more palatable?"

"They're still not going to agree on half of it," Alba said. "Or the Farians won't, anyway. Everything about their attitudes today said they were ready for a fight."

"They've come to the wrong place for that," Emmory replied.

Zin rubbed at the back of his neck. "I'd be happy if they agreed to a third and we secured an uneasy cease-fire."

I nodded. "The Solarians were pushing for the peace talks even before we got hit." Something was dancing around the back of my brain, but I couldn't get it to hold still long enough for me to recognize just what it was. I took another drink and hissed air out between my teeth. "*Dhatt*. The Farians wanted us involved. They got what they wanted—after a fashion. The Shen wanted us here, too. Either they all think I'm some kind of miracle worker, or they're just stalling for time."

"Why would they be stalling for time?" Alba frowned and sipped at her drink.

"I'm not discounting Your Majesty's negotiating abilities, but this is a tall order for anyone and you don't exactly have a lifetime of diplomatic experience. I'm more inclined to agree with Alba, but the only thing I can think they would be stalling for is to get their military in position for an attack." Heyai picked up the thread, her face carved into a frown. "We don't know anything about the Farians or the Shen in terms of fleet strength, so it's almost impossible to guess."

"But what if they are stalling?" I snapped my fingers. "When Aiz took me, he said, 'By the time they are willing to beg for your help it will be too late.' He was talking about our alliance with the Farians, but—"

"The Farians aren't exactly begging for help. But what if something has shifted the situation?" Emmory pushed away from his spot at the door and stood on my other side. "Something like Fasé's group gaining traction within Faria?"

"I don't know, the amount of money they offered Indrana was a little bit like begging," Zin said. "But I get your point, *hridayam*."

My *Ekam* shifted uncomfortably. I kept my eyes on the screen and the smile off my mouth at Zin's casual endearment.

"It makes no sense for the Shen to be the ones trying to stall. The Shen chose to engage the Farians here, after all this time. Why do that if they weren't ready to go to war?" Heyai tapped a finger on her lower lip in thought.

"Why do it here at all?" I countered her question with one of my own. "By bringing the fight here they had to know humanity would get involved, which means they want us involved."

"Otherwise they would have kept the fight in their own sector," Alba murmured. Then my chamberlain sighed. "Majesty, I know I've said this before, but I don't like it."

"I am right there with you," I replied.

Heyai tilted her head to the side. "When are you going to bring up the requirement about an immediate demilitarization of our sectors?"

"I was thinking first thing, just to get it out of the way."

"I'd wait," Heyai said. "A few days in, maybe? Let them work some of the issues out first and maybe relax some. By the third day or so the parties usually start to realize just how big a task they have in front of them and what's at stake."

I nodded and jotted down a note on my tablet.

"Majesty, do you mind if I steal Alba for a few minutes?" Heyai asked. "I had a few reports come across my desk today that may be of interest to you, but it would be more efficient to let her take a look rather than distract you from this."

I waved a hand and nodded absently. "Steal away, just bring her back. I can't survive without her."

"I'll see you in the morning." Alba squeezed my forearm.

"Thank you for your help today," I replied with a smile, and tapped my glass to hers.

"Always, Majesty."

I let the conversations between the others fade away as I stared at the competing lists. The Farians wanted justice—or revenge, depending on your definition—for the deaths of their gods. They also wanted to maintain the rigid hold they had on life on Faria, but I knew enough about revolutions to know that they were trying to hold on to oxygen in a vacuum with their bare hands. Change was coming; it didn't matter what they did.

Mia and Aiz wanted to come home, though for the life of me I couldn't figure out why they considered Faria home when Aiz had been gone for so long and Mia had never set foot on the planet. They wanted the Shen to not have to hide. They wanted the war to be over.

And then there was Fasé. I canted my head to the side. Fasé, whose people were looking to her to lead them. Fasé, who seemed so sure of the path she was taking. Was it because she could see the destination?

"Majesty, Fasé is here. Should I have Indula let her in?" Emmory asked.

"That was prophetic." I laughed at Emmory's confused eyebrow. "I was just thinking of her. Let her in. I have something for her to look at."

"This is a three-dimensional Chaturanga game," Zin murmured, still staring at the screen.

"Evening, Fasé. It's only the first day and I'm ready to punt your people out into the front yard. Do you speak Shen?"

"Evening, Your Majesty," Fasé said with a laugh as she came into the room. "I do. It was required for those of us who left the planet."

I reached my free hand out, touching my fingers to hers and transferring the digital recording of my day. "Let me find the time stamp on the conversation Aiz and Mia had."

"Is that Kag?" Fasé's eyes lit up in surprise. "I wonder—" Her eyes unfocused slightly as she cued up my recording. "It is him. Interesting. He's an old friend from home. I was told he'd gone, but obviously I didn't get the whole story." She looked up at me. "I think I found the part you were talking about, just after Aiz demanded his father's soul?"

"Yes." I nodded, stopping my own search. It was interesting that there wasn't any shock in Fasé's voice over that, and my curiosity grew.

"Mia says, 'You were going to wait.' I'm assuming she's talking about the demand for the soul. Aiz replies with—that *Das* is a hiss of annoyance, not really a word." Fasé frowned. "'You wanted to wait. I will go on.'" She glanced at me. "Next time, let them talk—they're being foolishly arrogant by assuming you won't have access to someone who can speak Shen. There's not enough context there. I can tell you there's obviously a disagreement about how to proceed, but not why."

"You're being extremely nonchalant about the fact that they demanded a soul," Zin said.

Fasé lifted both hands. "The Pedalion probably does have it."

We all stared at her.

"I haven't had nearly enough to drink for this." I tossed back the remains of my whiskey and headed back to the bar. "Why didn't you tell me about this earlier?"

"I honestly didn't know. We heard rumors of Javez's death but assumed that the Pedalion had actually killed him, not taken his soul hostage. But reflection on that tells me I should have probably assumed the worst of them. They know that the idea of his father trapped will drive Aiz mad and he'll do almost anything to get him back." Fasé perched on the edge of the dark brown couch, balancing herself easily with her knees under her chin.

"What about Mia? How does she feel about her father?"

"It's hard to say. She may be less attached given that half of her is human." Fasé smiled at me. "You're frowning. It's just reincarnation, Majesty. The concept should be easy for you," she said, a hint of laughter in her voice. "How else do you think Sybil and I got to be so old?"

"In theory, yes, I understand it," I replied. "Do I believe in it?" I took a drink and stared out the window at the stars sparkling in the sky. "I don't know, Fasé."

I'd promised Ganesh that I would do my duty if he protected my people, but where had he been when Cas gave his life for ours? Where had he been when Commander Resnik had faced down the Shen missiles with nothing more than a trio of unarmed freighters?

"Do you think we're all crazy?"

I cleared my throat and turned from the window. "Your gods are real, and your souls are things that apparently can be kept in little jars waiting for someone to demand their return. I'll roll with it for now. Mostly because it means while Aiz is dangerous, he's not entirely delusional."

Fasé studied me, an inscrutable look on her face that put Emmory to shame. "We can work with that," she said, finally, with a nod in my direction. "Whoever killed Javez Cevalla took his soul so he couldn't come back. This was, by all accounts, the reason for the renewed attacks by the Shen, and the spreading of the conflict into the human arms of the galaxy. I don't know if the Pedalion ordered the hit—though it wouldn't surprise me—but they gladly accepted the bargaining chip."

"How could a Farian have gotten that close to him?"

"Any number of ways; the Farian converts to the Shen side still look very much like Farians for a while. It would have been easy to slip someone in." She pondered the question. "At least from a visual standpoint. I suspect it was much harder than that. Why do you ask?"

"Curious," I replied. "Aiz and Mia seem more focused on getting the soul back than finding out who was responsible. Do you think that's because they already know?"

"It's possible. If they do, Aiz will throw it at Adora the moment he sees her. That's not the sort of opportunity he'd pass up. If they don't have the assassin they'll be hunting whoever it was, and they will find them. For now Aiz will push as hard as he can to get his father back because he knows these negotiations are his best chance. Killing someone is easy; retrieving a soul from the Pedalion—" She shook her head. "No one has ever accomplished it."

"They specifically started shooting around human targets to bring us into the fight?" I stared at the ceiling and blew out a breath, pushing aside the desire to ask Fasé more questions about souls that wouldn't help me manage these negotiations. "Or to push us right where we are now because they knew the Farians wouldn't sit down and negotiate with them otherwise."

"It certainly seems that way. It could also be that they hoped humanity would kick the Farians out of your spaces. The results of that would be disastrous. The Pedalion would be forced to admit there are other ways for us to dispose of our excess energy than giving it to humans. There are too many Farians and not enough gods left for them to take on that kind of burden." Fasé shrugged. "Either way, the Shen's plan worked, didn't it?" She tilted her head at me. "Was Mia flirting with you? Interesting."

I realized she was still watching the recording of the Shen and closed my eyes with a muttered curse at the curious looks my Body-Guards were now directing my way. "How about we not have that conversation," I replied, opening my eyes and refusing to look in Emmory's direction. "Mia is part human?"

"Yes, Majesty." Fasé was still grinning at me. "The Shen have intertwined their lives with humans, and Javez was with her mother during her brief life. I cannot say for sure if those who are the off-spring of humans and Shen carry their soul from life to life. Maybe they do and they don't remember it. Or they don't speak of it. But the original defectors, their souls remain the same as ours do."

"So, Aiz isn't Shen. He's a Farian."

"I would not say such a thing to him, Majesty." Fasé shook her head and squeezed my hand once before releasing me. "He would kill you for it. Granted, he'd probably bring you back to life right after, but I wouldn't recommend trusting him on that front."

"I'm pretty sure Emmory's going to kill him before he ever puts his hands on me again."

Fasé opened her mouth, closed it again, and looked to the side, some inner debate happening before she exhaled and spoke again. "You are technically correct. He was Farian. He chose to become something different, same as his father. Same as the other original Shen. Same as Kag is now, you can see the shift in him."

"That's why Aiz doesn't look like you?"

"He's chosen not to," Fasé replied to Emmory's question with a laugh. "And after so many years, I suspect it's just who he is now." Her face creased in thought. "Also, his manipulation of the gift veers wildly from what the gods intended. I suppose it's possible in a few thousand years I will look different as well, given the path I've chosen."

Part of my brain desperately wanted to ask just what she meant by that, but the rest of it was screaming about the volume of information Fasé had just hit us with.

"I think that's enough for tonight," Emmory said. "I don't know about the rest of you, but I've hit my saturation limit."

"It is enough," Fasé agreed. "There will be more revelations in the days to come, I'm afraid. Take the time while you have it, Your Majesty."

"Good night, Fasé."

Emmory and Zin walked her to the door and stood a moment in quiet conversation with the Farian before she patted them both in the chest and left the room.

I exhaled and stared at the screen for a long moment before I shut it down and looked at Emmory.

"Get some sleep, Majesty," he said. "We've got a long day ahead of us."

"Tell me about it," I replied, and headed for the bedroom. "I'm going to go drown myself in the shower."

Zin jerked as if I'd slapped him, and Emmory's sharp inhale was loud in the silence. I froze and pressed a hand to my eyes.

"Fuck," I muttered. "I am so sorry."

"It's all right, Majesty." Emmory found his voice first, but it was raw with emotion. We hadn't really talked about the aftermath of Wilson's attack on me, not in any detail. But they'd all watched me drown—fires of Naraka, the whole empire had—and it was unbelievably heartless of me of be so flippant.

"If anyone can joke about that, it's you," Zin said.

"Cowshit." Whiskey sloshed over the side of my glass as I crossed to him and wrapped my arms around his neck. "I'm sorry."

Zin hugged me back, his reply muffled by my arms. "Please don't ever do that again, Hail. The dying part, not the jokes."

"I'll do my best. Let me go so I can hug your husband before he pretends like none of this happened."

I felt Zin's rumbling amusement before he let me go and set my glass down on the table on my way to Emmory. My *Ekam*'s dark face was impassive, unreadable, but it had been nearly a year since he picked me out of the carnage of my ship and brought me home. A year of us together almost every day.

I knew what he was thinking and what he wouldn't allow himself to say even now.

"I'm sorry," I whispered, stepping closer and sliding my arms around his waist as I rested my head on his shoulder.

Emmory didn't say a word, but his arms closed around me, tightening almost to the point of pain, and he pressed his cheek to mine. His exhalation, when it came, was just the slightest bit shaky, and I heard him whisper something before he released me but couldn't quite make out what he'd said.

I knew better than to ask him to repeat it. Clearing my throat and retrieving my drink, I saluted them with it. "I am going to turn my bios off for an hour."

"Yes, ma'am. Just turn them back on or I'll have to come wake you."

"I'll see you both in the morning."

"Good night, Majesty," they echoed.

Flipping my bios off, I set my glass down on the edge of the bathroom counter and reached into the shower to turn the water on. The sound made my breath catch, but I didn't yank my hand back; instead I held it under the water. The drops splashed and bounced and rolled over my palm, dripping between my fingers to the shower floor.

I waited for the pain, the fear, the suffocating weight on my chest. It didn't come in a rush, but rather a slow, creeping thing I could feel crawling up from my toes.

"Okay, you can do this." I pulled my hand out, stripped my clothes off, and climbed into the shower.

39

I was up, watching Sol rise, cutting the Matterhorn out of the night sky with golden swords of light, when Hao came into the room. "Good morning."

"Morning," he replied, sitting next to me. "Sleep well?"

"A few hours; I'm grateful it doesn't take long to adjust to Earth time." I reached a hand out, brushing it over the bruise decorating his cheek. "What happened?"

"Someone tried to cash in on Po-Sin's bounty." He shrugged. "Before you say it, I'm not hiding in here like a rat in a cage. I suppose the Solies were onto something when they pushed so hard for standard times that weren't far off from Earth's. Though it's an exhausting thing on the outer rim."

"I remember. Can you believe that people climbed that mountain several thousand years ago with zero tech?"

"Our consistent flaw is our reckless stupidity."

"We are driven to explore, even at the risk of our own lives." I smiled. "It's one of our greatest strengths. What were you up to out there?"

"Checking on a few things." Hao grinned in return. "Rai said to tell you hello and thanks for the heads-up about the visitors in town."

"I can't imagine what they're thinking." I rolled my eyes. "If they accidentally take out a Solarian citizen they're going to be in a pile of shit."

"That's their problem. Gita was following me to make sure I didn't do anything wrong, by the way. I moved slow so she could keep track of me. I am a little hurt she didn't lend a hand with those two idiots."

"She knew you could handle it. Not to mention you would have just been snarly about the help. She would possibly forgive you faster if you stopped being an ass, you know? Swallow your pride, *gege*."

"Mind your own business."

"I hate that my trust in you is damaged. I can't imagine how she feels."

Hao cleared his throat and changed the subject. "We followed those leads Caspel passed on. I no longer have access to Un—to Po-Sin's accounts. However, Dailun was able to charm a bank teller into giving him a peek."

"What were you thinking? You'll get Dailun killed, never mind the poor girl at the bank."

"The boy at the bank can take care of himself," Hao corrected me absently. "And Po-Sin won't do anything to Dailun. He can't. Dailun has practical immunity while he's Traveling. He might get his ass chewed when he—if he—finally comes home, but that's it."

"Fine, what did you find out?" I poked him. "But if something happens to that bank teller, I'm holding you and Dailun personally responsible."

"I'll pass that along. He took Henri out for a drink." Hao's grin faded. "Hail, they paid Po-Sin a lot of money. This is the fifth account we've tracked down so far."

"What's a lot?"

"Current total is fifteen trillion credits."

"That's a fucking tenth of my Shiva-damned treasury." I looked away from the sunrise in shock. "How in Shiva's name do the Shen have that kind of money to throw around? And who else are they paying?"

"I don't know." Hao shook his head. "But they've got Po-Sin's support unless the first battle with the Farians somehow does enough damage to make him think that's not enough money."

"Can you find out where it's coming from?" The idea struck me, and I turned back to the rising sun.

"The tracking number on the transfer came from a bank I recognized." It was Hao's turn to stare at the Matterhorn as he mulled over the problem. "Yes, I think I can. Give me a few days."

"Check in with Gita." He glared at me. "What? She knows what she's doing. If you get stuck, ask her for help." I patted him on the knee as I stood. "I have to get ready. I'll talk to you later."

Hao muttered something in Cheng that sounded distinctly like *I regret all my choices in life* as he left the room.

"Oh, this is going to be fun," I subvocalized over the private com link with Emmory as first the Farians and then the Shen were ushered into the room from the two doors on opposing sides. Fasé and her people were already seated at the wide table.

The tension in the room shot up to the level of an engine room with an Alcubierre/White Drive going into failure. I dragged in a breath, set my shoulders, and sent a prayer winging up to Hanuman to keep Indrana safe and my head clear as I protected my people.

Adora took in Fasé's company, her mouth drawing into a thin line of disapproval, and she muttered something under her breath to the woman standing at her side.

"Good morning, Empress," Aiz said, his gaze flicking to Emmory, standing resolutely on my right-hand side. The positioning put him between me and the Shen, a fact that, judging by Aiz's wry grin, didn't escape him.

Adora and the Farians filled in the seats on the left side of the table.

Aiz's grin grew. "Good morning, Adora. It's a delight to see you again after all these years."

"Gamo re enis, retikós."

I didn't have to understand the words to understand that tone of voice. However, the other Farians gasped in shock, so whatever Adora had said wasn't good. Aiz's grin went almost feral in response and Mia shot me a helpless look. I sighed and tapped a knuckle on the tabletop.

"We have just gotten started," I said. "Adora, that's your first warning to watch your mouth. Same for you, Aiz. If you came here for a negotiation, act like it. Otherwise, get the fuck out."

"I was perfectly polite," he replied, but put his hands up when I put mine on my guns. "My apologies, Empress. Please continue."

"Everyone have a seat," I said, leaving one hand on a gun and looking around the room with a smile. "You all know me, and presumably you know each other, though we'll do a quick round of introductions before we get started. Before that, I will lay down the ground rules for these negotiations. I am the sole deciding voice in these chambers, the last word. I trust you all understand what that means, and that when I tell you to be quiet, you will do so without pause.

"As my chamberlain informed you yesterday," I continued, gesturing at Alba, who was sitting by my side, "each side is allotted three warnings during our morning session and three in the afternoon. They do not carry over, but don't feel like you need to use them. I promise you the more warnings I have to issue, the more cross I will get. Three warnings," I repeated. "The fourth will result in the entire delegation being removed from the room, at which point I will speak for you. Any decisions made after you leave will be on your own heads."

"We will not abide by decisions made without our input."

I smiled. "You will abide by whatever I tell you to abide by, *Itegas* Notaras, or you can leave now and deal with the Shen in your own territory. Your choice."

"Why do you get weapons?" The question came from Aiz, leaning back in his chair with one arm hooked over the back. Mia sighed and shook her head.

"I get guns," I said, staring Aiz down with a cold smile and putting a hand on the second SColt 45 I'd added on my left hip, "because I said so. You all wanted me in charge, this is what you get.

"After I am finished with the rules for these negotiations, I will go through each point on the lists. You are welcome to ask for clarifications on individual points, but you are not required to give any sort of answer at this time. Let's begin."

Six hours later, we'd been through the bulk of the demands on each side without further incident. Though the look Adora had shot in Fasé's direction when I announced the dismantling of the Pedalion had been filled with pure hatred.

The Farian requirement of Shen sacrifices had been met by Aiz with little more than a grim look and a shake of his head. Mia, however, looked sickened. Neither of them had done more than blink at the number difference at all, though Kag had frowned.

"The final issue for the Shen is the matter of the soul of Javez Cevalla," I said.

"What of it?" Adora snapped.

"The Shen would like it returned." I gave her a warning look that had zero effect.

The glare she turned on Aiz could have melted plasteel. "You can have your father's soul when the whole of the Pedalion lies dead and Etrelia is burning."

"Those are acceptable terms as far as I'm concerned," Aiz replied, laying a hand on Mia's arm before she could respond, and I watched her sit back in her seat, the first hints of hatred finally showing on her face.

So she does care about getting her father back.

Adora glanced my way and thought better of whatever she'd been about to say, folding her gloved hands together on the tabletop.

I waited a beat and then nodded as I got to my feet. "The session is closed for the day. I suggest you all retire and start thinking about which points you are willing to consider. I will see you in the morning."

The Shen and the Farians filed out. As soon as the room was empty I sank back into my chair and rubbed my eyes with my hands.

"Well done, Majesty."

"That was the easy part," I said, not looking up at Emmory. "Tomorrow when they reject all the demands out of spite? That's when things get really fun."

"Have a little faith," Emmory replied.

"I ran out of that a long time ago. We're talking about Indrana's future here. One that takes a dramatic turn for the worse if these groups go to war." I pushed to my feet. "I need a drink."

My *smati* pinged from an incoming com link as we made our way up the stairs to my rooms. A quick glance at the ID showed Agent Paez's information at the HCL facility, and I shared a look with Zin as I answered it. "Luis, hang on, I'm almost back in my rooms and I want to put you on the screen."

"Yes, Majesty," he replied.

Hao was leaning against the wall next to my door, legs crossed, and staring out the massive stained-glass window that overlooked the stairs. Gita was on the opposite side, pretending to ignore him. Poor Dailun sat in the middle and shot me a relieved look as he got to his feet.

I waved them into the room as I passed and transferred Luis's com onto the screen.

"Majesty," he said with a smile and a nod, his sharp dark eyes taking in the other occupants. "We're good?"

"We are, what do you have for me?"

"The results of the scan of that Farian outpost we spoke about, ma'am." Luis swallowed, a frown creasing his handsome face.

"Are you going to make me ask?"

"No, sorry, ma'am. It's just—we were able to catch a glimpse as we moved the telescope. There's not much there, but it's enough for me to be able to tell you that it wasn't any Farian ships I've seen before that hit the Persuor outpost."

"Was it mercenaries?" I asked Luis.

He shook his head. "It was—I'll just show you, Majesty. It's easier."

The screen split, showing the faint glow of the star behind the world where the Farian colony had been. A trio of ships, a design I'd never seen before, swooped in out of warp far too close to the planet for any sane pilot to be comfortable with.

"What the actual fuck," Gita cursed from behind me. "What are those things?"

They weren't normal Farian ships, with their rigid lines and sharp angles. These ships were designed for atmo, sleek as Indranan dolphins and so dark I could barely pick them out against the backdrop of space even with the light of the star. A blue light sliced out of each of them, stabbing down into the planet below with a precision no orbital bombardment could hope to match.

I was thankful for our visual, cold and clinical as it was, though I could all too easily imagine the chaos and pain down below. This was why there hadn't been any survivors of the colonies. Less than five minutes of that awful light and everything the ground below was nothing more than a smoking ruin.

"Dark Mother preserve us." Zin's whispered prayer echoed into the silence.

I met Luis's dark eyes. "You think it's the Shen?"

"I don't know who it could be, Majesty. It's no Farian ship we've ever seen, but that doesn't mean it's not theirs. We don't know enough about the Shen ships, though the design leans more toward their other ships than not. The alternative is that there's a third player in this game, and I like that even less."

"The Farians said they bombarded the colony from orbit." I jabbed a finger at the screen. "That's not the least bit like an orbital strike."

"I've never seen anything like that," Gita said. "Nothing in development, not even a whisper that anyone in the galaxy is even *thinking* of building something with that kind of firepower."

"If it is the Shen," Emmory said, his voice a rumble of concern, "They've got a lot more firepower than they've been letting on."

"If I had something like that, I wouldn't be sitting here at peace negotiations," I said, pointing at the ship and shaking my head. "Even if that's the only ships they've got, they could put a serious dent in the Farians, no matter what kind of defenses they're going up against."

"Unless they only have the three."

I turned to look at Hao. He was leaning against the edge of the couch, fingers tapping restlessly against the butt of the gun on his right leg. He gestured at the screen. "If the Shen only have those three, or for argument's sake if the Farians own those ships and are crazy enough to attack their own people. That's a good enough reason for keeping them as hidden as possible. If they flew them right at Faria they'd take a beating before they got to the planet. I can say that even not knowing what kind of defenses they have, because the same thing would happen if they flew on Pashati or Earth. I don't care what kind of firepower you have on a ship, it doesn't do you any good if you can't get past the defenses to take a shot."

"He's right," Gita said, the words filled with grudging respect.

"So far they've hit outposts and colonies. Things well away from planetary defenses of any kind, or even large masses of ships. My vote is it's the Shen, but we need more information."

"Agreed," Luis said.

"As weird as this sounds, I really hope that's not some new alien race deciding to make our lives more difficult," I muttered. "All right, we'll table this for further investigation. Luis, get this info to Caspel. Tell him I want every available resource directed at finding out who owns those ships and how many of them there are. Dailun, you and Alba get on this. Hao's busy with the money trail."

"Done." They all nodded at me. Luis signed off the link and I dragged a hand through my hair.

"Emmory?"

"Yes, Majesty?"

"I want to talk with Mia. See if Fasé can arrange that."

"May I ask why?"

I leveled him with an imitation of his Look but was met with calm patience. "I want to talk with Mia alone. Aiz isn't going to let me do that in the peace talks, but she might be more amenable."

"I'll speak with Fasé." He left the room, exchanging words with Johar as she came in. I'd been privately relieved when Johar passed on the opportunity to head back to Pashati and instead came to Earth with us. Protocol or not, my gut felt better having her with us, and her reputation was equally helpful in keeping the more reckless mercenaries off Hao's tail.

"Hail." She tapped her fist on mine. "Perimeter is secure. Told Emmory he needs to have a word with the Marines on the southwest corner. They didn't issue a challenge until I was well within killing range."

"I'm sure he will." I chuckled. Johar had taken it upon herself to run constant tests on the embassy's security. I was sure she was giving the Marine in command constant heartburn, but it gave her something to do—and as I'd told Emmory the first night here, a bored Johar was a terror none of us needed to deal with at the moment.

"Speaking of the money trail," I said, turning toward Hao and Dailun. "What's the latest?"

Hao pulled a tablet from his pocket and handed it to me. "I hit up three more accounts. Same general payments with the final total in the vicinity of twenty trillion."

Zin whistled. "That's a lot of credits. Where are they getting that kind of money from?"

"Especially if we assume that they're shelling out the same to the other mercs. *Hai Ram.*" I muttered. "They're laundering an awful lot for no one to be talking."

"I'm closing in on it," Hao replied. "I can tell you we've narrowed the origin of the payments down to two different companies. They're likely still fronts, but give us a little more time and we'll know for sure who the source is."

I passed the tablet over to Gita on my way to the couch; she glanced at it and then shook her head, her jaw tight with disapproval.

"What?" Hao's demand was sharp.

"Why should we believe you?" Gita demanded. "I'm just looking at a bunch of routing numbers. All I have is your word they go to the banks and companies you've got on the list."

Hao visibly gathered his patience. "I know how to track money, Gita. A little trust here would go a long way."

"That's funny coming from you."

"Are we going to do this now?" Hao raised an eyebrow. "I don't mind either way, just want to be sure you are okay with the audience."

"We're not going to do anything." She tossed the tablet onto the nearby desk and headed for the door. "Come talk to me when you have some kind of proof that's more than you wanting me to believe your word again."

"This is awkward," Johar muttered, low enough so only I could hear. "I wish they'd go back to having sex."

My choked laughter earned me a glare from Hao, which I met with an innocent smile.

"A little help would be appreciated, Your Majesty."

"You're doing just fine on your own," I said. "Go find some proof."

Hao snatched the tablet up, muttering under his breath as he stormed out of the room.

40

Bugger me." I set the cup of chai down, shaking the spilled tea off my hand with a second muttered curse.

"Stop pacing with a hot cup in your hand," Alice said, and winked when I shot her a look.

"It helps me think." Wiping the remains of the tea off on my pants, I picked up my cup again and resumed my pacing.

"With respect, Majesty," Caspel said from the other half of the split screen. "It makes me a tad dizzy to try to watch you when Alice isn't moving on her screen."

"I would get up and pace with you, Majesty, but—" Alice gestured at Ravalina, the newborn sleeping peacefully on her chest, and smiled innocently.

"I have enough trouble here without you two ganging up on me also," I replied, but I dropped into the desk chair, narrowly managing to avoid spilling a second time and sighed. "I cannot promise I won't shoot every single person in that room today."

This time Caspel's smile was sympathetic. "I've seen the video of yesterday, Majesty; you held yourself together quite well under the circumstances."

"Indranan lives are at stake, Caspel. I'm rather required to keep it together, I think."

"Well, yes, but it doesn't change the facts."

The third day of negotiations had not gone well. Adora had met me at the door with an accusation of trying to undermine the negotiations by wanting to speak to Mia directly. How she'd found out about it I still didn't know.

Not that I'd gotten to speak to Mia in the first place, because Aiz had interfered in that regard and sent me a nasty message about the need to speak with both of them or not at all.

Even Fasé had gotten in on the action yesterday and in the midst of the discussion about dismantling the Pedalion had earned herself not one but two warnings for calling Adora names I still couldn't find a translation for.

They'd made Aiz laugh, though he wouldn't tell me what Fasé had said and neither would Sybil.

I rubbed at the skin between my eyes with my free hand and sighed. "Thanks. I did get them to agree on a few things, so I guess that's a success. We'll see how today goes."

"Keep after them," Alice said. "I'll talk to you later." She disconnected her com and I turned my attention to Caspel.

"They don't care about these negotiations." I met Caspel's surprised look and rolled my shoulders uncomfortably. "The Shen, I mean. Both Aiz and Mia are so calm. They haven't gotten upset about anything at the table while the others are there. The confrontation yesterday about me wanting to speak with Mia alone had been the first time I'd seen Aiz even close to losing his temper since they'd recounted the story about the gods on the first day."

"Go on."

I closed my eyes a moment, recalling the last few days. "Adora is anxious. There's a weight on her, and the other Farians in her group are equally tense. This is important to them, even though they're not willing to cooperate. I honestly think that's just their arrogance getting in the way.

"Fasé and her group are invested." I scrambled for the right words to describe her easy smile and her intensity existing in the same space. "But they seem relaxed, like they—" I couldn't stop my laughter. "Like they know what the outcome is going to be."

"Which makes sense when you think about it." Caspel nodded. "But you think the Shen are just playing along?"

"I think so. I can't put my finger on it."

Caspel was as diplomatic as he was good at spying and didn't press me for more details. "It's your gut, Majesty. Would there be an objection from the Farians or the Shen to having Johar in the room today? She's as good as you are at spotting details others might miss."

"After all that haranguing I got from Caterina about proper companions and who I should have conversations with?" I couldn't resist the tease. "You're telling me to have Hao follow up on leads and to put Johar in the middle of a politically charged situation. Are you trying to get me in trouble?"

Caspel rolled his eyes at the ceiling. "They have skills that happen to fall into these specific occasions, Majesty, and I am always in favor of the right tool for the job." He grinned at me. "Besides, that was the matriarchs who were uneasy and while I don't blame them, I do understand where you were coming from."

"My sister knew what she was doing when she appointed you."

Caspel's smile was fond. "She would have been a good empress, Majesty. I hope you'll forgive me for saying that I am glad you are here to handle this, though."

"Forgiven." I knew what he meant. My sister would have been overwhelmed by all this chaos. Domestic administration of an empire in peacetime was one thing; negotiating a truce between two ancient warring alien races was something else entirely. "And thank you."

"Have a good day, Majesty. I look forward to reading your report this evening."

I disconnected the com link and looked over at Gita. "He was being serious, wasn't he?"

"Yes, ma'am. Caspel doesn't say things he doesn't mean."

The door opened before I could reply and Johar poked her head in. "Kisah said it was okay." She jerked a thumb over her shoulder with a grin. "But if I'm interrupting I can come back."

"No, come in," I said. "I've got a question for you anyway. Do you want to do me a favor today?" I asked as she shut the door. "Or do you have something else planned?"

"I don't, what do you need?"

"Alba's still busy with Dailun. Come to the negotiations with me and watch. I want a second opinion on some things."

"I can do that." Johar gestured at her plain black tunic and pants. "Do I need to change?"

I laughed and held a hand out to her, pulling her into a hug when she took it. "No, never change."

"I'd say the same to you, but you seem to be shifting in front of my eyes." She murmured, hugging me back. "It's not a bad thing, I think, but some days I miss Cressen."

"Some days I miss her, too," I admitted.

For reasons I couldn't understand, Fasé's contingent and the Shen were demanding land for the Shen on the Farian homeworld. Adora, obviously, rejected this the moment it was brought up, and the ensuing fight about it nearly disrupted the entire proceeding.

"Out!" I snapped, my patience gone. "We're breaking for lunch early. You stay right there," I said to Aiz as he started to get out of his seat. "Both of you."

He and Mia shared a look but complied, and I waited until the doors had closed behind Fasé before slamming both palms into the tabletop.

"Would one of you like to explain to me why you won't accept one of the other planets in the Farian home system for a settlement."

"It is just as much our land as it is theirs, Empress," he replied. "We have every right to be there."

"They are never going to agree to it and it still doesn't answer my question."

"It does," Mia countered. "You just don't like the answer, Majesty."

"Why would you want to put your people there in the first place?" I asked. "They will never get a moment's rest."

"You wouldn't understand," Aiz said, shaking his head as he got to his feet. "And in all honesty, Your Majesty, it doesn't matter. Your job is to facilitate these talks, not understand our reasons why."

"You asked me to do this, and I could make better arguments for you if I knew why."

A smile peeked through Mia's solemn expression. "You likely could, Majesty; however, it wouldn't make any difference. Adora will not yield on this point, so we will take our home back by force."

"You're abandoning the negotiations?" Fear tightened my throat and I fought not to show it on my face. If they walked out? I couldn't stop the worst-case scenarios from spinning through my head—images of Indrana at war were at the forefront, with the other human spaces not far behind.

"No." Aiz shook his head. "Absolutely not. We agreed to this in good faith and will stay for as long as the Farians do so. But they will walk away first and then we will go to war."

"All right." I held in the frustrated exhalation until they left the room.

"He doesn't give a shit about that land," Johar said, unfolding herself from her spot in the corner of the room. No one had remarked on her presence. I'm not sure anyone had even seen her. Johar was very good at making herself unobtrusive when she chose to do so. "Well, he does and he doesn't."

"What?"

"That land he just spent an hour arguing with the Farians about. He wants it, but he knows he's not going to get it and it's strange that that doesn't upset him at all. It doesn't upset either of them."

Johar scratched at her scalp, disrupting her short black hair. She settled into the chair Aiz had just vacated and mimicked his posture. Her legs were stretched out, and one arm looped over the back of the chair. Aiz had been sitting like that from the moment he'd joined us.

"I think you're right about the Shen being unusually relaxed," she continued. "This isn't a man who is invested in the outcome of something. This is a man who's killing time, who's waiting."

"Waiting?" I frowned, angry at myself for being distracted enough that I hadn't made the connection. "For what?"

"I don't know. Something. Whatever it is, he could give two shits about these negotiations, Hail." She shook her head and gestured around the room.

"He wasn't lying about sticking around," she said, waving a long-fingered hand at the door. "But only because he's pretty sure the Farians will back out first. You already know that."

"I do." Leaning my head in my hand with a groan, I dropped into my seat. "Shiva forgive me, they're all liars. I could ask them how the weather is and get eight different answers, all of them wrong. What I don't know is why the fuck they're bothering with this show."

"I wish I knew," she replied. "It makes me uneasy, Hail. That rolling gut-level feeling where the job is a little too easy and the payoff a little too good, you know what I mean?"

"Yeah." I mentally revised my tally of the members of my crew who were now feeling uneasy, and I did not like the results. "This is bullshit. A smokescreen. And he doesn't even care enough not to telegraph it. The question then becomes how in the fires of Naraka do I get out of it without getting everyone killed and starting up a war that will engulf the entire galaxy?"

Emmory muttered a curse that I echoed.

Johar got to her feet and stretched. "I'm going to do some looking around. I'll let you know what I find?"

"Do," I said.

Johar nodded and loped out of the room. I shared a look with Emmory. "What have we gotten ourselves into?"

"I don't know," he said. "Should we call this? Get out of here and let them fight it out? We could increase patrols for our freighters, pull things back to the empire as much as possible. Just wait it out?"

"If I thought it would work I'd be tempted to agree with you." I bumped my shoulder into his on my way to the window, leaning both hands on the sill and staring out into the street below us. "But I can't. The other human governments are expecting me to make peace here. Tomorrow I'm going to throw down in a roomful of aliens and tell them if they don't come to an agreement, then all of humanity is prepared to defend ourselves with force if necessary.

"They dragged me into this mess in the first place, Emmy. We don't know why, but we both know they're not going to let me out of it without a fight."

"That's what worries me," he replied. "I can't protect you here. There're too many variables, too many people. All one of them has to do is put their hands on you and it's over."

"If they wanted me dead—"

"Please don't say it." Emmory's laugh was pained as he joined me at the window. "I know they could, Hail. And I don't know why they haven't. What I do know is you have a knack for making people want to kill you. In this case it's all too obvious just how easy that would be for them."

"The good news?" I waited for Emmory to look at me before I continued. "I'm very good at not only avoiding being killed, but killing people back. Now I have an entire military at my beck and call. If the Farians wanted a war with Indrana, they would have done it when I refused them the first time.

"And the Shen? They want me involved, so we can be reasonably sure they're not willing to kill me? If anything, because of the epic shitstorm they know it would bring down on their heads."

"I hope you're right, Majesty. I really do."

"Same, Emmory." I rested my head on his shoulder for a heartbeat. "I never thought I'd say this, but I want to go home."

After lunch on the fourth day, I stood with both hands braced on the tabletop as the others filed into the room and took their seats. I'd been building up to this all morning, pushing and prodding and even teasing the assembled aliens into agreement on the issues they'd presented. My biggest triumph was getting Adora to agree to speak with the Pedalion that evening about a place for the Shen on Faria, even though it had come with a heavy warning from her that they were unlikely to budge on the subject.

"I appreciate you all making an effort to come to agreements on these issues," I said, gesturing at the screen behind me. The three glaring demands from each group were still marked as unfinished and I privately suspected they would remain so well after we'd concluded the negotiations. "Before we move on to them, however, I'd like to take a moment to let you know about humanity's requirements from these peace talks."

The Farians and Shen shared confused looks across the table before Adora spoke up. "Your Majesty, I don't understand."

"Of course you don't," I replied. "Because throughout this entire mess none of you have thought about the death and destruction you've brought to us. For whatever reason, you chose to bring your fight into our sectors of the galaxy instead of keeping it away from us as you have done for thousands if not millions of years. Don't interrupt me." I held up a hand before Adora could speak. "President Hudson has been in touch with the other leaders and we are all in agreement on this—get your war out of our space. Maybe we took your ships by surprise at the white dwarf binary star, but we defeated them and while we have no wish to go to war with you, we are not going to stand by and let our people become collateral damage in your war. The fight will go worse with all of humanity allied against you."

"Majesty, are you saying you'll go to war with us?" Adora asked.

"Humanity is not great at agreeing on things, but we have agreed that the next time your conflict costs human lives we will take up arms to defend ourselves." I looked at Aiz. "Whatever your agreement is with the mercenaries, tell them to take the fight elsewhere."

Aiz frowned at me. "We are no—"

"I don't need an argument from you right now. I need understanding of the gravity of this situation."

"We understand, Your Majesty," Mia said, putting a gloved hand on her brother's arm. "Fasé?"

"That works for me," Fasé said, and looked at the others. "Honestly, the pair of you should never have taken this squabble out of our system in the first place."

"How dare you," Adora snapped. "You are nothing more than a child. Stop acting like you understand."

"She understands what needs understanding, Adora." This was the first time Sybil had spoken during the negotiations, and the weight of her voice carried through the room. "She may be young, but she sees more clearly than those whose eyes have been clouded by too many years of hatred and anger." She folded her gloved hands in front of her and looked from Adora to Aiz and back again. "You both know what's coming. You both know what must be done. But you have let your egos and your obstinacy throw you into this death spiral."

Mia seemed shocked by Sybil's words, looking to her brother for guidance. Aiz lifted a shoulder, a sad smile peeking through his beard. "You are not wrong, *Máti*, but I chose this path and I will stay on it to the end."

"Even if it means the end of everything you hold dear?" Sybil laid her hands on the table, palms toward the ceiling. "Fires lay waste not just to the things we want to burn down, Brother, especially when they get out of control."

"There are some things that deserve to burn," Aiz said, his gaze flicking to Adora.

"You don't have the firepower to challenge us," Adora spat, coming up out of her chair and slamming both hands on the tabletop. "If you did, you'd already have done so. Stop your pretending, Aiz. You are a murderer and a heretic, and the best thing you could do for your people is show them how to be properly penitent in the face of the horrors you've committed!"

"Horrors?" Aiz laughed, the sound sharp and painful as he got to his feet. "You are a fine one to speak of horrors, Adora. You and the Pedalion traded your souls to those butchers you call gods so long ago you've forgotten anything remotely resembling mercy. How many have you murdered? Can't you hear their screams? Can't you see their faces when you close your eyes?"

The others surged to their feet, chaos descending on the room as the two groups shouted at each other in Farian and in Shen. Fasé sighed, shooting me an apologetic look as Sybil put her head in her hands. I got to my feet, waving a hand at Fasé to back away from the table, and she touched Sybil on the shoulder as she and the twins got to their feet.

Snagging my tablet, I passed it along to Zin. Alba had followed my lead without question and I pushed her behind Zin for good measure.

"Enough," I said. No one looked my way—they were all too lost in the argument, whatever it was. I wondered how long I had before they started pulling gloves off and trying to kill each other. The thought of my BodyGuards in that kind of deadly trap pushed me into motion.

I shared a look with Emmory, whispered an apology to Ambassador Zellin, and pulled my SColts free, aiming them at the massive chandelier. The reports themselves were loud enough but nothing compared to the crashing of several hundred kilograms of glass and metal into the middle of the table. It buckled under the impact, sending both Farians and Shen scrambling for cover. I stayed where I was, turning my head and lifting an arm to protect me from the spray of debris.

"I said that was enough." I holstered my guns. "You will all shut up *right now*. That is your second warning, and I promise you, you don't want to see what happens if I must issue a third." I let my gaze linger on each of them in turn before I exhaled and smiled. "Though, warnings aside, I believe that's enough for today. Go cool off and we'll start again tomorrow."

They all stared at me in shock as I brushed the dust off my jacket and turned to go.

"Furthermore, I expect you all to behave yourselves at the function the Galactic Relations Department is holding for you this evening. Some of you are several thousand years old; try to act like it." I turned and left the room, Emmory and Zin following behind me.

41

Y ou shot the chandelier out of the ceiling." Hao grinned at me,
Dailun beside him already trying to hold his laughter in and
failing. Gita was staring at me with a shocked expression I hadn't
ever seen on her face, and Ambassador Zellin had her face buried
in her hands. Her shoulders were shaking with what I hoped was
laughter and not tears.

"They wouldn't stop yelling," I replied. "And the gloves were
going to come off after that. I wasn't about to leave my people
trapped in the room with a bunch of raving aliens bent on killing
each other." I flung a pillow at Dailun when he finally burst into
laughter and then dropped onto the couch.

I covered my face with my hands. "I really am sorry, Ambassador, and I'll pay for the repairs."

"It's fine, Your Majesty. Honestly, if we had the room I'd
be tempted to just leave it as it is. It would serve as an excellent
warning."

Lifting a hand I shot her a look, entirely sure she was making fun
of me, which was both a relief and more than a little strange. "If
only the Shen and the Farians would pay attention."

The couch shifted as Hao sat next to me. "You've made some
incredible strides in the last few days, *sha zhu*. Don't discount those.
And remember, you're not going to fix this problem overnight. This
is just the first step."

"When did you start being logical and shit?"

He chuckled. "I've always been the more reasonable of the two of us." He patted my wrists until I dropped my hands. "I followed the money trail as far as I could go. I think she's finally happy with the proof."

"Gita?"

My *Dve* nodded. "It checks out. There isn't anything more we can do until we figure out how the Shen are getting the money. Every trail dead-ends before we can get to the source."

"There's a man I think can help who'll be at the party tonight. I'd like to come with you if it's all right," Hao said.

I nodded, but glanced at Emmory. "Will it be too dangerous?"

My *Ekam* shrugged. "I doubt it, Majesty. We'll be on Solarian territory with their guards. The mercenaries won't make a move, at least not without some serious blowback."

"It's easier to meet my contact there," Hao said. "It'll draw less attention in the long run."

"All right, you can come. Do you have clothes?"

Hao snorted. "Please, do I look like an amateur?"

"Go away." I waved a hand at the door, surprised when he obeyed. Gita followed him and I allowed myself to pretend that her shoulders were a little less stiff as they left the room.

"Keep your desire to meddle in that to yourself, Majesty," Emmory said.

I gave him my most innocent look, the one that had fooled hundreds of guards and thieves over the years. "I don't know what you're talking about."

My *Ekam* gave me the Look in return. "They're sorting it out on their own; let it be."

"Maybe." I got up from the couch and smiled at Stasia when she entered the room. "Or maybe they won't and I'll have to help. Either way, it's time to dress me up in my empress costume."

Emmory rolled his eyes at me. "We'll see you downstairs, Majesty."

"Majesty."

I took Zin's offered hand, holding my embroidered sari with the other as I stepped from the aircar. The heavy silk was embroidered with gold thread, the Indranan star shining brightly against the black. Stasia had woven my green curls into a bun at the back of my neck, and the delicate gold crown peeked out among the strands on top.

Hao offered his arm to Alba and threw me a wink as they fell into step behind me. We made our way to the tree-lined entrance beyond the gates of the Galactic Relations Department. The majestic building was part facility, part mansion, and tonight it was decorated to its fullest splendor. Lights streamed out into the soft summer night from a thousand hanging lanterns. The trees were still shedding their blossoms, so that with every slight gust of a breeze the air filled with what seemed like millions of pink petals.

Emmory was a solid presence at my side as we climbed the steps to where President Hudson waited with the Farians and the Shen. Adora's contingent, anyway; Fasé and her people had decided to stay at the embassy for the evening.

The Solarian Conglomerate head looked distinctly uncomfortable at being trapped between the two aliens, and I may have paused halfway up the stairs to brush an imaginary something from my sari simply because I could.

"Majesty," Emmory said over our com link as he bent to help me. I smiled at him, straightened, and finished my climb.

"Your Imperial Majesty." Chad's bow was elegant, almost too extravagant when compared to the stiff nods I received from Adora and Aiz. "The press asked for a photo op, and both *Itegas* Notaras and Ms. Cevalla agreed."

"Well, I'd hate to be the only person saying no," I replied.

Gita slipped into the space Emmory vacated as President Hudson took my hand, and I glanced in my *Ekam*'s direction. He was speaking quietly to a slender blond man my *smati* identified as Arkos Juno, head of the Solarian Guard Service.

I ended up on Chad's right side, with Adora next to me, and the smile on my face was perfect for the camera. The tension hummed through the air and if it wasn't captured in the photo, those around us knew all too well what hung in the balance.

"If I could introduce my wife, Your Majesty," Chad said as the cameras were ushered back toward the door and we proceeded into the building.

"Your Imperial Majesty." Laila Hudson dropped into a curtsy. "It's a great pleasure to welcome you to Earth." She was a tiny thing, with perfectly styled short blond hair and a robin's-egg-blue suit.

"Thank you so much for having me." I held out my hands, taking both of hers as I pushed aside everything else to focus on my duty. "These grounds are lovely."

"They are the cornerstone of the intergalactic complex. It was built in 3257 by President Inuwle. She was a great woman with an eye on the stars. The Solarian Conglomerate owes a great deal of its prosperity to her forward thinking."

Adora smiled at President Hudson's explanation. "She was a great benefit to humankind overall. We made first official contact with Earth during her terms as president."

"Ladies, as charming as this conversation is, I think we will excuse ourselves. I am in need of a drink after this afternoon's excitement," Aiz said with a bow.

I watched Adora's jaw flex as she held in whatever comment wanted to slip free, and I waited until Aiz had led Mia off before I murmured. "He does that precisely to get a rise out of you, Adora. I'd have thought after all these years you'd realize that."

Adora focused her platinum gaze on me, the silence stretching out for a full breath. Then she shook her head and smiled. "You would think so, Majesty; however, I have ever struggled where Aiz is concerned. He is in many ways my greatest triumph and my greatest failure."

"That sounds like a fascinating story," I said.

"It may be." She shook her head again. "However, it's not one for a party. Mrs. Hudson, thank you for your hospitality. I think I will go rejoin my people."

"They are very strange, are they not?" Laila asked softly after Adora had walked away. She still wore her perfect public smile, but the uneasiness in her blue eyes disrupted the illusion. "I know it's probably wrong to say so, but they feel quite dangerous."

"It is wrong. They are no more dangerous than any human," I replied, slipping my arm through hers with a smile of my own. "Why don't you introduce me around the room, Laila? Rumor has it I'm quite dangerous, too, but I think I'm slightly more of a people person than our other guests."

For the better part of an hour I let her lead me and Alba around the room from one conversation to another, from one group of important people who'd wrangled an invite to the function to another until even my *smati* was swimming in names and faces.

I was strolling past the balcony that led off the massive room, deep in conversation with Kalpak Saito, head of the farmers' union on Kurma who'd been on Earth on business and was almost unprofessionally delighted at a chance to talk to me about the new Tarsi agreement when the sound of rushing water filled my ears.

The sensation of cold water up to my chest was instantaneous and I had to force my feet to keep moving as my vision started to narrow to a single point on the far side of the room.

"Majesty, are you all right?" Gita subvocalized over the com.

"I need somewhere quiet."

"I am terribly sorry, Mr. Saito, I need to steal Her Majesty away," Alba said aloud, closing a hand around my upper arm.

"Quite all right, my dear." He smiled brightly. "It was a great pleasure, Your Majesty."

I managed a smile in Mr. Saito's direction but couldn't force any words past my throat. We made it into the hallway, Jagana and Kisah in front of us and Ikeki behind, before I stumbled. Alba caught one elbow while Gita slipped her arm around my waist.

"It's all right, Majesty," she said. "Can you take a breath?"

I tried, but shook my head when it stuck halfway down and tears filled my eyes.

"There's a library here, *Dve*," Kisah said. "Empty."

"Check exits. Ikeki on the door. Emmory is headed this way with Team One. Majesty, have a seat for me." Gita's voice was low and soothing as they lowered me into a chair.

"There was a waterfall outside, when we passed the balcony, ma'am, that was supposed to have been turned off for the party," Jagana's voice was equally low. "The noise triggered her."

I pressed my hands to my eyes but jerked them away when all I saw were the metal walls of Wilson's box and swore with enough viciousness to make Jagana gasp.

"Can you breathe for me, Majesty?" Gita repeated, unfazed by the curse.

I tried again, filled my lungs a little more on the second try, and sucked in a full breath just as Emmory came through the door.

I exhaled, trying to ignore the sudden chill running through me as the last vestiges of the flashback cleared themselves. "I'm all right, Emmy. Just a bad memory."

He dropped into a crouch at my side anyway, staring intently at me—or rather through me—as he assessed my status for himself. Finally, he smiled and pulled off his glove before he touched my face. His hand was warm, comforting on my cold skin.

"Flashback." It wasn't a question, but I nodded anyway.

"Hail, where are you?" Hao asked over the com link.

"Library, east side of the big room just past the balcony," I replied. "Hao's coming." I got to my feet, pulling Emmory up as I stood.

When Hao came through the door several moments later, I was standing by the window trying to pretend like I wasn't holding off a second round of tremors.

Hao's eyes flicked from me to Emmory and back again, but he kept his concern behind his teeth as a tall man in a severe black suit followed him into the room. "There you are, Your Majesty. I wanted to introduce you to a friend of mine."

The man tapped the heels of his expensive black shoes together and gave me a perfunctory bow. "Your Imperial Majesty. I am Marius Cavit. It is a great honor."

"Mr. Cavit is the CEO of Cavit Bank, one of the Solarian Conglomerate's largest financial institutions," Hao said.

"It's a pleasure to meet you." I waited for him to come up from his bow before I offered my hand. "Your bank is also one of the oldest institutions on Earth, isn't it?"

"You are well educated in our history, Your Majesty," Marius's accent recalled a brief stop-off outside Paris and the heady scent of baking bread. "And you're correct. I believe my ancestors funded a loan or two for yours during the expedition preparations."

"Did they?" I smiled. "I assume we paid them back, or are you here to collect?"

Marius's smile didn't waver, though I spotted the flicker of wariness in his blue eyes before he answered. "Hao asked if I would speak with you, Your Majesty. I hear you are in need of some proof as far as certain things go."

"I am." I shot Hao a smile he didn't notice because he was busy having a staring contest with Gita.

"Concerning some questions you've had lately on several large cash transfers?"

Translation: Cavit Bank did business with Po-Sin, which was

somewhat surprising, though not wholly unexpected. The more well-known banks could handle any legal money Po-Sin's various businesses made without fear of harassment from governments. And any illegal money was easily hidden through other channels.

For my part, I had preferred the smaller, unknown banks. Cressen Stone's funds were scattered among half a dozen systems under as many different names. I could have brought them all together, made the money more easily accessible and officially mine, but a part of me wasn't willing to believe things weren't going to slide out from under me.

The need for a safety net, it seemed, wouldn't go away after just a few months.

"I may," I replied with a cautious smile. "Not sure this is the best place for a conversation like that, though."

He smiled back. "It's actually far preferable, Your Majesty. I get far less attention speaking to you at a function like this than I would if you were to show up in my bank. It was my understanding you wanted confirmation of the companies responsible for several large deposits."

"That would be helpful."

Marius glanced over his shoulder before he continued. "The companies in question were BlueWater Incorporated and Penultimate Holdings."

I couldn't stop my derisive snort, and the man arched one black eyebrow at me.

"You know the names, Majesty?"

"One of them. Thank you, Marius. I appreciate the assistance, though I confess I'm curious as to why you're helping us."

"I owe Hao," he replied. "My daughter was kidnapped several years ago. He rescued her, made certain no one would ever attempt anything like that again."

"That was your daughter?" I'd heard the details of Hao's job after the fact when we'd met up for a job on Passault, minus the name of the girl he'd rescued. Hao was funny like that about his clients. It explained a lot as to why Marius would risk angering Po-Sin by working with us. Blood debts were something even Po-Sin would make an exception for.

Marius nodded, a brief smile creasing his sober expression. "Don't hesitate to let me know if you need anything else." He tapped his heels together again, bowed, and left the room without another word.

"Is that proof enough for you?" It was hard to tell if Hao's question was for me or Gita.

"It is." I answered before my *Dve* could. "Rai is such a pretentious ass. Penultimate Holdings." Rolling my eyes at the ceiling. "Does he even know what that word means?"

"It's hard to say. I don't have to point out that he doesn't have that kind of money. I thought this was going to lead us to our source, but we're going to have to keep digging."

"Can I just beat it out of Rai? Or let Jo do it?"

Hao chuckled. "I think I can handle it. Are you all right?"

I smiled at his concern. "I'm okay. The waterfall outside made things—" I waved a hand in the air, at a loss for words.

"Here, I brought you this," he said, holding out the mug he'd been cradling in his hands. Gita intercepted it, sipped it, made a face, and passed it on to me.

I took a drink with a smile, paused, and forced myself to swallow the mouthful instead of spitting back into the cup. "What horrendous thing is this?"

"They claimed it was chai," Hao replied with a laugh.

"They were wrong."

"Do you want me to take it, Majesty?"

"No, Gita, I'll hold on to it. At least it's keeping my hands warm." I couldn't help the grin I shot in Hao's direction. "This is not chai," I said, shaking my head.

"I'm going to dump it over your head if you don't watch it." Hao's gaze slid past me to Gita. "And don't think your BodyGuard there will keep you safe."

I slipped my arm through Hao's. "Don't pick a fight. I'm feeling better. Let's go back out to the party before someone notices I'm gone."

We headed out of the library and back out into the main room, exchanging greetings with people as we passed. Gita stayed at my side; the other BodyGuards fell back toward the wall behind me.

"Your Majesty." Adora approached, flanked by the other Farians.

"*Itegas* Notaras. Are you enjoying the party?"

"Well enough." She kept her gloved hands folded at her waist. "I would like to apologize for my behavior this afternoon; it was undignified. You are right about letting Aiz and our history get to me. I don't want to give the impression that the Farians aren't committed to the idea of peace, and it was pointed out to me that I may have done just that."

"I appreciate it," I replied, recalling Johar's words about Aiz not being invested. "We will pick up in the morning, see where compromises can be made, and start from there."

"Thank you, Majesty, both for your patience and for agreeing to this in the first place." Adora bowed, the gesture echoed by her companions, and the group turned and headed for the doors through the crowd.

I watched them go and spotted Mia, who was leaning against a table talking to a waiter, Aiz at her side. She looked away from the young man and smiled at me. I was distracted and nearly missed the waiter turning from them and pulling a gun from beneath his jacket.

"Gita?" I put my free hand on her arm.

Hao stiffened at my side. "Hail." He breathed my name a split second before the shooting started.

42

The screaming started with the first shots, guests scrambling for cover as waiters dropped their trays and opened fire. Aiz kicked the feet out from under the waiter as the man swung toward him with the gun. The waiter went down hard. Aiz grabbed for Mia and vanished in the mass of people rushing for the exits.

Hao spun away from me, kicking the nearest mercenary in the chest before he could bring his gun around to bear on us.

The AK-334 was an older-model laser assault rifle favored by Solarian-born mercs both for ease of use and for the low cost. The power magazines held 334 shot bursts, or a decent two-and-a-half-minute full-auto spray, though that kind of sustained fire tended to melt the barrel.

Hao finished off the merc with a shot from the man's own gun and immediately dropped into a crouch behind an overturned table, picking off targets as fast as he could find them.

I scrambled backward, pushing Alba toward the wall, looking for cover and a weapon.

Gita plucked the tray another waiter had thrown in her direction out of the air and hit an attacker in the face with it. The resounding clang rang out over the chaos.

Ikeki died with a choked gurgle, the only warning we had of the attacker behind us. I shoved Alba to the side. A Shen man I didn't recognize grabbed for Kisah, his dark eyes devoid of emotion. I smashed my mug of hot non-chai into the side of his head before he could touch her and he staggered back, blood dripping from the side of his face.

"Gita! Get her out of here!" Emmory shouted, tackling the assassin. The pair landed hard on the floor of the ballroom. They rolled several times, the Shen coming out on top.

Gita was tangled up with the merc who'd thrown the tray at her. Kisah and Jagana were calling out targets, firing at the mercs on either side of us.

"Kisah, gun!" I shouted, and my BodyGuard pitched hers in my direction without hesitation.

I caught it.

The Shen pressed his hand to Emmory's throat.

I squeezed the trigger and the Shen collapsed.

"Emmory!"

"I'm all right, Majesty." He pushed the Shen to his side and got to his feet, grabbing me by the arm and jerking me lower. "We need to move," he said.

Something exploded in the entrance, and the lights went down, plunging us into a darkness that was broken only by the moonlight streaming through the smoke. Emmory threw himself over the top of me as debris sprayed into the room.

Gita scrambled across the floor, one hand pressed to her side and blood flowing from a cut high on her cheek.

"Gita—"

"I'm all right." She spat blood on the floor. "Zin's holding the back corridor with Iza and Indula. We can get out that way or through the windows in the library."

"*Call in,*" Emmory said over the com link. "*I want everyone to call in.*"

"*There are more gunmen in the street,*" Riddhi said. "*They blew up an aircar right in front of the building, sir. Muna and Sahil are both with me. No injuries.*"

"Ekam Tresk, Captain Saito here. We have a shuttle headed your way for extraction. Please advise if you think more firepower necessary."

"Not right now, Captain Saito. I'm not sure the Solies will take kindly to our warship breaking atmo. Riddhi, make your way around to the back, stay low, stay sharp. Do not engage unless necessary. We've got a shuttle incoming from orbit."

"Copy that, sir."

I searched for Hao through the chaos, spotting him with Alba, the pair calmly picking off targets from behind an overturned table.

"Hao, we're moving." I jerked my head toward the door. He nodded in response through the smoke and waved a hand.

"I'll cover and follow," he said over the com. *"We've got more hostiles coming in through the opposite side."*

"Don't get killed," I ordered. *"And before you say it, I* am *the boss of you, gege."*

Hao's muttered curse was drowned out by the sound of him firing. Emmory shoved me through the door as the answering gunfire from the mercenaries slammed into the wall above our heads.

A moment later Alba dove through the doorway and I wrapped my chamberlain up in a tight hug. "Are you hurt?"

"I'm fine, Majesty." She gestured at her bare feet. "Though I'm better understanding your insistence on low heels."

I choked back a laugh. "Where did you learn how to shoot like that?"

"Gita's been teaching me, ma'am. I thought she told you," Alba replied.

"Hao, covering fire, move your ass." Gita knelt in the doorway, half hidden behind the frame, and fired back.

He slid through the door under her covering fire and I heard him say, *"You* are definitely not the boss of me."

"Asshole," she replied, but there was laughter in her voice.

We moved down the hallway, the sounds of my BodyGuards clearing rooms one by one was oddly soothing. I gripped Kisah's gun, my free hand on Emmory's back as we worked our way through the dark.

"Are you hurt?" he asked over our private com link.

"I'm fine. He didn't get close to me. He touched you. I shot him while he was touching you. You should be dead."

"Tell me something I don't know."

"He killed Ikeki." The grief was sharp and fresh, strong enough to poke holes in my adrenaline rush.

"I saw."

"Jamison favors the AK-334, Emmory. I'd put down credits this is his people. But I saw Aiz just before the shooting started; he took down one of the shooters."

"We'll debrief once we get out of here. Let's focus on that first."

Zin hit the door at the end of the hallway and nodded at Indula, who'd dropped to a crouch beside him. They slipped through; the alarms were still blaring and one more breached door didn't make any difference, but I still held my breath as Iza followed them and we waited a beat before Emmory started moving.

"Clear, no sign of Riddhi yet." Zin's voice was as cool as the night air that hit me when we came through the door.

"We're around the corner," she replied.

"Gita, hold this." I passed Kisah's gun over and unwound the sari, dropping it into a pile in the street. "Someone help Alba wrap some of that around her feet."

"Hail." Hao was already following my plan and passed over a knife, which I used to cut through the middle of my underskirt.

Gita had also figured out what I was doing and cut two narrow strips off my sari, tying first one and then the other around my ankles to bind my newly made pants. "You good, Majesty?"

"Better, yes." I noted the blood dripping to the pavement. "You're hurt."

"I'm fine, Majesty."

Before I could press her, a second explosion rocked the ground beneath our feet. Riddhi, Muna, and Sahli came sprinting around the corner.

"Ekam *Tresk, this is Shuttle 1145 from the* Hailimi, *Lieutenant Omei speaking. Can you give me a lock on your location?"*

"Roger that, Shuttle 1145. Did you catch that latest explosion?"

"Got a visual on it now, Ekam," Lieutenant Omei replied. "Looks like something in the Galactic Relations Department building went boom. Since you're talking to me, I'm assuming you're not inside."

"Correct, sending you our location now. There are hostiles, we will be on the move."

"We've got a squad of Marines aboard, sir, just tell us where to point them."

The shuttle flew overhead as we bolted from the side street and raced toward its landing site. It touched down, the door sliding open and Marines spilling out into the night. Relief flooded through me as we sprinted down the street toward the shuttle.

"Down!" Gita shouted, tackling me as the distinctive whomp of a railgun firing echoed through the night a microsecond before the shuttle exploded in a massive fireball.

The blast flung flaming debris and shrapnel through the air. As I hit the ground I saw a chunk of the shuttle slice a Marine in half.

"Vandi's hit!"

"Muna!" My Guard had been thrown several meters by the explosion. I rolled out from under Gita, scrambling on my hands and feet over to the young Guard.

"Perimeter. Now." Emmory snapped the order into the night air. "Ekam *Tresk to the* Hailimi *or any Indranan ships out there, Shuttle 1145 has been destroyed. Repeat, Shuttle 1145 has been destroyed. We are under fire from unknown force, heavy weaponry present. Request all possible assistance stat."*

"No, no," I whispered, spying the spike of molten metal that had impaled Muna on the left side of her chest. Blood bubbled around the wound, heated by the red-hot metal, and the smell of cooked flesh slammed into me with the same force as the railgun projectile that had just destroyed the shuttle. I grabbed Muna's hand. She choked, her fingers tightening around mine, and then died.

Somewhere in the dark part of my soul, a jagged tally appeared. One more person lost because of me.

"Targets at two and three," Indula called out, opening fire.

"Targets at four and six."

"Do not let them get around us."

"Hail, we've got to go."

"I know."

Whispering a benediction that was useless compared to the gun I pulled from Muna's other hand, I followed Emmory to the dubious safety of a parked aircar. The others joined us, along with the five surviving members of the Marine squad.

"Sergeant Nidha Sathi, *Ekam*." The woman wiped blood off her dark face with the back of her hand. "Captain's dead."

Indula and Iza continued to fire, covering Zin as he scrambled through the downed Marines and the wreckage gathering what weapons he could.

"The embassy is four streets down and six north. Embassy is reporting they are under attack by an unknown number of hostiles. Unable to get to us."

"They've got AK-334s and at least one shoulder-held railgun," Hao said, unloading two of the guns he had slung across his back and passing them to Riddhi and Sahil. "I'm guessing that's what the first two explosions were also from. My guess is it's an older-model Solarian Navy SCN 775."

"I would have said it was a Karsikov," I replied and he shrugged.

"Sergeant Sathi, take two of your Marines on point," Emmory ordered. "The other two I want running cover behind us. Majesty, I want you in the middle at all times. Zin, stay by her side."

"Got it," Zin said, his face hard in the flickering light of the fire.

"Iza, Indula, we're moving. You're on our six."

"Roger," they echoed back, alternating between shooting and moving until they'd followed us up the street toward the embassy.

We made it the four streets down.

"Fuck." Gita's hissing curse preceded her stumbling into me by a fraction of a second and I turned too late to catch her before she went down on a knee. Blood spattered the ground. I dropped to her side, listening to Emmory snap orders as the others scanned the street around us.

"Med kit!" One of the Marines fished hers out and passed it to me.

"Let me see." Hao knelt, kit already out, and I ignored my shaking hands as I took her knife and sliced down the side of her shirt, exposing the deep wound in her side. "Shrapnel?"

"No. Damn it," Gita muttered. "It was that squirrelly little shit at the party. I didn't think he got me that bad."

I took supplies as Hao handed them to me, patching Gita quickly, then passing the kit back to the Marine who'd handed it over. She took it with a nod, but the grim look on her face told me as much as the screaming alarms from my *smati*. My *Dve* was losing blood fast.

"Before you spout some noble bullshit about leaving you behind, get on your fucking feet," Hao said, sliding an arm around Gita's back and hauling her upright. "No one is staying behind as long as they have a pulse."

"Let me take her, Hao," I said, handing Kisah back her gun and swapping the other to my right hand. "You need your hands free."

He nodded sharply. I slid under Gita's right arm, wrapping my left around her waist, and we started moving again.

Halfway to the embassy Emmory shouted the warning as mercs hit us from an alley. Zin stepped in front of me, blocking the man who barreled out of the dark, and I saw the flash of silver in the streetlight just before the merc buried his knife in Zin's chest.

43

Zin!" I let Gita go, brought my gun up, and shot the man in the head.

Zin dropped back, falling to a knee. I tried to shoot the next attacker, but my gun was empty. I chucked it at his face as he started to bring his own up, following right behind the gun and tackling him. The impact drove the air from both our lungs, but I'd had time to brace myself for the hit and recovered before he did. However, my first punch bruised my hand on his body armor and I heard him chuckle. I swung my fist up, connecting with his nose. The crunch of cartilage interrupted his amusement, but before I could grab for his gun a boot slammed into my ribs, knocking me to the side.

My assailant didn't have time for a second kick. He fell back, a hole the size of my fist in the back of his head and I looked over at where Gita was calmly picking off targets from Zin's side. Alba was bent over him, her hands covered in blood.

I ripped the pouch emblazoned with a red cross off the dead merc's leg and scrambled back over to Zin.

His eyes were open, hands pressed to the area around the knife. "Let me see," I said, touching his hand and linking with his *smati*.

"Missed the heart," he replied. "Not by much, though."

"Missed the lung, too," I said, my smile laced with panic. "Look at you, lucky guy."

"Majesty, down!"

I didn't argue with Gita's order, and Alba followed me. We dropped against Zin's side as she fired a shot, killing the man whose nose I'd broken.

"Clear, ma'am."

I rose up, digging into the merc's med pouch with shaking hands and muttering a desperate prayer that they'd have what I was looking for. They did and I ignored the tears leaking from my eyes as I pulled out the hemostatic gauze.

"Alba, press down on his shoulders with all your weight. You ready?" I asked Zin, jamming the old-fashioned syringe filled with pain meds into his arm.

He nodded, pressing one hand down on the side of the knife and locking the other into my makeshift pant leg. I closed my hand around the knife handle, shutting out the sounds of the fight still raging around us, focusing all my attention on the blade. My *smati* showed me how dangerously close it was to his heart. If I pulled it out too fast or moved it wrong I was going to kill not only him but Emmory, too.

Even with the pain meds, it had to hurt, but Zin somehow managed to stay still as a stone as I slowly pulled the knife from his chest. His cry cut through the night as I finished, dropping the knife to the ground next to us. I slapped the gauze on, leaning on it with all my weight as the blood-clotting agents did their work.

If Zin's luck held, his Tracker augmentation was already hard at work on the internal injury.

"Sorry," I murmured, leaning in and pressing a kiss to his forehead.

"Don't be."

Emmory appeared, touching a hand to the side of Zin's face. I spotted his trembling fingers and reached out to squeeze his other arm.

"He's stable, but we're going to need Fasé or medical treatment as soon as possible."

"All clear on front," Sergeant Sathi called.

"All clear on left." That was from Kisah. "We are injury-free."

"All clear on back," Iza said. "Indula was an idiot and tried to stop a shot with his hand."

"I'm fine. Don't let her try to cut it off."

"Focus, people." Emmory's order was sharp. "We are still surrounded by hostiles, and the empress isn't safe until we get her behind the walls of the embassy."

"You're clear on the right, too." Johar's voice rose above the din. "Don't shoot me."

I looked up in time to see Johar and Dailun emerge from the shadows. She was dragging a mercenary by the throat, the man's hands desperately scrabbling at her arm, which was cutting off his air. "Emmory, you want this one alive?"

Johar was dressed in black from head to toe, blood streaming from her nose. An ugly black eye decorated the left side of her face. Dailun had a scarf covering his hair and exchanged a quick hug with Hao.

"Yes." Emmory practically snarled the word, getting to his feet and grabbing the man. Hao joined him, standing guard for my *Ekam* as Emmory slammed the merc into the wall of the nearest building.

"Jo." I reached a hand up to her and she smiled, taking it as she crouched.

"This is a shit-show. When I heard the shuttle blow I came out to give you a hand. Fasé and Stasia are safe in the embassy with the others. Embassy is under attack, but they're holding the line. It's going to take something massive to get through them."

"It's Jamison, isn't it?"

"I think so, plus half a dozen smaller outfits," she confirmed. "Are they making a play for you or for Hao, though? It would explain why the Shen were so insouciant at the negotiations."

I shook my head. "He seemed equally surprised by the attack; I saw him take out one of the shooters and then run with Mia."

426

Johar spit on the street behind her. "I haven't seen Jamison's ugly face yet, but you know how he is."

"He won't be here. When has he ever gotten his hands dirty?"

Johar rolled her eyes, then leaned past me to grip Gita's offered hand. "You look like shit, girl."

"Knife in side, I think the bleeding's stopped, though," Gita lied. We'd gotten the outside wound to stop leaking, but I knew she was bleeding internally. The wound was bad enough that her augmented systems couldn't keep up.

The sound of aircraft overhead distracted me, and I looked up.

"Solies finally got their shit together. They are not happy," Johar muttered. "I think the president got shot in the attack on the party. No word if he was killed. They're all in a fucking tizzy over it." She shrugged a shoulder, then looked over at Emmory as he returned. "We moving?"

"Solarians finally scrambled air support," he replied. "They should be able to draw away some of the fire on the embassy. Ground troops are incoming. According to our friend, there's at best two dozen of their men at the embassy." He jerked a thumb at the merc who was slumped over by the building.

"Let's get moving, then," I said. "Emmory, you take Zin. Johar can take Gita." I held my hand out to Hao and he put his AK-334 in it without question. I checked it, tucking the two magazines Hao passed me into my *choli*.

"Sergeant Sathi!"

"Yes, Your Majesty?"

"We're moving out." I ignored the Look I was getting from Emmory and the quick kiss he pressed to his husband's mouth as he helped Zin to his feet. "Continue on point; Hao, go with him. Be advised there are likely hostiles between us and the embassy, but see if you can let the embassy know we're on our way."

"Yes, ma'am. You heard the empress, move it."

We met scattered resistance the last few streets to the embassy.

I'd switched off the screaming alarms of my *smati*. The difficulty I was having drawing a full breath was all the information I needed to tell me at least one rib had been broken from the merc's kick.

Sergeant Sathi's team knocked in the back door of a building with a decent vantage point several doors down and across the street from the embassy, startling the five mercs who'd taken up position inside. I shot the sixth one as he charged in from another room, and the Marines made quick work of the others.

The Marines immediately lined up in the windows the mercenaries had vacated and began firing on the merc forces in front of the embassy. It didn't take long for Jamison's men to figure out we were there, with deadly results.

"Incoming!" Sergeant Sathi screamed on the heels of that terrifying whomp of the railgun firing.

I turned, tackling Gita and Alba. The blast slammed into the floor above us, and the building came down around us. Throwing an arm over my own head and burying my face in Johar's back, I rode out the dropping rubble, pain spiking through my right leg as something heavy slammed into it.

"Hail!" Emmory's shouted call over the com link was louder than necessary but I didn't shout back.

"I'm still alive." I coughed, covering my face with my sleeve as I waved the dust from the air. *"Johar, Alba, and Gita are with me. We're still alive."*

"Good. Everyone else call out."

"This is Sergeant Sathi. Corporal Uy is dead, sir." I was surprised by the burst of relief at Nidha's familiar voice on the com link. *"So are Patch and Hoole. I'm banged up, no major injuries, Private Srayh is out cold but her vitals are steady."*

"Hail, can you get out of the building?" That was from Hao on our private channel.

"Give me a minute." I tapped Johar's shoulder and she looked up from Gita with a worried frown then stood.

"She's lost a lot of blood, Hail," she said, keeping her voice low. "We have to get her to Fasé."

"I know. Help me see if we have an exit." I gestured upward. The building had partially collapsed and there were no exterior windows in the room we'd ended up in, but I could see light above and with Johar's help I scrambled up to the second floor.

There was no way out; the stairs had collapsed in on themselves and the back of the house had filled in any space that might have opened up in their absence. I muttered a curse.

"Emmory, Hao, we can't get out of here, at least not back down to you. Recommend you make it to the embassy for reinforcements and come back for us?" I couldn't stop the laugh. *"I think we're actually relatively safe here for the moment."*

"Majesty—" Emmory started, but I cut him off.

"I know you don't like it, Ekam," I said. *"But I am as safe as possible for the situation. Gita needs medical attention, and so does Zin."* A rumble shook the ground and I braced myself against the wall as a fireball erupted into the night sky. *"I think the Solies have finally gotten these assholes to turn tail and run. I'll keep looking for a way out of here, but I want you to move now. That's an order, Ekam, if you're going to make me do it."*

"All right, we're moving. If you find some way to get up and over to this side, the door out the back is clear. But do not move until I come back."

"If it looks like the building is going to come down on our heads, I'm moving," I replied, unable to stop from grinning.

Emmory exhaled over the com. *"We'll be back in a few, Majesty. I promise."*

"I know you will." I climbed back down and sat down heavily at Gita's side. "How bad are you?"

"Turned off the alarms." Her voice was slurred. "Not sure. Probably an hour, maybe more. Less if I have to keep running. Nothing a Farian and a blood transfusion can't fix."

"Stay awake for me at least," I said. "I don't want to have to carry your ass across the street."

"Make Hao do it, serve him right for breaking my heart."

I was reasonably sure my *Dve* wasn't aware of what she was saying. Johar's chuckle was edged with worry, and the look she shared with me proved she was sharing my fear.

If we didn't get Gita help soon, she was going to die.

"We're coming up on the embassy. It looks like the mercs pulled back when the Solies flew in," Emmory said over the com link. *"Majesty—"*

The building shook, raining debris down on our heads. Johar grabbed for Alba while I lunged to cover Gita—for a terrifying moment I was sure the entire building was coming down on our heads.

Then there was silence. I shook off the debris, scrambling to my feet and this time climbing to the second floor without Johar's help thanks to the shifted debris.

"Emmory? What happened?"

Fire and smoke billowed into the sky from the embassy. A second explosion rocked through the air, more fire scarring the night sky. I could hear Gita dimly through the rushing of the blood in my ears trying to raise the others on the com link.

"Emmory? Zin? Hao?"

Only the static of dead coms answered me.

44

*D*amn *it, Emmory, answer me.*" My demand was filled with a desperate desire to be wrong even as the awful certainty rose up in my throat like bile.

"Hail, what is it? What happened?" Johar yelled up.

"The embassy—" I choked on the words, faces and names colliding in my head, my brain screaming at me that it couldn't be happening even as the overwhelming rush of loss crashed into me and put me on my knees in front of the window.

Outside the embassy was gone, a smoldering pile of rubble in its place that lay scattered across the street.

The embassy I'd just sent my BodyGuards and my brother into. I stared out into the night, unable to move, to breathe. They were all gone.

"Hail!" Johar snapped at me, her harsh voice cutting into the darkness around me for just a moment. "Need you to focus. What happened?"

"They hit the embassy with something bigger than a railgun. I don't know, a rocket launcher, maybe? It's gone. I think—I think they were in it when—" My voice didn't sound like me; it was hollow, so filled with grief.

I swept it away, letting my rage fill the space, grinding the pieces of my heart into dust under a brutal heel. The sounds of gunfire outside were muffled by the blood rushing in my ears.

"Majesty." Alba tried to wrap her arms around me as I let out a shuddering breath, but I avoided her embrace.

"We need to get out of here. Jo, can you get Gita up?" I said, rubbing the tears from my face with the back of my hand.

Between the three of us, we managed to haul Gita to the second floor. I left them both with Johar until I found a way down. The rubble had shifted with the explosion of the embassy, opening a hole big enough for us to squeeze through back down to the ground in the corner of the room.

Johar helped Gita over; the bandage at her side was soaked through with blood and my *Dve*'s gold skin was ashen. Jo stuck her head through the hole, made a hissing noise, and popped back up. "It's about two and a half meters down. I'll go first. Alba, you help Hail lower Gita and then go."

She shimmied through, dropping to the floor while Alba and I maneuvered Gita around to get her feet in position.

"Anything?" I dared the question.

Gita shook her head. "Coms are completely off-line. I can see you and Alba, that's it. Jo's showing but she's not on the official roster. No one else is—" She squeezed her eyes shut, a tear leaking down to track through the dust and blood on her face. "It doesn't mean they're dead, Majesty. It could be a dampening field, anything. But we need to think about getting you somewhere safe, Hail. And I need medical attention. I can't protect you like this."

"I can protect myself just fine. We're not holing up anywhere, you don't have the time." I pressed my forehead to hers. Whatever lies Gita was trying to tell me, I knew Emmory and the others couldn't have survived that blast, and the grief magnified itself until I thought my heart was going to stop. "I'll handle it. You ready?"

She nodded and we got her through to the bottom floor. Alba shimmied through with my help and Johar caught her below. I followed quickly after passing my AK-334 through to them. "Stay here, I'm going to take a look."

"Majesty." Alba caught me by the arm. "Gita's right, we don't know that they're dead. We should call for support."

"We've done that. Someone hacked our coms," I replied. "First the shuttle and now the embassy just as the others were going in? I'm not going to chance it. Not until I know for sure what we're up against."

"Majesty, the Solarians—" Gita said.

"Fuck the Solarians! They let this happen!" I snarled.

Gita and Alba recoiled from my anger. Johar merely raised a curious eyebrow. I closed my eyes, dragging in one breath after another until I had leashed my fury and dragged it back under my boot.

"I'm sorry, *Dve*." I gave her a short nod with the apology, since I was unable to call her my *Ekam* even though I knew it was what I should do. "Stay here. I'll be right back."

"Hail." Johar passed me a knife, wickedly curved and serrated. "Don't lose this one."

I slipped into the dark. The sound of emergency sirens and the crackling of the fire at the embassy filled the night. Now I knew why Jamison's men had pulled back. They'd been expecting the embassy to blow, waiting for it.

This entire thing had been a mess from the start. I was done being the Empress of Indrana. Done being polite and constrained by rules and politics. They wanted a fight, they were about to get one.

I spotted the two mercs at the same time my anger flared again. Slamming the butt of my gun into the side of the first man's head bought me enough time to engage the second.

I didn't shoot him. The AK-334 would have betrayed my position, and my rage was calling for blood, blood delivered by fists and blade.

Johar's knife was perfectly weighted, the edge so sharp it cut through the throat and spine of the second merc with barely any effort at all. The smell of blood joined the ash and sulfur in the air.

"Oh gods."

I pivoted. The first merc was on the ground, scrambling away from me, his eyes locked on the fountain of blood as it finished spurting from his comrade's neck.

"Pray all you want, it won't save you." I shook the blade in my hand, spattering him with his comrade's blood as I stalked toward him.

The man fumbled for his gun, screaming when I jammed Johar's knife through his upper thigh and ripped it back out.

"It was a mistake, all right? I'm sorry. I'll go. I won't—I'm not going to kill you."

"You don't get it," I said, pressing the tip of the knife to the side of his throat as I took the Glock 667 from his holster. "You idiots blew the embassy and killed the only people in the universe who could have kept me in check. That's your last fucking mistake. However, I'm going to let you go. Tell your boss I'm coming for him, and there is nothing that can save you all from my wrath."

No live enemies, little sister. Hao's ghost whispered the order in my ear.

"Never mind. I'll tell Jamison myself." I cut the man's throat and stood, staring down at his dead eyes.

"Hands up." The voice behind me was accompanied by the whine of a Glock 667 powering up. "Turn around slo—"

I spun, bringing the Glock up as I did. Johar let the merc slide to the ground, his neck broken.

"I told you to stay with Gita."

"She told you'd need backup, and besides—" Johar jerked her thumb over her shoulder and I saw Alba supporting Gita behind her. "They are technically with me." She raised an eyebrow before she crouched at the dead merc's side and started stripping him of his gear. "Anyway, she was right, and I am not one of your BodyGuards to order around. Come here and put this on."

I let Johar slip my arms through the sleeves of the man's shirt and then buckle me into the vest. She grabbed me before I could step away. "I know that look, Sister. That hollow, dead-eyed, nothing-left-to-lose look. Don't give up hope on them and even if they are gone, you still have us. You still have an empire. Don't give up, okay?"

"I am not—" I couldn't make the words leave my mouth. Johar sighed and touched her forehead to mine as she released me.

"You are Hail Bristol, do not lose yourself to grief."

Sliding home the Glock, I went back to the other bodies to retrieve anything we could use. "Jo." I tossed her one of the med packs and cleaned her knife off on the merc's pants before passing it over. "Thanks."

"We'll get out of here and find a ship. Get this mess sorted. Unless you want to try for the Farians?"

The reminder that Fasé and Stasia had been in the embassy was almost enough to put me on my knees. For a moment I was tempted to agree with Johar's suggestion, go find Adora and pledge to them anything they wanted if they would help me wipe out Aiz and the rest of the Shen until there wasn't a speck of them anywhere in the black.

You can't trust them either, Majesty. You don't know who was responsible for this, Zin's ghost whispered in my ear, and I knew he was right.

"No, we'll get medical help for Gita somewhere. Where's the nearest hospital? After that, we'll find a ship or get in contact with the *Hailimi*." I shoved a second knife into the sheath in my new vest.

"Hail." Bakara Rai emerged from the shadows, a gun in his hand. It was pointed at me.

"You have impeccable timing," I said. "If you're here for Hao, he's dead and gone."

Rai stared at me in shock, the rogue pirate at a loss for words beyond "I am very sorry, Your Majesty."

"Rai, what are you doing?" I could feel Johar tensing by my side, but our guns were both holstered and there was no way to reach them before Rai shot at least one of us.

"Keep your hands where I can see them, Jo. I'm here for you, Majesty." Rai admitted, and then he smiled and tipped his head at me. "I see one BodyGuard, where are the rest?"

"They are also all dead."

"Maybe," Johar said.

"They're dead. The coms are working just fine." I snarled the words into the night air, their power growing every time I voiced the thought. Emmory and the others were gone. Why was I still running, still trying to survive? All I wanted right now was to stop, surrender, and let these faceless monsters kill me.

The Empress of Indrana doesn't roll over and surrender, Hail. My mother's ghost was stern in my ears. *And certainly, neither would the gunrunner Cressen Stone.*

She was right. I hated to admit it, but I couldn't stop. I owed it to the dead to keep going.

"Whatever the Shen are paying you, Rai, I'll triple it if you get us out of here."

Rai shook his head as more of his mercenaries melted out of the shadows, guns glinting in the moonlight. "Too late for that, Hail. Even if I wanted to, at this point the only way to save your Body-Guard is to surrender."

Gita's readouts suddenly flatlined in my head. I heard Alba's desperate cry and turned, heedless of the guns pointed at me.

Only to come face-to-face with Aiz Cevalla.

I threw my punch at his throat without thinking. He moved at the last second, so the strike that should have killed him instead only glanced off the side of his neck. I heard Johar behind us hit Rai low before anyone got a shot off, slamming him into the building.

The blow to the back of my head put me on my knees, and hands grabbed me, pressing me down into the street. I got one decent kick in before the warning whine of a gun I didn't recognize powering up sounded in my ear and I froze. I couldn't pinpoint the make of it, but that noise was clear enough.

"Majesty, a little cooperation will make all this a lot easier," Aiz whispered in my ear, and then the world went black.

45

I woke and surged forward, but the solid weight of cuffs locked me to the metal frame of a chair. The light hurt my eyes—too bright after the darkness of the street outside the embassy. This light had the familiar blue undertone of a ship and the floor hummed under my bare feet.

"Easy, easy, Hail," Johar murmured from behind me. "I've got my cuffs off; hold still and let me work on yours."

"Where are we?"

"Burner ship of Rai's. They brought us here after Aiz knocked you out. He brought Gita back from the dead, though, so that's maybe a trade-off? Either way, I think we should get out of here."

"I'm in agreement. Alba, are you all right?"

"Yes, Majesty." Alba sat in the corner, Gita's head in her lap and her face streaked with tears.

My *Dve* was unconscious but breathing, alive when she hadn't been less than ten minutes ago, though my *smati* still blinked desperate red warnings at me.

The door slid open and Johar muttered a curse, launching herself at Rai as he stepped through the door.

"Damn it, Jo!" Rai was still trying to untangle himself from Johar. The first tazer shot from the man behind him put her on the floor, but it took two more before she went down completely. Rai recuffed her, muttering obscenities the whole time. "Unnecessary.

That was gods-damned unnecessary, Hail." He glared at me, wiping the blood from his face.

"Don't you dare talk to me about unnecessary, you soulless piece of shit." I leaned forward as far as the cuffs would let me. "I'm going to take you apart with my bare hands."

"Business," Rai replied, but the smile he shot me was tainted with sadness. "I will extend my condolences again for the loss of your people, Your Majesty. That was not supposed to be part of the plan. But this whole thing went to shit the moment Jamison decided to light up the fucking party. I am going to wring—"

"Take your condolences and choke on them, Rai. Or better yet, shoot yourself in the head and save me the trouble." My cuffs rattled when I lunged forward, and the merc who'd moved to check my cuffs backed away. "I am going to set fire to your organization and *everyone else* responsible for this; I will raze it all to ashes. There will be nothing left when I am done with all of you except the warning of what happens to those who dare to harm what's mine!"

Aiz tsked as he came in the room. "I thought my temper was bad, Empress. But it is nothing compared to yours." He avoided my kick, retaliating with an open-handed slap that would have put me on the floor had I not been cuffed to the chair. "That's enough. Take another swing at me and I put a blast through your *Dve*'s skull first and then your chamberlain's and then that terror of yours. She killed three men before we got her subdued the first time."

I saw Rai's jaw twitch at the threat to kill Johar but kept my gaze locked on Aiz. "I am going to kill you."

Aiz grinned. It was a feral smile, and he grabbed me by the chin, leaning in until his face was inches from mine. "Watch your tone or I am going to put you back in a box and drown you over and over until you learn who is in charge here."

The sound of rushing water filled my ears, washing away everything else. It was broken only by the sound of Mia's voice.

"Aiz, what are you doing?"

439

"Teaching her some manners, Mia, because I am tired of this jumped-up criminal pretending to be a queen." Aiz released me and stepped back. His sister came through the doorway, shock on her elegant face. She was dressed in a gray uniform that matched her eyes. She was unarmed, not even a sign of a weapon, and I realized Aiz was the same way.

They are *the weapons, Majesty. Focus.* Indula's and Iza's voices collided in my head.

"She is the Star of Indrana, Aiz, and moreover we need her help. Show some respect. Your Majesty, I am so sorry. This is not how things were supposed to be." She reached around me for the cuffs, releasing me despite her brother's and Rai's shouted warnings. I surged forward, my left hand around her throat, and slammed her into the wall with a wordless snarl.

Aiz grabbed my other wrist, and everything stopped.

Everything.

My lungs refused to draw in air.

My heart stopped beating.

"Let. Her. Go." His voice was soft in my ear.

My hand opened of its own accord and Mia dropped, coughing, to the floor.

"I could keep you here for an eternity, trapped before the moment your brain realizes your heart is no longer beating. These moments usually flash like lightning, and are over and done before you humans realize what has happened."

"Aiz!"

I collapsed on the floor, wheezing, unable to get my lungs to cooperate. Aiz had been shoved to the side and through my tears I saw nothing but Mia's storm-cloud eyes. She cupped my face. Everything started up again, a painful lurching restart that felt so wrong that for just a second I wished she'd left me to die.

"I am sorry," she murmured, tipping my head back and pressing her lips to mine. Air filled my lungs again. Heat poured through me, chasing away the chill of death. "My brother gets upset when I am—well, he's very protective and it has been an awful evening. This is not at all how I wanted to speak with you. Take a few breaths, Majesty, the feeling will pass."

I threw up on her shoes.

Mia, surprisingly, did not recoil but kept her hand on the back of my neck, her fingers threaded through my hair. She murmured something unrecognizable while I tried to bring my rolling stomach back under control.

"Exhale, Majesty. It will be all right," she said in nearly perfect Indranan, no trace of her accent and halting speech of before.

I complied, the shuddering exhalation painful as my broken ribs reminded me they were still around, and then for a terrifying second I couldn't drag the next breath in. Mia's fingers tightened gently, and air flowed into my lungs.

"That's better." She got to her feet, pulling me along with her, though I had to brace myself on the wall when my legs protested. "Let's take care of this also." Mia cupped my face again and warmth rushed through me; the pain of my broken ribs vanished and my vision blurred as my head spun from the rush of power.

This was not the gentle warmth I'd felt from Fasé or any other Farian. This was wild and raw, the energy coursing through me with all the force of a tazer but none of the pain. It felt like the time Portis and I had been caught out in a lightning storm on Zartilia, racing for the ship as the rain slammed around us and collapsing on the cargo deck with spasms of relieved laughter.

Mia smiled, sliding her hand down my arm and backing up a few steps. "Behave yourself, please?"

I dropped into the chair, shaking. "Are you going to heal my people?" I managed the question through the sudden chattering of my teeth.

Mia moved toward where Johar, now recovered, knelt by Alba and Gita. The Shen stopped and looked back at me. "I am not asking for a favor in kind; I will heal your friends regardless. However, can I get a promise from you, Hail?"

"What?"

"Don't harm my people, and listen to what I have to say. You won't be injured any further."

I stared at her. My ability to tell truth from lies where the Shen was concerned was damaged, untrustworthy. Her kind gray gaze seemed genuine, but for all I knew it wasn't. Finally, I nodded, getting carefully to my feet.

"Done for the duration of my time here. Your people only though. Him—" I pointed at Rai. "Jamison, the other mercenaries are fair game. I will kill them if I'm given half a chance. And if you harm any more of my people, I'll do the same to you."

"Fair enough." Mia nodded once.

"I am fine, but Gita needs your help." Alba shook her head at Mia when the Shen reached for her.

Mia laid her hand against the wound in my *Dve*'s side. "You are in bad shape," she murmured. Mia closed her eyes, flexing her hand the tiniest bit, and exhaled. Almost immediately my *smati* registered Gita's vitals as stabilized, which should have been impossible.

Gita jerked, inhaling and then retching in much the same way I had. Johar caught her arm before she could hit Mia, but the Shen was already out of arm's reach.

"Don't bite," Mia said to Johar with a grin that was far too charming, and touched her fingers to Johar's forearm.

Johar's eyes fell closed, and a shudder ripped through her. She tensed, coiled like a snake about to strike as Mia moved toward Gita.

"Ah, ah." Rai wiggled his gun. "Stay there, Jo. I'll shoot you again."

"Me cago en la hostia de tu puta madre." Johar spat the curse in his direction and Rai winced.

Mia looked at Alba again. "You are hurt; I can ease it."

"Alba, let her," I said. The healthier we were, the better our chances of escaping.

Mia touched Alba's offered hand, then smiled at me as she got to her feet. "We'll leave you alone for a few minutes while we get off-planet, and then we will move to my ship. I'll expect your cooperation, Majesty, yes?"

"Fine," I gritted between clenched teeth.

Aiz didn't back down when I looked at him. Instead he crossed the space between us, smiling when we were eye-to-eye. "If you ever harm my sister, I will take several lifetimes and hold you in that space between life and death. Then I will snuff your life out and go about my day. Are we understood?"

I wasn't going to let him see just how terrified I was of his promise, so I simply stared at him. "You couldn't face me in a straight fight, but I'm up for it if you can find your balls."

"Enough, both of you." Mia sighed, stepping between us with a shake of her head. "Aiz, she has every right to be angry." She shoved him back, wrapping her fingers around my upper arm.

I stared down at her; she was close to her brother's height but several centimeters shorter than both of us.

"Majesty, please do not push my brother, he is rather reckless and impulsive. Bringing you back from the dead once per day is more than enough, I think?"

I shook her hand off, still staring at Aiz. Surprisingly, he nodded—first to me and then to his sister—and left the room.

The moment the door closed, I bolted across the room, falling to my knees at Gita's side.

"It's all right. I'm all right, Hail," she murmured, wrapping her arms around me and squeezing me tight.

I felt the grief start to rise again, tears filling my eyes, and tried desperately to shove it all back behind the locked door of my heart. "I thought I was going to lose you, too. I can't, not with everyone else gone."

"They're not gone. We don't know for sure. We'll get through this, I promise."

"What's the plan?" Johar's hands were warm on my back.

"I promised to cooperate," I said. "You three didn't. See if you can find a way out of this mess."

"Hail." Gita gave me a Look that split my heart in two while making me want to laugh at how close it was to the one Emmory used to give me. "We're not leaving you here. We'll stay together, whatever happens. Emmory would kill me if I left you."

"Emmory is dead, *Ekam.*"

She flinched at my reply and I felt the shift of takeoff for a moment before the internal compensators kicked in, and it was as oppressively heavy as the grief weighing me down.

Get up, Majesty, find a way out of this. Emmory's ghost managed to be equally sympathetic and uncompromising. His words jerked me to my feet, the two women following me up.

The door slid open and Rai came in, two men with guns behind him. Johar spat at his feet. He sighed. I crossed my arms over my chest and stared at him.

"Brought you clothes," he said, setting the pile in his hands to the side and reaching back to take the two pairs of boots from the man on his left. "These should fit you and Alba; let me know if they don't."

"Okay." I didn't move to take them, and Rai finally set them next to the clothes with a second sigh.

He straightened, dragging a hand through his dreads. "Hail, look, I don't know what happened, but we were not here to hurt you or your people. Jamison wasn't supposed to be involved in this but he came stampeding in like he always does. We're not sure about survivors of the embassy explosion. I can't find any traffic about it. I am truly sorry—"

"You want absolution, go find a priest," I said coldly. "You won't get it from me."

Rai nodded, backed out of the room, and stood watching me as the door slid closed.

I glanced at Johar. "Surveillance?"

"This is a burner ship. Unmarked. Untraceable," she replied with a shake of her head. "It's too clean. He wouldn't have a reason to spend the credits on an upgrade like that."

Alba and I sorted through the pile of clothing. I tossed a new shirt to Gita before stripping out of my shoes, shredded underskirt, and *choli*. "Rai's seen it all anyway," I muttered.

"What?" Gita stammered, and Alba choked.

"She has, too," I said with a grin, waving a finger in Johar's direction.

Johar was laughing so hard she was bent over at the waist while my people stared at me, their eyes wide in astonishment. I shimmied into the cargo pants Rai had brought and then pulled the long-sleeved gray top over my head.

"I did have a life before all this." My humor fled as I patted her on the shoulder and dropped into the chair to put on my boots. I fumbled the clasps. "Fuck."

Keep moving, ma'am, don't stop. Don't fall apart. Kisah's ghost issued the demand and I blinked back the tears, though a few escaped to fall to the floor.

I waved Gita off before she could drop at my side. "I'm fine." I fastened my boots. They fit perfectly. And stood. I straightened my spine, lifted my chin, and threw my grief around me like armor. The door opened immediately when I banged on it, two Shen on the other side. They were unarmed, hands bare, dressed in the same uniform Mia had worn.

"Your Majesty." The taller of the pair gestured down the corridor. "If you'll come with us, we are docked with *Thína* Mia's ship now and we will disembark shortly."

We moved into the cargo bay, Rai's men stiffening when I came into the room, and I smiled that practiced Cressen Stone smile. It didn't matter that they were all armed to the teeth; I met the eyes of each and every one of the mercenaries and they all looked away first.

"That is impressive," Aiz said, hopping down from the ledge above us and landing on the balls of his feet with only a whisper of sound. "My sister is already on her ship, Empress. Let's get you moved before one of these poor bastards shits himself."

Rai stood by the docking tube, his arms crossed over his chest and his mouth pulled into a grim line. "Hail."

I ignored Aiz and the protests of the Shen guards, peeling off to get in Rai's face. "Start running," I said. "As soon as I'm free I'm coming for you. This is all the head start you get."

"It's more than he deserves," Johar said over my shoulder. "Come on, Hail." She slipped her arm across my waist, gently tugging me back out of Rai's personal space.

"You all know me or at least know of me." My voice carried through the air as Johar walked me backward. "Pick whichever name you want—Cressen Stone or Hail Bristol. We are the same person. You know the death and destruction I am capable of raining down on unlucky heads. You've heard the stories of the Bolthouse Gang. Believe me when I say it will be a thousand times worse for you. Start running. Killing this man won't save you." I jabbed a finger in Rai's direction. "The only thing that will buy you some time is to run as far and as fast as you possibly can. This is the only mercy you get from me.

"I'm coming for you. Run." I turned on my heel and walked away.

46

Aiz seemed to be reading my moods better and didn't say a word as we walked across the docking bay of the Shen ship, or maybe he just wasn't in the mood for a fight himself.

Part of me wished he'd give it to me. My promise to Mia hadn't included defending myself or my people, and if I could goad Aiz into a fight, so much the better.

If I was lucky, maybe he'd lose his temper and kill me.

Hail. The voice of Zin's ghost in my head was filled with sadness, and the accompanying kiss to my temple made me stumble. *No giving up, you have an empire to think about and right now you have people to keep alive.*

"Majesty, are you all right?" Gita's voice came over the com link but for a second I couldn't figure out why her voice was in my head when she was right there, alive. I stared blankly at her shoulder for a long moment before I shook myself.

"Fine. I'm fine." I subvocalized, feeling both women tighten their grip on me for a moment before they released me.

How was I supposed to say I'd just been distracted by ghosts?

"Focus, Empress. We've a bit more to do before you can rest." Aiz patted my face, eliciting a hissing curse from Gita, who slapped his hand away.

That same unfamiliar power whine sounded as the Shen around us brought their weapons up. The movement was smooth and practiced and screamed of years of training. A chiming tone echoed through the air and the unfamiliar ship seemed to hum around us for a moment before settling.

Putting my hand on Gita's arm and stepping forward to block her from Aiz, I met his smirk with a calm look. "The negotiations were bullshit. You were stalling. You're ready to go to war."

"We've *been* at war. This is different. I told you the Farians won't realize they need help until it's too late," he replied. "The negotiations were bullshit, Your Majesty, but only because their arrogance blinded them. We have been preparing for this for a hundred years. All Mia's people needed was a little more time to get the last piece of our newest ships working."

"I've never seen guns like that."

Aiz's mouth twisted into a grin. "My design. Would you like to see it up close?"

"Sure."

"The Koros 101 is a fifty-shot energy-pulse rifle. Completely lethal but harmless to equipment and ideal for spaceships. It has a cousin for ground combat that is even more powerful." Aiz snapped his fingers, taking the offered gun and passing it to me. He slid a hand into my hair, gripping it tightly when my finger closed on the trigger. He leaned in, heedless of the gun I now pressed to his throat.

"I know you want to, so do it. Pull the trigger. Kill me. Kill yourself. We'll both come back from it, but the taste of death might be enough to slack that rage I see in your eyes—at least for a little while."

"Hail, no." Alba breathed my name, a plea for sanity, and I teetered on the brink for an endless moment, staring into Aiz's brown eyes.

"For some reason I promised your sister I wouldn't hurt you. I keep my word." I took my finger off the trigger but didn't hand the gun back. Instead I looked it over carefully, recording every millimeter of it with my *smati* so I could examine it later.

"I could give you schematics for it, if you'd like. I'm quite proud of it, but I'd be interested to hear what a professional like yourself thinks."

"I thought I was just a jumped-up criminal?"

"I was angry." He took the weapon back, trailing his fingers along my jaw as he released his grip on me. "There were unexpected complications at the party; that attack caught me completely by surprise and I dislike being surprised. Mia is right, you were born with noble blood, no matter what else you've been through. I should and I do respect that as well as your experience."

My *smati* pinged with the incoming message and Aiz winked, handing the gun back to the Shen next to him and continuing down the corridor.

I followed him, knowing that Gita and Johar were sharing a worried look behind my back. *"Record everything you can, you two. I don't know how long they're going to let us have our* smatis, *but we'll figure out some way to store all this."*

"Yes, ma'am," Gita replied.

"Hail, watch out for him." Johar's voice in my head was filled with concern. *"Don't let him put you off balance."*

I didn't reply to her. I couldn't. I knew what Aiz was doing. I also knew I was already off balance, and nothing in the galaxy could make me right again.

"Anyway, the cousin for that model is amazing. The pellets are tiny." Aiz spun, holding up his thumb and finger a centimeter apart. "But the velocity turns them into little bombs. We did the field tests on Hagidon; you should have seen the carnage. I suspect one could take a fighter out of the air with it if you knew where to shoot."

"Or a shuttle," I said quietly. "Though the railgun that took out my shuttle was the newest Karsikov model."

"Yes, so I heard. You won't believe me, but this Jamison doesn't work for us." Aiz pressed a hand to the panel on the door in front of him and it slid open. "Empress, welcome to the bridge of the *Infinite Hope*. Flagship of the new Shen war fleet."

"I'll be gods-damned," Johar whispered.

I only just kept my own exclamation behind my teeth as I stared at the sight through the curved glass opening that stretched in a 180-degree arc across the bridge. The cluster of planets hung in the black, little jeweled orbs scattered across velvet.

"Majesty, where are you?" Fasé's dead voice floated through my head and I shook it, trying to focus on what Mia was saying.

"What?"

"I said I should have left the screen up. I think I messed up showing off my bridge with that view." She pointed at the planets.

"Where are we? We didn't—I didn't feel us float into warp." There wasn't anything like this close to Earth anyway, nothing within even a week's journey at top speed.

"You wouldn't have." Mia smiled and gave me a conspiratorial wink as she slipped her arm around mine, ignoring Gita's poorly contained snarl as she walked us across the bridge. "One of the many things the Farians have hidden from you. We don't use warp bubbles; they're...inefficient, and honestly a rather dull way to travel. It would have taken us far too long to reach home from Earth had we gone that way."

She gestured with her free hand at the planet in the viewscreen. "Welcome to Sparkos, Your Majesty. It's just an outpost, I'm afraid, not really home, but it's solid ground and fresh air."

I looked at Mia out of the corner of my eye; she wore the smile of a woman who knew she held the advantage and was content to wait to see how things played out.

"What do you want from me?"

"We'd like you to join us, Your Majesty, to bring justice to unjust gods. Ask your gut if this is the right path for you to take."

My gut was silent, reeling from the loss of more than I could bear. Somewhere in the grief, I heard Sybil's voice and realized Mia's words were but an echo of the future she'd spoken of so many months ago.

I saw a Star in the cold, empty black of space. A blue-green jewel of a planet. Home to warriors capable of shattering worlds. There would be no hiding for virtuous monsters or unjust gods from the accelerated expansion. I saw a light that is not light spreading. We all fight—we will all die. We surrender—we will die. There is no true shelter for sides that will collapse without each other to lean on.

And then, right on its heels, Dailun whispered, *Less violence, not more, Sister.*

"I won't help you," I said, my voice rough.

"You will, Majesty. I've seen it." Mia's reply cut through me. "Look closer and you will see we are prepared to fight for as long as it takes for you to agree."

I could pick out with my naked eye half a dozen planets around the massive red giant star. Between them, floating in the black and only slightly illuminated as they passed in front of the planets and star, were the ships.

There were dozens of them, and more shadows in the distance: sleek, black things that reminded me of Indranan dolphins. Ships like the ones that had destroyed the Farian colonies in a matter of minutes. I swallowed. The Farians had horribly misjudged the Shen, both in numbers and in technology. Now I knew why Aiz had just been killing time, why the negotiations had been a ploy.

The Shen were ready for war, and there was nothing in the galaxy that could stop them.

The story continues in...

DOWN AMONG THE DEAD

Book TWO of the Farian War

Keep reading for a sneak peek!

ACKNOWLEDGMENTS

Thank you, dear readers, for listening to these stories. My dentist said he loves reading books from his patients because even if he doesn't enjoy the book he learns something about the author. We leave little pieces of ourselves among the pages and this book is no exception.

To my husband, Don, for being the calm in the storm, for sometimes being the storm, for showing my stuck and stubborn self the value of balance and improv. You are the love of my life to the heat death of the universe and beyond.

To my family for your support and love, for your endless patience when so often my phone went unanswered or my reply was "I'm sorry—I have to write." You are amazing, and I am so lucky to have you in my life.

To my agent, Andy Zack, thank you for your tireless and relentless advocacy for my career. I couldn't ask for anyone better to do this with.

To my editor, Sarah Guan, who is simply the best. Thank you for making me work harder, for challenging me to connect the dots I don't see (or sometimes ignore), and for bringing Hail's story to life. Also to Jenni Hill, Ellen Wright, Nazia Khatun, and all the others who work at Orbit—you are as much responsible for this book as I. Without your hard work and love we'd be stuck out in the black.

To my friends—all of you—but especially to Lisa, Beena, and Blair for taking the time to read and provide me with valuable feedback. To Cass, Rook, and Jenny for always making Sirens so much fun. To Athena and Nikki and Dex for being sisters of my heart.

I've missed some, I know. There's not enough room for all of you but know my heart is full.

To Dilip Gohil and his friend for their awesome translation work on the Bristol family motto and pronunciation of Indranan words. Thank you for giving your time to something so important to me.

To LJ Cohen, for always answering my injury questions with "well, it depends," and then going on to give me eighteen different options to choose from. You are a rock star and I adore you.

To my Patreon Crew, thank you for your unfailing support, for your enthusiastic participation in my side project, and for being so damn awesome. You all rock and I love you.

extras

meet the author

Photo Credit: Donald Branum

K. B. WAGERS has a bachelor's degree in Russian studies, and her nonfiction writing has earned her two Air Force Space Command Media Contest awards. A native of Colorado, she lives at the base of the Rocky Mountains with her husband. In between books, she can be found lifting heavy things, running on trails, dancing to music, and scribbling on spare bits of paper.

if you enjoyed
THERE BEFORE THE CHAOS

look out for

DOWN AMONG THE DEAD
The Farian War: Book 2

by

K. B. Wagers

I t was purely by accident I crashed into the patrol. My instincts were in control and I disarmed the startled woman with ease, knocking her to the ground and powering up her weapon.

"Your Majesty?"

I blinked stupidly at the woman who looked like Kisah, reminded myself she was dead, and then stiffened at the echoes of other Hessian 45s powering up. "Don't move," I snarled when she started to get up.

More Shen, Hail. Don't trust them. Don't let your guard down. Portis rested a comforting hand on my shoulder.

"Shiva, it is her. Everyone, guns down."

"Majesty?"

I held the gun steady as I backed away from the Shen who looked like my dead BodyGuards. "No."

"Hail." Not-Emmory had his hands up. "It's us."

"No. I saw the embassy blow. My *Ekam* is dead. Aiz blew your damn secret about looking like anyone you want to. I'm not falling for this again. Take one more step and I will shoot you."

"Little sister—"

I shot not-Hao before he finished his first step. He stumbled back, a hand pressed to his shoulder, with curses that the real Hao would have been proud of flying from his mouth.

"Next step in my direction and I shoot you in the head," I said. "I promised Mia I wouldn't hurt her people, but I've already broken at least one promise lately, and you are trying my patience."

"*Sha zhu*, I am going to kick your ass."

The pistol whined to life again in my hand. "You keep that name out of your fucking mouth. That is not your name to use."

"What is wrong with you?"

We stared at each other. My heart slowed in my chest and my muscles tensed as I prepared for a fight. For a moment I thought not-Hao was going to come at me, gun or no gun, but then the Shen wearing my *Ekam's* face took charge.

"Hao, enough." Not-Emmory's voice was sharp. "Zin, take Hao back to the ship."

"Ah-ha." I waved my gun. "Nobody's going anywhere except for me."

"Hail." Not-Emmory blinked at me, his hands still up. "He's going to need medical care."

"You can move after I'm gone," I said.

"Please?" he asked. "I'd like to talk."

"Fine," I said finally, and the pair disappeared into the jungle. "You have one minute."

"Are you hurt?" Not-Emmory asked, his voice soft.

"I'll be fine." I smiled mirthlessly. "These are scratches compared to what I've been through the last few months."

The violence that ripped through not-Emmory's face startled me enough that I took several steps away from him.

"We could help you," he said.

I laughed. Aiz's energy had coursed through my veins for the first hour after I'd left him, and my injuries from the fight were long healed, but the wound on my side was still hot with pain. "I'm fine. Time's up."

"I know." Now his smile was gentle.

I had a split-second to regret letting not-Emmory have his victory, and then not-Zin crashed into me like a freight train. He hit me from the side, knocking us both over a downed tree, and I landed hard on my injured side.

Not-Zin had a hand locked on my gun arm, fingers digging into my forearm until my hand went numb. I gasped, the gun dropping into the jungle undergrowth, and tried to kick at him. But he knocked my foot away with his own and then planted it into the back of my knee. My other leg was pinned against a log, not-Zin putting pressure on it with his thigh.

I slapped at him with the only thing I still had free, my left arm, even though the movement shot fire through me.

"Majesty, stop."

A hard hand grabbed my wrist and twisted my arm behind my back, but I only fought harder, and the Shen surprisingly released it instead of letting my bones snap.

My captors were cursing in Indranan, which was also a surprise, but I was too far gone in the fighting rage Aiz had beaten into me to examine it for long. Not even the powering up of a

Hessian 45 stun setting was enough to still my thrashing, and I almost got free of not-Zin's grip.

"Shiva's sake, Emmory, just do it before she gets free. I've survived worse."

The pain coursed through me, stiffening every muscle in my body for a screaming eternity. I felt not-Zin collapse on top of me as the same shock ripped through him, but before I could recover, someone rolled him to the side and quickly cuffed my hands and my ankles.

The stunned silence settled heavily around us until I turned my head to the side to spit the loam out of my mouth, my laughter following after. "You bunch are going to get an earful from Aiz. No broken bones? You didn't even *try* to kill me! What is wrong with you?" I started to roll over, but someone's boot landed in my back.

"Majesty, I think it's best if you stay right there."

"That sounds like Indula." I craned my neck to get a peek at the Shen wearing my dead Guard's face. "He hated fireworks, loved harassing Iza, and was a horrible singer."

"I'm hurt, Majesty. I thought you liked my singing." He grinned at me.

I spat blood in his direction. "You are not Indula, because Indula's dead. Iza's dead. Emmory and Zin are dead. Hao is dead. They all died and left me behind. You are not Indula. He is nothing but ashes and rubble back on Earth."

The Shen with Indula's pretty pale eyes looked away from me, his smile sliding into a horrified look that twisted something buried inside my chest.

"Sir?"

"We'll handle it. Let's get her up. We're going to have to carry her back to the ship. I don't trust her not to run if we take those cuffs off her legs."

"Smart man," I said, smiling into the dirt.

"Emmory, what the fu—What did they *do* to her?" Not-Zin was breathing hard when he hissed the question.

"I don't know, but I'm going to be asking our prisoner that question."

They lifted me up, hands sliding under my armpits. I turned my head and closed my teeth on exposed fingers. Not-Indula swore and dropped me. I crashed into the Shen on my other side and tried to roll away, but she grabbed me, wrapping her arms and legs around my torso.

"Dark Mother, Emmory, she bit me!"

Not-Emmory crouched at my side with a sigh. He grabbed me by the chin with one gloved hand, holding me still as he released a cloud of *sapne* with the other. I tried to hold my breath, but the flare of pain as his fingers tightened on my bruised face made me gasp, and I inhaled the foul lavender smoke.

As the world dropped away, the last things I saw were the sad brown eyes of my dead *Ekam*.

Follow us:

f **/orbitbooksUS**

𝕏 **/orbitbooks**

▶ **/orbitbooks**

Join our mailing list
to receive alerts on our
latest releases and deals.

orbitbooks.net

Enter our monthly
giveaway for the chance
to win some epic prizes.

orbitloot.com